LOCUS ORIGIN
— THE NEVER BORN —

LOCUS ORIGIN
THE NEVER BORN

CHRISTIAN MATARI

Locus Origin – The Never Born is a work of fiction. Names, places and incidents either are products of the author's imagination or are used fictitiously.

Published by OZ-OM Books.

ISBN 978-9935-9067-0-0

www.locusorigin.com

In memory of my grandfather.

May your star always shine brightly down upon us.

ACKNOWLEDGEMENTS

I would like to thank my editor Luke John Murphy for going above and beyond to make this book into what it is. Without your diligence and hard work, this novel would have never gotten published.

I would also like to thank Mark Molnar, whose amazing concept art has truly made Locus Origin come alive.

Last but not least, I would like to extend my thanks to all those who offered their advice and support, most especially to Björgvin Björgvinsson.

Prologue

I have heard it said that birth is the most beautiful and natural thing in the world. Mine was neither.

I can remember lights so bright they burned my eyes, the buzzing of the fluorescent bulbs flickering in rapid succession high above, and the blurred shadows of figures looming over me in a state of panic, silhouetted against the strong light source. A high-pitched noise droned somewhere off to the side of the room, its pitch rapidly gaining momentum. Most of all, I can remember how cold and frightened I felt.

It was a strange feeling, gasping for breath with lungs which had never before tasted air.

The sudden sharp pain in my abdomen felt as if something were pressing up against my insides. As my stomach muscles began to spasm, my arms and legs started to convulse, beating uncontrollably against the freezing-cold operating table. My vision became blurry and the droning noise in the distance had become an even steady pitch.

The dark emptiness of my existence, my entire life up to this brief moment in time, returned to me once more, so inviting, comforting even.

A single tone cut through the oncoming silence. A sharp cry from one of the fading figures looming overhead drowned out the muddled outbursts of the others. It was the first distinct word I had ever heard.

"CLEAR!"

My entire body convulsed as waves of electricity shot through my chest, pulsating throughout my entire body. My arms and legs flailed outwards, fingers and toes stretched out as far as they could reach.

As quickly as it had all begun, the convulsions stopped. My arms and legs went limp. The clanking sound my ankles made as they slammed against the table echoed throughout the room.

The obscured figures repeated the process several more times, each one more draining than the one before.

Finally, I embraced the alluring darkness.

Many would find it odd that I can remember my first moments in such great detail. Normally, you are not supposed to remember your own birth. Most people don't have any memories of their first few years of life. Then again, most people aren't brought into this world as fully-grown adults.

I was born to a machine.

Chapter 1

The enormity of the bright featureless hall was such that he could barely make out its boundaries as he peered from under the covers. His body reacted sluggishly, but the throbbing pain he had felt in his head had all but dissipated. Warm air flowed through vents in the high ceiling, one of them situated right above his bed.

He arched his back, bringing his numb face directly in front of the gust of fresh air. He breathed deeply. The pain he had felt before had receded.

He became aware of the others. All around him, people in white gowns lying on beds with metal frames. Most seemed as bewildered as he was. All of them were bathed in the soft yellow glow of the fluorescent lights.

There were hundreds of them. Thousands even.

A plump nurse dressed in a white gown, which appeared to be a few sizes too small for her, came to the side of his bed as he lay deep in thought. She startled him as she threw his covers to the foot of the bed.

"Marcus Grey," she bellowed. Her shrill voice rang in his ears.

He looked questioningly into her stern, weathered eyes.

"Your name dear," she explained to him. "Your name is Marcus Grey, model number 6-26. Please try and remember that," she ordered as she unbuttoned his gown from the neck down.

She produced a green jar with a white lid that she attempted to open, without much success.

"Damn these things. Why do they always have to make them so difficult to open?"

She beckoned a scrawny orderly, who seemed very out of place, over to assist her with the jar.

"You gave the doctors a bit of a scare there Marcus," she informed him as she dipped four of her bulging fingers into the jar and proceeded to rub its contents onto his chest. It felt cold at first, then slowly it began to sting, a slight burning sensation on his skin.

It was then that he noticed the stitches. A T-shaped scar clear across his chest. It didn't hurt, but the soothing tingling sensation from the ointment being not-so-delicately massaged onto his skin brought about some discomfort.

"There," she exclaimed, wiping her fingers on her dress, "that should heal up nicely in a week or so."

After she finished buttoning up his gown, she put the covers back in place and ordered him to get some rest.

A short distance away, a pair of heavily-set orderlies were busy restraining one of the newly-awoken men, whose muscular frame made him seem more like a wild animal than a man. He clamped his jaw shut, grinding his teeth as he struggled against the orderlies. His muscles tightened, his gown tearing at the seams as he struggled for freedom.

He screamed as an elderly nurse with curled strawberry-blonde hair approached carrying a syringe. Wrinkles formed around her full red lips as she frowned, increasing her pace. Almost as soon as she began injecting the contents of the syringe into his vein, the frantic behemoth of a man stopped resisting. His muscles began to lose their tension.

The orderlies refused to loosen their grip. Instead, they eased him backwards into his bed before tying him to the cold steel bars on each side of the mattress with thick leathery straps.

"It's always the 6-17's that have to cause problems," the nurse grumbled as she pried his eyelids open, making sure that the drug was having its full effect.

"Sorry Pearl," one of the orderlies replied, somewhat abashedly. "The doctor said he'd be out for another hour or two."

Pearl just shook her head, frowning at each of the two broad-shouldered orderlies in turn before veering off out of sight.

Due to the commotion, Marcus had almost missed the approach of a pair of gaunt men dressed in pale green robes. One was fairly old, with easily discernable wrinkles on his brow and circling around his steel-gray eyes, which seemed to lack any sign of emotion. His silver-gray hair swayed as he walked under a vent.

"How long does it take to grow them?" the younger of the two men inquired, tilting his tall narrow head in anticipation of a response.

"The entire cloning process takes roughly seven to eight years. At a ninety-three-percent growth acceleration rate, a big step up from the original fifty eight percent," the older man explained as he focused on the small metallic slate in his hand, which gave off a sickly green glow, illuminating his face.

"Why are most of them bald?" the young man asked, looking perplexed as he scanned the room.

Marcus eyed the occupants of each bed surrounding him and, sure enough, most of the heads he counted were almost completely devoid of hair.

"The accelerated growth causes a form of acute alopecia, due to the strain on the nervous system. It also makes it easier to clean the tanks," replied the old man, kneeling over one of the patients, forcing the prostrate figure's jaw open and peering inside his mouth too closely for comfort. The dulled patient did little to object to the poking and prodding.

"So… some of them will always be bald?"

"Oh, no, they're just hatched that way. In fact, the ones you see here who do have hair were hatched prior to the ones that don't. Some models take longer to regain consciousness, up to a week or so's difference."

Marcus ran his fingers over his scalp and felt the brushing of stubble forming on his skin. It was a surprisingly pleasing sensation, and he caught himself smiling as he probed every aspect of his cranium with his fingertips.

"What about muscle atrophy?"

"Electronic stimulation takes care of muscle development," the doctor answered. "If it weren't for that, it would take months of physical therapy before they could even walk."

"How is it that they're able to perform so soon after hatching?"

"Ah, that's an excellent question. We call it 'resonant memory'." explained the older of the two, a hint of pride in his voice.

"Resonant memories?"

"Indeed. You see, each clone has been imprinted with a set of skills specifically tailored to his or her designated function. That includes language skills."

"But none of them appear to be able to speak, Doctor," the young man stated, still visibly confused.

"Yes, you see that's because resonant memories don't grant the recipient instant proficiency, but rather instill a dormant quality which the subconscious mind slowly develops into the fully functioning skill."

"I don't understand. How does that help? I mean…" the younger man paused to think of a better way to explain his dilemma. "How is that any different from learning something from scratch?"

"Well, all of these clones right here know how to speak. They just don't yet know that they know it," the doctor informed him with a smirk. "They can understand everything you say to them, but it may take several days before they can begin to formulate their own speech patterns."

"Interesting. So it's a form of accelerated learning process?" the younger doctor asked, rhetorically.

"Not at all," the other corrected. "You see, there are varying degrees of familiarity. Language is usually slow to develop, as it requires a fair amount of cognitive processing and practice. More focused skills such as first aid, engineering, even combat skills, can come quite naturally."

"Just how naturally, Doctor?"

"For instance, if someone were injured, a clone might spot a first aid kit and immediately know how to treat the injury without any prior training whatsoever."

"Fascinating. Sort of like waking up with amnesia. But then why do we need such an extensive training facility?"

"We leave nothing to chance. Just because a clone knows how to shoot straight doesn't mean that a bit of practice won't do him good. Besides, it helps to train them as a group. It builds morale. We're at war here, we can't afford any mistakes."

"What about personality?"

"Needless to say, every clone is a blank slate. However, they are fairly quick to adapt and develop a unique persona, but that's more of a question for our resident psychiatrist, Dr. Rupert Wells. I'm sure you'll run across him as you start to settle in."

The two doctors had finished examining a handful of patients, and began making their way towards an exit which Marcus noted was guarded by a single man dressed in body armor comprised of gray and faded-orange plating. He carried an SGC K-660 medium carbine, a weapon Marcus instinctively recognized as lethal in close quarters.

"Is it true that none of the clones have received telomere therapy?" the young doctor continued his barrage of questioning.

The older doctor promptly hushed him, checking their immediate area for reactions. "We're not supposed to discuss that openly."

Marcus lay still, pretending to sleep.

The two doctors walked past the guard, who pressed a glowing red circular button on the wall beside the doorway, which immediately turned blue. The heavy metal door sprung open, producing a loud whizzing sound and a series of echoing clanks as it locked into place, a sequence repeated shortly after the two doctors had exited the room as the door clamped shut once more.

Marcus pondered the significance of what he had overheard. He understood the meaning of the word "clone", but not its ramifications in relation to himself.

He surveyed the grand hall in which he lay, peering into the dull faces of the occupants of each bed in turn.

He began noticing a pattern.

Every two rows or so, he saw a person with the exact same face as before. It was unmistakable. He wondered, had he not heard what had gone on between the two doctors, how long it would have been before he would have noticed it?

Although he had never seen his own face, he was able to gauge what he must look like from his identical clones merely by following the pattern of bed assignments. There he was: light-olive toned skin, dark stubble growing on his head, bright blue eyes and pleasing features.

Although satisfied with his appearance, Marcus couldn't help but wonder why someone had thought it necessary to make more than one of him. Was he somehow flawed? Inadequate? So many questions were racing inside his mind, but they would have to wait for answers. He was exhausted. He leaned back onto his pillow and slowly allowed his drowsiness to get the better of him.

Chapter 2

Marcus grimaced at the taste of the thick gray paste as it slid down the back of his throat.

"It's not supposed to taste good," smirked the clone seated across the table, "but they say it's good for you."

He was a raggedy-looking dark-skinned man. His long narrow face and close-set brown eyes suggested a frivolous nature. His plump nose looked slightly bruised, as if he'd been punched not too long ago. He furrowed his brow as he licked the gooey substance off his spoon, pretending to enjoy it.

Even at only a quarter of the size of the hospital dome, the mess hall was still an impressive structure. Guarded at each entrance by a pair of armed custodians, the flow of hungry clones streaming through the food line was carefully managed.

"I don't see them eating it," replied a blond-haired, pale-skinned clone seated on Marcus's left. His boyish features exuded innocence. The light-blond stubble on his upper lip and chin appeared neatly groomed.

"Who are they?" inquired Marcus gesturing towards the guards. It was a question that had weighed heavily on his mind.

"They're the breeders," explained the dark-skinned clone. "I'm Taz by the way, Taz Sobieski," he introduced himself. "What's your name?"

Marcus paused briefly. It was the first time anyone had asked him his name, and he had to struggle to remember it.

"I'm… Marcus. Marcus Grey," he finally stuttered, as he pondered how the breeders went about assigning their names.

"That's a good name. Much better than Sobieski," Taz grinned. "What about you?" he asked the pale clone on Marcus's left.

"Meer, Steven Meer. Although I'm thinking about changing it," he proclaimed.

"You can change it?" Taz asked, obviously intrigued.

"I don't see why not. I hear they generate them randomly anyway."

"Would you look at that," Taz blurted out, gawking at a fair-skinned girl making her way through the lunch line towards their table.

Her skin glistened every time she passed underneath one of the lights. Her short, curly brown hair indicated she'd been hatched at least a couple of months before them. There was something about the way she moved, so strong-willed and determined, that caught Marcus's attention.

She slammed her tray down on the table, claiming an empty spot next to Taz. She was barely in her seat before she had begun scooping the vile goo into her pert mouth. Marcus couldn't help himself. His eyes were fixated on her full, pouting lips. He was mesmerized. It was as if he had seen beauty for the first time in his young life.

Suddenly her lips were no longer moving, frozen in place, a gaping hole as she held her spoon right in front of them. She was staring right at him.

"What the hell are you gawking at?" She shouted at Marcus, so everyone could hear.

Their entire section of the mess hall went silent. Everyone at the table was staring at him. Marcus became very much aware that he still hadn't replied, or even moved for that matter. His hand jerked, spilling his glass of white opaque liquid clear across the table.

"Way to go Marcus," shouted Taz as he and the fair skinned girl sprung to their feet in a vain effort to avoid getting wet.

Great, Marcus thought. Now not only does she think I'm a pervert and a klutz, but she knows my name. He hung his head in shame, covering it with one hand.

"I'm sorry. I didn't mean to…" he tried to apologize.

"Shut your face," she raged back at him. "Now I'm going to be late for class, you moron!"

Her face was flushed with anger as she stormed off.

"Hey gorgeous!" Taz shouted. "If you need a hand changing, I'm at your disposal."

She flicked her wrist back and produced her middle finger, a gesture only Taz was familiar with, apparently having been on the receiving end of just such a gesture a number of times in his short life.

The ruckus had attracted the attention of the server, a loud man with pudgy cheeks that wrinkled as he sneered in their direction. He stood poised behind a long counter at the far end of the hall, scooping up globs of the gray, gooey paste onto platters for the seemingly never-ending line of clones, all dressed in the same drab clothing.

"She's probably into girls," mumbled Taz as he sat back down in his seat."

"Who is she?" Marcus blurted out.

"I don't know who she is, but I think she's a pilot," answered Steven.

"How do you know?" Taz probed, still staring at her backside as she ducked through a nearby exit.

"She was wearing a pilot's uniform," Steven replied, without looking up from his plate.

Marcus looked back down to his gray jump suit, which seemed indistinguishable from the one the girl had been wearing.

"Am I a pilot too?"

"No," Steven corrected him. "Her suit had a pair of white stripes running from her shoulders all the way down her arms. Ours only has one stripe. I guess that means we're plain soldiers."

"How do you know all this stuff?" asked Taz, astounded.

"I'm curious. I ask questions," confessed Steven, still focusing on his food.

"I ask questions too, but everyone just tells me to shut up and mind my own business," Taz retorted.

"That's probably because you're too busy flirting with them while you're at it."

Taz grinned in quiet response. He finished the last scoop of gray paste from his plate and stood up from the table.

"Hey, you can't blame a guy for flirting when he's surrounded by nurses and girls in uniform all day long."

He shot one last smirk at Steven, who remained unimpressed, before tossing his tray onto the pile by the exit. He gave the guards a wide eyed glare as he departed the mess hall.

"How can he focus on girls at a time like this?" wondered Steven, shaking his head in disbelief.

"Yeah," replied Marcus, his cheeks blushing, his mind still very much focused on the fair-skinned young pilot whom he had so unwittingly angered mere moments before.

"Steven, why are we here?" Marcus inquired hesitantly.

"Isn't it obvious? We've been bred for war."

"War?" Marcus let out. "A war with whom?"

"I'm not sure yet," Steven confessed, clearly somewhat disturbed. "But I'm going to find out. We're scheduled for orientation tomorrow.

I assume that means we'll get a chance to see more of this place. I have a feeling things will be clearer then."

"What if I don't want to go to war?" Marcus blurted out.

"I don't think we have much of a choice," said Steven, clapping his hand on Marcus's shoulder.

Marcus felt an immediate connection with Steven. His pale gray eyes seemed so soulful, full of wisdom and generosity. Despite his reservations at the idea of being forced into becoming a soldier, Marcus caught himself smiling. At least they were all in this together.

"I wouldn't worry too much just yet," Steven said reassuringly, leaning closer to whisper in Marcus's ear. "But keep your eyes and ears open. We have to find out as much as possible about this place. If we have to be soldiers, the best thing we can do is to watch each other's backs."

Marcus kept smiling. He'd been bedridden for a little more than two weeks due to his initial complications. The other clones in the hospital dome had been free to move around the 'green zone' of the hospital dome and mess hall, chatting, getting to know each other and some of the friendlier staff, and generally adjusting to their new bodies and lives. This was the first time Marcus had eaten in the mess hall, having finally been deemed well enough to leave the hospital dome, and he felt overwhelmed at the newness of everything. It was also the first time he'd really spoken to anyone, apart from answering questions about his health from the doctors and nurses.

"Cheer up Marcus, and eat your food. One thing's for sure, we're going to need all our strength."

Marcus closed his eyes and devoured the rest of the foul-tasting goo. As he forced the last spoonful down his throat, an enormous hand grabbed his shoulder, gripping it firmly. Marcus turned and found himself overshadowed by the monstrous behemoth of a man he had witnessed the two heavily-set orderlies overbearing a few days earlier.

"You…" he gestured to Marcus, his tray dwarfed by his gargantuan hand. "You're in my seat."

"Wha…?" Marcus began to say, but he was cut short as the monster of a man lifted him up and tossed him to the floor like a ragged doll.

"Hey! Who the hell do you think you are?" shouted Steven, rising up in Marcus's defense.

Marcus rolled over to lie on his back, propped up on his elbows. He was just in time to see Steven jumping up on the bench to stand level with the huge man's face, defiance shining in his eyes. Marcus couldn't believe that someone he had just met would put himself in harm's way in his defense, especially against a man of that size.

"Why don't you pick on someone your own size?" Steven shouted, glaring maniacally.

The towering giant scowled, his nostrils flaring as he sized up his opponent. His eyes were drawn briefly to the nearby guards. Finally he huffed and turned to leave.

"That's right. Walk away before I climb up there and teach you some manners," Steven called after him.

The giant paused briefly, but didn't turn, storming out of the mess hall instead.

"That was amazing," Marcus gasped. "I can't believe you did that."

"Just because he's big, doesn't mean he can push people around," Steven smiled, his hand outstretched to help Marcus back to his feet.

Chapter 3

Takahashi Muromoto had accomplished extraordinary things during his long life. He had built up his corporation not only through ingenious corporate maneuvering, but also by some of the most innovative designs in the robotics industry that Terran society had ever seen. Even his top engineers had trouble following his work, which they claimed was both revolutionary and decades ahead of its time.

What had come as an even greater surprise to everyone was that as his competitors began losing ground, Takahashi had offered them mergers, encouraging them to fold their companies into his, on very generous terms. This not only strengthened the Muromoto Group, but ensured that there would be a minimum of ill will between him and the majority of his competitors. Within two decades the Muromoto Group had become the leading robotics manufacturer in the entire Terran solar system, and despite Takahashi retaining controlling interests, his former competitors had flourished under his leadership.

Yet Takahashi missed those times when his work revolved more around actual design work, before his wife's untimely death. Still, there was only one person he felt he would be able to trust with managing all that he had created. But his daughter Mariko wasn't quite ready yet. Or perhaps she was, and he just couldn't admit it. Could it be that it was he who wasn't ready to let go? He had been in the driver's seat going on ninety years now.

He'd been unplugged from the network for a brief moment, pondering the future, when the call came.

"Takahashi?"

"Yes?" he replied, regretting having instructed the girl to call him by his first name.

Only his wife and daughter called him Takahashi, or Taki for short. But it had been years since his daughter had called him that. She was becoming increasingly formal with each and every visit. Visits that seemed to be shorter and further between with each passing year. It bothered him to no end.

"You have a conference call with Mr. Kessler and Mr. Mulland."

Takahashi paused briefly, still concerned with what he had managed to uncover during his long stint of submersion inside the Terran Information Network. Half a dozen monitors, each reporting on different aspects of Terran society, flickered as he rose to his feet. His leg muscles cramping up, his knees buckling.

He'd been under too long.

"Give me a moment," he requested as he loosened the tie around his neck.

"But sir, they were…"

"I need a moment!" he cut her short. "Tell them to wait."

As two of the most powerful figures on Beta Terra, neither Mr. Kessler nor Mr. Mulland was accustomed to being kept waiting, but Takahashi was confident that, in his case, they would make an exception.

"Yes sir," the girl replied. She had only been his secretary for a few months, but she was already getting on his nerves.

No, that wasn't it. She reminded him too much of his daughter, of his little girl when she was still young and called him Taki, before she decided to pursue her career, before his wife died. Perhaps that's why he'd told his secretary to call him by his first name.

He knelt on the marble floor. He hated how cold it felt. He hated everything about the luxurious penthouse suite at the top of his corporate empire. It wasn't home to him. After his wife died he had become increasingly reclusive, sleeping at the office, or not sleeping at all. He couldn't even remember the last time he'd gone home. There were simply too many things there that reminded him of all that he'd lost. It was better this way. At least his life still had meaning.

He rose to his feet, grabbed an ornate crystal glass from the counter and poured himself a stiff drink.

"Put them through," he said calmly, as he downed the contents of the glass, grimacing at the strong aftertaste. Seconds later the primary viewscreen, which took up the entire eastern wall of his office, came to life. The two men displayed on the screen were equally agitated, although that was the only attribute they shared.

"Mr. Mulland," said Takahashi, greeting the man on the left side of the split viewscreen, a pudgy, middle-aged man with a heavily receding hairline and poor complexion. Mulland merely nodded his head in acknowledgement, his multilayered chin wriggling as he looked quickly left and right, as if to assure himself that he was indeed alone.

"...and Mr. Kessler," sighed Takahashi, greeting the square-jawed man on the right, a man so rigid he looked as if he should be occupying a display case in a museum.

"I trust you both received a package this evening? Judging by your stern visage, you've apparently both viewed the contents, despite my instructions to the contrary."

Both men lowered their heads in quiet acknowledgement of Takahashi's keen observation.

"Good. I thought you might. I only hope for your own sakes that no one else was present when you did so," exclaimed Takahashi, smiling slyly. He knew full well what the ramifications would be if anyone else had seen the contents of the packages he'd had sent.

"You can't be serious about this? Do you really expect that…"

"I expect that you follow my instructions to the letter, Alan," stated Takahashi, interrupting Mulland. "After all, it's nothing you haven't done before."

"Yes, but this time you're asking me to go behind the W.R.D., and, more importantly, if Division 6 finds out what you're up to, I can't even begin to tell you the insurmountable amount of shit we'll be in!" Mulland shouted, thoroughly unnerved, before making an abrupt attempt at regaining his composure.

Takahashi turned his back on the viewscreen, directing his gaze to the magnificence of the cityscape of Sol, the capital of Beta Terra. He knew full well that Mulland was heavily involved with Division 6, and his feeble attempts to persuade Takahashi otherwise would not stop him from pursuing his goal.

"You will do as I say Alan," repeated Takahashi calmly, "otherwise I hope you enjoyed your most recent encounter with your beloved Astrid, for it will be your last as husband and wife. When she finds out what sort of operation Mulland Biotech is running, she won't think twice about leaving you out in the cold."

Alan Mulland took in Takahashi's threats with a grave expression.

"…which brings us to Mr. Kessler." stated Takahashi, recognizing the sound of a cigar being lit.

19

It had surprised him that Kessler hadn't been smoking when he had first appeared. After all, there were two things Kessler was never seen without: a cigar in his mouth, and the holy cross around his neck. The hypocrisy of the latter was not lost on Takahashi.

"This goes against everything I believe in. More importantly, this goes against everything my family stands for. I refuse to be any part of it." Kessler proclaimed, slamming his fist on the table and fervently suckling his beloved cigar.

"You will if you want to retain controlling interests in Kessler BioChem." Takahashi informed him, abruptly spinning on his heels, just in time to see Mr. Kessler raise an eyebrow.

"What are you talking about?"

"It's no secret that the Lareko family holds a thirty-nine percent stake in your company. What may surprise you, however, is that over the past four years I myself have slowly acquired an additional twelve percent – through various shell corporations, of course."

"This is an outrage!" Kessler bellowed. "You can't blackmail me, you filthy son of a bitch!"

"On the contrary, my dear Kessler, that is exactly what I can, and am, doing. You see, I know you despise the Lareko family and everything they stand for. Either you do as I say, or not only will I see to it that the Lareko family receives controlling interests in Kessler BioChem, I'll give it to them absolutely free of charge."

Mr. Kessler's complexion turned a shade of red that Takahashi believed he'd never seen before, at least not on a human being.

"On the other hand," he interjected to prevent Kessler having an aneurism, "do as I ask, and I shall hand over the shares to you."

Mr. Kessler breathed heavily without answering, his regular skin tone slowly returning.

"Well…" he finally spat. "It looks as if you've given us no choice."

"You always have a choice, just not a very good one," Takahashi sneered.

The main viewscreen went blank. Takahashi found the silence uncomfortable. He poured himself another stiff drink and approached the window. He let his gaze wander across the magnificent cityscape. It was almost midnight, yet the skyline was buzzing with a countless swarm of hovercraft. Even this late at night the city was so alive.

He caught his reflection staring back at him in the window. His wrinkled skin and pale complexion felt almost alien to him. Who was this man staring back at him? So much time had passed. So much work in preparation for… it was only a matter of weeks now, until his whole life's work would finally come to fruition.

He ran his hand through his thick, mangy hair. Despite his old age, it hadn't thinned at all. It had even retained most of its natural dark color, albeit with a few silvery strands highlighting his temples. Mariko had used to say that it made him look almost regal.

He threw back the shot of whiskey and tore off the tie which had been hanging loose around his neck. He folded up the sleeves of his shirt, all the way up to the elbows.

"Suzie!" he shouted out into the hallway.

"Yes Takahashi? Will that be all for tonight?" she inquired as she came gallivanting from the hallway.

Takahashi looked at her for a moment, captivated by how much she reminded him of his daughter, back when she still used to call him Taki. She had the same shoulder-length hair, the same rosy cheeks, the same innocent smile.

"Almost," he replied. "I have one more call to make."

"Very well sir," she replied, turning to leave the room.

"…and call me Taki."

Chapter 4

The tour was led by Private Sebastian Kean, a short, red-headed clone whose model Marcus had seen only among the custodial staff. He had small, sunken eyes and only a hint of a nose, which seemed to disappear abruptly just above his gaping mouth and crooked teeth. His chin was virtually non-existent, merging seamlessly with his pale neck. His face was covered in freckles, so much so that, from a distance, he appeared permanently flustered. To Marcus, he looked as if he would cower in fear at the first hint of battle. Perhaps that's why his model was being used for such menial tasks.

"Listen in! Welcome to Alamo Station, a true testament to the drive and fortitude of the human race. Today I will be guiding you on a tour of the Station's primary facilities. Now, if you'll follow me, this corridor will take you from the mess hall to the training facility where you'll be spending most of your time in the coming days." Sebastian shouted over the crowd of more than a hundred clones he had been assigned.

"You'll notice the guard station roughly halfway down the hall. You are going to need to show your I.D. to the guards stationed there in order to get through. The same applies if you wish to leave the mess hall through the southern exit," Sebastian droned, reciting the same speech he had so obviously told countless times before.

Marcus had caught up with Steven just as the tour was about to begin. Meer had seemed pleased to see him, even patted him on the shoulder as he shook his hand and smiled.

"This is exciting, don't you think?" he asked Steven as they made their way towards the guard station.

"Definitely," replied Steven, trying to fix everything he saw in his memory. "Now we can finally find out what we're up against. Keep your eyes peeled."

Marcus smiled and mimicked Steven's attempts at discovery. With luck they might find a weakness, something they could exploit.

"Since this is your first time outside the green zone, please form a line and the guard will issue you your Ident chip," Sebastian proclaimed, springing to life as if awoken from a deep slumber. The last part of his statement had clearly stirred up something important from his memory. "Do not lose your Ident chip, people. Believe me, you don't want to go through the bureaucratic mess that that entails."

The Ident chip was a small reflective square, encased in a dark rubbery substance around the edges, roughly the size of the tip of his finger.

"Hey Marcus," came the familiar voice of Taz Sobieski. His dark hair had grown a bit since Marcus had seen him last, and had begun curling at the tips.

"Look at the ass on her!" he exclaimed, a bit too loudly for anyone in their proximity to have missed.

He was pointing to an auburn-haired beauty with a shapely figure, some ten meters ahead, who promptly turned to reveal her lightly freckled face. She squinted at Taz, who realized at once that she had heard him.

"Much better than that pilot girl, don't you think?" he whispered for everyone's benefit, unabashed.

She was attractive, there was no denying that, but there was something about the pilot girl that had preyed on Marcus' mind.

24

Perhaps it was just that he'd made a fool of himself in front of her. Regardless, he was determined to see her again, if only to apologize. To show her that he wasn't like Taz.

"Next up is the training facility," shouted Sebastian as the swarm of bewildered clones made their way through a pair of pressure-sealed doors at the end of the long hallway.

The doorway led them into a gigantic structure, dwarfing the recovery room many times over. Transparent walls in steel frames divided the massive structure into dozens of segments of varying sizes, all accessible via a series of corridors and walkways, some of which were suspended in midair.

The entire group was dumbfounded at the sight, not only at the size of the chamber, but also at the level of activity inside each compartment. Some held rows of desks and chairs, with clones watching or listening intently to a person who either stood at the head of the room in front of a wide viewscreen or paced about, gesturing every which way. In other rooms, dozens of clones ran around and performed athletic feats utilizing all manner of contraptions.

"Impressive, I know," confessed Sebastian, filled with so much pride one could almost believe he had built the entire thing himself. "Take it in people. You may enjoy looking at it today, but I promise you, in a week or two, you'll have had enough of this place to last you a lifetime. Trust me, I know."

Marcus couldn't help but notice a hint of resentment in the young private's tone.

"Alright, next up are the barracks."

Kean led them out of the hall through a different exit, further along the side of the enormous structure, and into another hallway. This one was different from the one they'd taken to the training facility, a cylindrical tube made out of a transparent material, allowing its occupants to see outside the Station for the first time. The dark-gray rocky terrain beyond the transparent walls was covered periodically with a grayish moss-like substance. A thin layer of pale-blue mist lightly shrouded the scene. Marcus' gaze was drawn upwards, first to the magnificent star-studded sky, and then to the majestic blue orb looming high overhead. Large flakes of dusty brown cut through the shimmering blue, creating irregular shapes across the orb's surface, a halo of bright blue and orange surrounding its rim.

"That, ladies and gentlemen, is Alpha Terra," proclaimed Sebastian to his crowd of mesmerized onlookers. "If you're lucky, you won't ever have to set foot on its surface."

"Why's that?" asked a curious Steven, distracting the guide's audience.

"Well… because… you just don't." Sebastian stuttered, taken aback at the interruption. "Trust me, there's nothing good on Alpha Terra. Not since before the war."

"Why?" Steven persisted.

"It's a wasteland, ok?" barked Sebastian, starting to lose his patience. "The whole planet was bombed from orbit in the early days of the war. Now can we please keep questions to the base and its facilities? Everything else you need to know will be covered during basic training."

Sebastian didn't wait for an answer, simply turning on his heel and stomping away down the length of the corridor, making loud clanking sounds each time he slammed his small feet onto the metallic grating covering the floor of the tube.

Trailing after him, the clones were lead through yet another security checkpoint where each and every one of them was made to produce their Ident chip. The surly pair of guards appeared to be closing in on the end of their shift. They each carried a metallic pad with a viewscreen on one side in their hand. When the Ident chip was brought within arm's reach of the device, the screen facing the guard flashed green.

"Move along, move along," the pair repeated, almost in unison.

Periodically, a uniformed man or woman would emerge from the other end of the tunnel and be allowed ahead of the line. Most of them were on foot, but a few rode on motorized carts with small beds on the back, laden with crates and drums. All paused briefly to be scanned by the guards before continuing with their business.

After passing through the checkpoint, the crowd swarmed along another identical tube. Up ahead, yet another monstrous structure cast its eerie shadow over them. This one was cylindrical in shape and at least ten stories tall, its whole outer wall transparent. Marcus could just make out the shapes of people inside, some rushing along the walkways encircling the entire structure, others strolling lazily along, still others standing at the enormous windows and admiring the view, deep in conversation with a fellow clone.

"Amazing!" Marcus gasped, just as a midsized freighter flew overhead.

"Come on Marcus," urged Taz as he bumped into him. "Don't stop now, the line's moving."

The group made their way into the barracks. Inside, the curvature of the hallway was almost invisible due to its sheer size, to the point that Marcus was unable to see the people at the far end of the hallway as anything more than dots.

Ramps allowed access between the levels for both people and motorized carts. The entire outer wall consisted of thick plates of reinforced glass, giving the occupants a spectacular view of the Station, which, it began to dawn on Marcus, was even more enormous than he'd imagined.

Over half a dozen superstructures were connected via tunnels and hallways, as were the dozens of smaller buildings strewn about the landscape, bathed in the cold blue glow reflected by Alpha Terra. Rows of shuttles and small freighters spiraled through the sky, some inbound and awaiting clearance for landing, others jetting off into space and disappearing from view in a matter of seconds. Marcus wondered if the fair-skinned pilot was on board one of them. Perhaps they'd never meet again. He hoped they would.

"Alright people, gather round," barked Sebastian. He stood poised by the inner wall, which Marcus now noticed was lined with a row of metal doors at short intervals for as far as the eye could see.

"These are your standard quarters," he informed them as he opened one of the doors.

The crowd pushed and shoved, making it virtually impossible for Marcus, who had lagged behind the group, to catch a glimpse of the interior of the small room.

"Each and every one of you will receive your own room for the duration of your training." Sebastian's voice faded as Marcus took a few steps away from the crowd, towards the window. He couldn't seem to tear himself away from the splendor of the night sky.

What a miraculous vision, he thought. What great things awaited him among those stars?

Steven placed his hand on the railing next to him. "That's freedom right there," he whispered, gesturing out into space, "all we have to do is take it."

"Take it?" Marcus wondered.

"I'll find a way," Steven confided, his crooked smile hinting that he was already coming up with ideas.

"Maybe it's not as bad as you think... being a soldier I mean," replied Marcus, not sure if it was Steven he was trying to convince, or himself.

"We'll see."

* * * * *

The promenade was the highlight of the tour, a wide, open structure teaming with life as thousands of clones roamed about freely, frequenting a variety of shops, restaurants and bars on each of the structure's many levels. Marcus had never seen so many colors in one place. Bright neon signs advertised the names of each establishment, desperately attempting to overshadow those next to it. He was hit with a welter of smells that made his mouth water in anticipation.

The people seemed so relaxed. Some of them weren't even in uniform. Tables and chairs were neatly organized in their designated areas, filled with cheerful clones who seemed to be enjoying themselves immensely.

Marcus spotted a clone identical to the behemoth who'd taken his seat in the mess hall. This one sat surrounded by a group of five others, all intently listening to another Taz, who was frantically attempting to impress them. The behemoth had a brown cylindrical object in his mouth, with smoke periodically emanating from it, and a bottle of golden liquid in one hand. A blushing blonde sat on his lap, her arms around his massive neck.

"The promenade is available to you during your time off," Sebastian explained. "Now, I urge you to be on your best behavior here, as there are usually some civilians around."

"Civilians?" asked a clone Marcus hadn't noticed before. His skin was a rich dark brown, darker even than Taz's.

"Corporate liaisons to the military mostly," Sebastian informed them. "You didn't think that the Republic paid for all of this did you?"

Instinctively, Marcus knew that a corporation was a privately owned institution, created to provide products and services to the masses for the betterment of the Terran race. Or, he wondered, was that just what they wanted him to think? Were the other clones thinking the same as he was? If they were all imprinted with the same understanding of Terran society, were they all reacting the same way? Were the differences between them merely physical? If so, were the other 6-26 models identical to him in every way?

He looked at another 6-26 in the group. He seemed just as perplexed as Marcus was. He wondered if they even shared the same scar. Instinctively Marcus started to rub his chest, running his fingertips over the raised skin where the seams had been. Maybe the scar somehow made them different.

"…the two corporate towers on the north-east corner of the promenade house the offices of those corporations involved with the military hierarchy."

Marcus zoned back in on Sebastian's ramblings.

"Does that answer your question?"

"Yes Private," replied the dark-skinned clone, who seemed just as confused as before he'd asked his question, despite their guide's detailed explanation. He stood as still as a statue, alone with his thoughts. His taught, muscular frame seemed almost too big for his ebony skin, which was tightly stretched across each of the many bulges of his arms. His sunken eyes seemed apathetic, as if he was asking his questions more to pass the time than out of any genuine interest.

"Oh, before I forget," added Sebastian. "Your Ident chip also functions as a credit chip. That means you can use it to buy food, drinks or personal items here on the promenade. You will each receive five hundred credits a month. Use it sparingly."

Marcus spotted the behemoth from the mess hall loitering at the back of the group. He looked down at the minute chip in his monstrous palm and smiled, quickly shifting his gaze to take in all the possibilities this new-found information had to offer.

"Now we're talking," he muttered, starring at his identical twin with the cigar in his mouth and the blonde on his lap.

Chapter 5

The quarters were little more than two by three meter cells, with walls made from a non-reflective metal. Each room had a bed which could be pulled out of the right wall, while the left wall had a viewscreen embedded into it. Its touch-screen interface allowed the room's occupant to enjoy a wide selection of material at their leisure. The far wall of the cell served as a bathroom. A metallic toilet protruded from the wall, and a grouping of small holes in the ceiling ejected a steady stream of water at the push of a button.

Marcus had neglected to push his bed back into the wall the previous evening, the first time he'd activated the shower, so when he awoke, lying on the hard bed, his sheets were still damp from the night before. As he rose to sit on the edge of the bed, it gave way to his weight, bulging ever so slightly and emitting a squeaking sound. Experimentally, he pushed his weight up and down on the bed in rapid succession to reproduce the noise. After a moment he stopped and sat quietly, wondering how the bed would hold up against the weight of the behemoth from the mess hall – who, along with Steven and Taz, was in Marcus' squad – and whose name, Marcus had discovered, was Jago. A strange name, he thought, amusing himself as he leaned forward to pull a small lever on the wall beneath the viewscreen.

A wide drawer rolled out. Inside were several identical uniforms in his size, a bar of soap, and a bundle of coarse towels. He grabbed the soap before pushing the drawer shut again and retracting his bed back into the wall.

He enjoyed the shower, the warm sensation of the flow cascading down his naked body. The night before he'd used up all of his water before knowing fully what to do with it. They were only allocated five minutes of water in the morning, and then another five after training. This time he quickly lathered himself in soap, and then soaked in every second before the stream finally ceased.

The viewscreen flickered to life as he was halfway through putting on his uniform.

"Basic training will commence in ten minutes," a female voice recited twice before the viewscreen again went blank.

* * * * *

Marcus stood in line at the back of a formation of eighteen men and women. He'd noticed there were no duplicates amongst them, although what significance that held he had yet to discover. At the far end of the hall an identical group had lined up as well, all eagerly awaiting instructions. The hall was a huge chamber, over a hundred meters along each wall. The floor was divided into white tiles, each half a meter square. In the center of the room two men stood in conversation by a motorized vehicle attached to a pair of closed carts.

The men opened a latched hatch on each of the carts before acknowledging that they were ready to begin. One of them strutted to the far side of the room as the other, a gangly looking man wearing a black uniform decorated with a single silver medal, approached Marcus' group.

"Good morning," he addressed the clones, his booming voice reverberating throughout the chamber. "I am Drill Sergeant Alexander Dawn. You will address me as 'Drill Sergeant'."

"Yes, Drill Sergeant!" a lone clone at the center of the front line of the formation bellowed.

Marcus leaned forward to see who it was. His uniform was impeccable, neatly pressed and a perfect fit. He had brown hair, perfectly groomed and cut as if chiseled out of stone, and his narrow face and long chin were set in an earnest expression, suggestive of a serious nature. His high forehead glistened under the strong lights, as did his high cheekbones.

"Sergeant David Lance, I presume," acknowledged Drill Sergeant Dawn, eyeing his datapad.

"Yes, Drill Sergeant," Sergeant Lance bellowed once more.

"So, you're the one leading this disorganized group of misfits?" the Drill Sergeant asked rhetorically. "Good, let's see how you all do. Take your men, don the proper equipment and let's begin." He ordered, gesturing towards the carts at the back of the motorized vehicle.

"Yes, Drill Sergeant!" Sergeant Lance replied, before hurling a stream of insults at the entire group of clones, bullying them into motion.

The proper equipment consisted of a padded vest with a bulky sensor embedded in the center of the chest, a plain-looking closed helmet with a built-in visor, and a weapon loosely resembling a simplified version of the SGC K-660 medium carbine. Marcus had trouble donning his vest. It was too loose, and kept writhing around on his slender torso. The helmet fit like a glove, but the visor obstructed most of his peripheral vision and tinted the rest of what he could see.

34

The carbine was heavier than he'd expected. It had a small display screen mounted above the chamber, which gave him a readout of the amount of ammunition left in the clip and the temperature of the barrel.

"Press the button on the lower left side of your helmet," boomed the Drill Sergeant.

Marcus fumbled around awkwardly, trying to find the button with his fingertips while still holding on to his carbine with his other hand. There, he had it. He pressed it and instantly the visor on his helmet lit up. The dark tint that had obscured his vision faded away, and a number of readouts and overlays appeared, the helmet's built-in computer merging them with the view through the visor into an augmented reality. A blue triangular icon glowed above each of his teammates' heads. As soon as he focused on one of them, their name, rank, model number and role assignment were displayed above the icon.

This is amazing, Marcus thought as he scanned the group.

Albano, Reid. Model Number: 6-11, Rank: Private, Role: Sniper, the readout indicated as he scanned the dark-skinned clone from the promenade.

Marcus focused on a short clone who seemed less familiar with his carbine than the others. *Vod, Taylor. Model Number: 6-19, Rank: Private, Role: Medic.*

"Hey Steven," Marcus shouted, too loudly, trying to overcompensate for the helmet covering his mouth. The whole squad winced and looked at him as they tried to cover their ears, despite the futility of the gesture: the sound had come from the speaker system inside their helmets.

"Yes Marcus?" Steven replied calmly, in a slightly patronizing manner.

"Oh, sorry," apologized Marcus, still too loudly for comfort. "What does it say about my rank and role?"

"You're a private and a soldier," Steven replied. "What about me?"

"The same," Marcus answered, buzzing with excitement.

Marcus focused on Taz, curious as to what role he had been assigned.

Sobieski, Taz. Model Number: 6-28, Rank: Private, Role: Scout.

"Taz, you're a scout," Marcus informed him.

"Nice! You know what that means, don't you?"

"No, what?"

"That means you have to do as I say," Taz joked.

"Actually, Private," came the booming voice of Sergeant Lance as he grabbed Taz's chestplate, jerking him to one side so that the two of them were face to face, "you have to do what I say!"

"Yes Sergeant." Taz conceded.

"Alright, listen up," the Drill Sergeant shouted over the clamor, the clones falling back into formation. "As I'm hope you're all aware, a Terran Forces squad operates in three teams of six. The Sergeant commands his team personally, while the squad's two corporals each command another. Sergeant, nominate two of your men as acting corporals. You and they in turn will each choose an acting private first class to support you in the running of your teams. Now, this is important people, should a corporal die, the PFC is automatically bumped up to corporal. The same goes for the senior corporal to sergeant. That means you *will* follow their orders."

"Yes, Drill Sergeant!" Lance spun about and surveyed his troops. "You," he said, pointing towards a *Dimitrov, Tony. Model Number: 6-*

12, Rank... flickered from *Private* to *Corporal, Role: Command.* "...and you," Lance pronounced, gesturing with his carbine towards *Spielman, Adam. Model Number: 6-23, Rank: Corporal, Role: Command.*

The two newly-assigned Corporals proceeded to promote a clone Marcus didn't recognize – *Hiroshi Kitamura*, flashed his helmet – and Reid Albano, the sniper, to Privates First Class. Lance scowled, clearly not ready to delegate authority. He finally waved a hand, almost at random, at Tara Simone, the shapely auburn-haired girl with the freckles, nominating her the squad's third PFC.

"Excellent," the Drill Sergeant stated. "Then we're finally ready to begin. Someone get that truck out of the way."

Following the truck's removal, Drill Sergeant Dawn pressed his index finger on a series of touch-sensitive buttons on his datapad, and, with a smooth hum, the floor tiles began to shift. Marcus stared as a line of tiles right in front of him began to ascend, forming a wall three meters high. All around the room, some tiles rose while others fell, creating a three-dimensional labyrinth with no discernable markings, its walls as white as the floor and ceiling of the hall. Marcus realized that the only way to orient himself inside the maze would be to keep track of the edges of the ceiling and the chamber's outer walls. It wouldn't be much help, but at least he should be able to estimate his position relative to the rest of the room.

"All right men. The objective of today's exercise is to reach the center of the labyrinth." Dawn informed them. "The enemy, represented today by Sergeant Baker's team, will do everything in their power to stop you and get there first," he stressed.

The monstrous Jago, lugging a large weapon obscured by his even larger body, broke out of line and stormed off towards the labyrinth's entrance.

Raynes, Jago. Model Number: 6-17, Rank: Private, Role: Support Gunner.

"Stop!" roared the Drill Sergeant.

Jago came to a stumbling halt.

"Where the hell do you think you're going, dumbass?"

"Kill the enemy?" stammered Jago.

"Sergeant Lance, tell this prehistoric animal that until given an order, he is to remain still." the Drill Sergeant commanded.

"Yes, Drill Sergeant! You there, you big ape, get your sorry ass back in line before I shoot you myself!" Sergeant Lance screamed at the top of his lungs.

"Yes boss," grumbled the humiliated Jago as he dragged his enormous tree-trunk legs back into line with the rest of them.

Drill Sergeant Dawn scowled at him for a brief moment before continuing. "Now, as soon as the lights go off, you may proceed to your goal."

Marcus felt his heart begin to beat rapidly at the thought of having to complete their task blindly. Although his resonant memories had given him the knowledge that these were training weapons, going up against another copy of Jago didn't sound particularly appealing to him. Who was to say that the brute wouldn't just use his fists to pummel him into a bloody pulp?

The room went dark.

"Go, go, go!" Lance cried.

A stream of confused clones poured into the opening of the labyrinth.

Marcus paused for a second as the visor of his helmet began to shift his field of view from pitch black to a green-tinted display of his surroundings. He saw Steven at the rear of the throng beckoning him to follow.

"Stay close to me Marcus," Steven suggested as he turned to enter into the maze.

Marcus sprang after him, not wanting to get left behind.

"Dimitrov, you take those two down the next left. Albano, take those two and head on to the right." Lance was at the front of the procession, meaning Marcus couldn't see who he was pointing to. Where was he supposed to go? "The rest of you follow me, we'll hold position near the center while the others perform a pincer maneuver," the Sergeant's voice sounded over the speakers in Marcus' helmet, a clear measure of authority in his tone despite the lack of clarity in his orders.

Marcus wondered how the Sergeant could possibly expect his plan to work when the maze could easily lead the main group to a dead end, leaving the rest of the squad outnumbered and busy getting shot to pieces, or worse.

"Sergeant?" he hesitated.

"Yes Private?" Lance snapped.

"Wouldn't it be wiser to send the scouts first…?"

"Private, do as you're told! This is my command and you are to follow MY orders. Is that understood?"

"Yes Sergeant," replied Marcus, flustered that the Sergeant would so easily dismiss his input.

Up ahead, the corridor dove sharply downward and split into two directions. To the left it veered around a corner, while to the right it seemed to slope further down before veering off to one side.

"PFC Albano, Grey, Meer, you three take the right. The rest of us will take the left." Lance barked.

Marcus was pleased that he and Steven had been grouped together. He found it comforting. They stalked down the winding corridor, which twisted and turned before doubling sharply back on itself. Reid Albano, who had been leading them, stopped abruptly. The path rose steadily in front of them in a dozen or so steep steps, which Marcus instinctively knew could give them an advantage over the competing team. Judging by the height of the steps, they'd be well above floor level at the top.

"Contact!" chimed the voice of Corporal Dimitrov. "Sergeant, we're boxed in."

The sound of heavy fire could be heard in the distance.

"Suarez and Clarke are down. Please advise."

"What? How the hell did you lose your team already?" yelled a distraught Sergeant Lance.

"Ambush Sergeant, they came at us from two sides at once!"

"Stay put Corporal, hold your position."

"Yes Sergeant." Dimitrov grunted.

"Spielman, take five and show Dimitrov how it's done!" Lance barked. "And you, Dimitrov, stay put and don't screw anything else up until Spielman gets there!"

Marcus listened worriedly as Dimitrov calmly fed Spielman and his scratch team directions to reach the left-flanking team's last position. "...then a left, and I'll be fifty meters dead ahead of you."

However, the instant the comms went silent, a barrage of shots rang out.

"Aaaaah!" Spielman's voice cried frantically. "They got us! They fucking got us all! I'm...runn..." his comms went dead.

"Fuck!" moaned Sergeant Lance. "Stay calm everyone! Just stay calm!"

Albano, who'd been quietly creeping up the steps ahead of them while Marcus and Steven listened to the unfolding drama, gestured for the other two to join him. From that vantage point they could see over the center of the maze, and, sure enough, the enemy team was closing in fast as Marcus and Steven joined the sniper.

"We've got to hold them off." Albano aimed his weapon, a mock sniper rifle, at the other team and prepared to fire.

"Hold who off Private?" yelped the confused Sergeant.

"Sergeant, the enemy is closing in on the objective. I count at least five of them. We're going to try and hold them off as best we can."

"Good work Priv-" the Sergeant's acceptance was drowned out by the sound of Reid's rifle being fired several times.

Marcus watched as the nozzle spat a beam of red light at its target, and realized that the sound of gunfire was being produced by the speakers in his helmet. As two of the enemy squad crumpled to the ground, he wondered how they could engineer it so that the position of the sound corresponded to the physical location of the weapon being used.

"Suppressive fire, damn it!" Albano yelled as the three remaining members of the enemy team began firing back.

Marcus drew a bead on his intended target and squeezed the trigger. The gun kicked as each imaginary bullet went off. He was amazed at how natural it felt. He emptied his clip in a few short bursts, released the clip and replaced it with a spare from the pouch that hung from the side of his vest, slamming the new clip into place.

It all felt so natural.

Steven and Marcus worked in unison, forcing the enemy to keep their heads down long enough for Albano to get ready for his next shot. As each new clip slid into place, Marcus could make out the readout on the weapon's small display screen updating itself.

Albano fired.

"Two to go." He informed them, his tone utterly void of any emotion.

Instantaneously, Marcus's visor flashed red.

"You've been terminated." a raspy synthesized voice explained to him.

His viewscreen went black. The lack of any light source made it impossible for him to even see his hands in front of his face. The only thing still functioning was the sound system. He heard several more shots, some of them from right next to him, obviously fired by Meer and Albano. The others came from behind them. His communications were cut off, but from the direction that the shots were being fired from he could tell that the enemy had managed to sneak up behind them. Soon the only shots being fired were those of the competing team.

Marcus lowered himself carefully to the ground and waited for the game to end. He didn't have to wait long.

He had barely managed to bring his pounding heart rate down when the lights flickered back to life and the walls of the labyrinth began to sink back into the floor.

"That was just... pitiful," Drill Sergeant Dawn proclaimed from the edge of the rapidly-disappearing maze. "Is that the best you can do?"

Marcus removed his helmet in order to grab a breath of fresh air. Next to him Reid and Steven were getting back on their feet, helmets in hand. Both of them seemed just as disappointed as Marcus felt.

42

"You know, that wasn't a bad idea you had there, Grey," noted Reid in quiet surrender. "Sending the scouts in first to get a feel for the place – I'm guessing that's how they managed to ambush us as easily as they did."

"Quiet down," commanded the Drill Sergeant as the squad crossed the now-level floor to gather around him. "All of you had better get your heads out of your asses if you plan to stand a chance against the real enemy. You've got to swallow your pride and take orders. And for God's sake, learn to use each and every one of your team to the best of their ability. You can bet your ass that's what the enemy will do. The enemy is as savage as they come. They don't even know the meaning of the word 'pride'."

"Except we still don't have a clue who the enemy is, because you haven't told us shit!" barked Taz in frustration.

"Hell Sarge, these boys are greener than Toby's shorts after a week in the tank," interjected Taz's twin from across the hall, where the other team were also picking themselves up and removing their helmets. "Why don't you give us a real challenge?"

"You were the real challenge, Ramirez. Now shut your mouth. The only way these boys are going to learn is through adversity." The Drill Sergeant snapped, his patience about to expire. "As for the identity of the enemy, you'll find out all about that during tomorrow's lessons. For now, suffice it to say that even Ramirez and his men would be humbled in their presence." The Drill Sergeant looked worried, as if something weighed heavily on his mind. "All of you, report to Drill Sergeant Paxton in room eighteen for marksmanship training. I'm done with you for the day." Dawn buried his face in his palm, rubbing his temples as he strode out of the simulation room.

"Maybe you should be leading this team instead of Lance," Reid muttered as he pushed between Marcus and Steven. The two of them exchanging worried looks.

"I'm not so eager to find out more about who it is that we're up against," confided Marcus.

"Neither am I," replied Steven, carefully keeping an eye on the Drill Sergeant as he exited the simulation room.

Chapter 6

"They are the most ruthless, savage creatures that humanity has ever come across. They are called the Nyari." explained the educator, a grim-faced, disciplined woman with graying hair bound in a ponytail. Deep lines encircled her bulbous eyes, and the dark sacks beneath them were a testament to her tireless dedication to her job. "They are also the only sentient life form Terran society has encountered to date."

Marcus sat between Steven and a brunette whose model he hadn't come across before. She had vibrant brown eyes with what looked like small flecks of gold in them, soft, delicate skin and alluring features. A light pattern of faded freckles covered the bridge of her petite nose. She was listening intently to the lecturer, unlike many of the others.

"Am I the only one who finds this all a bit overwhelming?" whispered Marcus, leaning over to Steven so the lecturer wouldn't overhear.

"This whole thing, our very existence, artificially created to fight an enemy whom we've never even met? It's one big cosmic joke," replied Steven, perhaps a tad too loudly.

The lecturer squinted her eyes in their general direction. Luckily the auditorium seated hundreds of clones from dozens of squads, and he and Steven were sat towards the back.

"I don't think it's funny at all," said the brown-eyed girl as she leaned towards Marcus, a mysterious smile making its way across her full lips. "I think it's great," she added, snapping back into place, focused once again on the lecture.

"What? You can't be serious!" mumbled Marcus. "What could possibly be great about our situation?" he asked Steven when he realized she wasn't going to answer him.

"You mean that we've been created to serve our people, that we have the opportunity to perform acts of insurmountable heroism against a foe vastly superior to us – that doesn't excite you?" the girl replied before Steven could say anything.

"You there, in the back," scolded the lecturer, "Keep quiet."

Marcus kept his mouth shut, thankful for the break in conversation. He didn't even know how to begin answering the girl anyway. When the lecturer finally focused her attention elsewhere, the brunette turned back to him, whispering softly so that only he could hear.

"Then think of it this way. If there wasn't an enemy so vastly superior to us, the Terran Republic would have no need for such a grand army, thereby negating the necessity for both your creation and mine. You and I would never have existed, and so we'd never have met."

Marcus was dumbfounded. Had she just implied she liked him?

"Pay attention!" she hissed when she realized he was still staring at her.

"Your average Nyari is a 2-2.4 meter tall killing machine," the lecturer droned on, having obviously given this exact lecture more times than she cared for. "Although their outward appearance may resemble that of an insect, these vicious humanoids have internal organs not unlike our own: heart, lungs, four sets of kidneys, three stomachs. Their powerful legs not only allow them to run at high speeds, but also to jump a remarkable distance. So be warned, never,

46

ever, get into close range with one of these beasts." She indicated a diagram of a Nyari foot soldier.

"Unlike we Terrans, the Nyari have four arms, which end in a set of three fingers tipped with razor sharp claws. They are formidable opponents in hand-to-hand combat, as well as expert climbers. The upper set of arms, protruding from the shoulders, is longer and bulkier than the lower set. These creatures are amazingly strong, easily capable of lifting up to four times their own body weight. What's more, they have high endurance levels and a surprising tolerance for radiation."

The image on the viewscreen flickered to a photograph of a Nyari foot soldier charging towards whoever had been holding the camera. Marcus found the image disturbing. The creature was mid-jump, its forearms outstretched, ready to dig its razor-sharp claws into the photographer's flesh, in what were probably the last moments of his life. Its two beady, black little eyes were filled with hate.

"Note the row of vertical mandibles extruding from the mouth," the lecturer continued. "Six above and six below the mouth, and an additional pair of powerful pincers to dig into the victim's flesh, allowing the Nyari to lock onto its prey while a second, smaller pair of pincers tear the skin away, leaving a gaping wound."

Marcus felt queasy. He couldn't help imagining the gruesome scene that must have followed the image on the screen, particularly the terror that the poor photographer must have felt in that instant. Two rows in front of him, one of his lookalikes gagged, visibly just as disturbed by the implications of the image as Marcus was.

"Luckily for us, these mouth-parts also allow the Nyari to create a variety of sounds. By manipulating their formation, a Nyari is capable of speech not unlike our own."

"How is that good?" someone on one of the front rows interrupted.

"Ah, yes. A scout model," the lecturer murmured, doubtlessly having been asked the same question a hundred times before, most likely by the same type of clone. "I'm glad you asked," she replied insincerely before resuming her lesson. "Since the start of the war, our intelligence services have been able to capture live specimens, which in turn has given us the opportunity to study their language. Through language we gain the invaluable ability to interrogate our prisoners."

"But if they speak and we can understand them," Steven interjected, "can't we reason with them?"

The educator tilted her head, rolling back her eyes in silent contempt.

"Unfortunately all our attempts to negotiate have failed. The enemy is a savage and ruthless killer, hell-bent on one thing, and one thing only…" She paused for dramatic effect, an act rehearsed and repeated so many times over the years that it had lost any measure of sincerity. "…the total annihilation of every Terran man, woman and child."

She eyed the room, noting that her statement hadn't quite hit home.

"We are fighting for our very existence. This isn't about territory or resources. This is not a war of religion. This is not about who's right and who's wrong. This is about staying alive."

"See," the brown-eyed girl whispered, "we get the chance to be the saviors of our species. Can you think of anything nobler?"

"I guess not," replied Marcus, his eyes still very much on the terrifying image on the viewscreen.

"So, let's resume, shall we?" uttered the lecturer, pointing towards the creature's carapace on a new slide. "The Nyari body is covered in a hard, chitinous shell, which can range from a muddy yellow to a medium brown. Unfortunately, this formidable shell protects nearly

48

their entire bodies. Note that even the elongated head is enclosed in a pair of curved plates which meet at the center, creating a groove which runs the length of the skull from the mouth to the back of the head, where the plates transform into a mesh of thorny barbs. Two slits for the eyes, and another two for a pair of antennae protruding from the top of the head. Our intelligence has shown that these antennae provide the Nyari with an almost supernatural awareness of movement in their surroundings, making ambushes difficult at best and flanking maneuvers nearly impossible."

"Suicidal, more likely," Marcus quipped to the girl with the brown eyes, who shot him back a faint smile.

"As far as weaponry goes," the lecturer droned on, "these are some of the items in the Nyari arsenal."

A slide showing a barbed spear with a sectional shaft slid into view.

"This is called a 'Stiak'," she explained. "The Stiak is a particularly cruel weapon, most often tipped in a very potent neural toxin that paralyzes its victim. Next we have a strange device called a 'Rot Nitlik'," she carried on as the image of a crude-looking spherical device with a rusted metal cover came into view. "These grenades generate a gel-like substance on impact, which pins targets in place as the Nyari move in for the kill."

Another image, a metallic disk with barbs studding its edge, appeared on the screen.

"This is a common weapon in the Nyrai arsenal," the lecturer continued. "It's called a 'Rot Mak'. It is a thrown chakram-like drone which tracks and hones in on its prey. Next, we have what is undoubtedly the most vicious of all the Nyari weapons, the 'Sker Mekett'."

The image of a sword-like weapon, lacking a sharpened edge but bearing a chainsaw's bladed links along both edges, came into view. "A Sker Mekett is capable of cutting through our Ridgeway body armor as if it were made of that gray paste you people enjoy so much in the mess hall," she mused. "Now, I'm sure the sharper ones among you will have noticed that the Nyari weapons we've been discussing do not include any firearms. I assure you that this is not an oversight, but reflects our actual experience on the ground. We don't know why the Nyari seem to disdain firearms in ground combat, especially given that their ships use ranged weaponry in advance of our own, although we suspect it's something of a cultural taboo."

The four Nyari weapons seemed so alien to Marcus. Each was coated in an apparently biological substance resembling the Nyari's chitinous shells, serrated barbs jutting out in strategic places, as if designed to intimidate and cause pain as much as to kill.

"What can you tell us about their homeworld?" asked one of the scout models on the front row.

"Yes, of course, their world. The site of all of our most recent engagements," the lecturer replied, as she started pacing back and forth on the small circular stage, as if pondering how to proceed with the answer. "The Nyari system is home to six planets in close orbit around its yellow star, of which their homeworld, Nyramar, occupies the second orbit. The entire planet is one huge tropical jungle, with trees as thick as seventy meters, and heights of up to seven hundred and fifty meters. However, the Nyari mostly stick to the forest floor and lower canopies, carving their cities into the immense tree trunks of the oldest trees, some of which can house as many as tens of thousands of Nyari. Their dwellings are linked via underground tunnels and overhanging walkways, making settlements very hard to spot, especially where the edge of the city meets the jungle proper."

"How is it that these savages are so hard to fight? Can't we just bomb them from orbit?" asked one of the command models from the front rows. "They don't seem to be that much more advanced than us."

"Looks can be deceiving," replied the lecturer, resuming her pacing. "The fact is that the Nyari are an old race. Exactly how old we have yet to determine, but their technology is superior to ours, in some areas markedly so – their interstellar capabilities for example. Whereas we use station-based mass accelerators to shoot our fleets to a point on the outskirts of their system, they use a ship-based version of this same technology, allowing each ship to 'jump' independently from wherever they are, a technology we have yet to be able to replicate. In practice, however, the radiation expelled by these drives mean that the Nyari use the two barren planets in their system as jumping-off points, allowing them to slingshot their ships out from the planets' gravity wells, thereby increasing their acceleration without risking the population of Nyramar.

"The good news is that despite their technological advantages, much of the Nyari's equipment is inherited, passed down from father to son, a testament to their slow rate of industry. We will, in a sense, wear them down over time.

"Alright we're out of time. Class dismissed. Don't forget to read up on Nyari physiology," she shouted over the rustle of the crowd, eager to be let out of their seats after the long lecture. "Memorize it people! It may mean the difference between life and death one day!"

Marcus paused after rising from his seat, turning first to the girl and then back towards Steven. He closed his eyes, screwing up his courage to ask her for her name. Or even just to speak with her again before she left the auditorium. He wasn't sure if he'd ever have the opportunity again. He set his shoulders, opened his eyes, and turned to face her.

"Eve," she said, grinning from ear to ear, before he could open his mouth.

"What?" he mumbled, unsure of what she was referring to.

"My name," she explained, "in case you were too nervous to ask."

Chapter 7

"It's called Callisto," Steven explained to the small group at the table on the promenade.

He and the team's medic, Taylor Vod, had been discussing the makeup of the Terran solar system, and were arguing about the name of the moon their training facility was based on.

"Luna orbits Beta Terra, Callisto orbits Alpha Terra," he corrected the young medic. "You've got them mixed up."

Taylor was a stubborn man and didn't easily give up on the argument. Marcus wondered if he wanted to demonstrate his mental superiority to compensate for his short physique. He also smoked way too much. In fact, outside of training, Marcus couldn't remember a single moment when Taylor had been without a cigarette in his mouth. The smoke bothered Marcus. He kept trying to waft it away with his hands. Either Taylor didn't care, or he was too entrenched in his argument to notice.

"You've got it all wrong," Taylor retorted. "Demeter orbits Beta Terra."

"I think you ought to lay off the cigarettes, they're starting to mess with your head," replied Steven in frustration, "Demeter is one of the seven moons of Oberon. It's highly radioactive. You can't even land a ship there."

"Cigarettes have no effect on your mind, and you're wrong," the medic insisted before leaning back on his chair and folding his arms, clearly indicating that he was through trying to argue sense into Steven, who was happy to conclude the argument.

"Would you look at that?" moaned Taz, gesturing towards his lookalike at the bar across the way, conversing with an attractive young blonde. "Doesn't it bother you?"

"Doesn't what bother me?" queried Steven.

"All these jerks walking around with your face. It's disgusting."

"Or maybe you're walking around with his face," Steven jested. "He might be older than you, you know."

"Screw that. I'm way better looking than him. Therefore it's my face. Something's gotta be done about this," Taz mumbled, having had one too many drinks.

"Like what? It's not like you can change your face."

"Who said anything about my face?" he retorted, snatching Taylor's cigarette from his mouth and flinging it into a nearby glass. "I'm gonna rearrange his," he added, grabbing the ashtray off the table.

The others looked on as Taz stood up and crossed to the bar, holding the ashtray behind his back as he swaggered up behind his lookalike and poked him on the shoulder.

"He can't seriously…"

CRACK!

Taz's ashtray connected square with his twin's jaw, the resulting sound making it clear that the poor man's jaw had nearly snapped in half.

The blonde screamed in terror as Taz ran down the promenade, leaving his victim trying to prevent his blood from spurting all over the poor girl.

"That guy's fucking insane," bellowed Taylor, who was still morning the loss of his last cigarette. "He's supposed to be our scout?" he added, still outraged, as a pair of guards came rushing down the promenade.

*   *   *   *   *

The Training hall crackled with tension. Their squad had been performing better recently, but their win-to-loss ratio was still far from adequate, mostly due to Sergeant Lance's poor judgment and lack of leadership.

"Today's training will be the last in this series of exercises, designed to help promote cooperation and unity among your squad," Drill Sergeant Dawn barked. "And although you could have performed better in the past, I believe that today you will prove yourselves ready to serve in the Terran military."

Across the hall, another Drill Sergeant was occupied in motivating his squad before the simulation began.

"Yesterday there was an incident on the promenade involving a pair of 6-28 models."

Taz fidgeted, trying to keep his hands still at his side.

"This is unacceptable," the Drill Sergeant carried on. "Although we have yet to ascertain the identity of the assailant, rest assured that every measure is being taken to resolve the situation," he affirmed as he paced back and forth, coming to a stop in front of Taz, who was obviously having great difficulties keeping his composure. "It is only a matter of time before we have a suspect in custody." He paused. "Now, the games," he turned his back to Taz and took a few steps away from the squad. Taz sighed in relief. "Today, you will be up against Sergeant Lain and his men. I want a clear and concise victory," stated Drill Sergeant Dawn as he raised his datapad prior to executing the simulation. "Make me proud!" he concluded as he pressed the series of imaginary buttons on his datapad that would rearrange the room into a maze of indistinguishable walls and steps.

Marcus could feel the rise in his heartbeat. His breathing increased in interval. Already the rubber foam lining of his helmet was starting to stick to the skin of his neck as he began to perspire.

The room went dark.

The whole team waited the full three seconds it took for their helmets' night-vision to come online.

"Alright, I want three teams," commanded Sergeant Lance. "Sobieski, Albano, you two take the lead for Corporal Dimitrov on the left. Dimitrov, take Meer and Grey with you. Orseau and Hughes, you take the lead for Corporal Spielman on the right, with Kitamura and Suarez. Clarke and Simone will scout out the front, while the rest of us bring up the rear. Move out people, let's not keep the enemy waiting."

The squad moved into position. Marcus was pleased with Lance's orders, not only because Steven was part of his group, but also because the Sergeant had ordered a scout to lead each team through the labyrinth. Although he thought that pairing them up with a sniper was a mistake. In quarters as close as those inside the labyrinth, the sniper rifle's long barrel would be a disadvantage if they ran into an ambush.

Dimitrov's team's trail turned swiftly to the left after a thirty-meter steady march down a straight corridor, which descended a quarter of a meter with each step. Down was bad, Marcus thought, keeping an eye out on the walls above, half expecting to see an enemy sniper poised for attack. No, they couldn't be that far into the maze already.

The corridor veered left yet again, bringing them to another thirty-meter corridor running parallel to the hallways they'd followed from the entrance.

"Crap," blurted Taz. "This is a dead end."

The maze was quiet, no shots being fired. The only sounds they heard were those of their own heavy breathing and the beating of their hearts.

"Dimitrov, bring your squad up the rear, following our trail," Lance ordered. "We came to a crossroads earlier and proceeded directly across. Take the left. I've got a sneaking suspicion that the enemy is going to try and come around behind us."

"…ontact, contact!" the speakers flared.

"Report!" Sergeant Lance shouted back.

Marcus's team was already well on their way back to the starting point when they heard the shots. They were faint, probably at the opposite end of the maze.

"I say again," the Sergeant recounted. "Who is this, and what is your situation?"

There was no reply. The gunfire had subsided and the maze was again quiet as the grave.

"I repeat, what is your situation?"

"They're dead Sergeant," Steven answered. "Can't you hear that?"

"I can't hear a thing."

"Exactly," replied Taz. "Their comms have been disconnected."

"Fuck!"

There was a distinct pause.

What do we do? Marcus asked himself.

"Dimitrov, take your team and check on Spielman. I want you to nail those bastards."

"You got it Sergeant," Corporal Dimitrov acknowledged.

Taz and Reid sprung forward, increasing their pace to a fast jog, pausing briefly at every corner to cover each other.

"See anything?" the Sergeant howled.

"Not yet Sergeant," Taz chimed in, "but we should be there any…"

Taz and Reid stopped dead in their tracks. Taz had his left hand raised to indicate that the rest of them should approach with caution. Dimitrov and Marcus peered around the corner. It was a lowered clearing, roughly four by five meters, with three points of entry. Spielman, Kitamura, Hughes, Orseau, and Suarez lay on the floor. The spinning triangle on Marcus' visor indicated their status was '*Deceased*'.

"It's Spielman's team. They're dead Sergeant," Corporal Dimitrov confirmed. "They're all dead. No sign of the enemy."

"Shit. Alright, well continue the flanking maneuver and…"

Sergeant Lance's comms went dead. The sound of heavy fire could be heard no more than twenty or thirty meters away, towards the center of the chamber.

"Fuck, fuck, fuck!" a voice shouted into the comms. It was Jenna Raleigh. Marcus recognized the voice of the naïve young blonde as she screamed again and again in total panic.

"Calm down!" Dimitrov yelled into the comms.

It worked. Either that or she had just been shot, effectively cutting off her comms.

"What's your status?" Dimitrov barked. "Jenna?" he repeated when all he could hear was gunfire, and the sound of something heavy being slammed against one of the walls.

"It's Jago," she finally replied. "When the Sergeant was shot, he snapped and charged the enemy. They shot him immediately but he just kept on going, fighting blind. He knocked out Becks by mistake. The enemy took out Clarke."

"Alright Jenna, calm down. We're on our way. What's your current location?"

"I don't know. I ran off as soon as Jago started beating up our own team," she replied.

"Simone, Vod, Taber, come in," Dimitrov ordered, checking their status.

"We're still here. We fought free, and we've got a good line on the objective, but so does the enemy. We're in a stalemate at the moment, but I'm pretty sure they've got some men maneuvering to outflank us."

"Hang in there, we're coming," concluded Dimitrov, gesturing for Marcus and Steven to move forward on the flank while he took Taz and Reid back through the maze to help break the stalemate. "Move fast boys, keep your weapons at the ready, and fire at anything that moves!"

"Yes Corp," Marcus replied, tilting his weapon up as he moved to stand beside Steven.

"Well Marcus. If you want to be a hero, now's your chance," Steven smirked before charging headfirst down the path ahead.

Marcus followed fast on his heels. Whether it was due to their night-vision or simply their fast pace, Steven was nothing more than a blur ahead of him, rushing from one corridor to the next, not even stopping so Marcus could guard his back when they came to junctions. In fact, he moved so quickly that Marcus could barely even register it when he shot down two of the enemy combatants upon clearing a corner.

"Slow down!" Marcus yelled. "You're going too fast."

Steven paused and turned to face him. "It's just a game Marcus."

"I know, but I want to win," Marcus confided, a bit disappointed that his friend wasn't taking this more seriously. "They're counting on us."

Steven quickly raised his carbine at him, pointing it straight at his head.

"What are you-"

The gun went off.

Marcus cringed as if he had really been shot.

Steven's outstretched hand pointed at the sniper he had just shot, positioned right behind Marcus on a raised platform some twenty meters away.

"I thought you were going to shoot me," Marcus prompted.

"Shoot you? I would never do that. Come on, I have an idea."

The two ran off once more, down a set of winding tunnels leading them deeper into the maze.

* * * * *

Simone, Taber, and Taylor had dug themselves in deep behind a waist-high wall, with Taylor guarding the rear while Taber and Simone exchanged potshots with a group of at least five enemy combatants right across the center of the maze. Even though the objective, a green holographic diamond, was a mere seven meters away in the center of the contested clearing, neither team could risk running into the open in order to claim victory.

It had been several minutes since they last heard from Corporal Dimitrov, which, in conjunction with a heavy round of fire they'd heard earlier, had lead them to believe that they were the only members of their squad left. It was still possible that the nerve-wracked Jenna Raleigh was still cowering in some distant corner, assuming the enemy hadn't found her, but they weren't expecting her to be of much help.

"We have to do something," yelled Taylor.

"Like what, genius?" Simone belittled him. "We're outgunned, and we have no idea how many more men they have repositioning themselves to take us out."

"That's exactly why we can't just sit here and wait for that to happen!" Taylor retorted.

Simone looked at him gravely, trying to come up with even a vague idea for a strategy which could lead them to victory.

"I've got nothing," she finally concluded. "Taber, we're going in."

Taber nodded his approval. This was do or die, the moment of glory. The three weary soldiers changed their clips and took a deep breath, ready to storm the enemy.

At the very same instant they emerged from cover, Steven appeared from behind the enemy. Marcus had given him a boost, using his hands to propel him completely over the wall behind their opponents' position, which was as close as they'd been able to sneak without being spotted. As Taber, Taylor and Simone let loose a hail of imaginary rounds on the enemy from the front, Steven emptied his clip into them from their rear.

It was all over.

Marcus could hear the cheering as the remnants of his squad claimed the objective. Victory was theirs.

"Well done gentlemen. Very well done," Drill Sergeant Dawn congratulated them as the light returned to the simulation room.

Sergeant Lance didn't seem all too pleased with the success of his team, no doubt due to his lack of involvement in their victory.

"Raynes, Jago," Dawn barked when the squad had gathered back at their starting point.

"Yes boss?"

"You've got to learn to control that temper of yours," the Drill Sergeant commented. "The ability to keep a cool head in battle is essential to every engagement. That applies to you too, Private Raleigh."

Jenna appeared from under her helmet with a shameful look on her face.

"I'm sorry," she apologized. "He's just... so... big!" she explained, looking up at Jago.

"Size is rarely the most determining factor for the outcome of a battle, Raleigh."

"Yes sir," she conceded.

"Now, seeing as this was your last training simulation, I have an announcement to make. Tomorrow you are to report to the grand auditorium at fifteen-hundred hours for a motivational speech by General Santiago. After which you will have until noon the following day to decide whether or not you wish to serve in the Terran military."

The Drill Sergeant's last remark rang in Marcus' ears. The perplexed look on Steven's face told him he wasn't the only one who was confused.

"We get to choose?" he asked.

"Of course you get to choose. The War Replication Act, Article 4, Section B, states that a clone shall have the choice between a life of freedom on Alpha Terra, or a term of service in the Terran Forces, after which he or she shall be granted full citizenship on Beta Terra or the colony of his or her choosing."

"But," Steven paused, "I thought Alpha Terra was a wasteland?"

"It is, Private," replied the Drill Sergeant, eyeing Steven suspiciously. "Alpha Terra is a post-apocalyptic wasteland, overrun with deserters, thieves, smugglers and vagabonds. If you choose to live out your life among such rabble, rather than here among these great men and women of honor, then I hope luck's on your side Private, because we sure as hell won't be."

Chapter 8

The squad had waited in anticipation for the clock to strike 3:00 pm. The auditorium was a grand hall, large enough to accommodate several thousand spectators. A raised central stage occupied the area opposite the two adjoining entry ramps. On each side of the stage a pair of massive red banners edged with black and white stripes sported the symbol of a two-headed eagle encircled in white, five stars floating above the twin heads. Rows upon rows of red-cushioned seats ascended from the stage towards the back of the hall. On the stage, near its center, stood a single figure with graying dark hair wearing a black uniform with three red stripes along the side of its sleeves.

The clones marched in, double file, between the lines of ceremonial guards arranged along each side of the entry ramps. The guards, clones themselves, were dressed in the Ridgeway Terran Infantry standard battle gear and sporting SGC K-660 medium carbines. As Marcus marched past the guards, he thought about how strange it was that his resonant memories sometimes provided him with such detailed information about the things he saw.

Taz had managed to locate enough seats for their entire squad just off to the right of the stage, but not so close that they could clearly make out the stage's sole occupant. Marcus sat between Steven and Taz, who was propounding the theory that the clones' whole existence was nothing more than an elaborate game, created for the amusement of the Beta Terrans. As far as Marcus knew, Taz could be right. Marcus wondered if this element of paranoia had been bred into Taz's model on purpose. Perhaps in order to make him a better scout. Edward Suarez, a foul-mouthed, arrogant clone who thought he got along great with everyone, sat down in front of Marcus, giving him a conceited smile as he did so. Too bad his popularity was all in his head.

As soon as their squad had gotten to their seats, the clamor from the crowd began to rise. The rapidly-filling auditorium was an impressive sight. Marcus didn't know how many clones there were, but definitely somewhere in the thousands. He wondered how many lookalikes he had in this very room. He could easily make out the four closest to him.

For the first time since his birth, he caught himself thinking about the origins of his model. Was there such a thing as the original 6-26? If so, he would surely be long dead by now.

The murmur of the crowd started to subside. Eventually the massive black void behind the stage came to life, first as a flicker of bright light, then the soaring symbol of the two headed eagle on a crimson background. The image faded quickly to a live feed of the figure on stage.

He was a middle-aged man, with silvery gray lines running through his otherwise black hair. His stern, steel-gray eyes lent him a commanding presence. He wore silver medallions emblazoned with the emblem of the Terran forces on his shoulders and more medals than Marcus had ever seen on one person before. The collar of his uniform protruded upwards in the back and on the sides, following the curvature of his neck.

"Welcome Terrans," his booming voice echoed throughout the hall. All eyes and ears locked onto him.

Sergeant Lance was seated on the other side of Steven, and Marcus noticed a euphoric grin creep its way onto his face, his eyes wide open, soaking in the scene.

"I am General Enton Santiago, and I am here to welcome you all to Alamo Station. Alamo Station is not only the heart of the Terran military, but also home to the War Replication Department, or W.R.D.. The W.R.D. is charged with the important duty of creating, developing and nurturing clones for the betterment of our race."

The General paused dramatically, surveying the crowd, having no doubt not only rehearsed, but also given, this very speech countless times before. Still, his recital was far superior to the lackluster performances of their lecturers in the training facility.

"Now, tomorrow at noon, you will all be given a hard choice, perhaps the most difficult, definitely the most important choice you will ever make. Each and every one of you has the right to choose whether you wish to serve in the Terran forces, upon the completion of which you will be granted full citizenship, along with all the rights entitled to you as such. Or…" the General recited, pausing yet again, this time looking down at the floor in a show of veiled contempt.

"…or you can choose freedom. Now I know full well how tempting that may sound to some of you, but I assure you, freedom may award you the right to live your life according to your own decisions, your own standards, your own morals, but it will strip away all that you have come to know, to trust and rely on. Should you so choose, you will be escorted down to the surface of Alpha Terra, where you may live out the rest of your days in cities scorched by fire, on fields once lush but now barren, in wastelands strewn with rubble and debris where every day you will have to resort to scavenging for food like rodents, among deserters, criminals and every other lowlife imaginable." The General sneered at the thought. "A life of freedom is a constant confrontation with the harsh elements that will wear you down just as easily, if not more so, than a single tour of duty."

He bit his lip, shaking his head to emphasize his point.

"A tour of duty consists of four years of service in the Terran military, where you will have the opportunity to strike at the very heart of our enemy, the merciless Nyari, whose bio-mechanized ships laid ruin to our once-beloved homeworld, Alpha Terra."

Whether his display of sadness over the mention of the Nyari attack was genuine or not, Marcus couldn't tell, but it stood to reason that such a dramatic event would live on in the hearts of every Terran for centuries to come.

"Choose service, and all of your needs shall be met. You will be clothed. You will be fed. You will have a warm bed to sleep in. You will be compensated. You will know camaraderie the likes of which you have only just begun to imagine. Most of all, you will have... a purpose!"

The cheering of the crowd applauding the General's well thought-out words as they rose from their seats resounded throughout the hall with incredible might. The General stood still, allowing his audience a moment to regain their composure before continuing.

"And after you have fought and bled together as brothers and sisters, you will be celebrated as heroes and saviors of the Republic and welcomed into a life of free citizenship on our new homeworld, Beta Terra!" Santiago's voice shot up in a thunderous roar as he voiced those two last words, a roar superseded only by the explosive applause from the thousands of enthralled onlookers.

In that moment Marcus felt as if they'd all made the choice to serve, all except Steven, who still sat quietly in his seat, a troubled expression on his brow. Marcus plumped back down into his seat, and began to contemplate his life, his entire existence, up to that moment.

They had been created to serve, a service made to seem noble and selfless. Yet the more he considered their choice, and the freedom offered, the more he began to see it for what it really was. Although painted so grimly, Marcus believed the choice was given, not out of generosity, but rather to give those who had chosen to serve a sense of honor and pride in the belief that it was their decision to do so.

*   *   *   *   *

A flawless procession of logistics department carts passed Marcus and Steven by as they leaned back on the polished metal framework of the bench just outside Marcus's quarters in the barracks. Outside, the view of the base gave way to Alpha Terra, just as the sun was disappearing behind it. The rays appeared to ignite its atmosphere in brilliant hues of golden red and blue. The planet itself was equal parts dark blue, dull brown and gray in color. A few small branches of bright orange shone through amidst the dim and uninviting landscape, cracks in the earth through which fiery molten lava erupted from time to time.

After nearly a month of gray and white steel walls and fluorescent lights, the magnificence of what they were seeing had stolen the clones' breath entirely. The schedule for the rest of the day was void of any activities, giving them time to think before officially registering their decision the following day.

Marcus had meant to meet up with the rest of his squad on the promenade, but after freshening up he had found Steven waiting outside his quarters, perched on the bench, staring into space.

"Just think, Marcus," sighed Steven, breaking the silence. "We could be there tomorrow."

The corridor was silent. Marcus didn't know what to say. The idea of leaving the squad and living in such uncertainty didn't sound too appealing, but leaving Steven, his only friend, was even less palatable.

"Free to wake up when we choose, go where ever our heart takes us, and meet people who, at one point, were as exhilarated about their decision as we are now."

Marcus's eyes were drawn to a small but distinct flare of bright light close to the planet's edge.

"That's the Wako," explained Steven. "Callisto's orbit should take us close enough to see it more clearly tonight," he continued, unable to hide the sadness in his voice.

"What's the Wako?" asked Marcus, unable to contain his curiosity. He wondered again how Steven knew so much about everything.

"The Wako is a weapon, a gun so big it took over twenty years to construct."

"What does it fire?" Marcus asked.

"Us."

"What do you mean? It shoots clones?" Marcus's confusion grew.

"The Wako is a mass accelerator. A cannon, designed to propel ships all the way to the Nyari system. They say that it can achieve velocities multiple times the speed of light. Without it, we would have lost the war a long time ago."

"How long does it take? The journey I mean."

"About six months. Without the Wako it would take hundreds of years," claimed Steven, his sadness evaporating.

"But how do they get back?"

"They have another accelerator there, hidden on the outskirts of the system. They built it in parts and assembled it on the other side. Each part was just small enough to be fired off by the Wako here. Pretty clever, don't you think?" he mused.

"How do you know all this?" Marcus asked him, astounded with the intricate details of Steven's understanding of Terran history.

"While the rest of you were busy spending your credits on drinks, cigarettes and fast food, I bought this," Steven exclaimed, producing a sleek, miniature version of the datapad Marcus had so often seen in the hands of the Station's personnel.

Marcus looked at the device with fascination. The display screen showed a variety of selectable items for the user's viewing pleasure.

"It has network access that allows me to connect with the Terran archives. I've been pretty busy reading as much as I can, to try and make sense of everything," Steven explained as he pocketed the device. "Although, after tomorrow, I don't think I'll be getting much use from it."

"Why's that?" Marcus asked him.

"I doubt there are any network access points on Alpha Terra."

There was another silence, during which Marcus' mind wrestled with the impossibility of deciding whether he'd rather leave his squad or his friend.

"It's getting closer now," he muttered as the Wako slid closer into view.

It flared once more, and this time applause erupted from a group of custodians who had paused to take in the sight. The Wako was indeed magnificent, so immense you could easily fit an entire battleship inside. The square outlines of its barrel extended a little over eight kilometers, with various turrets and docking bays, themselves immense but dwarfed by the scale of the station, cluttering its surface from end to end. Marcus could make out the silhouettes of a pair of cruisers waiting their turn to be flung towards Nyramar against the station's huge bulk.

"Beautiful, isn't it?" sighed Steven.

"Steven, why is it that you're so against serving in the military, but you seem so utterly fascinated with every aspect of it?" Marcus blurted. He thought he'd made a fair, and intuitive, point.

"It's hard to explain," Steven replied, pausing briefly as he contemplated how best to answer. "I want to be free," he said finally, "but I also want to explore, discover new things, to learn the truth – the real truth, not the truth the military decides for us."

Marcus didn't understand.

"If I serve, they'll ship me off to war, where I will be forced to fight for a truth that the military has fed us. I will die a horrible death, just like so many millions of clones do each and every year."

Steven was right of course. Marcus had heard the rumors himself. The war with the Nyari was no joke. With a projected casualty rate of eighty seven percent, the thought of going to war seemed suicidal. Marcus dragged his attention back to his friend, who was still talking.

"No, I will not serve. Tomorrow I will go to Alpha Terra, and hopefully someday I can find a way to improve the rights of clones. Give them more choices than they have now."

"I'm coming with you," Marcus blurted out, before he'd even realized he'd decided.

Steven smiled.

"Did you know that Terrans don't even originate from Alpha Terra?" Steven said, breaking the awkward silence. "We don't even come from this galaxy. We come from some distant planet called Earth, millions of light years away."

"How is that even possible?" Marcus countered. "Did they have a mass accelerator orbiting Earth?"

"No, the colony ship that originally brought us here was powered by a salvaged alien drive."

"Alien?"

"Apparently the Earthers discovered an alien craft of some kind, disabled in their system. They kept the primary drive for study, but built a colossal seed ship called the *Lazarus* and rigged the backup drive from the alien ship on the *Lazarus*."

"But then why did they send it all the way out here? And how did the colonists survive such a long journey? Surely it would have taken hundreds of thousands of years." Marcus's mind was overburdened with questions, questions which demanded answers.

"The Earthers were able to access the navigational data from the alien craft. This very system was its point of origin. That's why we're here, to establish contact. Only, when the *Lazarus* arrived, there was nothing here. There weren't any colonists on board anyway, only DNA samples. The artificial intelligence on the *Lazarus* was instructed to create clones as soon as it arrived," explained Steven, with a great deal of enthusiasm. "The whole thing is one big cosmic joke of truly galactic proportions," he mused.

Marcus couldn't help but laugh. "But then, how long did it take? I mean, surely these Earthers will have figured out the alien drive technology by now. Why haven't more come here?"

"1184 years. That's how long the journey took," Steven explained. "And nobody has heard anything from Earth since. Of course, our communications technology is way behind the drive technology that got us here. It will take millions of years before our first message even reaches earth. So I wouldn't sit around waiting for a reply," Steven jested.

"Wow," sighed Marcus. "So why haven't the Terrans here developed the alien drive technology themselves?"

"Ah, excellent question," commented Steven. "They were about to. They had their most brilliant scientists working on the drive on the Lazarus day and night. Apparently it was damaged after the landing on Alpha Terra, during the founding of the original colony. But, as luck would have it, the drive and the entire research facility, including most of the data, were all destroyed in the Nyari invasion."

They sat in silence, quietly observing more cruisers being hurled away on their six month journey to Nyramar.

"They say that they always make toasts on the promenade whenever the Wako flares," revealed Steven.

"They must be drinking a lot tonight then," Marcus mused.

Then he grinned. He could feel the excitement now. Tomorrow was a whole new day, a whole new life. He would be following his best friend on a great adventure. The knot in his stomach began to dissipate, replaced instead with hope for a future full of untold possibilities.

Chapter 9

"How can you dismiss us this easily?" Sergeant Lance shouted into their faces.

The infuriated Sergeant had just received Marcus' and Steven's documents, both sets of which indicated their choice of freedom. The two friends were on their knees, their hands cuffed behind their backs. They had reported to hangar bay 3-14 just a few minutes earlier, and once the Sergeant had read their documents, the squad had turned against them.

The bay was a warehouse-like structure, some fifty meters square, with a ceiling over ten meters high. It was cut in half by a thick glass wall running between two reinforced-steel girders. A door in the center allowed the troops entry into the far compartment, which housed a B-14 Barracuda dropship.

Marcus could see the ship's landing gear and undercarriage clearly from where he knelt, but the rest of the ship was obstructed from view, as the clones' side of the hangar bay was split into two stories. The upper floor housed bunk beds, enough to sleep twenty clones. The lower floor was divided into two areas by an internal partition, the larger holding a scattering of benches, tables and battered lockers, as well as a narrow steel staircase to the storey above and the doors leading to the rest of the Station and the ship. Beyond the partition, which was broken by a doorless entryway, was a semi-enclosed area housing showers and latrines. The floor of the whole lower storey was covered with dirt-stained tiles that had accrued layers upon layers of grime and sweat over decades of continued use. Marcus wondered just how many squads had called this place home before them.

"Is this really necessary?" bellowed Taz, obviously distraught over the whole ordeal.

"They're traitors to the cause," Sergeant Lance spat. "They don't deserve to be treated any better."

"They're not traitors," argued Reid. "They have every right to choose."

"Every right?" blurted the Sergeant. "After all we've been through together?"

He was furious. It was clear to Marcus that the Sergeant had seen their decision as a personal attack, a rejection of his leadership.

"Where's the Ape?" the Sergeant cursed as he paused his pacing, not seeing the behemoth standing a few meters behind him.

"Right here boss," replied Jago, who had become accustomed to the nickname.

"Put them in the showers. It disgusts me to have to look at them," the Sergeant ordered him.

"Yes boss."

Jago pushed them forcefully aside, tipping them over. He then proceeded to grab Steven and Marcus by their legs, each monstrous hand easily encircling both of their feet, dragging them into the showers with their backs scraping against the cold grimy tiles. He didn't show much restraint as he hoisted them up, propping them none-too-gently against the walls of the shower compartment. A sharp pain shot through Marcus's skull as his head made contact with the wall. The lights in the shower area flickered on.

At some point the tiles on the wall had been white, but now they were more of an uneven yellow, with streaks of brown running down to the floor from the rusted metal pipes. Three small toilet stalls took up the breadth of the wall across from the showers. The lights continued to flicker, buzzing chaotically.

Jago hunkered down to look them each in the eye. It was the first time Marcus had seen his enormous crooked nose and square jaw up close. His bloodshot eyes stared at him, studying him.

"Stay put and shut up," he finally spat. "One word and I'll put your heads in the shitter," he snarled as he rose to his feet, towering over them, completely blocking out the flickering light.

He turned the shower nozzle on and off a few times, letting streams of ice cold water pour over them. He chuckled as he turned to leave.

"Forget them," Steven whispered to Marcus, not wanting to draw Jago's attention. "In six months they'll all be dead anyway." Marcus wanted to reply, but the thought of having his head crammed down a toilet that probably hadn't been cleaned properly for years, if not decades, convinced him not to. "No matter how terrible Alpha Terra may be, rest assured, they're in for far worse."

The two friends sat in quiet resignation, watching through the doorway to the main area as their former teammates opened their lockers and began donning their gear. The dark-gray and faded-yellow standard infantry armor looked menacing. Especially when worn by Jago Raynes.

The chestplate consisted of two segments, the seam between them running down the middle of the chest. A backplate of the same design was fastened to the chestplate by straps across the wearer's sides, and both plates were bolted to a high, crescent-shaped neck guard that ran around the back of the wearer's neck. The eagle insignia of the Terran forces was engraved in black on the left segment of the chestplate. The shoulder plates – 'pauldrons', Marcus' resonant memories informed

76

him – extended from the neck guard across the shoulder and down the upper arm, while a pair of bracers covered the outer forearm from elbow to the wrist. The upper-body armor was strapped over a padded jacket made of dark-gray leathery material. The pants were made of the same material as the jacket, but with a thick ribbed lining running down the sides, and faded yellow plates protecting the knees and shins, merging seamlessly with armored boots.

The helmet was a matching dark gray and faded yellow, with a built-in three-point laser-sighting unit mounted next to a tinted visor. A large latch extended from either side of the helmet's chin-piece like mandibles, allowing a sideways-facing cylindrical canister to be snapped into place, and a small but durable-looking antennae protruded up from the back left side of the helmet. A series of small pouches, hanging from the belt or fastened to the chestplate, carried spare ammunition.

Save for the size difference, the squad members all looked identical once they'd finished putting on their gear. No marks to indicate rank. Marcus knew that this was deliberate. The ranks were displayed holographically, so that the enemy had no indication of who was in charge.

Suddenly the bay's entry door opened, and in walked a familiar female pilot, with dark curly hair now much longer than when Marcus had first met her. With her was a scrawny, young-looking clone with protruding ears and an elongated chin.

"Pilot Zorita Spencer and Copilot Scott Adler, reporting for duty, Sergeant," she barked confidently as she came to attention in front of Lance.

Marcus's heart skipped a beat. Not now, he thought. Why did she have to show up now when he was tied up on the floor like some kind of animal?

"Are you any good?" inquired the Sergeant, removing his helmet to look the new additions in the eye.

"Any good?" she sneered. "Sergeant, I'm the best damned pilot this military has ever seen. Am I right Minty?" she claimed, shoving her copilot off to the side so she could march up to the window to get a better look at her ship.

The copilot averted his gaze in embarrassed apprehension. Taz removed his helmet to get a better look at Zorita's shapely behind as she leaned up against the glass admiring the ship.

"Who cares about her piloting skills, that ass is smoking hot," he said to the room at large.

She turned to face him, a sly smile on her gorgeous lips.

"That it is Private, that it is," she replied, taking a few well placed leisurely strides towards him.

Taz didn't see her right hook before it was too late and he was lying on the floor on his back.

"…and if I ever catch you looking at it again I'll tear off your legs and shove them up your ass."

Sergeant Lance couldn't contain his laughter.

"Are you sure you wouldn't better suited as a soldier?" he finally asked when his laughter had subsided.

"No sir. I don't bother with small arms. I prefer lots of speed and heavy artillery," she proclaimed, gesturing towards the cannon attached to the barracuda's underbelly.

"Good enough for me," Lance acknowledged. "Alright men, grab your assigned weapons from your lockers and let's get these cowards onto the ship."

While the rest of the men were busy familiarizing themselves with their weapons, Jago grabbed Steven and flung him over his shoulder. Marcus was amazed at the ease with which he had lifted his friend from the stained floor.

"Albano, you grab the other one," ordered Sergeant Lance.

Reid set his sniper rifle aside and entered the shower area, kneeling in front of Marcus.

"I'm sorry for this," he whispered, grabbing Marcus around the waist and using his legs to lift him up over his broad shoulder. "May God be with you," he added softly, before marching out of the showers.

God, thought Marcus. He knew what the word meant, but had never really pondered its implications. Until now.

*   *   *   *   *

The barracuda was an uninterestingly blocky vessel, with no wings or visible means of maneuverability. Its bluntly pointed nose sloped back to join the main body of the craft, the underside of the nose heavily plated, the topside forming the windscreen of the cockpit. Apart from the nose, a raised tail was the only visible characteristic that Marcus was able to make out as Reid carried him onboard.

Inside, the barracuda sported two decks, the lower of which was accessible via a wide entry ramp which swung down from the front of the craft's main body, and two wide sliding doors on the vessel's flanks, with bars mounted above them on the ceiling for rappelling gear. A row of benches lined both sides of the deck on either side of the side doors, with lockers bolted to the bulkheads aft of the doors and a metal desk and chair bolted to the floor in the back serving as a makeshift office, workbench or surgical table depending on the task at hand. The second deck above could be accessed only via hatch and ladder, located in the rear corner of the deck.

Although his resonant memories informed him that the second deck housed two rows of cryo-stasis pods as well as the ship's cockpit, Marcus never made it that far. As soon as they were all on board, Lance ordered Marcus and Steven to be cuffed to the rappelling bar over the port door.

"We're good to go Spencer," the Sergeant called, linking his armor's built-in comms to the ship's intercom.

"Aye aye Sergeant. And call me Raven."

The ship's engines came to life with a low-pitched droning hum. The electronics fired off in a cascading series of high pitched noises. The entry ramp began to inch upwards, with the accompanying clanks and whirring sounds, until it shuddered closed, lying flush with the deck. As the atmospheric seals suddenly pressurized, Marcus could feel a tingling sensation coursing throughout his entire body.

The ship's gravity drive engaged, and Marcus could feel the barracuda begin to hover in place. He could hear the hangar bay door opening. It wouldn't be long now. He wondered what the smell of fresh, non-recycled air would taste like, how it would be to feel the wind on his skin. Steven had described that morning what it would be like, taking that first step onto a new world. Marcus couldn't help but feel excited.

Raven, he thought. He would never see her again. Nor Eve for that matter. He missed Eve already. He wondered what she was doing right now. No doubt she would forget all about him. Maybe she already had.

* * * * *

The journey was a mere two-hour trip, but to Marcus it felt like forever. The weightlessness of open space was as frightening as it was exhilarating.

His former comrades, slouching on the benches lining the bulkheads, were silent for the most part, all except Taz, who regaled his teammates with tales of his alleged female conquests back on the Alamo, and Reid, whom Marcus believed he heard say a prayer. Was Reid praying for him? He wasn't sure, but the thought helped calm his nerves. He liked Reid. The two hadn't gotten much of an opportunity to get to know each other, and perhaps that was Marcus' own fault.

Gradually the barracuda began to vibrate. Marcus could sense the reverberations passing through him, passing from the wall into his skull.

"What's going on Zor... I mean Raven?" the clueless Sergeant asked.

"We're entering the planet's atmosphere Sergeant. Nothing to worry about," replied the pilot over the ship's intercom.

"How far are we from the DZ?"

"Just a few minutes Sergeant, I'll let you know. Geez, talk about..." muttered Raven, a bit slow on the release of the comm button.

The vibrations grew exponentially in strength, to the point where the ship appeared to be shaking uncontrollably, tossed around by some unseen force. Marcus could clearly make out the anxiety on everyone's face but Reid's. The dark-skinned clone had his hands together, palms facing each other, seemingly as calm as could be.

A few moments later, the shaking dissipated and the barracuda once again flew smoothly. Marcus hadn't even noticed the gradual return of gravity during the commotion, but it was undoubtedly there now.

"Almost there Sergeant," stated Raven. "We're right above the LZ. I'm easing her down now."

Sergeant Lance got up, and, while holding the rappelling bar for support, began making his way towards the soon-to-be-free men. He pressed a button to the side of the wide doorframe on the left side of the ship, just next to Steven's head, before pulling a lever. The door slid open.

A warm dry gust of desert air blew in through the opening. It smelled different than Marcus had imagined. Almost stale. Still chained to the bar by his wrists, Marcus couldn't see outside over his shoulder, but the barracuda was still descending.

"Alright, you first," ordered the Sergeant as he grabbed Steven by the shoulder, turning him around so that he could release the cuffs. "What do we have here?" exclaimed the Sergeant, snatching Steven's miniature datapad from his pocket after unfastening his cuffs. "I don't think you'll have much need for this anymore," he sniggered as he raised his foot and promptly ejected Steven from the ship with a quick thrust of his boot.

"Nooo!" yelled Marcus, throwing himself towards the open door, the cuffs yanking him back before he could see what had happened to Steven.

The ship hadn't landed yet. How high up were they?

Sergeant Lance loomed over Marcus, who was hell-bent on resisting.

"Stand the fuck down, or I'll have one of my men shoot you," the Sergeant yelled at him.

Marcus eased up as the Sergeant proceeded to unfasten his cuffs, sending him crashing to the floor.

"Get up," he ordered.

Reluctantly, Marcus got on his feet, one hand firmly on the rappelling bar. He leaned over to look through the opening.

The ship hovered a mere two meters or so off the ground.

The high pitched whining of the ship's engines had drowned out the thud when Steven had hit the ground. He lay there on his side, rubbing his knee.

It was then that Marcus caught his first view of the landscape. The ship appeared to be hovering in the middle of what he guessed might have been a city square. All the buildings in the vicinity were little more than crumbling ruins. Scorched vehicles and debris littered the streets as far as the eye could see. Everything was covered in dust. He could make out a few skeletal remains amidst all the clutter. The whole place reeked of death. Steven had managed to stand up and was looking intently towards Marcus, ready to catch him to help break his fall.

"Jump Marcus!" he shouted. "Forget about them. They'll all be dead in six months!"

Marcus clutched the rappelling bar with both hands, looking back at Sergeant Lance, then down to Steven.

"They don't stand a chance Marcus!" reiterated Steven, "The Nyari will kill them all!"

"We're not going to fight the Nyari!" Lance yelled over the sound of the engines, much to their surprise. "Our squad has been designated for corporate service!" he added. "We won't even be leaving the Terran system."

Could it be true? Marcus wondered. Was Lance just making it up out of spite? Or was the squad truly not meant for the war? It had never occurred to him that they might be sent anywhere other than Nyramar.

Lance began shoving Marcus out the door.

"Wait," shouted Marcus in desperation.

"What now?" sneered Lance. "Don't tell me, sudden change of heart?" The sarcasm in the Sergeant's tone was unmistakable.

"I... I don't know," muttered Marcus.

"What are you waiting for?" shouted Steven. "He's lying to you!"

Marcus's mind was going a million miles a minute. On the one hand, if he stayed with the squad he would be betraying his best friend, his only friend. On the other hand, what had sounded before like a harsh life of freedom now looked more like a slow, but certain, death. Even the hot stale air stung with every breath he had to force himself to take.

"I... I've changed my mind," Marcus let out. His surrender pained him. He turned his head. He couldn't bear to look Steven in the eye. He was so overwrought with guilt over disappointing his friend that his knees buckled.

"Are you sure Grey?" probed the Sergeant. "The punishment for desertion-"

"Yes, I'm sure," Marcus interrupted him, his voice quivering in anger, anger aimed more towards himself for his cowardice than with Lance for withholding the truth. "Take me back to the Alamo."

"Marcus, no! They're using you! They're using you!"

Those were the last words Marcus heard from Steven as the door slammed shut and the barracuda began its steady climb back into space.

Chapter 10

Marcus found himself sitting on the bench outside his old quarters, the very same bench he and Steven had shared the night before. He had no reason to be there anymore. His quarters had been assigned to someone else, someone new and clueless, probably still weeks away from having to make the same gut-wrenching decision he'd been forced to make.

He felt betrayed. If only the Sergeant had told them earlier, none of this would have had to happen. Maybe if Steven had known that they weren't headed for Nyramar, he might have chosen to stay. Maybe then Marcus wouldn't be feeling so wrought with guilt. He felt like storming back to hangar bay 3-14 and commandeering the ship and blasting off to Alpha Terra. Maybe it wasn't too late?

The corridor in front of his room was empty. Most of the clones were sound asleep by now. A lone custodian busied himself trying to repair one of the drones which normally cleaned the floors in the hallway.

Marcus stared quietly into space. He found a spot on one of the land masses on the desolate planet where he imagined Steven would be, probably still standing there, cursing his name, his very existence.

He would have been better off if they had sent him off to war. Then at least he'd be dead in six months. He wouldn't have to live with the guilt for the rest of his life, wouldn't have to live on a base orbiting the world where he'd left his only friend to waste away and die... alone.

"Is this seat taken?" a familiar voice asked.

Marcus raised his head, and looked into the comforting smile of the girl who had, once upon a time, in a classroom on the other side of the base, teased him for not wanting to serve.

"Eve," he blurted out, not quite sure what to make of her sudden reappearance.

"I haven't seen you in a while," she stated, smiling at him, her beautiful brown eyes flaked with gold so soothing to look at.

"I've been… busy," he lied, unsure whether or not she could sense his remorse, his guilt.

"Me too," she replied, taking the empty seat next to his.

Marcus's nerves got the better of him and he involuntarily started fooling around with his new wrist communicator, a device he'd received upon his return to the Alamo.

"I'm glad you chose to stay," she sighed, looking down at her lap, equally tense.

"I dunno," he answered.

"You don't know?" she inquired.

"I… I had chosen to leave, but… at the last minute I changed my mind."

She placed her hand on his, preventing him from fiddling with his wrist comm.

"I'm glad you changed your mind, otherwise I would never have seen you again," she professed, her grip tightening around his hand.

Her hand was warm and clammy to the touch. Marcus could feel the tension in his body slowly beginning to dissipate. She liked him. There was no denying it.

"How did you know it was me?" he asked her.

"What do you mean?"

"Well, there are probably hundreds of guys on the Alamo that look just like me," he explained to her.

"But none of them are as vulnerable as you. You always look like you have the weight of the entire galaxy on your shoulders. And your eyes..."

"My eyes?"

"They hide an old soul."

She was staring so intently into his eyes that he felt as if time itself had stopped, just for them. He wanted so badly to confide in her, to tell her what he had done, even if she would curse him for his cowardice. Instead he said nothing. He did nothing, paralyzed by her gaze.

"Marcus," she urged.

"How did you know my name?"

"I asked."

"Whom did you ask?" he inquired.

"That dark-skinned guy from your squad, the one who can't keep his hands to himself."

"Taz?"

"Yeah, that's the one," she acknowledged.

"He didn't try to..."

"Oh yes he did, and when I said no, he hit on every one of my friends," she chuckled.

"One of these days his mouth is going to get him into some serious trouble," Marcus mused.

"What about your mouth?" she continued, leaning in closer, her full lips and blushing cheeks so close to his that he could smell the peach-scented aroma on her skin.

"My mouth?" he muttered.

"Yeah, why don't we see if we can find so…"

He pressed his lips against hers before she could finish. Every fiber of his being wanted her. He placed one hand on her brow, brushing her hair away from her eyes before laying it to rest firmly on her cheek. With his other hand, he grabbed her hip firmly, pulling her towards him, while she wrapped her arms around his neck.

*　*　*　*　*

Sergeant Lance had received orders to report to the offices of GeoDynamics, one of the largest of the Terran super-corporations. As he made his way towards the two corporate towers just outside the promenade, he couldn't help but wonder if his appointment to corporate service in lieu of going to war would have a negative effect on his ambition to gain rank and recognition within the military. No doubt the lack of risk and opportunities to demonstrate his superior leadership qualities would slow his advancement considerably. On the other hand, being so close to HQ could prove to have its advantages. As long as he kept the corporate lackeys happy and did his job, he'd be a Lieutenant soon and could make Captain in no time. He'd have his own cruiser or even his own battleship, with a crew of hundreds, even thousands, taking his orders. He might have been born with only nineteen clones under him, but he'd be damned if things were going to stay that way for long. He sniggered as he approached the bridge leading to the two towering structures.

The guard at the entrance snapped to attention, and cleared him to pass through the checkpoint. Lance wondered what his first assignment would be. Maybe he was to guard the new orbital space platform under construction in orbit above Titan, or break up riots on

Coraya 6. Maybe he'd oversee the terraforming of Selene, or even hunt down smugglers clear across the solar system.

As he approached the T-junction where the corridor leading to the towers divided, he scanned the display screen on the wall that indicated what was where. Aeon Astronautics, Bionare Polymers, DynaCorre Industries, Garvan Motors. There it was, GeoDynamics. North tower, seventh floor. Lance eyed his wrist comm, which also had a built-in chronometer. Six minutes early. Best to be on time, he thought, not wanting to be late for his very first assignment.

He stopped in the middle of the corridor to peer out through the window. At least twenty stories high, he counted before giving up. The northern corporate tower was a cylindrical structure of reinforced glass and steel, the windows reflectively opaque so no one could see what was going on inside.

The corridor pierced through the outer walls of the tower, ejecting the eager Sergeant into a central antechamber, bathed in a warm, soft golden glow. The center of the chamber contained a fountain which rose some eight meters into the open center of the tower, spewing forth cool clear streams of water which frothed as they collided with a seemingly chaotic arrangement of natural rocks in the basin's center. Golden beams of light originating from just below the ring of water encircling the rocky formation were the only source of light in the otherwise murky chamber. A row of four double-wide elevators on the opposite wall allowed access to the building's many floors.

Lance hailed one of the elevators by pressing a button at the side of the door. Impatiently, he strode over to the fountain and curiously dipped his fingers into the cold pool of water at its edge while he waited for the elevator to arrive.

"Mr. Lance," prompted a feminine voice from behind him, startling him and making him spin on his heels, splashing water all over the floor. "You are Mr. Lance, are you not?"

Her silky smooth, pitch-black shoulder-length hair glistened from the halo of light spilling from the open elevator. Her pale skin was free from even the most minute imperfections, and long, curled eyelashes adorned her slanting eyes, indicating the oriental origins of her genetic material. She blinked as she looked him over from head to toe, obviously expecting someone more... competent.

"Sergeant Lance, Ma'am," he corrected her, immediately biting his tongue in regret.

"Sergeant Lance. Very well," she complied, brushing a few droplets of water from of her dark-gray business suit. "I am Diana Torres, corporate liaison between the Terran military and GeoDynamics."

"Um... pleased to meet you Ms. Torres. How can I be of assistance?"

"Follow me please," she instructed, stepping back into the elevator, beckoning him to do the same.

Lance brushed an imaginary speck of dust off of his uniform and straightened his collar before entering the elevator. A push of a button and a short moment of awkward silence later, the door opened into the offices of the GeoDynamics Corporation. The reception area was an oval room with a curving reception desk made from dark-brown wood with a stone top. The floor was paved with tiles of the same stony material, save for a circular opening in the center of the room, from which the corporation's logo was projected, sleek and elegant lettering with a cresting arc hovering above it. The Sergeant had to hide his admiration for the elegance of the ambiance.

"My office is just through here, second door on the right," Torres said, ushering him forward.

Her office was no less impressive than the reception area. A pure-white, fine-grained carpet lined the floor from the door all the way to a raised section near the windows, which reached from the raised platform to ceiling, giving a spectacular view of the cold and unforgiving landscape of Callisto. The side walls were made of the same type of dark wood as the receptionist's desk. A pair of abstract paintings on the left-hand wall offered a stark contrast to the otherwise minimalistic décor.

Torres took long, sensual strides towards the raised section of the room over by the window, upon which rested a desk made from one solid piece of curving glass. Three revolving cup-shaped chairs of white leather surrounded the desk.

"Please, have a seat Mr. Lance," she gestured as she circled the desk to take a seat on the opposite side.

The Sergeant took a seat. He didn't even think twice about correcting her a second time for not referring to him by his rank. She placed her palm over a black disc-shaped device with silver edging. A blue glow shot up from its center, scanning her hand.

"It's quite a simple job really," she explained as rows of semi-transparent holographic icons appeared floating in mid air above the device.

She poked a few of the icons in rapid succession. Each time she did so the rows were replaced with an entirely new set and formation of icons.

"Ah, here it is," she said, pressing one of the icons with a seemingly unnecessary display of force.

A large glowing sphere, as cloudily transparent as the system's icons, appeared with seven smaller orbs orbiting it. She tapped the third sphere out from the central one. The other orbs vanished from sight as the one she had selected rapidly grew in size. A mesh-like grid texture faded into view, with a glowing red pulsating dot slightly above the equator on her side of the orb.

"This is Triton," she explained. "The third moon of Oberon. It's a barren rock, utterly devoid of any distinguishing features, save for its numerous craters. It does, however, hold some interest for GeoDynamics due to its possible mining opportunities."

She poked the glowing red dot, and the holographic display instantly zoomed in on it.

"We've done plenty of surveying there in the past, but we've never really come up with anything substantial enough to justify an excavation. However, we've only covered about thirty-four percent of the surface, and we'd like you to take your team down to this position to do some more surveying for us."

"That doesn't sound too complicated," the Sergeant assured her.

"Good," she confirmed, double tapping the red dot which brought up a small menu.

"I'm sending the coordinates to your barracuda's nav system. A technician from GeoDynamics will bring the scanning equipment to your hangar. Although the system is largely automated, it's best if you have your team's technician operate it."

"No problem there," the Sergeant answered. "Our technician is…" he began to explain, but was cut short.

"The survey cycle requires sixteen hours of uninterrupted operation to run its course. Please return the equipment immediately upon your return, as any information it gathers is the property of GeoDynamics and should be handled as strictly confidential," she warned him. "Oh, there is just one more important little detail," she added. "It is inadvisable to prolong your stay on the surface of Triton."

"Why's that?" he ventured, a tad flustered that she'd cut him off mid-sentence.

"The moon emits some residual radiation. Which is one of the reasons we haven't fully surveyed it yet."

"Radiation?" the Sergeant inquired, alarmed at the revelation.

"It's nothing to worry about. If you don't stick around too long, that is. Our estimates show that the body, when properly protected by armor such as yours, can withstand up to twenty one hours of exposure. Just be sure to issue anti-radiation pills to your squad," she reassured him.

"I… I'll make sure of it," Lance concluded as he prepared to leave Ms. Torres's office and recall the squad to hangar bay 3-14 for their first mission.

Chapter 11

Marcus sat on the edge of the bed. Its seemingly frail metal frame had, to his surprise, supported both of their weight with relative ease. Eve lay facing the wall, perfectly still, clutching the covers. He wasn't sure if she was asleep or not.

Her quarters were indistinguishable from his old room in the barracks. He wondered why most of the base looked so new and clean, while the hangar bays and the areas designated for the clones on active service were so old and worn. Maybe it was all an illusion. Perception, he speculated, had to be important up until the moment they chose to serve. After that, function replaced appearances.

Still pained by the guilt of abandoning his friend, Marcus had been unable to get a moment of sleep the whole night. He'd simply sat on the edge of the bed in silence.

The viewscreen on the wall was turned on, with the volume at its the lowest setting. The news was currently reporting on allegations that the Tomiko family, one of the wealthy and influential families in Terran society, had risen to power and fortune through dealings with nefarious narcotics distributors. The head of the family, a Hajime Tomiko, was posing for the cameras on the steps of the Grand Tribunal Center in Sol. Rain poured down heavily as he denied any allegations against himself and his family, claiming instead that the Tomiko family had earned their place among the elite through ingenuity and sheer business sense.

Every once in a while, the image would shift to scenes of the Terran capital. Marcus found it even more enormous than he had envisioned. Thousands of vehicles hovered in parallel lines, coming and going in a never-ending parade as the rain poured from the cloud cast sky. The confining shapes of the city's buildings, many of which soared as many as two or three hundred stories, were an impressive sight. There had to be millions of Terrans just in the capital alone.

So why did they need to make more, just to ship them off to war? Were the free Terrans too afraid to fight for themselves? He couldn't think of any other reason. Perhaps he simply didn't want to. He liked seeing them in this new light. Cowards, the lot of them, he thought. It was all their fault that he'd been forced to abandon his friend.

Yet he knew deep down that that wasn't true. He had only himself to blame. If anyone was a coward, it was him. But if, even just for a minute, he toyed with the idea that it wasn't his fault, he got a brief respite from the waves of guilt and melancholy.

"Grey," a voice emanating from his wrist comm boomed through the room.

Marcus quickly covered it with his hand to drown out most of the noise. He didn't want to wake Eve up. She looked so peaceful lying there. Free from regret, free from the anger that burned inside him.

"Private Grey, report," the voice of Sergeant Lance repeated.

He pressed the comm up to his mouth and got up off the bed, walking over to the corner of the small room with his back to Eve.

"This is Grey," he answered.

"We've got a mission Private. Report to the hangar. We're leaving in an hour," the Sergeant proclaimed.

"Yes Sergeant," he acknowledged before switching off the comm.

Eve turned in the bed, stretching her delicate arms into the air, yawning briefly before taking a deep breath.

"What was that?" she inquired as she propped herself up on her elbows.

"That was my Sergeant," he explained. "We've received our first assignment. We're leaving in an hour."

"That's great news!" she cheered, rising up to sit on the side of the bed.

Marcus couldn't help but avert his gaze. Although he'd seen her naked in the heat of passion earlier, it now seemed inappropriate somehow.

"Aren't you excited?"

"Excited?" he wondered.

"You're finally fulfilling your role in destiny," she professed.

"But," he hesitated. "This probably means I'll never see you again."

Her puzzled expression clearly gave way to her lack of understanding for the dire situation they had landed themselves in.

"What do you mean?"

"Well, you have two days until it's your turn to choose," he explained. "And I'm leaving for what's likely going to be at least a month-long assignment. Corporate service missions aren't going to take us to Alpha Terra, and everywhere else in the system takes weeks to reach. They don't use the Wako for missions in our system unless it's an emergency, and even if they used it to get us wherever we're going it would take weeks to return to the Alamo."

Her expression transformed from puzzlement to disappointment.

"So, you see, by the time I get back, you'll already be well on your way to Nyramar."

The silence that followed was unbearable. It seemed to Marcus that every time he would get close to someone, fate would snatch them away from his life.

"But I will be back Marcus," Eve said, disrupting the silence.

"Maybe in a year or so."

Marcus knew she could make no such promise. But for a moment he entertained the thought of her returning to him, jumping into his arms as he welcomed her home.

"The tour is four years," he interjected.

"Yes, but they're constantly making exceptions for those who have shown great bravery in battle."

"Don't do anything stupid. I'd rather you be careful and hide behind someone else if that means you'll be safe."

Even though he had no concept of how long it would take for four years to pass by, Marcus assured himself he'd wait for her.

"I'm not signing up just so I can let someone else be the hero," she objected. "I want to be the best soldier I can possibly be."

The thought disturbed him. He just knew that she wouldn't be coming back. Not alive in any case. But he refused to think about it. He knew there was no way he was going to be able to talk her out of it anyway. She was always so eager to serve. He envied her of that. He wished that he too could find such a strong purpose in his life.

He sat down beside her. Without saying a word, he put his arm around her shoulders and hugged her tight, perhaps for the very last time.

Chapter 12

Hangar bay 3-14 was filled with commotion when Marcus came running through the door. The squad was busy donning their armor and gearing up for the mission.

"You're late!" Lance bellowed.

"Sorry Sergeant, I got held up," Marcus tried to explain.

"I won't abide tardiness in my squad Private. See to it that it doesn't happen again," the Sergeant rebuked him.

"Yes Sergeant. Sorry Sergeant," Marcus apologized as he opened his locker to retrieve his equipment.

The SGC K-660 carbine was the same weight as the training model, but his armor was significantly heavier than the simple vest-and-helmet combo he'd worn during the simulations.

"What's up with your face Spielman?" inquired the Sergeant, gesturing to the red hand print on Adam's left cheek.

Marcus surveyed the Corporal's feminine features. The unfortunate clone had a pert and awkwardly shaped nose. Marcus had misjudged him when they'd first met, doubting the smaller man's combat capabilities, but the Corporal had proven that his lightning reflexes more than made up for his inferior muscle mass. His wiry frame allowed him to perform acrobatic feats which would give him the opportunity to strike at the enemy from nearly impossible angles.

"I was at the Zonaka, chatting up a 6-18, Sergeant," he replied.

"I see she left you with something to remember her by," the Sergeant jested.

Corporal Spielman wasn't amused.

"Alright men, grab a canister from the crate by the door. They've been specifically calibrated to mix with the atmosphere on Triton. Your helmets' built-in filtration systems will filter out any harmful agents in the air. This will allow you to breathe for up to twenty eight hours once we're there."

It took Marcus a few minutes just to figure out what went where, and his squad was already busying themselves loading an orange box-shaped device with retractable legs onto the ship.

"What is that?" he asked as he followed his squadmates into the barracuda's half of the bay.

"It's a survey scanner," the Sergeant informed him. "If you'd been here on time you wouldn't have missed the briefing."

"Sorry Sergeant," repeated Marcus. "What is the mission?"

"We're heading to one of the moons of Oberon to take some geological readings for one of the corporations. It's a snooze job if you ask me, so don't you do anything to fuck it up."

"I won't Sergeant."

Marcus found a corner of the deck where he wouldn't be in the way, and turned the atmos canister clockwise until it clicked into place, connected to the valves on the underside of the chin section of his helmet. Once that was done, he secured his Kessler A-14 combat knife, with its twenty-four centimeter blade and serrated edge, in its sheath, which hung from a strap around his right thigh. The rest of his gear consisted of four Nova Labs B2 Annihilator fragmentation grenades and an SGC N-11 medium handgun. A duffel bag contained his non-essentials: a sleeping bag, fusion lamp, a small tent and enough field rations for a whole week.

Some of the others had received more specialized equipment. Taylor had a medical scanner strapped to his hip and carried a durable first aid kit. Eric Taber, the squad's technician, carried an assortment of scanners and tools in pouches and slings on his armor. Jago, as the squad's designated Support Gunner, had been issued with a drum-fed Voss Viking KRS-56, an enormous high-calibre machinegun. Marcus' resonant memories made him look for a tripod or mount, but he couldn't see one anywhere in the assorted gear scattered around the hangar bay. It seemed that Jago was intending to simply fire the huge weapon from the hip.

Marcus looked back through the glass wall separating the squad's quarters from the hangar as Sergeant Lance sealed the airlock between the two compartments. The squad began making its way up the ramp to board the ship.

"Ready to witness some awesome piloting skills?" Zorita proudly proclaimed as she passed them at the base of the entry ramp.

Taz kept his mouth shut, not wanting another display of their pilot's physical combat skills.

"Let's make this one smooth and easy Raven," the Sergeant suggested, following her up the ramp.

"I don't fly any other way Sergeant," she bragged.

The squad secured their weapons in a weapons rack on the first deck before climbing the rungs of the ladder through the hatch up to the stasis chamber. The stasis units on the second deck were egg-shaped pods, split in half right down the middle. The back section, which was fastened to the hull, was made from a reflective metal alloy, lined on the inside with a rubbery black foam, with a man-shaped depression in its center. The front sections, made from hardened glass, were hanging from the air a full meter and a half away from their back sections, attached by a pair of servo arms. Clearly they'd only close when the occupant was inside. Ten pods lined each wall, flanking a narrow deck leading to the cockpit.

There was something eerily familiar about them, thought Marcus as he placed his helmet in a niche underneath the pod he'd been assigned. It wasn't anything from his resonant memories. Perhaps some remnant from when he'd first been hatched. He pressed his back up against the man-shaped depression in the back section of his pod. To his surprise, the rubbery foam gave way to his motion, altering its form to fit the shape of his armored body perfectly. He watched as, one by one, the rest of the squad entered their pods. Near the far end of the deck a slightly larger pod had been installed for Jago. Even so, the huge man had to hunch in order to fit inside.

"We're gonna have to put you on a diet, Ape!" Lance chuckled from a neighboring pod.

Jago wasn't amused. He merely grunted in acknowledgement.

Marcus could count four unoccupied pods. One each for the pilot and copilot, and a third for Taylor, the squad's medic, whose charge it was to oversee the stasis process for everyone's safety. The last pod would have belonged to Steven.

Marcus tried as best he could to swallow his guilt, to let go. He couldn't allow his failure to affect the mission, and risk getting someone killed. He just couldn't live with himself if that were to happen. No, for now he would have to set his guilt aside. There really was nothing he could do about it anyway.

"Fire up the engines Raven," the Sergeant ordered as he leaned back into his pod, the black foam enveloping his lithe frame.

"You got it Sergeant," came Raven's reply.

The now-familiar series of high-pitched tones sounded as she engaged the ship's electronics, followed by the low droning hum of the engines echoing throughout the ship. As the hangar door began to open, Taylor started to make his way down the row of pods opposite to Marcus, executing the stasis parameters. As he drew nearer to the middle of the row, Marcus was able to watch as he pressed a series of buttons on a side panel on the back section of each pod, monitoring the feedback on his datapad. As soon as the parameters had been entered into each pod, the servo arms lowered the transparent front section into place, merging with the rear half. A quick wheezing noise, followed by a muddled thump, could be heard as each pod sealed itself shut. That way, if there was a hull breach, the passengers would remain safe until rescue could arrive.

Marcus stared at the pod opposite his. It was Milo Clarke, one of the squad's scouts. Shortly after Milo's pod had sealed itself shut, he simply drifted off to sleep. A digital readout embedded in the glass of the pod displayed the status of its occupant, as well as a timer showing how much remained of the stasis cycle. Six weeks and eight hours. That was the estimated duration of their trip.

Eve would be long gone by the time he would return.

Marcus couldn't help but wonder whether cryo-stasis was anything like the unconscious state in which clones were kept during their growth. It was his turn now. Taylor entered the parameters on the panel on his left side. The glass section began to close shut.

If waking up from stasis was similar to being born, then would entering stasis be somehow the same as dying? Marcus pondered as the muffled thump indicated that his pod had sealed itself shut. His eyes were wide open, staring out through the glass as Taylor disinterestedly monitored the readout on his datapad.

The hairs on the back of Marcus' sweaty hands rose. A tingling sensation swelled in his gut as the soft whizzing sound of the gaseous compounds spewed forth from the vent at the top of his pod. Marcus held his breath. His mouth was clamped down so hard that he thought not even the Ape could pry it open. He didn't want to experience what it would feel like to die. His heart raced, beating so hard and fast he was certain that it would soon leap clear out of his chest.

But eventuality won out. He gasped for air. The gas began filling his lungs. His vision blurred. Finally, he welcomed death's sweet embrace.

Chapter 13

Waking up from stasis bore only a passing resemblance to Marcus's initial hatching. The same numbness of the body and drowsiness of the mind accompanied it, but the physical complications that defined his first moments of consciousness did not present themselves, much to his relief.

He waited as the glass section of his pod rose to its open position. He felt as if he could sleep for an entire day. He watched as the rest of the squad awoke from their sleep as well, while Taylor, the first to arise, scurried between them, taking their pulses and prying open their eyelids to shine a pen-shaped flashlight into their pupils, gauging their reactions. Raven assisted her copilot out of his pod and, after a series of stretches – during which Taz carefully undressed her with his eyes when he thought no one was looking – the two of them preceded through the door to the cockpit.

Although the B-14 had originally been designed only to land and take off, ferrying troops from orbiting ships to the ground and back, the Terran Forces had made numerous alterations to its design over the years. Many of the ships, Marcus' squad's included, had been refitted with extended fuel cells for extended service within solar systems.

It had been a long journey. Their trajectory had had to be calculated precisely before thruster burn could be initiated, or they would have wound up far off course. Once the burn sequence had been completed, the ship was powered down. Everything except minimal life support for the stasis pods and the ship's navigational computer and onboard sensors had to be taken offline to save power. The navigation computer had then been programmed to automatically awaken the sleepers when the destination had been reached, the timers on the pods being merely failsafes. Marcus knew that, in the event of an emergency, the computer was programmed to wake up only the two pilots as well as the squad's technician and highest ranking officer. This time, however, the drift through the solar system had been uneventful and the ship had reached its destination on schedule.

Through the small round window at the back of the second deck, Marcus was able to make out his first view of Oberon's third moon. It was a dark and foreboding orb. Its dim, cratered surface had a thin purple atmosphere which shimmered in the sunlight. Long thin streaks, pure white in color, cut through the atmosphere in random places. Marcus had never seen anything like it. The sight intrigued him no end, and he started to feel excited about landing on this little ball of rock in the far reaches of the Terran system.

"Keep yourselves strapped in people. This might get a bit bumpy," Raven warned them over the ship's intercom.

Taylor had just finished checking on the last person's vital signs as Marcus squeezed past him to reinsert himself into his pod. The black substance swelled around him, ready to cushion him against any turbulence.

"No complications," announced Taylor. "Everyone's vitals are in order."

"Excellent. You'd better strap yourself in too," Lance ordered.

The ship's thrusters came back online with a sudden jerk. Jago was wearing the strangest expression Marcus had ever seen on the gargantuan man's face. It was one of mixed thrill, fear and excitement.

"Can you feel it men? Gravity is a bitch. Yee haw!" yelled Corporal Spielman as the ship began to shake. "I just hope Raven doesn't screw up the landing or we'll all be looking like that gray paste they used to feed us back in the mess hall."

The squad chuckled in amusement.

"What the hell is that stuff anyway?" Taz asked.

"Probably some of the Ape's bodily secretions," said Taylor in jest.

"Gross, Doc!" resounded most of the squad in unison.

"Alright people, cut the chatter. We've got a job to do here," Lance ordered.

The entire ship began shaking uncontrollably as it entered the atmosphere, more so than it had done when they had landed on Alpha Terra.

"Um, people, hold on to something. We're coming in a lot faster than we should be," Raven professed. Marcus could hear she was seriously worried, scared even.

"Something's not right," blurted Taz.

The Sergeant unfastened himself from his pod and gradually made his way towards the cockpit. The ship jerked back and forth, tossing left and right, making it difficult for him to stay on his feet, despite the servo arms of the open pods lending him ample support to steady himself. The cockpit door slid open and he was gone. The rest of the squad ground their teeth in anticipation of what was to come.

The shaking became increasingly forceful and the bolts that held the stasis pods in place started to come loose, rattling profusely. Fear loomed in the eyes of the entire squad as they began to realize that the end might be near. The ship's engines whined so high that it started to hurt Marcus' ears.

The maneuvering thrusters went off one by one as the pilots tried desperately to regain control and adjust their reentry. An orange-tinted warning light in the ceiling blinked on and off, and somewhere in the back a high-pitched siren began to wail, doing little to calm their nerves. All Marcus could think of was how much he wanted to go back to stasis. At the moment it seemed a far better option than getting splattered all over a crater on some forsaken moon.

The sudden whirring of the landing gear extending and then locking into place seemed inconsequential given the tremendous speed they were traveling at. Marcus felt as if the turbulence alone would be enough to break the ship apart. He closed his eyes in anticipation of the impact, clutching the edge of his pod with all of his might. This was it, he thought. This was the end.

Without warning, the ship slammed down, hard.

The landing gear did little to soften the blow. The entire ship screeched as it plowed through a field of rock for what seemed to last forever. The stasis chamber was showered in sparks as every member of the squad held their breath. The deafening screech of metal grinding against rock pierced through the ship, until suddenly the ship ground to a halt.

The ship stood still. The squad held their breath, waiting for the wheezing sound that usually accompanied hull breaches. A series of sparks burst forth before quietly dying down.

Silence.

The siren was no longer wailing and the warning light had stopped flashing. No one even dared so much as breathe. They just looked in wonder at those occupying the pods around them.

"Anyone of you girls need a band-aid?" came Taylor's voice, breaking the silence. "Or something to calm your nerves? A stiff drink perhaps?"

The whole squad peered out of their pods just in time to see the medic, leaning against the side of his pod as calmly as could be, light himself a cigarette. The doors to the cockpit slid open and Lance emerged, beads of sweat pouring down his brow.

"Is everyone ok?" he asked Taylor, still breathing heavily.

"Apart from some bruised egos, everyone seems fine," Taylor told him, a cloud of smoke hovering in front of him.

"That's good," replied the Sergeant, breathing a heavy sigh of relief.

He took a few seconds to regain his composure as the squad tumbled out of their stasis pods.

"Ok, listen up everyone," he ordered, claiming everyone's attention. "Raven did a great job under the circumstances. It seems that the extreme density of this moon resulted in a much higher gravity than we expected. That, coupled with some malfunctioning sensors, made us ill-prepared for this landing. We don't yet know the scope of the damage," he explained, burdened by the severity of the situation. "Now, we've still got a job to do here, and not much time to do it. Dimitrov, I want you and your team to escort Taber to the survey site, and help him get things up and running as soon as possible."

Dimitrov nodded in agreement, immediately grabbing Marcus, Taz, Reid and Becks to follow him and Taber down to the first deck to prepare the probe.

"Ape, Spielman, follow me." Lance went on. "We'll go have a look at the damage."

Jago and Spielman fell in line behind the Sergeant.

"The rest of you, stay put!" he barked as he climbed down through the hatch to the lower deck.

Marcus could feel the increase in his weight due to the increase in gravity. It felt like he weighed twice as much as he normally did. His legs buckled under the weight. The others were experiencing similar problems, particularly Jago, who must have weighted half a ton in the moon's high gravity.

On the lower deck the effects of the crash became more apparent. The signs of impact were clearest on the left wall, where a large dent in the hull ran almost the entire length of the deck. They were indeed profoundly lucky to be alive.

"Sergeant, I'm ready to seal off the upper deck and prepare oxygen conservation for deck one. Does everyone have their atmos canisters installed?" asked Raven over the ship's intercom.

"Good to go Raven," the Sergeant answered after making sure everyone was wearing their helmets and that their canisters were properly secure.

"Alright, I'm gonna need you to hold your breath for just a few seconds," advised Raven.

The atmospheric pumps began emptying the lower deck of breathable air. A few seconds later she was back on the comms.

"Deck one is clear. I'm opening the hatch. You can breathe normally now."

The wide door on the starboard side of the ship started to slide open. Triton's toxic atmosphere, a wispy purple mist, poured in through the crack. When mixed with the compound in the atmos canister and inhaled, it smelled faintly of rusted metal. Marcus worried whether or not the damage to the ship would be too severe for them to be able to return to the Alamo.

"Alright men, let's go take a look at the damage," barked the Sergeant.

Spielman and Jago climbed out through the side door and helped ease the Sergeant down to the surface.

GeoDynamics: Survey Probe 8602, Marcus read on the side of the probe as Taber made sure it hadn't been damaged during the impact.

"Looks good," he finally proclaimed. "No visible damage."

It took four of them to lower the probe down to the surface. It felt like it weighed a ton under the severe gravity conditions. Their armor did little to ease their efforts in carrying the equipment to a suitable location. They were within the area proscribed by GeoDynamics, but had to get far enough away from the ship so that it wouldn't interfere with the readings.

It took them the better part of an hour to locate a good spot. They finally placed the orange-painted probe in the center of a small impact crater, lowering the adjustable legs to support its weight. Marcus wasn't sure whether the frail-looking legs would hold, given the increase in gravity. Taber slid open a small panel on the surface of the probe, which revealed a small keypad and display.

"Hold it steady," Taber snapped as Taz made sure that the legs were secure and the device wouldn't topple over at the slightest nudge.

The tech fiddled around with the keypad, comparing the layout with the instructions on his datapad.

"How much time?" Dimitrov inquired.

"Not long," replied Taber. "I'm just making sure that everything is in order. The device should be pre-configured. I just need to know if our landing messed anything up. But I think we got lucky."

"Yeah right," scoffed Taz, looking back towards the damaged ship.

"You guys can head back to the ship. I'll just be a few seconds."

Corporal Dimitrov nodded his approval and the rest of the team began making their way back.

Marcus noticed Spielman and Jago in front of the ship, a handful of the others helping them trying to mend a crack in the forward panel. To his surprise the landing gear, although bent and badly damaged, had not broken off in the crash, leaving the ship's only turret, a small cannon hanging from the center of the barracuda's underbelly, relatively intact.

All of a sudden Marcus spotted the same thin, graceful white streaks in the upper atmosphere he'd seen from the barracuda, now appearing one after another. Like the ripples of fingers playing in a pool of water, spreading out as they trailed clear across the sky. He stopped to admire the spectacle. Corporal Dimitrov came up from behind him, slapping him on the shoulder.

"Everything ok there Grey?"

"I'm fine," said Marcus, assuring the Corporal. "I was just admiring the sky."

"The sky?" inquired the Corporal, following Marcus's gaze to the peculiar formation of thin white lines.

He paused briefly as he realized what was occurring.

"Run!" he roared suddenly. "Everyone, back to the ship! Now!"

"I just finished. What's the..." Taber's words were cut short as one of the thin majestic white lines roared out of the sky and blew clear through his helmet.

His limp body hung momentarily as if suspended by invisible strings, before falling solidly to the ground. Marcus could hear the gurgling sound as blood spewed out from the gushing wound.

"It's a meteorite shower!" shouted Corporal Dimitrov, sprinting for the ship as fast as he could.

111

Chapter 14

The squad huddled together on the ship's lower deck, trying to come to terms with Taber's death.

Marcus couldn't help but blame himself. He should have realized that the thin streaks of white had been miniature meteorites burning up on contact with Triton's thin atmosphere. He could have warned everyone. Perhaps they were even the cause of the equipment failure that had contributed to the crash.

Was he the only one who'd spotted them? Had he spoken out when he first noticed them, could all of this have been averted? The notion that this was all somehow his fault haunted him, tortured him. The whole squad would have been better off if he'd left with Steven.

Steven, he thought. Steven had been right all along. They were all going to die. Only after six weeks, not six months.

Sergeant Lance paced back and forth. His helmet was off since the deck had been re-pressurized upon their return to the ship.

"And you're certain that he managed to activate the probe?" he inquired.

"He said he was finished," Dimitrov replied, hanging his head in mournful reservation. "He was on his way back when… when he collapsed."

The Sergeant took in the news, standing in front of his men and rubbing the stubble on his chin.

"Then all we can do is wait, and hope that the meteor shower subsides," Lance stated, his expression filled with worry. "Spielman,

Jago, what's the status on those repairs?" he asked, quickly changing the subject to what he clearly saw as the more pressing matter.

"The repairs should hold Sergeant," the Corporal informed him, "but the landing gear is pretty banged up. There's no way we'll be able to retract it."

"Which will no doubt cause problems for the pilots," stated Lance.

"Raven says that we'll burn up a lot more fuel, plus steering will be more difficult. Other than that, she's mostly worried about having to land this piece of junk again," exclaimed Spielman.

"We'll have to make do with whatever repairs we can manage in the short amount of time we have," Lance decided.

"We still have fourteen hours to go on the probe's survey cycle. I suggest we see what we can do about the landing gear in the meantime," suggested Corporal Dimitrov.

"We'll work in shifts," acknowledged the Sergeant. "Two teams work while one team rests, with rotation once per hour. The ship should provide us with at least some protection, but we may have to patch up some holes if one of those meteors punctures through the hull."

"You heard the Sergeant," shouted Corporal Dimitrov. "Let's get to work!"

* * * * *

Still struggling to cope with the loss of their technician, the squad fought to make the best repairs they could. Marcus had volunteered to go fetch Taber's tools and scanners, but Sergeant Lance would hear nothing of it. He'd dismissed Marcus' offer with a curt "I'm not risking any more of my men."

The meteorite storm was at its peak, ferociously beating down on Triton's deserted landscape. Somewhere far off over the horizon they could hear the occasional explosion as a larger rock collided with the surface.

"We should wait," complained Taz. "We shouldn't be outside under these circumstances. Can't we just go back inside and get some rest and come back out when it stops raining fire from the sky?"

"No," Lance barked.

"Well why the hell not?" Taz asked. "There's no reason we have to get this done right now!"

"Because the radiation will kill us if we don't get out of here soon!" the Sergeant roared.

"What radiation?" Dimitrov asked, sounding worried.

"The residual radiation on this god-awful moon," the Sergeant spat.

"Weren't you going to tell us this?" Dimitrov cried, outraged by the Sergeant's lack of disclosure.

"I didn't deem it necessary to worry you over something that should have been inconsequential," the Sergeant replied, standing firm in the belief that he'd done no wrong.

"Well... how much time do we have then Sergeant?"

"We still have three hours left on the survey cycle," the Sergeant explained. "Four hours after that, we'll start to feel the effects of radiation poisoning."

"Seven hours?" Taz burst out. "There's no way we can get all this fixed in under seven hours Sergeant! It just can't be done."

"Yes it can, Private Sobieski, because we don't have a choice. We get it done, or we die. It's that simple. Now I suggest you shut your mouth for once and get to work!"

Marcus had never seen anyone work as hard as the squad did following the Sergeant's revelation. With seven hours to go and no end to the swarm of meteorites pounding the ground in sight, the outlook wasn't good.

During each shift, more and more meteors slammed into the ship's hull. Even though they were each smaller than a pebble, they dug deep into the ship's armor. Cracks appeared along the surface in some places, cracks that could severely weaken the ship's structural integrity.

The squad tirelessly welded shut each crack and patched every hole, using emergency materials from a locker in the barracuda's lower deck until the meteorite storm finally began to dissipate. There had been no more loss of life, but a few close calls kept them all on edge. With a little over an hour left on the survey cycle, Lance ordered Dimitrov and his men to retrieve Taber's body.

It looked more like a ragdoll than a person, thought Marcus as they arrived at the scene of Taber's untimely demise. His corpse had been hit several more times while it had lain out in the open. Puncture wounds through the chest and the left hip were stained with dark-crimson blood. The top portion of his head was missing, and bits and pieces of bloody meat and bones were strewn about on the ground where his left leg used to be. It was heavier than Marcus had imagined. It took four of them to carry it all the way back to the ship.

They were met halfway by Corporal Spielman, Jago, and some of Spielman's men. They had been ordered to retrieve the probe. Shortly after Marcus and his team had laid Taber's body to rest on the lower deck, securing it by strapping his armor to some bolts in the floor, Spielman's voice sounded on the comms.

"We're at the survey site Sergeant. The probe's a little banged up but it appears operational. There's an orange light, and it says 'analyzing' on the interface. There's also a display of mineral composites, saturation levels, depth, and a whole bunch of other jargon on the readout."

"I think it needs a bit more time," the Sergeant replied.

"Yes sir. We'll wait until it's in the green."

Dimitrov and his team joined the others who were still frantically trying to make repairs to the ship. He'd brought Taber's equipment and was attempting to use it to perform some technical readouts on the ship, but either there was something wrong with the scanners or he simply lacked the required resonant memories to use them.

"The light's green Sergeant," Spielman voice came over the comms. "The readout says 'Analysis complete'."

"Good work Corporal," the Sergeant replied. "Bring it on home... and be careful with it!" he added, before ordering the rest of the men to wrap up the repairs.

Marcus inspected the ship. From the look of it, things could go either way.

"Our job here is done," bellowed the Sergeant. "It's time to gear up and buckle down. I want everyone back in their pods ASAP!"

"Yes Sergeant!" the squad replied in unison, half relieved to be going home, half worried that their repairs wouldn't hold up.

The men clambered through the side door and secured their equipment in the cabinets as Raven sealed the lower deck shut and began the re-pressurization sequence. The hatch to the second deck swung open as, one by one, the squad climbed through.

Marcus paused by the tiny window near the back of the upper deck, taking one last look at Triton's desolate surface, the moon which had claimed the life of one of their own. He was among the last to insert himself into the black rubbery foam of his stasis pod. The lining gave way to his weight, even more so due to the increase in gravity.

He stared at Taber's empty pod, then at Steven's. He wondered how long it would be until his pod would be among those left empty at the end of a mission.

Raven brought the ship's engines online with the familiar low droning hum, and fired off the thrusters. The ship shook violently as the gravity drive fought off the heavy pull of Triton's super-dense core. Slowly but surely, the shaking began to subside and the barracuda made its steep climb back into space.

Once they were surrounded only by unforgiving vacuum, Raven announced that the repairs were holding and there appeared to be no leaks. The whole squad cheered and praised her skills as a pilot for getting them back on their way to the Alamo. Taylor handed out the anti-radiation medication. They each received three small white pills from a bottle bearing the logo of Mulland Biotech. Reid said a silent prayer as Raven made the calculations prior to initiating the thruster burn which would send the ship on their long drift home.

Moments later, the two pilots emerged from the cockpit and climbed into their stasis pods. The experience had taken its toll on the cocky Raven, who was visibly shaken from the whole ordeal. One by one, Taylor began to initiate the squad's stasis cycles, sending them drifting off to the long sleep they would endure on their way home.

Chapter 15

Marcus arose to utter chaos on the upper deck. His stasis pod stood open. Through his stasis-blurred vision, he could see that all the other pods were open as well. The alarm was sounding. The emergency lights flared.

As his vision began to clear, he could see that neither of the pilots, nor Sergeant Lance, were anywhere to be seen.

"What the hell's going on?" shouted a bewildered and disoriented Taz.

"I don't know!" Dimitrov shouted back over the wailing siren. "Grey," the Corporal pointed at Marcus. "Go check on the cockpit. Find out if the Sergeant and the pilots are ok!" he ordered, unclamping himself from his pod.

The Corporal floated in the air, completely weightless.

"The magnetic floor is offline!" Reid yelled as he grabbed hold of one of his pod's servo arms, pushing off to propel himself down to the back of the ship, where Jago spun in the air, apparently unconscious after hitting his head on one of the bulkheads. Droplets of blood encircled him, drifting aimlessly.

Marcus unbuckled the safety strap which kept him locked in place, enveloped in the black rubbery lining of his pod. He managed to drag himself out of the pod towards the cockpit, only to have to pry the door open. The motor which controlled the door wasn't functioning.

Inside the cockpit, the Sergeant was screaming hysterically at Raven, demanding an explanation for how this could have happened. In his newly awoken state, Marcus didn't quite understand what had gone wrong. His head was spinning, a throbbing headache sneaking up the base of his spine. Then he noticed it. The entire front panel of the ship had come clean off and was drifting off into space right in front of the cockpit window.

"The entire lower deck is exposed to vacuum, don't you understand that? It just won't work!" Raven yelled back at Lance, her face flush with anger and frustration.

"The second deck is sealed, so we should be fine, right?" Lance responded, more to reassure himself than the pilots.

"No. I mean yes, we're sealed off, but the nose coming off has torn something else loose," Raven tried to explain. "We're venting oxygen fast!"

"Can we patch it?" the Sergeant asked. His hand gripped the back of Raven's seat as he stared worryingly into space at the slowly spinning sheet of metal suspended no more than five meters in front of the window.

"How? With what?" she replied. "The leak is somewhere behind this instrument panel. "We'd have to tear this place apart and even then, there are no guarantees. We could end up making it worse."

"Can we seal off the cockpit and send out a distress signal?"

"We could, but then we'll have to rely on someone being close enough to pick us up," she explained. "Plus, the air we vented from the lower deck when the panel came loose is bound to have screwed up our trajectory, and the nav computer is out, so who knows where we could end up. Even in stasis, we could drift all the way out the other side of the solar system."

"Well, what the hell else can we do?" Lance shouted right into her ear in desperation.

"Well, we haven't gotten that far from Oberon. We could still make it to one of the lunar colonies. I think that's New Io over there," she explained as she pointed towards a small, dust-colored moon somewhere in the distance. "Landing without a nose is gonna be a real bitch though. And we'll lose that precious survey probe of yours. Everything on the lower deck will burn up once we hit the atmospheric boundary of that moon."

"What about us?" the Sergeant inquired.

"The upper deck is shielded separately, but there's no guarantee we'll make it," she replied. "It depends on how much heat we generate when we hit atmosphere. Without a heat-shield, reentry could kill us all."

Lance sighed heavily.

"New Io… isn't that where they found that alien artifact?" asked Adler, interrupting the Sergeant's chain of thought.

"No, that was Helios. And those are nothing but rumors and propaganda!" he snapped.

"They were talking about it in the Zonaka, back on…"

"Will you shut up?" Lance interrupted him. "That has nothing to do with our current situation."

"Sorry Sergeant," the copilot apologized.

"No, we can't lose that probe. Not after everything we've been through," Lance mused.

"What about Eric's body?" asked Marcus, finally making his presence known.

"Grey? What are you… why are you awake?" the Sergeant shouted, somewhat flustered.

"We're all awake Sergeant."

"Fan-fucking-tastic. Emergency protocol isn't supposed to wake the entire squad up. Now we'll have a lot less oxygen to go around," Raven shouted.

Suddenly it came to him.

"I have an idea!" professed Marcus.

"Not now Private," the Sergeant brushed him off.

"But the forward ramp…" he pleaded.

"The forward ramp is damaged Grey. It won't go down!"

"But maybe it can go up," suggested Marcus, receiving mixed looks from his audience.

"What do you mean up?" Raven asked.

"If we dismantle the hydraulics that are holding the ramp closed, level with the deck, we might be able to force it to swing up instead, high enough to act as a heat shield, effectively blocking off the entire lower deck," Marcus explained.

"That's a crazy… no, that's fucking insane!" Raven shouted. "Let's do it!"

"Wait, what?" Lance moaned. "You can't go down there Grey. The lower deck is exposed to vacuum."

"Our suits can be sealed Sergeant. Raven, do you think you can get us to New Io before we run out of oxygen?"

"I can do it!" she blurted, without even stopping to think.

It felt important to Marcus that Taber's body received the respect it deserved. To leave it to burn up on reentry felt somehow like betrayal. He couldn't go through that again. He would not go through that ever again! If protecting Taber's body gave the rest of the squad a better chance of survival too, then his mind was made up.

"You're a lot braver than I thought, Grey," the Sergeant admitted.

Marcus nodded and quickly pushed himself back through the cockpit door.

As Taylor aided the squad back into their stasis pods, Marcus grabbed his helmet and proceeded towards the hatch to the lower deck. He put his left hand on the hatch and his right on his helmet's atmos canister, ready to seal his suit and break the hatch seal as soon as the squad was in place and Raven had depressurized the upper deck.

He felt pride swelling up inside him. As afraid of death as he'd been in the past, knowing that he was risking his life, not only for the good of the mission, but, more importantly, for the honor of a fallen comrade, somehow made all his fears evaporate. In that moment, fear had no meaning for Marcus. It was as abstract a notion as it would have been to a machine.

Moments later, when everyone was once again firmly fastened into their pods and Taylor had initiated a twenty-minute stasis cycle, Marcus removed his atmos canister and rotated the valves to sealed mode.

"Now!" He yelled.

Raven engaged the depressurization procedure. How peaceful they all looked, thought Marcus as the air escaped from the stasis chamber. Protected by their stasis pods and their dreamless sleep, the squad had no idea what was about to happen. Then the hatch blew open and Marcus pulled at the edge, diving straight down through the opening.

The damage was immense. The entire front section of the lower deck was exposed to vacuum through a gaping hole where the slanted wall above the closed hatch had been. It was beautiful, seeing the stars so clearly. He felt as if he could lunge out from the ship and swim among them.

The ship abruptly changed course.

"Hold onto something," Raven bellowed on the comms.

Marcus banged his head against a bulkhead as he was tossed to the side. The view from the front changed quickly to that of Oberon's magnificent orb. The towering gas giant filled the view, swirling waves of deep blue, purple and orange radiating as far as they eye could see. Marcus was able to make out the outlines of New Io, silhouetted against the giant bright ball of gas.

As the ship's thrusters burst into action so did Marcus, berating himself for having spent way too much time admiring the view. He kicked against the bulkhead, sending himself soaring towards Taber's body.

He landed almost on top of it, and immediately began fumbling for his tools. Not knowing what else to do with them, the squad had returned them to Taber's pouches and cases once they'd finished their repairs on Triton. Marcus spotted the powered screwdriver he needed for the hydraulics, and immediately launched himself forward to begin fumbling with the clamps attaching the pistons to the ramp.

The first piston came loose with relative ease and Marcus shoved it aside, but the second, now the only thing keeping the ramp from swinging open, was much more difficult to unscrew. It was clearly taking the weight that both pistons had previously born together as the thrust from the engines and the increasing gravity of New Io resisted Marcus' efforts to loosen the clamps.

New Io was getting closer now. The soft brownish yellow tinge of the little moon, measured up against Oberon's bright swirling clouds of gas, seemed almost inviting.

"How are we doing down there, hot shot?" Raven shouted over the comms.

"Good. Got one side dismantled. Working on the other one now," Marcus replied.

"You're doing great. Just let me know when it's done. I'll try and stave off the landing until you're secure behind the ramp. Just don't forget that we're running out of O^2 up here," she advised him.

"Roger that."

Perhaps if he were somehow able to exert some upward tension on the ramp, the hydraulics might come off easier. It would also prevent the ramp from hurtling outwards instead of inwards.

Marcus scoped the scene and spotted a piece of rappelling rope sticking out from one of the cabinets at the far end of the deck. Knowing at once what he could do, he sprung forward, sailing through the air towards the cabinet. His aim was slightly off and he ended up crashing directly into the GeoDynamics probe, which collided with the far wall with a great deal of clatter. No time to secure it now, he thought. If he didn't manage to hoist up the ramp, it will burn up anyway, as would he, and possibly the rest of the squad too.

He seized the rope on the second attempt, and jumped back to the ramp, holding one end of the unraveling piece of rope feeding out from the gap between the locker door and its frame, the other end still inside the cabinet. He threaded the rope through an equipment hook in the ceiling and down into and around the socket for the hydraulic piston he'd already removed, and then across ramp to the remaining piston. Pulling as much slack through as he could, Marcus stood and reached up to tie the end of the rope to a second hook in the ceiling, so that by pulling on the loose end of the cord he could lift the ramp inwards. But as he stretched up, the rope jerked out of his hand. It was stuck. The cabinet door was barring the rest of the rope from unraveling.

There must be a knot on the other end, he thought.

"I'm going to have to land real soon there cowboy!" Raven yelled on the comms.

New Io now filled the gaping hole of the broken nose section. He could clearly see the desert landscape and small wisps of thin white clouds.

"Almost there!" he shouted back as he pulled with all his might on the rope, but to no avail. It was completely stuck in the locker's door, the length of the deck away. Even if he was able to get to the cabinet in time, it was latched shut.

Something, anything, he thought. There had to be a way. He was running out of time.

There it was, on the floor beside him, strapped onto Taber's belt. His sidearm.

Still holding onto one end of the rope so that the whole thing wouldn't come undone, Marcus knelt down, pulled out the handgun and aimed for the lock on the cabinet. He pulled the trigger, once, twice, but the crack of gunfire failed to materialize as the gun refused to fire.

"Oxygen!" he shouted to himself. The gun won't fire without oxygen. "Shit!"

He fumbled around, hoping there was a hose line somewhere on his armor that would allow him to vent enough oxygen onto the weapon for it to fire, but found nothing of use. Finally he remembered the atmos canister he'd removed from his helmet earlier. Wrapping the rope around his forearm, he snatched the cylinder from his belt and proceeded to smash it, end-first, on the floor, cracking the seal. He could only hope that its contents would allow the combustion he needed to fire the sidearm. He aimed the wheezing canister at the weapon, took aim at the locker once more, and fired.

The shot went off.

Time seemed to stand still as he wasn't sure if he had hit his mark. Then the rope sprang free as the door of the cabinet flew open, the loose end tangled up in a knot half the size of his first. Without a second to waste he tied the end of the rope in his hand to the second hook and seized the loose end, pulling on it with every last fiber of his being. As soon as it was taught, he secured it with a knot and leapt for the final piston.

"Grey, do you hear me? Listen, it was a valiant effort, but we're down to our last few seconds of O^2 up here," Raven said.

"JUST A FEW MORE SECONDS!" he screamed into the comms.

"I have no choice but to land… I'm sorry," she said, the ship lunging downward.

There was no time to answer, no time to think.

He grabbed the powered screwdriver and went to work on the last bracket, loosening each of the four heavy bolts that held it in place. The first two came loose, and he could make out a small lake on the surface of New Io. The third came loose and he could feel his armor beginning to heat up as sparks started to fly into the lower deck from the open nose section. As the last bolt came undone, the rain of sparks had become so intense that it blinded him. The heat was becoming unbearable. Kicking the piston aside, Marcus grabbed the rope and pulled hard. The ramp barely budged.

Again he pulled, locking his arms in place and kicking around, bracing himself against the ceiling for leverage, putting his whole body into the effort. He could feel the tendons in his legs, arms and neck tightening, ready to tear, as he screamed, pulling with every last breath of oxygen left in his lungs. The ramp moved a centimeter or two.

He was done. Even holding the rope in place was taking all of his rapidly fading strength, his vision tunneling as heat and asphyxiation killed him. In just a few seconds, he would be nothing more than dust in the wind over New Io. He surrendered his life to fate.

But Fate, it seemed, had a different plan.

Without warning, something miraculous happened. As if it had a will of its own, the ramp began to rise. The inertia and friction of the ship colliding with the atmosphere had created a force that pushed on the ship's underbelly, forcing the ramp up inside the lower deck. Its speed increased until the ramp collided with the ceiling with tremendous force, almost tearing a hole through to the second deck.

Marcus was flung back, crashing against a bulkhead at the rear of the ship, utterly exhausted. The heat began to dissipate as the ship sailed through the atmosphere. With a tremendous effort, he reached up and opened the seal on his atmospheric valve to let in the cold, fresh oxygen of New Io. He lay there quietly, breathing in the dry desert air, silent and content at having saved Taber's body, as Raven struggled to guide the ship in for landing.

Raven managed a better landing than she had on Triton. Instead of an uncontrolled, screeching slide across a scattered surface of rock, the squad's arrival on New Io was a semi-controlled slide across sandy dunes. Unfortunately, the barracuda's abrupt collision with a wall sent Marcus sailing through the air once more, head-first into the ramp.

Chapter 16

Although the oval chamber occupied the southeastern corner of his penthouse suite, Takahashi had been avoiding the arboretum for years. It was an odd room, out of place with the rest of the suite. Rows of bushes lined the unadorned stone walls, and a cobblestone path surrounded a central dais from which grew a single majestic tree. A series of simple old candelabras were mounted on the walls, bathing the chamber in a soft, pleasant glow.

The chamber was carefully maintained by a gardener who regularly swept the pathway and tended to the plants, all save the stately tree standing alone in its center. All those in the Muromoto household knew that no one was allowed to disturb the tree, bar Takahashi himself.

As he entered the chamber, he reflected upon the many nights he had spent pruning it, trying to get the shape just right by stimulating growth in the right places and stunting it in others. Now, free from his interference, the old tree's gnarled branches had grown naturally, spoiling the delicate shape Takahashi had spent years developing. Still, it was time now. There was a lot of work to be done.

Takahashi knelt by a small cupboard next to the entrance and retrieved a pair of old shears which had been gathering dust since his last visit. He approached the old tree cautiously, gazing at its chaotic beauty. It was wrong. It had always been wrong. The old man had believed his memory of the monumental tree to be infallible, but the more he cut and pruned, the more his memories seemed to shift, realigning themselves as if to torture him.

He was getting old. He looked as if he was approaching the twilight of his years, but he felt sharper than ever, and with the proper telomere therapy he could still have decades left. Decades, Takahashi pondered. He hoped it wouldn't be that long. Although he still had a job to perform, he hoped that the time would go by quickly. Perhaps, fate willing, he would be with his beloved Lilly soon.

"Taki," prompted his secretary from the doorway, disturbing his thoughts.

Takahashi let the pair of cutters drop to the ground, slightly shaken by her use of his nickname, despite his invitation to her to do so.

"Yes?" he asked, turning to meet her gaze.

Her rosy cheeks did little to hide her shyness. She had never been inside the arboretum before.

"There's a Mr. Larry Harkin here to see you," chirped the innocent young woman.

Takahashi raised an eyebrow. It was a name he hadn't heard for the longest time.

"Show him in please," he urged her, wiping the leaves from his white silk shirt, now stained with tree sap.

A few minutes passed before the guest arrived in the doorway. He was a middle-aged man, completely bald, with deep worry lines on his oily forehead. His large ears drooped, his bushy eyebrows had grown almost as wildly as the tree Takahashi had been pruning, and his cheeks bared purplish veins. The two men, old acquaintances who'd met in similar circumstances all too often, didn't bother with greetings. As with their previous meetings, it was clear neither party was taking any particular enjoyment from the encounter.

"I see you've started this old nonsense again," Harkin chortled, breaking the awkward silence.

Takahashi didn't reply. He merely smiled halfheartedly.

"I have some matters to discuss with you, regarding C-CORE," Harkin began, fidgeting with the change in his pockets, stretching his pants outward in a peculiar fashion.

The quaint little man always had a way about him which defied social norms, Takahashi mused.

"Go on," he bid him.

"We received your request to resume your old position at the Composited Correlation of Entities, but the others doubt your motives," muttered Mr. Harkin, pedantically giving the agency its full title while fidgeting with his coins and rolling his feet on the hard stone floor.

"Oh?" smiled Takahashi. "And I suppose they sent you to interrogate me?"

"They're worried. Why now, after all this time?" coaxed the round little man.

"I never really left," claimed Takahashi. "Not the cause, in any case. I merely refocused my attention on alternative means to the same end."

Mr. Harkin eyed him suspiciously, leaning forward comically to get a better look.

"I would be lying if I told you that Lilly's passing hadn't slowed my progress initially, but, after having spent some time away, I've kept rather busy since," Takahashi added.

"What are you up to, old man?" Harkin probed.

"The Republic feels that C-CORE's exploratory missions are becoming too costly. Some very powerful people say that we have yet to see the fruits of our labor. None of the vessels we have sent have ever established contact, let alone returned," Takahashi said, turning towards the old tree.

"We've tried explaining to them that the sheer distances involved mean that, even if any of the ships manage to send a communication, it could be decades, or even centuries, before their signal would reach us," Harkin faltered, moving to stand beside him.

"And how have those affirmations been met?" Takahashi inquired, knowing full well what the answer would be.

Harkin didn't reply. He looked sternly at the branch in front of him, reaching out to pluck one of its leaves, rolling it between his fingers before allowing it to fall to the ground, joining the hundreds who had fallen prey to Takahashi's cutters.

"The Republic keeps pushing the ethical issue of sending people on one way trips. Even though everyone on those crews, military or civilian, is a volunteer, it simply unnerves people to think about it," Takahashi answered for him.

"So what is it that you propose we do about it?" Harkin protested smugly.

"It is pivotal that the missions continue," Takahashi proclaimed. "We tell the Republic what they want to hear."

"And what is that exactly?" Harkin sniveled.

"That we'll cut back on spending. We'll reduce the number of missions. All the senate really cares about is the money," Takahashi suggested.

"That won't be enough," Harkin argued. "The senate has been pushing the ethical issues vehemently in public."

"They have no qualms about sending millions of clones to their deaths to defend the Republic, but send a few of their own into deep space and suddenly they've grown a conscience," sneered Takahashi. "Very well then. We won't send any more citizens into deep space. We'll use the clones."

"The clones?" Harkin asked , startled at the thought.

"Why not? People can't argue that it's a fate any worse than what awaits them on Nyramar. Surely that will fit in nicely with their selective ethics," Takahashi sneered.

"But… they're clones," Harkin gasped, clearly aghast at the thought.

"Tell the others that the Muromoto group will be donating fifteen percent of its annual profits to the CORE upon their acceptance of my request," Takahashi concluded. "We'll see how much they still doubt my motives."

Takahashi knelt down to retrieve the cutters from where he had dropped them. Before Harkin had disappeared back through the doorway Takahashi was once again pruning his tree, lost in thought.

Chapter 17

"The man asked you to state your business Private Grey!" the familiar voice of Sergeant Lance resounded through Marcus' head, followed shortly by a chorus of laughter from what he could only assume to be from the rest of his squad.

He was lying on his back on the forward ramp, which had fallen down to its open position. He must have been lying on it when it blew open and slid down on his back, head-first into the sand. The whole squad surrounded him, laughing and applauding in turn.

"Fantastic job soldier," affirmed Corporal Dimitrov.

"Not bad, not bad at all," Lance confirmed, still chuckling as he reached down with his arm extended to help Marcus to his feet.

The whole world spun around before his very eyes as he slowly regained his balance. Marcus removed his helmet, breathing in the hot desert air.

"You did more than just save the mission there Grey," stated Raven. "See that huge crack in the heat shield over there?" She pointed towards an obvious crack in the second deck's shielding. "We'd all have been killed if you hadn't done what you did."

Embarrassed at all the flattery, Marcus acted as if he hadn't heard it, instead turning to look around. After all, this was his first time setting foot on a world containing a real Terran settlement. The structures surrounding the squad were an odd mixture of crumbling sun-baked stone walls and metal silos and walkways. The entire area was walled off in a chaotic manner and sand was the most predominant feature, lying everywhere in drifts and heaps.

It was high noon, and the sun was scorching hot. The orange and purple orb of Oberon towered overhead, the majesty of its rings lending an almost sacred presence to the scene. Over the walls surrounding the squad, Marcus could see several groupings of lush palm trees swaying gently in the breeze as a flock of birds soared among the few wispy clouds overhead.

"What did you say this place was again?" Taz asked.

"According to the nav computer, it's called the Last Oasis. It's the largest settlement on New Io." Raven replied with a hint of sarcasm.

"Well, I think it's amazing, whatever it is," exclaimed Marcus.

"Amazing or not, we're only staying as long as it takes to patch up this hunk of junk," Lance interjected as he slammed his fist into the side of the ship.

No one missed the clanging noise of something coming loose and hitting the floor on the lower deck.

Suddenly Marcus noticed the local dock workers, a group of four extremely tanned men whose faded brown overalls were covered with dirt and grease. They wore dark braided beards, and a reddish-brown cloth they'd wrapped around their heads to form a kind of hat. One of them, a scrawny middle-aged man with wrinkled skin and a crooked nose, held a small book and pen.

"Sir, I must insist that you state your purpose on New Io!" the odd-looking man insisted. "The authorities will not be pleased with the military meddling in our affairs."

"Relax buddy," said Sergeant Lance, patronizingly. "We're not here in any official capacity. We just need our ship fixed and refueled and we'll be on our way."

The dockworker looked towards his coworkers for support as they hovered around him aimlessly.

"You must speak with Rory, the refinery manager."

"Refinery?" Lance asked.

"This is a GeoDynamics refinery facility," the dockworker replied.

"Really now?" the Sergeant proclaimed, realizing his luck. "That is most interesting. Go fetch this Rory of yours so that I can have a word with him," Lance ordered in his most intimidating manner, taking a step forward to loom over the diminutive dockworker.

"We want no trouble with the military, sir. I will ask that he come see you at once. Stay here please," begged the cowed old man, holding his hands up in an appeasing manner as he took a couple of steps backwards to put greater distance between himself and Lance.

He muttered something to one of his coworkers, who immediately ran off further into the compound.

"Our first mission and our damned ship's totally wrecked," Lance stated, turning to face the barracuda, which was firmly lodged, nose first, into the perimeter wall of the GeoDynamics compound. A thin plume of smoke billowed from the front of the ship, which had borne the brunt of the damage. Surprisingly, the landing gear had withstood the impact of the landing once again, at least enough to save the turret. Still, it was apparent that the ship would neither take off, nor land again, without a major overhaul.

"Don't worry boss, we'll get it fixed," Jago rumbled reassuringly.

"Hopefully it won't take too long. We still have to deliver the probe to our contact on the Alamo," the Sergeant replied. "Still, I guess we have had at least some luck. Landing in a GeoDynamics facility means I should be able to contact our corporate liaison. That is, if this Rory fellow will allow me the use of his communications tower."

135

"I'm sure it won't be a problem," Dimitrov assured him. "And, in the meantime, at least we managed to crash-land somewhere more interesting than last time."

Marcus thought the Corporal was right. He found himself pulled in every direction at once. This world offered a whole range of new and exciting possibilities.

All of a sudden, the humming of a motorized vehicle heading in their direction caught the squad's attention. In the distance, the dockworker who'd run off to fetch Rory was returning, running alongside a rusty open-topped motorized cart with a single seat protruding from its center, on which sat an overweight middle-aged man. His sun-baked skin was wrinkled beyond belief, his auburn beard covered his mouth entirely, and his graying hair was topped off with a striped cap with sweat-stained edges. Unlike the dock workers, his peculiar overalls were red, and stained not with dirt and grease, but rather with sweat and what looked like food stains. He wore tinted circular lenses on a rubbery band around his head, no doubt meant to protect his eyes from the glaring sun.

The small but fast-moving vehicle screeched to a halt some two meters in front of Sergeant Lance, blowing up a thick cloud of dust.

"My, my, what have we here?" the weird-looking old man inquired, his pungent aroma easily overpowering every other scent in their vicinity.

"Are you Rory?" the Sergeant prompted.

"'pends," blurted the odd man.

"'pends?" Lance asked , taken aback by the man's strange demeanor.

"'pends on whether you folks is here to stir up trouble or not," stated the old man, staring intently into Lance's eyes.

"No, no trouble at all," Lance informed him. "We just need repairs, and to borrow the use of your communications tower to contact Alamo Station. I need to inform my superiors of our situation."

"Hmmm…" the overweight man sighed, scratching his beard.

A leftover piece of bread came loose from within its folds, which he promptly snatched up from his lap and put in his mouth.

"In that case… I'm Rory. I manage the facilities here. You do as I say and I'll have my workers sort you out. Although I'm afraid we don't have the parts y'need to fix yer ship, or what's left of her. Our supply ship is at Coraya 4, picking up supplies. It'll be close to three weeks b'fore she can bring back the parts y'need," he explained.

"Three weeks?" bellowed Sergeant Lance. "That's way too long."

"Well I guess ye could contact the Alamo and see if they can send someone out here with the parts, but I wouldn't hold me breath if I was you," Rory chuckled.

"Can you escort me to your communications tower? I'll contact my superiors. With any luck, there's a supply ship close by which could get us out of your hair sooner," the Sergeant proposed.

"I guess that'd be alright. Follow me. Oh, and try to keep up, will ya?" yelled Rory as he backed up his cart, deftly spinning it about and blowing up another thick cloud of dust.

"Spielman, you and your team follow me. The rest of you, guard the ship while we're away," the Sergeant ordered as he ran off after the cart speeding off into the distance.

Corporal Spielman and his men took off after them in hot pursuit, before the rest of the squad even had time to acknowledge the order.

*   *   *   *   *

The scorching heat from the desert sun hovering directly overhead was too much for the squad to bear. They all agreed that it would be far better to have one team cooling down inside the ship while the other stood guard outside. Even so, they had to rotate guards every thirty minutes, as their metal-plated, fully-enclosed armor simply wasn't built to withstand such high temperatures. It was a full two hours before they spotted the Sergeant returning.

"Problem?" Corporal Dimitrov called, having removed his helmet like the rest of the squad.

"You could say that," Lance spat as he closed the distance, coming to a stop in front of the squad. Spielman and his men formed up beside him. "Alamo can't spare a ship at this time. We've been ordered to lay low until the GeoDynamics supply ship can return with the parts we need," the Sergeant informed them.

"What took so long?" asked Corporal Dimitrov.

"Comms delay. We're pretty far out from the Alamo, so there's a seven minute lag in response time," the Sergeant answered. "But at least we have one thing going for us. We can complete our mission here instead of on the Alamo. I contacted our GeoDynamics corporate liaison, who wasn't at all too pleased with our current situation, but admitted that our troubles were unforeseeable and therefore not our fault. She asked that we hand the survey probe over to the facility manager here."

"Well, that's good news," Dimitrov replied.

"It is," replied the Sergeant. "The dockworkers will take it into storage. We have three whole weeks to kill. But don't let that get to your heads just yet. We will have to make guard duty arrangements. I want one team with the ship at all times. Dimitrov, you and your team have first watch. The rest of you can have a look around, and get some rest before your shifts."

"Yes Sergeant," acknowledged Dimitrov, disappointed at having to delay his exploration of the Last Oasis.

"I'll send Spielman and his men to relieve you in eight hours," Lance told him. "Alright men, I want you all on your best behavior. Let's move," the Sergeant bellowed.

Marcus watched as the other two teams wandered off into the compound while he and the rest of his team remained guarding the smoldering ruins of their ship. Shortly afterwards the dockworkers returned and unloaded the survey probe onto a pushcart and began hauling it off to a warehouse.

Marcus couldn't wait for Corporal Spielman and his men to get back.

Chapter 18

Eight hours in the smoldering heat did little to lessen Dimitrov's team's excitement. They spent the hottest part of the day in the ship's shade. When the blazing sun began to set on the horizon, they heard the familiar call of Corporal Spielman and his men.

"Hello there. Ready to be relieved from guard duty?" Spielman asked, lugging his weapon as he strode towards them, swaying from side to side.

"Everything ok there Corporal?" Dimitrov asked , not sure what to make of Corporal Spielman's swagger.

"Fine, fine. We've just been sampling the local brew. A strong, fiery drink they call Raketta," Spielman answered. "You really ought to try it."

"I'm sure we will," replied Dimitrov. "Well men, let's not make Corporal Spielman have to ask us twice, shall we? You heard the man. Guard duty's over."

Marcus' team sprung to life, reborn from the slumbers of the hot afternoon shift and eager to be let into the settlement to experience all that it had to offer.

"Oh, one thing before you go," Spielman added. "The locals don't allow any weapons or technology in their village. You'll be asked to leave them within the GeoDynamics compound. You might as well leave it all here with the ship where we can keep an eye on it."

"No technology?" asked Taz in astonishment. "Not even comms?"

"Nope, no technology whatsoever," answered the swaying Corporal.

"What about that Rory guy? He drove around on a powered cart," Dimitrov insisted.

"Well, he's not a local. He's a Beta Terran, and a representative of GeoDynamics. He doesn't follow the local customs. And he doesn't leave the GeoDynamics compound. You can carry whatever piece of tech you want here, just have to leave it behind before you exit the compound," Spielman explained.

"Alright," Dimitrov sighed with a puzzled expression. "Why don't the locals allow technology in their village?"

"They're some manner of religious lot. 'Muslani', I think Rory called it," Spielman went on. "They call themselves the 'Children of the Wastes', if I remember it correctly. They're not exactly politically aligned with Beta Terra. They think of themselves as free people, and they don't much take kindly to the presence of GeoDynamics on their moon. Nor to our presence, for that matter. We had a hard enough time just ordering drinks at the local bar."

"Understood," Dimitrov acknowledged. "We'll do our best not to arouse any hostilities."

"Good luck with that," added Corporal Spielman. "The Ape already duked it out with one of the locals who didn't like him eyeing his daughter."

"Why am I not surprised?" Taz muttered, shaking his head.

"Anyway, Lance's team will take over from us in eight hours, so you guys get two whole shifts to yourselves." Spielman slurred. "Lucky bastards! They've got real beds at the inn too…"

"Well men, leave your equipment in the ship. Let's get out of these tin cans and change into our uniforms, then have ourselves a look, shall we?" suggested Dimitrov.

*   *   *   *   *

Having seen the whole of the GeoDynamics facility, Marcus now had a good idea of the general layout. It was roughly rectangular compound, and the barracuda had come down in its empty northeast corner. West of the downed ship was a large warehouse built against the compound's north wall, and beyond that stood a cluster of smaller storage buildings. In the northwest corner was an unremarkable two-storey stone building, standing amidst a clutter of rusted debris, with three steps and a ramp leading to the double-wide entryway. A sign above the door read 'GeoDynamics Main Office'. To the south of the main building a steel-grated gate four meters wide barred entry to the Last Oasis through the compound's west wall. A small guard post, a hut barely large enough to accommodate its sole occupant, was situated to the right of the gate, between it and the main office.

South of the gate stood a tall comms tower, perched atop a small building that served as the compound's link to the rest of the system. Running along the southern wall stood a row of low, dirty buildings containing the refinery facilities, followed by three designated landing pads. Each of these was entirely encircled by stone walls, five meters high, with maintenance and service-related structures built into their inner rims. A gated entrance between each pad and the rest of the compound allowed the owner of the docked vessel some manner of security. Either that, or it gave the facility manager control over who was allowed entry to the compound.

Three huge storage silos, each at least twenty meters in height and ten in width, stood in a line along the southern side of the warehouse, facing the jumble of storage buildings and landing pads. The round tanks were painted white, but with a colored stripe circling the upper

142

half, no doubt indicating their contents. The one opposite the largest refinery structure was rusted from top to bottom, its white paint peeling off to reveal the tarnished metal underneath. The tanks pinched the center of the compound into a narrow bottleneck between two open spaces, one to the west in front of the gate, the other to the east where the barracuda had crash landed.

As Marcus and his team approached the tiny guard hut next to the gate, they could see an elderly dark-skinned man so thin that he was hardly more than skin and bone sat behind a pane of glass, his bloodshot eyes half closed. When Corporal Dimitrov knocked on his window, the little man jumped, almost falling off his stool. He stared at the clones one by one for a few seconds before remembering where he was and what he was there to do. He leaned forward to push the button on the desk in front of him to activate his microphone.

"Welcome to the Last Oasis, only port on New Io," he said – a greeting well rehearsed, if rarely spoken. "Please present your papers or Ident chip," he barked through the small speaker, its wires exposed, hanging from one of the rafters overhead.

Corporal Dimitrov knelt in front of the window, handing his Ident chip through a small gap beneath the pane of glass. The elderly guard leaned forward, squinting his eyes to see if Dimitrov's face matched that on display on the ancient-looking computer in front of him. At some point the device had been a pasty white color, but years, if not decades, of the sun's rays fracturing on the glass had discolored the lettering on the keypad, as did yellowish stains, no doubt accrued from frequent contact with the guards' sweaty fingers.

"Please step up to the side here sir, and onto the metal plate," the guard requested, gesturing to one side where, half covered in sand, was a black metallic plate about one meter square.

Dimitrov stepped on top of it and the guard, who had leaned forward to make sure that he really was in place, pressed two of the buttons on his keypad simultaneously, resulting in an erratic array of bleeps and clicks from the device the Corporal was standing on. The guard stared intently at his monitor.

"You're clear. No weapons or prohibited items. You'll of have to wait for the system to receive your identification from the military. It should take no more than fifteen minutes or so. Please step aside sir," the guard said, without a trace of interest or enthusiasm. "Next please."

* * * * *

The gates to the compound closed abruptly behind them. They emerged from the GeoDynamics facility into an open square, somewhat off center in the town, just as the sun had set on the horizon. The sun-washed structures bathed in starlight and the orange and purple radiance of Oberon seemed almost romantic.

Almost every house had a courtyard walled off from the street, filled with rows and rows of fruit and vegetable bearing plants just visible through half-open gates. The soft yellow glow of candlelight emanated from the windows, their green-painted wooden shutters wide open in a display of the simple, secure community that resided here. A chorus of laughter from playing children and the clatter of housewives setting the table for dinner could be heard throughout the street. Wet clothes in a multitude of warm, earthly colors had been hung out to dry outside almost every household. A lone malnourished cat and her three young kittens followed the team's every step as they threaded the narrow streets following Spielman's directions toward the Black Lotus

Inn, the only establishment in town that they'd been told would serve outsiders.

The few locals out on the streets were quick to give their passage a wide birth, and those who spotted them from their windows closed their shutters in a quiet protest against this new presence in their town.

Chapter 19

The Black Lotus was a three-storey structure of sand-scrubbed stone, nestled on a street corner. A large terrace on the first floor housed several long tables and benches. Grape vines wound around the dark wooden supports, continuing up to the second-floor balcony where they clung to a mesh of wired netting sheltering the gallery, hung with large quantities of luscious purple grapes for the patrons to pick at as they sipped Raketta well into the night. Lanterns hung over the terrace, basking its patrons in an orange glow and casting eerie shadows, which writhed as the lanterns swayed in the gentle breeze. Somewhere not far away, a wind chime clanged and cicadas chirped in the bushes.

As the few locals who sat on the terrace spotted the team's approach, they slammed their coins on the table in protest and disappeared into the night, leaving behind their unfinished drinks and half-filled bowls of dried fruits and nuts.

The floorboards creaked as Marcus and the others stepped onto the terrace. The sweet aroma stemming from the kitchen was so alluring that it made Marcus's mouth water. Having only ever tasted dry rations and the mess hall slop on Callisto, the exotic food he could smell being prepared by the Black Lotus staff left him mesmerized, eager to sample everything they had to offer.

Inside, the team was greeted by the sight of a wide hall, littered with ottomans and comfortable-looking sofas embroidered with intricate floral patterns. Strewn across the seating area were plush silken

146

cushions in a wide array of colors. The seats were arranged to form three seating areas, each surrounding a brass cylindrical object covered with ornate carvings and with a glass sphere filled with water at its base. On top of the peculiar looking device there was a receptacle of sorts, covered in burnt ashes. From each of the devices, a long rubbery pipe extended a couple of meters and lay haphazardly on the nearest sofa or ottoman. On the left of the room stood a lavish staircase of ashen wood, varnished to a high glossy shine. Opposite the entrance were the reception counter and the doorway to the kitchen.

The lobby was deserted after the departure of the locals, but they could hear a clatter emanating from the kitchen, followed by muddled voices and a deep laughter. Marcus wondered where Lance and his team were, before deciding that if Spielman was anything to go by, Lance and the others had probably already drunk their fill and were sleeping it off somewhere.

Corporal Dimitrov approached the reception desk, upon which there lay a ledger bound in leather with brass edging, and a bell to summon assistance. Dimitrov looked back at the rest of them. His questioning gaze betrayed his indecision as to whether or not he should ring the bell. When no one said anything, he put his palm down on top of it, and it produced a high-pitched sound which seemed to hang in the air for a long time.

Suddenly, Marcus felt something poking him in the back. Turning around in silent surprise, he was confused to see that there was nothing there. Looking forward again, he saw that the others were still stood in front of him, unsure of how to behave as they waited for someone to answer the bell. Then there it was again. Something or someone was poking him in the small of his back, slightly harder this

147

time. He turned sharply, half attempting to surprise whoever or whatever it was that was doing it, but still, there was no one there.

"Mistah, you want to try the shisha?" a squeaky voice inquired from somewhere below him.

Looking down, Marcus finally noticed the small, dark-skinned boy, no more than eight years of age, who had been standing directly behind him. His big brown eyes, unafraid of the strangers who had entered his town, were quite heartwarming. Markus was caught completely off guard. It was the first time he, or any of the team, had seen a child in real life. The sight was both comical and endearing at the same time.

"A what?" asked Marcus, not sure exactly what a 'shisha' was.

The others turned to marvel at the sight of the young boy.

"The shisha," the boy repeated, pointing at the peculiar device in the center of the closest seating area. "The pipes! I have strawberry, apple, liquorish and cinnamon, but I'm out of lemon," He said, rifling through the contents of a large belt pouch, inside which Marcus could see small blackened lumps.

The boy took a couple of them out of the pouch, pressing them up against his nose and proceeded to smell them, leaving a dark smudge on his upper lips and nose.

"This one is liquorish. It's very good," he informed Marcus, proffering the little lump in his outstretched hand. "Ten credits."

"I, ah, my credit chip is in the ship. We were told we're not allowed to bring any technology into the town," Marcus tried to explain to the youth.

"That's right," said Corporal Dimitrov, he and the others gathering around the little boy, curious to see what was going on. "So how are we going to pay for our rooms and food?"

148

"...or the wine?" added Taz.

The swinging doors to the kitchen flung open as the innkeeper, no doubt a relative of the boy to judge by their strong resemblance, emerged. He wore a dark-green robe of silk, and a circular hat with a flat top of the same color.

"Good evening sirs, I am Omar Ashwari. How may I help you?"

"Um… yes, well, I'm not sure actually," Dimitrov blurted, turning to face him. "You see, we aren't allowed to bring our credit chips, but we are in need of rooms, and some food."

"And drinks," added Taz again, from the back of the group. The Corporal shot him a look that obviously was meant to get him to keep quiet.

"That's no problem sir," replied Omar. "We can send the bill for your rooms to the GeoDynamics facility. You pay them with your credit chip, and they pay us in our form of currency. That's how it is usually done here with visitors. Not that we get many."

"Excellent," Dimitrov smiled, pleased that everything appeared to be working out. "So, what about food – and drinks?" he added before Taz had the chance to chime in.

"You can order whatever food, drink or service you desire here sir. We will simply have it added to your room number, and it will be added to the bill," explained Omar. "Just be aware that the refinery manager will not allow your ship to leave until all bills have been paid."

"You can have the Shisha added to your room too," proclaimed the little boy, tugging at the back of Marcus's belt.

Marcus turned to him, smiling.

"In that case, I'll try the liquorish. But give me a chance to get a room and freshen up first."

"Sanjey, leave the customers alone," barked Omar, scolding the eager young boy. "Let them settle in first."

"Sorry dado," moaned the little boy, turning and running away to sit on a small foot stool by the terrace window.

"My apologies for my son, he can be a bit too eager at times," explained Omar.

"That's quite alright," professed Corporal Dimitrov, smiling. "We'll need five rooms then please."

* * * * *

The room was as small as his old quarters on the Alamo had been, back before he'd chosen to enter into a tour of duty. After spending the night with Eve, Marcus had yet to sleep in his bunk in the squad's cramped, dirty hangar bay. Still, this room felt more open, less confined than anything on the Alamo, not only because the door didn't have a lock, but also because on the wall opposite the wide bed, covered in fresh white linen, an open window let in a light breeze of warm desert air. The window had a wooden frame, covered in fine netting to keep insects out. The frame could be lifted out from the bottom to access the shutters hanging outside if one wanted to block the window entirely.

Tearing his eyes away from the first open window he'd ever seen, Marcus spotted a basin filled with water stood on a table by the bed. He splashed some water from it onto his face. The salty taste on his lips as the water washed away the dried sweat reminded him just how hungry he was, and how eager he was to sample the local cuisine. He hung his jacket inside the narrow closet by the door and proceeded downstairs, his stomach growling with anticipation.

Chapter 20

They had ordered over half of what the Black Lotus' menu had to offer. The table was covered in brown-glazed ceramic plates adorned with colorful symmetrical patterns. On each one, a different dish added to the orchestra of aromas.

Pan seared yellow cheese, wrapped in dough. A chopped salad of fresh tomatoes, cucumbers and onions, covered with grated white cheese and olives soaked in oil and vinegar. Cured lamb, broiled over a bed of rice, cooked in vegetable stock adorned with a wedge of lemon and a seasoning of cinnamon and hot peppers. A pie made of buttered dough and pigeon meat, lathered in powdered white sugar mixed with cinnamon and orange juice, and so many others, each dish more exquisite than the next, a virtual explosion of exotic tastes.

The five men gorged themselves for what seemed like hours, recounting their story since departing from Alamo Station, laughing and sipping Raketta well into the night. None of them would have believed they would end up in a situation such as this when they had set out from Callisto.

"Well Taz, it looks like you got your wish," proclaimed Marcus, taking a bite of a small fish that had been coated in batter and fried in oil.

"Absolutely! This is much better than what I used to drink in Zonaka," replied Taz, taking another sip from his Raketta and closing his eyes, shaking his head violently to resist the strong bite of the bitter wine.

Marcus felt guilty that their presence there had driven off all the local customers. Although they had made up for it to some extent by ordering with such complete lack of restraint. They found a great deal of solace sitting there on the terrace. The warm atmosphere, the star-cluttered sky, now void of Oberon's presence. The streets were empty, save for the malnourished cat and her three young, who had come trotting up from around the corner of the house opposite. She approached without caution to rub herself up against their calves, meowing softly as she begged for food while her young played at the base of the terrace, hunting each other in a tireless game of cat and mouse.

"They're amazing!" Reid let out, staring intently as Marcus fed the cat one of the small fried fish. She snatched it from his fingers and gobbled the whole thing up in a matter of seconds. It was as if she'd never seen food before.

"I wonder where they get the fish," Taz blurted out of the blue, more interested in the food than the display of feline playfulness.

"What do you mean?" Dimitrov asked. "Where do fish normally come from?" he added sarcastically.

"No. I mean, this whole place is one big desert. So how do they get fish?" Taz reiterated, with continued interest.

"I suppose they probably import it," proposed Reid, shrugging his shoulders.

"I saw a big pool of water when we were coming in for landing," Marcus explained to them. "I guess, since they call this place the Last Oasis, it must be built on the banks. The locals could have introduced the fish into the water when they settled this place."

"Sounds reasonable," Dimitrov conceded.

This got Taz onto the process by which the Terrans terraformed planets and moons, and how it was all a conspiracy orchestrated by the Terran Republic to introduce mind control agents into the atmosphere. Marcus began dozing off as the discussion quickly turned into a heated debate. He had never felt so content, sitting in the balmy heat, his stomach filled with exotic foods and his head swimming from the effects of the Raketta. Then, without warning, a sharp numbing pain shot through his temples.

* * * * *

"He's dead! Can't you see that? They're all dead!" a voice shouted at him. Disoriented, Marcus looked around to get his bearings. The muddled sounds of distant gunfire echoed through his mind as someone emptied a full clip of carbine rounds. He looked down and saw that he was holding the lifeless body of little Sanjay, streams of blood trickling from an open wound on his neck.

"Forget about him, we need to get back to the compound, stat!" Dimitrov screamed right in his face as he grabbed him by the shoulder, pulling him away from the Black Lotus, blood soaked bodies littering the terrace.

"They're all dead Marcus. We have to go before..." Corporal Dimitrov was cut short as something jumped at him from out of nowhere.

His blood curdled screams begging Marcus for help.

"Tony!" Marcus shouted.

* * * * *

"Easy there, I'm right here. No need to shout," Dimitrov assured him, sitting on the edge of the table, still sipping his Raketta.

"You alright there Grey? You look a little pale," Becks inquired, eyeing him with concern.

"I… I must have fallen asleep," Marcus explained hesitantly. It was the only reasonable explanation for what he had just experienced.

"And do you always call out for Corporal Dimitrov in your dreams? Because frankly, I find that very disturbing," said Taz, and the whole team broke into laughter.

"It's nothing," Marcus assured them. "Forget about it."

"No, no. I wanna hear more about this," said Taz, obviously in the mood to make more jokes at Marcus' expense. "So, what were you and the Corporal doing in this dream that requires you to call out his name with such excitement?"

"Leave it Sobieski," Dimitrov ordered him. "I think Grey's been through enough for one day. I think we can all forgive him if he's a bit shaken up. He did save all our lives, after all. Or have you forgotten about that, Private?" the Corporal scowled at Taz.

"Sorry Corp," he replied.

"Don't tell that to me, tell it to Grey."

"Sorry Marcus. Just havin' some fun," Taz mumbled.

"Just forget it," replied Marcus.

The conversation slowly died down. The five of them sat there, nibbling at the leftover food, sipping a last bottle of Raketta, feeding the rest of the small fried fish to the cat. Once she had had her fill, she started to bring the morsels over to her kittens, who promptly fought over the mangled pieces.

Marcus noticed a figure at the end of the street, lurking in the shadows, slowly approaching the inn. Marcus slid his hand down to

154

his thigh, to where his sidearm should be – but they had all been required to leave their weapons behind in the ship. The figure slowly came into light, and the knot that had begun forming in Marcus' overly-full stomach dissipated immediately. It was an old man. A local, dressed in tattered robes. His wrinkled, sun baked face was tense, and he was smiling almost maniacally as he approached them.

"What's his problem?" wondered Taz, who had also spotted the old man approaching.

The others turned to see who Taz was referring to. The old man took small, slow steps, his long graying beard flowing in the cool evening breeze, as did the end of his tattered turban, which had come loose.

"He seems harmless," Corporal Dimitrov commented. "Just ignore him."

They continued to watch the old man's progress until he came to a stop at the edge of the railing separating the terrace from the street. He leaned over the railing with an outstretched arm and grabbed Marcus's wrist. Marcus's first instinct was to pull away, but he fought the urge and allowed the old man to take his hand. The bearded figure leaned forward and spoke in a raspy voice which sounded of old age and demented wisdom:

> Eat little larvae. Eat. Eat!
> You will need your strength for what's to come.
> On the morrow, the star of wisdom will fall.
> Then the freak show will come to call.
> Nine and nine came crashing down.
> How many leave, is up to the one-eyed clown.

They stared at him with utter amazement. They didn't know what to make of the eccentric old man and his riddles. He stood there, smiling at them, slowly letting go of Marcus's arm. He turned to leave, shuffling back the same way he had come, as if he had come only to speak with Marcus. The team sat there in silence, exchanging puzzled looks as the old man slowly crept back into the shadows whence he came.

*   *   *   *   *

The first smoke of the Shisha pipe left them each coughing and wheezing. The sweet taste of liquorish it left behind was an interesting addition to tonight's wide array of new flavors. Sanjay, the young boy who had sold them the lump of liquorish-flavored coal, chuckled as he watched the newcomers attempting to use the exotic pipe.

"You don't need to inhale," he said, smiling from his footstool.

"What? How then?" asked Marcus, curious to learn how he was supposed to use the device.

"Just suck on the pipe, but don't breath," explained little Sanjay. "Instead, let the smoke slowly escape from your mouth. Like this," he said, jumping from his footstool to snatch the pipe from Taz's fingers.

He put the end to his mouth and sucked hard, his cheeks blowing up like two plump red tomatoes. He handed the pipe back to Taz and slowly opened his mouth, letting the thick white smoke trickle out slowly. It clung to the air like a serpent, writhing and twisting around itself until Sanjay blew the rest of the smoke out of his mouth, dispersing the serpent into a misty haze.

"See!" he proclaimed, proudly.

Sanjay's technique proved to be easy to follow, and they each sat enjoying the liquorish-flavored smoke of the Shisha pipe long into the night, until it was time to crawl into bed. As soon as his head hit the fresh, white-linen covered pillow, Marcus was asleep, his head filled with new experiences for his dreams to play out.

Chapter 21

Marcus arose the next morning to the sound of angry villagers shouting downstairs, and Sergeant Lance's voice attempting to soothe what sounded like an angry mob.

"Calm down sir. I'm certain that none of my men have anything to do with your goat escaping from its pen," Lance was saying, somewhat unconvincingly.

Marcus gathered up the few personal belongings he'd brought with him, splashed some water on his face, and headed downstairs to view the spectacle in person. Lance had his hands full. He had been backed into a corner by five of the local men, and had his hands raised in protest as the mob drew closer and closer. Omar, the receptionist, stood at Lance's side, shouting back at the mob.

"Please, not in my inn, take it outside," he pleaded with the angry men.

"We want them gone," shouted the tallest of the five, his beard and moustache shaking violently with every fiery outburst.

"They should not be allowed to leave the compound," added another.

"Every time these outsiders enter our village, something bad happens, and when they're military, it's as if they were never taught any manners," bellowed a third.

"Please," Sergeant Lance begged. "We really don't wish to cause you any trouble. If you could just give me until the end of the day, I'm quite sure that I can help track down your lost animal and I promise

158

to have a word with my men and discipline those who have done you wrong. You have my word!"

The locals eased up somewhat at this, taking a couple of steps back, their shoulders relaxing, their arms dropping to their sides.

"Very well. You have until the end of the day," warned the tallest one, looking to the others for support. "Otherwise, we will go to the Sheikh."

"The Sheikh?" the Sergeant asked, unfamiliar with the title.

"Sheikh Abdul Ba'ari. He is our leader, a highly religious and important man. His word is law," the tall one informed him.

"There is really no need for that," Lance assured him.

"We will see," said the tall man, backing off and preparing to leave.

Omar moved to follow them as the Sergeant relaxed, breathing a sigh of relief. The men left the inn with Omar fast on their heels, whispering promises of free drinks the next time the men would visit his establishment, provided they would leave the foreigners alone – at least while they remained on his premises.

Lance finally noticed Marcus standing at the bottom of the stairs, watching what was going on.

"Ah, Private Grey. Just the man I wanted to see," the Sergeant said.

"Oh, why? Have I done something wrong?" Marcus asked, hesitantly.

"On the contrary! I was so impressed with your performance yesterday, rescuing us, that I'm promoting you to Private First Class," announced the Sergeant. "I've already spoken with Corporal Dimitrov about it, and he agrees with my assessment."

"Thank you Sergeant," replied Marcus, flattered by the Sergeant's recognition of his efforts.

"You will, of course, not let me down. Will you, PFC Grey?" asked the Sergeant in a patronizing tone. "As Private First Class, if anything were to happen to Corporal Dimitrov, then you will have to take his place as Acting Corporal. Are you sure that you're up to the task?"

"I won't let you down Sergeant" replied Marcus with resounding conviction.

"Excellent," Lance replied. "Oh, and one more thing. With the loss of our technician, I will need someone to undergo the training necessary to take his place. I went over the breeding logs with Doc Taylor, and we reviewed the pre-stamped resonant memories of everyone on the squad. The results showed that your model has a high natural aptitude for working with electronics and technology."

"Really?" asked Marcus, surprised that the Sergeant knew things about him that he didn't even know himself.

"Yes, really," Lance affirmed. "It's therefore our consensus that you undergo the necessary training to fulfill the role for the squad."

"I'll try Sergeant, but won't we simply get a replacement?" Marcus asked hesitantly.

"Clones are bred in batches of eighteen, Private. Full squads. There aren't a lot of spares running around. The senate has passed laws regarding how many of each type of clone can be bred at any one time. Getting a replacement could take months, even years. Until then, you're the best I've got," answered the Sergeant, shifting his stance as well as his tone. "Now, unless you wish to continue questioning my orders, Private, then I suggest you report to Taylor. He's waiting for you at the ship."

"Yes Sergeant" replied Marcus. "Sorry Sergeant."

"Now, if you'll excuse me, I've got to go round up the rest of the troops before these backwater morons turn on us," the Sergeant exclaimed, marching up the stairs to wake up whoever might still be asleep.

*　*　*　*　*

The Sergeant's harsh words about the locals had Marcus worried. Sure, these people lived off the beaten track, but that didn't mean that their way of life was any less noble or meaningful than those of any free Terran. If anything, in Marcus's view, these people were to be respected for their choices, and admired for their complete lack of dependence on technology and weapons. They'd learned to live together in peace and harmony. How could anyone find fault with their way of life? He considered the ways of the Children of the Wastes as he made his way through the town's narrow streets towards the GeoDynamics compound.

On his way he passed by a circular building with a high, domed roof. Inside, through a set of double doors twice as high as a man and carved with intricate patterns so precise and detailed that he could easily imagine it would take a skilled craftsman the better part of his lifetime to create them, Marcus observed as two dozen of the local men sat on their knees on ornate rugs, all facing the same direction. They bowed forward with their arms stretched out in a pleading manner, then rose and knelt in unison, like a calm wave gently caressing a sandy beach. Marcus stood there in silent wonder, watching and pondering the meaning of this strange, yet soothing, ritual.

Eventually, a boy, dressed in simple brown robes, came out from a small alcove inside the building. The boy noticed him and rushed over to the giant doors and began closing them. His angry glare was all that was needed to tell Marcus that he wasn't welcome there. Disappointed, he continued towards the GeoDynamics compound as the sun began its steady climb over the horizon.

"Shoo, shoo. You are despicable," he heard someone shouting from up ahead.

It came from the house opposite the compound. Clearing the corner, Marcus saw a heavy-set man, holding one of the horns of a goat, trying to pull it away from Jago Raynes, who lay passed out and spread-eagled on his back in the man's vegetable garden, the goat trapped under one enormous arm. One of Jago's legs was lying in a puddle of muddy water as the goat licked his face repeatedly.

"What have you done to my tomatoes you big oaf?" yelled the heavy-set local, letting go of the goat and turning to inspect the damage. "Those were my finest tomatoes," the man moaned in anguish, putting both hands on top of his head in disbelief.

Marcus shook his head, not sure whether to interfere or simply leave things be. At last, when the heavy set local began to nudge Jago with his boot, Marcus felt compelled to intervene.

"Sir, please allow me," shouted Marcus, approaching with haste. "I'm sure I can wake up the... uh, big oaf."

"You'd better! And whose goat is this?"

"I think I may have an idea who that goat belongs to," Marcus, told him, proceeding to give a detailed description of the man from the inn.

An empty Raketta bottle proved to be the perfect instrument with which to wake up the squad's support gunner from his alcohol-induced stupor. Having filled the bottle with the muddy water from the puddle, Marcus poured the contents all over the behemoth's face.

"I swear, I can too ride a goat!" the Ape shouted as he rose abruptly from his slumber. "Oh, it's you," he mumbled, confused. "What, where am I... and why am I covered in..." he said using his hand to wipe his face before giving it a thorough sniffing. "What is this?"

"Come on Ape," suggested Marcus, chuckling and shaking his head. "The Sergeant is looking for you... and the goat."

* * * * *

After making sure to send the Ape on his way to see Lance, and that the goat found its way back to its rightful owner, Marcus finally managed to get back to the ship.

Taylor had been impatiently awaiting his arrival.

"Where have you been? You were supposed to start your shift over half an hour ago," he complained testily. As part of Lance's squad, the medic had been on guard duty since the early morning, and was clearly impatient to get some sleep. "Corporal Dimitrov and the rest of your team are already inside."

"Sorry Doc," Marcus apologized, approaching the ship where the medic had been waiting for him outside. "I ran into a fellow soldier who'd gotten himself into some trouble with the locals. I couldn't just leave him to handle it on his own. At least, not in his condition," Marcus said, with a slight, unintended, smile.

Taylor gave him a questioning stare, which Marcus felt compelled to interrupt before the medic could question his story any further. "So, um, the Sergeant said you had some training material for me?"

"Yes, follow me," Taylor beckoned, turning to enter the ship.

Inside, Corporal Dimitrov and the others from his team had already found comfortable positions to spend the day's guard duty. The

Corporal lay alongside the wall with his weapon in his lap. His helmet was propped under his head for support. Taz and Becks sat on the floor playing a game with cards Taz had purchased in one of the stores on the promenade back at the Alamo. The only one who had his guard up was Reid, the sniper, who sat by the entry ramp with a keen eye on the entrance to the compound.

"Good day there, PFC," Reid barked. "You're late. Shift started 32 minutes ago."

"Hey there Grey," sighed Taz, barely looking up from his game. Becks merely turned his head and nodded in Marcus's direction. The only sound coming from Corporal Dimitrov was a sporadic light snoring.

"Sorry about that guys."

"Don't worry about it," Taz muttered. "Reid's just in a bad mood because he drank too much Raketta last night.

"Never mind all that," interrupted the medic, grabbing Marcus's arm and pulling him towards the workstation at the rear of the lower deck.

"Look here," he gestured, turning on the embedded computer console.

"I've pulled out some basic training manuals for you. While you're on duty I expect that you study them carefully."

Marcus moved to the swiveling chair, which was mounted on a short rail in the floor which allowed for it to be moved forward and backward about a meter or so without ever coming loose. He moved it back a bit and took a seat. The heading on the console screen read '*Basic Electronic Security*'.

"Use the arrow keys to scroll up and down. When you're done with this one, I'll get you started on '*Human-Computer Interaction*' and

'*Basic Decryption Methodology*'," Taylor informed him. "Thanks to recent advancements in genetic manipulation we're all bred with increased learning capacity. It shouldn't take you more than a shift or two to get through each of these manuals."

"Don't worry Doc. I promised the Sergeant I wouldn't let him down, I've no intention to break that promise" Marcus stated defiantly.

"That's good to hear, but you don't have to act like a smart ass! Now, if you'll excuse me, I have to go back to the Black Lotus. Apparently Simone and Clarke got into an argument which ended in a bit of a scuffle. Clarke is in need of some stitches."

Chapter 22

"Guys, wake up! The boss is coming back with the others," shouted Jago, who'd reached the ship at a run near the end of their shift, Edward Suarez in tow.

"Has something happened?" asked Marcus, looking up from the console screen, having gotten halfway through his second revision of '*Basic Electronic Security*'.

"Are you kidding?" Suarez barked, flustered. "The Sergeant is furious. He's kept shouting something about a goat and us going way overboard on the bill at the Inn. He'll explain everything when he gets here."

"Thanks for the heads up," Taz called, clearing the floor of any evidence that would indicate that he and Becks had spent the whole shift playing cards.

Corporal Dimitrov rubbed his bloodshot eyes as he rose up from his sleep. "Oh man, this hard floor is a real killer for my back." He stood up, yawning and going through a quick series of stretches. "Ok men, you heard Suarez. Let's look alive."

A few minutes passed before Reid spotted the Sergeant approaching with a full entourage of Corporal Spielman and his men.

"Corp, they're here," Reid warned.

"Well then, let's not keep the Sergeant waiting. Let's go out and say hello," Dimitrov ordered, approaching the open entry ramp at the front of the ship.

They headed down the ramp in single file as the rest of the squad came to a halt, forming a huddle around them. The Sergeant stepped forward, the grim expression on his face doing little to lessen the tension.

"All right, listen up, and listen good!" Lance bellowed as he spun on the spot, turning to make sure all of them could clearly see how enraged he was. "Some of you seem to think that just because I'm not around twenty-four-seven, that means you can get away with improper conduct and disgracing your uniforms. Now I'm not about to name any names," he bawled, shooting the Ape a subtle but particularly nasty glare, "suffice it to say, you are all equally at fault. Take a good look at the man standing to your left. This man is your brother, just as the man on your right is your brother. You are responsible for your brothers, just as they are responsible for you. If you see your brother about to disgrace me, my squad and his uniform, it is your duty to stop him. If you cannot behave properly when I'm not around, then I will punish all of you. Is that understood?" he shouted, his voice quivering.

"Yes Sergeant!" the whole squad replied.

"I can't hear you! I said, do you maggots understand?" he yelled at the top of his lungs.

"Yes Sergeant!" the squad shouted back, as loudly as they could muster.

"That's better." The Sergeant stopped and put his hands on his hips. "Now, there's an urgent matter that I need to go over with you. This being our first time on a settled world other than Callisto, it's understandable that some of you may have gone a bit overboard with your spending. The Terran military pays each and every one of you a generous allowance of five hundred credits every month. An allowance that some of you managed to exceed in a single day of drinking and reckless spending. Granted, a large portion of the bill comes from reparations for damages incurred by your little visit to the Black Lotus Inn, the only place in this wretched town that would actually accept our business."

Marcus wondered how anyone had managed to exceed their allowance in a single night. His whole team hadn't even spent that much altogether.

"Now, seeing as most of you cannot afford another night on the town, nor can our reputation as Terran soldiers afford another hit like that incurred from yesterday's behavior, I have decided that instead of allowing you to sleep in the warm, comfortable beds of the inn, eat their exotic food and drink their spiced wine, those of you not on guard duty will make camp a quarter mile west of the settlement, where you will remain until your next shift starts. Is that understood?"

"Yes Sergeant!" the squad shouted in acknowledgement.

"Good. Now, I want absolutely no contact with the locals. You are not to talk to them, engage with them or even look at them, unless they specifically come to you first, in which case I expect you to be on your best behavior."

"Yes Sergeant," they replied in a slightly more relaxed tone.

"All right then. I'm glad we've got all that sorted out. Spielman, you and your men will relieve Dimitrov and his men. Corporal Dimitrov, Ape and the rest of you, grab your tents, sleeping bags and rations, and make your way to the camp site. I'll be there in about an hour or so and I want to see those tents up by the time I arrive. Corporal, see me when we're done here and I'll give you the coordinates for the camp site I've chosen. Now move out!" Lance ordered as he turned to

168

march out of the compound, leaving the men frantically searching for their gear.

*   *   *   *   *

The march to the camp site went more quickly than Marcus had anticipated. The sun had begun to set on the horizon, bathing the sky in brilliant hues of orange and pink. The cool desert breeze was a welcome change to the scorching heat they had been forced to endure during their guard duty.

"Thanks for helping with the goat," whispered Jago, having slowed his pace so he could match Marcus's position in the procession.

"Don't mention it," replied Marcus, relieved to see that the big Ape was capable of basic human emotions, like gratitude. "We're brothers after all, like the Sergeant said. We should look out for one another."

"Ya, I guess," said Jago, scratching the back of his neck. "Just don't tell the others."

"I didn't... I mean, I won't," Marcus corrected himself.

"Good," replied Jago, nodding his head in approval before hastening his pace to catch up with Jenna Raleigh, who according to rumor, had taken quite a shine to him the day before.

"That's so typical for a 6-18," noted Taz.

"What?" asked Marcus, not understanding what Taz was talking about.

"The 6-18... Jenna!" he went on until Marcus caught on.

"What about her?"

"They all go for the big guys. Well, that, or the guys in charge."

"What are you getting at Taz?"

"They're flawed. They're so freaked out about going to war that they latch on to whoever they think can save them if push comes to shove."

"So? There's nothing wrong with being scared, Taz."

"I hear they're going to discontinue them," confided Taz.

"What do you mean... discontinue?"

"They're gonna stop making them. No more 6-18's. It's a shame really. They're one of the better looking ones."

Marcus had never considered the possibility that his actions reflected not only on himself, but also his entire model. The thought of causing the cancelation of his whole line only spurred him more to perform to the best of his abilities.

* * * * *

The camp location the Sergeant had picked out for them was a long, flat stretch of grass and sand on the banks of the oasis, which curved around northern side of the settlement. Marcus found the sound of cicadas chirping all around them comforting as he looked towards the settlement, where a few bright spots of light shone from second-storey windows, just high enough to be seen above the settlement's outer walls.

The water was perfectly calm, reflecting Oberon's towering form above them. Marcus was overcome with a feeling of wellbeing as he started unpacking his tent.

* * * * *

They all stared intently at the bright ball of light that had appeared in the evening sky moments before.

"What is it?" Dimitrov blurted, looking up from his half-erected tent and losing his grip on one of the poles so the whole thing collapsed in on itself.

Marcus could just make out a tail of trailing fire behind the globe, a menacing vision of impending doom that was rapidly growing in size.

"Wow!" shouted Taz. "What the hell is that thing?"

"The star of wisdom," Marcus's words escaped his mouth without even realizing it.

"What?" asked Taz, still staring in astonishment as the falling star flared brightly as it overshot them at tremendous speed. They all turned to observe the star's awe-inspiring descent, a thick black trail of smoke cutting clear across the skyline.

"Should we be running for cover or something?" Taz inquired, breaking the silence.

"I don't believe it's going to touch down anywhere near here, judging by its trajectory," Reid assured them. "We should be perfectly safe here."

"That's a relief," sighed Taz, joining them once more in silent wonder as they gazed at the horizon, waiting anxiously for the moment of impact.

"The old man said this would happen," Marcus whispered, a second before the horizon exploded in a brilliant display of fire and smoke.

The ground shook as a wave of kinetic energy shot through their camp, knocking them all off their feet and tearing down the few standing tents, most of which landed in the oasis several dozen meters behind them. The deafening thunder of the impact left Marcus's ears buzzing. He lay on the ground in shock for what seemed like several minutes, trying to understand what had happened, and how it was possible that the old man had foreseen it. More importantly, why had he told them that it would happen? Why them?

"Everyone ok?" Dimitrov called out as he got back to his feet.

They all answered to let him know that there were no injuries.

"We should tell the boss," barked Jago, full of excitement.

"Eh, I'm pretty sure that wherever he is, he couldn't have missed the gigantic explosion that just took place, Ape," the Corporal replied sardonically. "Besides, the Sergeant is probably on his way over here as we speak, remember? He said he was going to come and inspect the camp."

"Oh... right," Jago replied, feeling embarrassed at having been outshone by Dimitrov.

"We should wait here," Dimitrov declared. "The Sergeant should be here any minute. While we wait, we should try and save what tents we can."

*   *   *   *   *

Sure enough, Sergeant Lance showed up at the camp about ten minutes later, panting heavily, having run most of the way.

"At ease men," ordered the Sergeant between labored breaths. "Did you get a good look at what happened?"

"Yes Sergeant," replied the Ape, beating Dimitrov to the punch. "The star fell and exploded on the ground, Sergeant."

The squad stared incredulously at Jago. They all knew he wasn't the brightest, but none of them had expected him to state the obvious quite so... bluntly.

"The star? What star?" asked the Sergeant, bewildered.

"Sergeant, if I may?" Dimitrov offered. "What the Ape is trying to say is, we noticed what looked like a meteor, or falling star, entering the atmosphere roughly fifteen minutes ago. Without access to our comms, we were unable to inform you of its presence. The meteor shot across the sky at tremendous speed and touched down approximately sixty or seventy kilometers due southeast of our position, resulting in the explosion you witnessed. The explosion caused a shockwave, plowing through our camp and tearing down our tents, flinging some of them into the oasis. Luckily, no one was hurt in the explosion, sir."

Jago withdrew, taking a step back having been outperformed by Corporal Dimitrov yet again, this time in front of the Sergeant.

"Very well," Lance said, after pondering Dimitrov's detailed description of the event. "It seems meteor showers are a risk everywhere, not only on Triton. I'm amazed that people would actually want to live here."

"Yes Sergeant," Dimitrov replied. "Although this one was a lot bigger than the miniscule rocks that rained down upon us on Triton. If it had struck within a few kilometers, I'm not sure we'd still be standing here."

"I still want this camp up and running. Borrow some tents from Corporal Spielman's team if you have to. Those of you off-duty will have to share tents with those on shift," the Sergeant decided.

"Sergeant," Dimitrov interjected.

"Yes, Corporal?"

"Permission to take my team out to inspect the blast crater?" Dimitrov asked hesitantly.

"Permission denied, Corporal," replied the Sergeant. "As you said, that crater is sixty or seventy kilometers from here. Without vehicles, it would take days for you and your men to make the journey there and back."

"Perhaps we could borrow some riding mules from the locals, Sergeant, and..."

"I said no, Corporal," Lance barked, irritated. "Have you forgotten that I ordered you not to have any contact with the locals?"

"No Sergeant," Dimitrov replied. "Sorry Sergeant."

"Just get this camp up and running."

"Yes Sergeant." The Corporal turned to the others. "Alright men, you heard the Sergeant. Let's get these tents up. Becks, you and Taz go and see if you can fish some of those tents out of the water," the Corporal ordered as Sergeant Lance turned back towards the settlement.

As the camp began to take form once more, Marcus couldn't help but keep one eye on the horizon, in the direction of the crash site. That night, as he fell asleep, cold and still half-starving having only eaten field rations, he thought long and hard, trying to remember the rhyme the old man outside the Black Lotus had recited for them.

Chapter 23

Three days in the scorching heat had reduced the squad to a poor state. The pungent aroma of old sweat permeated the entire camp site. They had gone without so much as eye contact with any of the locals when they marched through town on their way to guard duty and back. They had to rely entirely on their own company, and slept whenever possible. Marcus wouldn't have expected to get so tired from doing so little work. The combination of the heat and lack of any real activity did nothing to motivate the squad, who lay in and out of the searing sun, playing games and spinning tales.

Corporal Dimitrov had produced a mouth organ on the first night. Every night since, as the squad had begun lighting a campfire from broken branches and leaves they'd gathered on the far banks of the oasis, he started to play, usually an upbeat melody for starters, then slowing to a softer, sadder tune by the time the stars shone brightly overhead.

The Sergeant had spent little time in the camp, preferring the cool shade offered by the Black Lotus. He rationalized his stay there by claiming that he needed to improve relations with the locals. The squad knew better. Every day around the time the squad ate their evening meal he would come waltzing into camp, his breath reeking of Raketta and his attitude increasingly condescending.

On the evening of the fifth day, he strode into camp with an almost empty bottle of Raketta still in his hand, swaying from side to side.

"Dimitrov," he shouted as he crossed the perimeter. "Why are the men not assembled when I arrive?" he barked, slurring his words.

"Sorry Sergeant?" the Corporal responded, not seeing the importance of the Sergeant's request.

"I said, why are my men not standing at attention? Or do you think that I don't deserve a proper reception when I come to inspect my troops?" the Sergeant slurred.

"I'm sorry Sergeant. I mean, I didn't know you were coming," Dimitrov explained, approaching the Sergeant.

When he reached him, the Corporal leaned in towards the Sergeant and whispered something into his ear.

"I'm not drunk!" yelled the Sergeant, striking Dimitrov across the face.

The Corporal took the blow unflinchingly, then simply stood, his head turned away from the Sergeant in submission. Lance stared at the rest of the squad, who were looking on aghast, his eyes filled with silent contempt.

"How dare you judge me?" he shouted, turning on Corporal Dimitrov. "I am your commanding officer." The Sergeant took a few steps away from the Corporal, who still hadn't flinched. "I may have had a glass or two," he confessed, stopping clear in his tracks, his eyes closed and his head tilted as he paused for a brief second before continuing. "...but that's only because I'm attempting to make a good impression with the locals."

The rest of the squad tilted their heads down, staring at their own feet. No one dared look up, afraid that the Sergeant would see their expressions for what they truly were. Marcus knew that if he would look up, even for a split second, Lance would see it in his eyes. What

176

little respect he had once had for the Sergeant was now gone, replaced by a mixture of contempt and pity.

No, no one dared look up as the Sergeant took a few more steps back.

"At least I'm not trying to have my way with the farm animals," chuckled Sergeant Lance. "Spielman, Dimitrov, I want you and your men to give me five laps around the oasis."

"The oasis Sergeant?" Dimitrov asked. "That's about twenty miles sir. In this heat…"

"Then I guess you better start running Corporal," the Sergeant sneered. "NOW!"

They stood there for a few seconds, unsure of whether or not the two Corporals would comply with the order, given the Sergeant's inebriated state.

Slowly but surely, Dimitrov and Spielman started walking, then speeding up to a jogging pace.

"That's better!" shouted Sergeant Lance as the rest of the squad followed suit.

The last Marcus saw of the Sergeant that day was him turning back towards the village, still clutching the bottle of Raketta in his hand.

* * * * *

The next morning, they were hastily awoken by Spielman and his men.

"Wake up, quickly now. The Sergeant's coming," Suarez whispered as he beat the side of Marcus's tent with his open palm.

Before Marcus was even fully awake he was outside and standing at attention, in line with the rest of the men from his team.

"What's he doing out here this early?" inquired Taz, none too discretely.

"Shush, not a word," Corporal Dimitrov ordered in an attempt to silence the paranoid Private.

"Probably drank all the Raketta in town, and now he's heading out for the next settlement," Spielman mused.

Dimitrov shot him an angry glare as Lance entered the camp.

"Good morning Sergeant," Dimitrov barked in an attempt to start their encounter with the Sergeant on the right foot.

"Good morning Corporal," the Sergeant replied somberly. "Although I'm not sure if I would say it is indeed a good morning."

"Is something wrong Sergeant?" Dimitrov inquired, sincerely worried.

"Oh, just some local troubles. One of Rory's miners didn't come back last night. Rory's all up in arms about it. Said something has to be wrong for Old Sam not to show up on the dot. Plus, some of the locals are complaining about missing cattle," the Sergeant replied dismissively.

"Cattle, Sergeant?" Dimitrov asked.

"Just a couple of cows. Of course the locals are blaming us for it. I don't suppose any of you were stupid enough to disobey my orders and be messing around with the livestock, have you? None of you followed the Ape's example?"

"No Sergeant, of course not sir," the Corporal replied.

It was strange how calm and composed the Sergeant could be when he was sober, compared to the arrogance and compulsiveness he displayed when under the influence of the Raketta. Still, something about the Sergeant's behavior did strike Marcus as odd, drunk or not.

178

Over the past few days, he'd become increasingly unsympathetic, first towards the locals, and then towards the squad.

"I promised Rory that I'd send someone out to look for Old Sammy. Spielman, you and your men can go south and look for him, will ya? Shouldn't be more than a few clicks," the Sergeant ordered, gesturing to a seemingly small rocky outcropping, jutting out of the sand on the southern horizon.

"You should find him at the dig site."

"Yes Sergeant, will do," Spielman acknowledged.

"One more thing," added the Sergeant, raising a finger in the air and staring randomly into the distance as if trying to remember what he was about to say. "Rory said something about recovering Sam's mining vehicle. In case something's happened to Sam. Take care of it."

"A mining vehicle?" Spielman questioned in wonder. "But I thought technology was forbidden outside the GeoDynamics compound."

"GeoDynamics pretty much do whatever they please. Why do you think the locals dislike them so much?" Lance explained. "Just get the job done."

"Yes Sergeant," the Corporal replied. "But what about weapons sir? If something has happened to Sam and the livestock, how are we to protect ourselves?"

"That's an excellent question Corporal," replied the Sergeant with an idiotic grin. "I'm sure you'll come up with something." Lance spun away, already heading back to town.

"Can you believe this guy?" Spielman asked, rhetorically, as he began to organize his team for departure.

"Something's wrong," Dimitrov pronounced. "But we better do as he says. There's nothing we can do about it out here, short of having the Doc give him an evaluation."

179

"Yeah, but he'd better watch it. Talking to us this way is one thing, but I wouldn't want to be him if he tries talking to the Ape like that," Spielman joked.

*   *   *   *   *

It was late in the evening when Spielman and his men returned to camp. There had been no sign of Old Sam at the dig site, but they'd found a trail of blood stretching from the door of the broken-down mining vehicle, which lay wedged in a small crevasse. Spielman and his men had been unable to recover the vehicle, and there'd been no sign of Sam himself. The Corporal ordered his men to take some rest while he headed into town to bear the bad news to Sergeant Lance.

"This whole thing has something to do with that falling star," Taz blurted once Spielman had left. "I'm telling you. What did that crazy old man by the inn say? The star will fall from the sky... You're all gonna die... something like that?"

"Shut up Taz," Becks put him down, not in the mood to listen to any more of Taz's hysterics. "That guy was clearly insane."

"Yeah, and I suppose we were all hallucinating when we all saw the big fiery ball of light fly across the sky," Taz retorted sarcastically. "What do you think Grey?"

"Me?" Marcus hesitated to answer, as he wasn't really sure what he felt. "I... I'm not sure what to think. I suppose it could all just be a coincidence," he offered, half-heartedly. But in the deepest, darkest corners of his mind, he knew that was a lie. It wasn't a coincidence. The old man had foretold that this would happen. What was worse, Marcus somehow knew things were going to get worse, a lot worse. This was the calm before the storm.

Chapter 24

In the days that followed, reports of missing livestock became more frequent, and tension among the locals reached new heights. The Sergeant had lessened his drinking, but the squad easily perceived his agitated state. It was on the morning of their tenth day on New Io that Sergeant Lance entered the camp, seemingly sober, calm and collected.

"The Sheikh has invited me to a meeting," he announced as he stood in the center of the camp after performing his daily inspection. "I am allowed two escorts."

The Sergeant looked each of them in the eye, weighing his options for what seemed like several minutes before finally blurting, "Corporal Dimitrov, choose one of your men to accompany us to the Sheikh's palace. The two of you clean up and meet me by the ship in two hours' time."

* * * * *

Marcus was surprised that Dimitrov had chosen him to accompany the Sergeant. Although he had a feeling that the Corporal had taken a liking to him, Marcus was sure he wasn't the best candidate to act as a guard for Lance. Becks had always performed better than him in close combat training, and Reid's skill with the rifle surpassed Marcus' by a long shot. Taz's keen eye made him the best choice to spot a trap or an ambush. Out of the whole team, Marcus was the least logical choice. It worried him that the Corporal could have chosen him based on his feelings rather than his merit. It bothered him so much that, as they walked into the Last Oasis, he asked Dimitrov outright. "Corporal, why did you choose me?"

"Why shouldn't I have chosen you?" the Corporal bluntly replied.

"I... well, I don't think I'm the best candidate to act as a bodyguard," Marcus stated.

"Neither do I," the Corporal responded, his answer taking Marcus completely by surprise.

"Then why did you..." he asked, but the Corporal interrupted him, already anticipating the question.

"Because the Sergeant doesn't need a bodyguard," he explained. "He may think that he does, but if there is going to be trouble at the Sheikh's palace then I don't think there'd be much we could do about it anyway, especially given the fact that we don't have access to our weapons."

"I hadn't really thought about it that way," Marcus confessed as he pondered the Corporal's explanation.

"Given the Sergeant's temper of late, I thought it more prudent to bring someone who's calm under pressure, empathetic, and has a knack for problem solving," Dimitrov said, shooting Marcus a friendly smile. "And besides, I don't think our visit to the Sheikh is purely a social call. He wants something. Something he can't get from anyone else."

"Like what? How do you know?" Marcus asked, amazed that the Corporal had such a firm grasp of the situation.

"The Sheikh is the spiritual leader of these people, people who don't want anything to do with us out of fear that we'll interfere with and taint their way of life. For such a man to openly ask for a meeting with us, he must really be desperate," Dimitrov explained.

"The missing farm animals!" Marcus exclaimed, confident that they would be the topic of today's meeting with the Sheikh.

"Exactly. Although, I'm afraid it's more than just a few missing cattle by now. I'm certain this is all connected with the falling star. If only the Sergeant would see reason, and let us to go and scout it out!" the Corporal sighed, still full of resentment towards Lance.

"I think you're right, but I still think the Sergeant made the right call when he stopped us going. We need a vehicle to scout something that far away. In this scorching heat, we might not even make it back if we went on foot."

"That's why I chose you today, Grey," Dimitrov replied. "I need your help convincing the Sheikh to allow us the use of our weapons and equipment."

"But, the Sergeant..." Marcus tried to interject.

"The Sergeant is losing it," Dimitrov snapped. "You've seen it, we all have. We need to convince him that this is what we need to do, or who knows what will happen to these people once we're gone. What's going to happen when whoever, or whatever, is doing this runs out of livestock?"

"But even if we manage to persuade them, we don't have a vehicle," Marcus pointed out.

"We'll borrow one of Rory's mining trucks," the Corporal replied.

It was obvious that Dimitrov had thought this through. It sounded like the best course of action, and the only way to gain some measure of control, over both the situation and Sergeant Lance.

* * * * *

Sheikh Abdul Ba'ari's palace was a veritable fortress of mud-brick towers of varying sizes, all connected by six-meter-tall walls, complete with medieval battlements. Two honor guards, dressed in unadorned white robes, stood at attention in front of the four-meter-high entryway. Each of them carried a curved sword, which they drew from their sheaths when Lance, Dimitrov and Marcus approached.

"I thought you people didn't use weapons?" the Sergeant sneered, smugly. "We were told that your religion forbids it."

"Our religion forbids war, murder and acts of violence. Our customs forbid weapons, for they are the instruments of death. Only the Sheikh's Hajari are allowed to carry weapons, and we are only allowed to wield them in defense of the Sheikh and his people," the bulkier of the guards proclaimed, beaming with pride.

"And I suppose it's up to you to determine when and how you are able to justify their use?" the Sergeant asked, clearly not expecting an answer. "Never mind, we're here at the Sheikh's request," he went on, promptly dismissing any further comment the Hajari might have made.

"Very well," the guard acknowledged, breathing a heavy sigh of surrender before bowing humbly to the Sergeant. "His Holiness Sheikh Abdul Ba'ari is waiting for you."

The second Hajari raised his arm, and proceeded to knock on the door with the back of his clenched fist, his judging gaze never leaving Lance for as much as a second. A slit on the door opened briefly, and a pair of eyes peeked out to inspect the arrivals.

After a moment, the massive wooden doors swung slowly open, creaking loudly. It was obvious they were not accustomed to frequent use, and that the Sheikh's Hajari had only closed the doors when the settlement was visited by outsiders, which, it seemed, did not happen often.

Reluctantly, the aging servant who had allowed them entry stepped forward to introduce himself.

"I am Aman, servant to his Holiness. Please follow me." He said with a slight lisp as he withdrew a set of oval glass plates mounted on a metallic frame from the sleeves of his plain white robe. He fastened the peculiar device onto the bridge of his nose, and peered at them through the lenses.

"I thought they didn't use technology," the Sergeant whispered, obviously unnerved by the hidden implications of the odd device, which lacked any obvious function or means of activation.

"Excuse me, Mr. Aman, but what is the nature of that device? And why are you using it on us?" Corporal Dimitrov asked as politely as he could, trying not to seem too nervous.

"Are you referring to my spectacles?" Aman asked, unfastening the device and holding it at arm's length, inspecting it from afar. "You've never seen spectacles before?" he asked with astonishment.

"Well, yes," Dimitrov confessed. "I saw some on the promenade back on the Alamo, but they were much bulkier and darker. Each type had a different purpose. Some let you see in the dark, others could see right through walls. But yours are so slim and clear. And we were led to believe that your people did not use technology."

The servant relaxed, and let out a peal of laughter.

"Technology? I suppose they are, but they don't have a hidden purpose. Without them I can't see past the end of my nose," Aman proclaimed as he put the spectacles back on his nose with his right hand, and inspected the fingers of his outstretched left hand, smiling to himself at the ignorance of the supposedly techno-savvy outsiders.

"Follow me. I'll take you to see the Sheikh," he prompted, now a lot more relaxed in their presence.

The Sheikh's courtyard was a wide square, covered with ornate stone tiles and colorful flowerbeds. A raised terrace with a towering fountain was accessible via grand steps opposite the palace entryway. To the left, shaded corridors hid behind white-painted pillars of ornately carved stone. To the right, a central structure divided the rest of the courtyard into two open areas, with a roofed open-air lounge between them. A lavish swimming pool occupied the farther area, whereas the closer was covered in freshly-cut grass, broken only by a cobblestone path, along which Aman led them towards the covered lounge.

Under a canopy of vines clinging to the ceiling, the Sheikh lay on a bed of ornate pillows made of silk atop a floor covered in beautiful rugs woven with detailed patterns. He wore purple robes made from the finest silk, which draped generously over his plump belly and thick features. A purple cloth was wrapped around his head to form a hat similar to those worn by the locals. His neatly-kept full beard had thick streaks of gray mingled with its otherwise pitch-black color. His face looked as if it had been chiseled from the same rock that made up his palace, with straight, square lines framing his cheekbones and chin. His nose, large, straight and prominent, stood atop small, black-painted pouting lips. His beady, sunken eyes hid below a protruding brow, fixed on the three clones from the moment they set foot in his lounge. His face twitched. He closed his eyes and turned his cheek, raising a hand to beckon them forward without a word.

"Please, take your seats," Aman invited as he ushered them further into the lounge, towards the Sheikh.

Seated on plush pillows, separated from the Sheikh by a dark, reflective wooden table standing barely twenty centimeters off the ground, the Sergeant gave the Sheikh his greetings. "Your Holiness," he smiled, with a hint of sarcasm in his voice that Marcus hoped the Sheikh and his servant wouldn't pick up on. "We are here at your request. How may we be of assistance?"

There was a tense pause as the Sheikh weighed the sincerity of the Sergeant's words. Luckily, it seemed that the emptiness of his greeting went unnoticed.

"You and your men have caused my people a lot of pain and discomfort," Sheikh Abdul Ba'ari stated in a phenomenally deep, raspy voice, his words hung in the air as he pondered how best to proceed. "It is my judgment that you and your men must make amends," he continued.

"Judgment?" Lance spat, nearly bursting with outrage. "I was not aware that I had come here to be judged!"

"Whether you were aware or not is not my concern," the Sheikh replied, calmly lifting a small porcelain cup of tea to his lips, creating another awkward pause as he took a series of small sips while Lance gaped at him. "What matters is that my people have been wronged, and you owe it to them to make up for it."

"This is ridiculous," the Sergeant blurted. "I don't have to stay here and..." but he was cut short as Dimitrov grabbed his arm, leaning towards him and whispering something in his ear.

"What did you have in mind?" the Sergeant finally grunted, when the Corporal had finished.

"I am pleased to hear you have come to your senses," the Sheikh remarked stoically.

"During the past week, my people have endured hardship not only at your hands, but also at the hands of the desert. Livestock has gone missing. The rate increases with each passing day. Yesterday, a young boy from one of the outlying farms went missing as well." The Sheikh paused.

For a moment, Marcus thought he caught a glimpse of concern in his eyes.

"This has got to stop. I want you to send some of your men to investigate these disappearances... and stop them at any cost. With luck, you will find the missing boy alive, and he can be returned to his family."

The Sergeant leaned forward, a smirk Marcus worried would seem menacing on his face.

"I'll do it," he announced, staring the Sheikh straight in the eyes before adding, "On one condition."

"State your terms," the Sheikh responded, unshaken by the Sergeant's forwardness.

"We'll use our weapons and equipment," the Sergeant replied, straightening his back.

"Impossible," bellowed the Sheikh angrily, his calm finally shaken. "I cannot allow you to defile the customs of my people."

"If there really is a threat out there, then I don't really need your permission. As highest ranking military officer present, I can declare martial law, giving me and my men the right to bear whatever arms and equipment we see fit," the Sergeant shouted, slamming his clenched fist down on the table.

"Sergeant, you know as well as I do that New Io is not under the Republic's rule. Your laws do not apply here," the Sheikh replied smugly. "If you were to declare martial law, you would find yourself before a military tribunal as soon as the crisis was over."

Sergeant Lance was dumbfounded.

"Hm. I see that my knowledge of your laws confuses you," the Sheikh added. "I learned a long time ago that it can be highly beneficial to know as much as one can about Terran laws and customs."

"He's right," Dimitrov whispered to Lance. "Even if we..."

"I KNOW HE'S RIGHT!" the Sergeant screamed into the Corporal's face.

Dimitrov froze, Lance realizing he'd gone too far. The redness of his flushed face paling quickly as his muscles unclenched.

"You can't expect us to go out there to investigate an unknown threat without allowing us to protect ourselves." the Sergeant finally protested.

"What about the Hajari?" the Corporal interjected.

"The Hajari are needed here," the Sheikh informed him. "The Last Oasis is the largest settlement on New Io. The majority of the Children of the Wastes reside here. The Hajari are here for their protection, not mine. They cannot be spared."

"What about nominating us as Hajari?" the Corporal blurted on the spur of the moment. "That would at least allow us to carry those curved swords, wouldn't it?"

"The Hajari are the most devoted servants of the people. To nominate an outsider as Hajari would be an even greater outrage," the Sheikh snapped. "But I see your point." He thought long and hard before coming to a conclusion. "I will allow those of you who go to seek the cause of the disappearances a temporary reprieve. You will be allowed the use of your own blades, these combat knives. But your firearms must remain within the GeoDynamics compound."

"Thank you sir," the Corporal consented, pleased to have wrung even this small concession from the Sheikh. He clearly thought it was a good sign that the Sheikh was willing to negotiate at all.

"Do not make me come to regret my decision," the Sheikh added, waving Aman to escort the clones from the premises.

Lance's nostrils were flared with rage, and his eyes were locked on the Sheikh. "Do not make me regret mine," the Sergeant snarled before storming away in anger.

* * * * *

Once they were safely out of earshot of the Hajari and well on their way back to the GeoDynamics compound, the Sergeant once again showed his true colors.

"Since when did I task you with the negotiations?" the Sergeant barked at Dimitrov.

"Sorry Sergeant," the Corporal replied. "I only meant to help."

"I brought you along as bodyguards in case the Sheikh thought he could bully me into bowing to his every demand," the Sergeant snapped, grinding his teeth. "But since you are so quick to volunteer your assistance, even when it hasn't been requested, then I am quite sure that you won't mind volunteering your team for this investigation for his *Holiness*," Lance sneered. "I hope you remember this the next time you open your mouth when you're not supposed to."

Chapter 25

The outlying farmsteads surrounding the Last Oasis were little more than crumbling huts, each surrounded by a few acres of barely sustainable crops. Fenced-off areas connected to the habitats usually held some form of farm animal, typically goats. All the farms the team passed had enclosed boxes of wired mesh, inside which a handful of chickens were kept.

It didn't take the farmers long to spot the team as the soldiers traveled through their land. Clearly, they were an unwelcome sight. One farmer even flung dung from his goat pen at them, shouting obscenities as they marched along a track a few dozen meters from his farm.

Yet despite their squalid living conditions, these people were real human beings. Perhaps that was what had been missing in his short existence, Marcus thought, a sense of realism. It occurred to him that not only was his physical body a construct built by some lab technician and nursed to adulthood by a machine, but that his memories and impressions were equally artificial.

If a being was not the creation of the chaotic forces of nature, but had been carefully fabricated through deliberate planning and machine implementation, could such a creation really be thought of as a human being? Even Marcus' life after hatching had been planned, perhaps for decades in advance, through the polishing and refinement of procedures and protocol. At least, it had been up to the point where the squad had crashed on this moon. Perhaps his existence was more akin to that of a computer? Constructed and programmed to perform a specific function, its freedom to choose nothing more than an illusion.

"I'm telling you, this Sheikh guy just wants us as far away from the others as possible. He's trying to split us up so his guards can take us out a few at a time!" Taz bellowed, interrupting Marcus's somber train of thought.

"Will you shut up with the stupid conspiracy bullshit? I swear, I'm gonna beat the shit out of you if you don't stop," Becks yelled back, fed up with Taz's constant paranoia.

Taz snapped his mouth shut, frustrated that none of the team were taking his worries seriously.

Eventually, they approached the path leading to the homestead of the missing boy and his family. The fields were empty. Through a window they could see a lone candle flickering inside the feeble hut. The door stood slightly ajar, so Dimitrov knocked on the doorframe to avoid pushing it open.

A local man in his forties appeared in the gap, peering out to see who had come calling at this late hour. As soon as he saw them, he slammed the door shut without a word.

"Mr. Habanji, I'm Corporal Dimitrov," the Corporal called through the sun-bleached wood. "We're here at the request of Sheikh Abdul Ba'ari. He asked that we help locate your missing son."

After a pause, the silence was broken by a muffled argument between the man and a woman inside the hut.

Marcus surveyed the area surrounding the farm. It was smaller than those they had been passing on their way to their destination, some twelve kilometers southeast of the Last Oasis.

The door burst open without warning, and a woman in tears flew out, Habanji frantically trying to stop her speaking to the team. She was a vision of fading beauty, lines formed by decades of worry drawn across her face.

"You will find my boy?" she cried, the despair in her voice enough to touch even the hardiest of men.

It was the first time Marcus had witnessed such love between a mother and her child. He knew the love of family was something that he himself would never know. The best he could hope for was the camaraderie of his unit.

"We will do our best Mrs. Habanji, I promise you," Dimitrov assured her. "Can you tell us where the boy was last seen?"

"You, this is all your fault!" her husband yelled. "You outsiders come here and bring your curse upon our lands!"

Marcus couldn't help but think that Habanji could be right. Bad luck seemed to follow them around wherever they went. First Triton, and now this.

"My boy, he loved to play over by the old Ranek tree on the hill overlooking the farm." Mrs. Habanji overrode her husband's objections. "I saw him through the kitchen window during the day," she explained, her eyes filled with tears and her voice breaking with worry. "By the time I called out for him to come home and eat supper, he was nowhere to be seen."

Dimitrov turned to view the old tree at the top of the hill, some distance away. It was a blackened gnarled tree with leafless branches, casting an eerie shadow over the hill as the sun began to set on the horizon.

"It's not like little Raja to wander off alone," she continued. "You will find him, won't you? You have to find him!"

"We'll do our very best Mrs. Habanji," the Corporal reassured her, as Mr. Habanji finally managed to pull his wife back into the house and slam the door shut, narrowly missing the Corporal's fingers, which had been resting on the doorframe.

The team sighed in unison. It had been a long trek from the Last Oasis, and their task was only beginning. How they were supposed to find one lost boy in the middle of the scrubby desert was beyond them.

They were already more than half way through their water supplies when they reached the Ranek tree. A small groove at the bottom, next to a thick root which dug itself only halfway beneath the soil, proved to be the most likely location for the boy's antics. A few weathered toys lay strewn about the area.

"Taz, see if you can spot the boy's trail," Dimitrov ordered.

Taz knelt down and began studying the ground for any signs of the boy.

"It's going to be difficult following a trail once the sun sets," he said.

"Then I guess we'd better act quickly," the Corporal grunted, shooting Taz an angry glare. "The boy's life may be at stake."

"Yes Corp."

Marcus admired how genuine the Corporal's concerns seemed. Unlike the Sergeant, he seemed genuinely sympathetic to the Children of the Wastes.

"Corp, I've got something!" called Taz, who had wandered off a few meters from the rest of the team.

They all scurried around him as he pointed to several trails of tracks.

"These aren't human," the scout said, staring intently at the grouping of tracks leading off into the desert.

194

"What are they, Taz?" Dimitrov asked.

"Unknown. But see here," Taz gestured at one of the more visible prints. "Three sharp claws. They're dug in deep, too, as if whatever it was that made them was either very heavy, or getting ready to jump."

"Jump?" exclaimed the Corporal. "You mean attack?"

"I would say so, Corp. The other prints aren't as deep as these."

"How many of them were there?" Reid asked, his concern clearly visible.

"I think three, but the tracks are difficult to make out. I can see them more clearly here, where there's still some soil, but as soon as they veer off into the desert, they get pretty faded."

"We should head back and inform the Sergeant," Becks suggested.

"And leave a young boy to be killed by some wild animal?" the Corporal asked, incredulously. "Not on my watch."

"But Corp, by now they'll have…"

"We're going Private. That's an order!"

Marcus was proud to serve under Corporal Dimitrov. He was clearly a man of principle and honor. Unlike Sergeant Lance.

*   *   *   *   *

The sun had just set, and Oberon's radiant form was nowhere to be seen. The dim emptiness of the desert, lit only by starlight, filled Marcus' mind with mystery and a sense of adventure. He wasn't afraid, any more than he had been when he'd moved the barracuda's ramp to save the squad. His conviction urged him onward. Somewhere out there a young boy needed them. He only hoped there was still time to save him.

Taz scouted ahead. He'd been reluctant to head up the team, but Dimitrov had ordered him to do so. Without their helmets and their built-in night-vision and thermographic modes, it was difficult to see any distance.

Taz stopped at the top of one of the dunes in front of the team, kneeling low and gesturing for them to move up. The rest of the team rushed towards him.

"There's something down there," he explained as they arrived behind him.

A small valley lay before them, the shadowy outlines of a carcass lying in its center just visible. They could make out the buzzing of flies swarming around it, and the stench of decay hung in the air.

"Is that the boy?" Marcus whispered.

"No, it's too big. Probably a camel or a cow," Taz replied.

"We should go take a look nonetheless," Dimitrov ordered.

They slid, silently and cautiously, down the far side of the dune. Although they were only armed with their combat knives, all of the clones were well versed in T.R.A.C.S., a form of unarmed combat developed by the Terran military. That, in addition to their numbers, gave Marcus the confidence to slip over the crest and down into the valley. As they reached the bottom of the dune, Marcus thought he saw movement, a shifting in the shadows lurking around the carcass. He hesitated briefly in his advance. As he saw his teammates continue on, he forced himself to follow them.

"I think we should go back," he called softly. "I don't like the look of this."

"It's just a dead animal," Becks proclaimed.

"Something isn't right. What could have dragged it all the way out here, so far from the farm?" added Marcus.

The team turned to face him.

"Look, Marcus, it probably just got out of its pen, wandered off too far and died of dehydration," Becks replied. "There are five of us out here, so if anything's gonna happen I'm pretty sure we can take care of it."

Over Beck's shoulder, Marcus saw it again. It was definitely moving, whatever it was.

"There's something there!" he yelled, pointing towards the rotting carcass.

The others spun around and peered into the darkness.

"Where?" barked Taz, as they took a few careful steps towards the body, squinting their eyes to try and make out the shadows surrounding it.

There was no more movement. Was he imagining it?

All of a sudden, a terrifying shriek cut through the silence, an intense blast of sonic energy. Becks and Taz, who had been at the forefront of the team's advance, fell to their knees in agony. They all dropped their knives, clutching their ears in gut-wrenching pain from the blast. As they did so, a menacing shadow leapt from the rotting carcass right onto Becks.

Marcus could see it clearly now, a creature almost a meter tall with two powerful legs and grayish white skin wrapped over its muscular frame. Its gaping maw, lined with an array of small, sharp-looking teeth, locked onto Becks' neck. He screamed as blood gushed from the wound. The creature wagged its thick white tail, eager to consume its meal, its frail arms dangling at its sides.

Marcus froze, the ringing in his ears wracking him in pain. The whole thing had happened so fast he didn't know how to react. The creature's featureless milky-white eyes, set either side of its elongated head, level with its huge mouth, focused on him, as if to say 'You're next'.

The others were equally stunned. Taz was staggering back to his feet, still recovering from the massive blow to his eardrums. He'd gotten about halfway up when another shadow sprung from the carcass. It struck him headfirst, square on his chest, knocking him over and stunning itself in the process.

Marcus rolled to his feet, and saw that Corporal Dimitrov's lips were moving. He was screaming something at Marcus, but the buzzing sound in his ears stopped him making out even a single word. The Corporal ran towards Becks as Marcus spotted another pair of the predatory creatures slip into view. They took a few careful steps away from the carcass towards the group, their torsos swaying from side to side as they eyed their potential meals with interest.

Marcus ran to Taz, just as the disoriented creature which had knocked him over got back on its feet. He grabbed Taz's arm, pulling the scout to his feet as fast as he could. The two of them looked over to Reid, who was trying to drag the Corporal away from Becks. Dimitrov had been trying to tear the creature on the unfortunate clone loose, but had only made Becks' wound worse in the process.

Marcus had never before seen so much blood. Although his resonant memories told him that the human body held roughly five liters of blood, they'd done little to prepare him for seeing it all oozing from Becks' gaping wound. The other creatures drew closer. The two late arrivals prepared to circle them, trying to cut them off from any means of escape.

The creature that had attacked Taz earlier now stood poised to attack, its mouth open, and its strong legs bent and ready to jump, its short arms poised. Its focus shifted from Taz to Reid, as the sniper tried to tear the Corporal away from Becks.

"Reid!" Marcus shouted in warning, hoping his hearing had returned.

The creature lunged, aiming for Reid's extended arm, but before it reached him, Reid spun around, grabbing the creature by its jaw and neck in mid-air. Marcus couldn't believe it, it was as if Reid had had eyes in the back of his head. The creature fought back, its arms and tail flailing about wildly, trying to claw its way loose. Reid embraced it, hugging it tightly in his muscled arms.

Marcus heard the snap as Reid twisted its head, breaking its neck. The creature went limp in his arms, except for its tail, which continued to flap for a few seconds before it too fell still.

The two creatures who had begun to circle the team hissed loudly, backing off a couple of steps, just as three more appeared in the background.

"Now's our chance," Taz yelled. "Corp, we gotta run!"

Dimitrov finally loosened his grip on the creature that was still gnawing at Becks' throat. He realized the dire situation they were in and let go of his adversary.

"Run!" he bellowed.

Reid and Marcus managed to snatch their combat knives from the ground as they started running as fast as they could. They stumbled away desperately, leaving Becks behind for the creatures to feast on.

Chapter 26

They ran right through the early hours of the night, all the while sure that the creatures were right on their heels. God knows how many more of them could be out there, thought Marcus.

"What the hell were those things?" Taz screamed when they finally paused to catch their breath.

"I don't know. I've never seen or heard of anything like them," Dimitrov panted.

"I've had it with all of this. Crash land here, crash land there, eaten by space monsters here," Taz blurted hysterically.

"Calm down Taz," the Corporal ordered.

"No I won't calm the fuck down, I won't calm the fuck down until I'm back on the Alamo," yelled Taz.

"We need to warn the Sergeant," Dimitrov decided.

"We need weapons," exclaimed Reid.

"They did look pretty pissed when you snapped that one's neck," Taz gasped.

"Come on guys, let's keep going. There could be more of them out there," the Corporal said.

They picked up the pace again, jogging the last couple of kilometers to the Last Oasis.

*   *   *   *   *

It was slightly after midnight when they showed up outside the Black Lotus Inn. They'd blown right past the squad's camp site. The Children of the Wastes were already fast asleep, all except Omar the innkeeper, who was leaning back in his chair behind the reception counter. Sanjey was fast asleep on one of the couches in the lobby when Marcus and his team came bursting through the front door.

"Have you seen Sergeant Lance?" Corporal Dimitrov shouted.

Omar fumbled with the book he had been quietly reading.

"What? Oh, the drunk fellow. Yes he's upstairs, room… eh… 207," Omar informed them as they rushed on past him, Taz almost tripping on the stairs to the second floor.

Sergeant Lance didn't answer the door on the first knock, nor the second. It wasn't until Corporal Dimitrov was pounding heavily enough to wake the entire floor that they decided to risk opening it themselves. Like all of the rooms in the inn, Lance's room had no lock. The Sergeant lay on his bed, an empty bottle of Raketta on his chest, clutched in his left hand.

"Wake up Sergeant!" Dimitrov shouted, grabbing Lance by the shoulders and shaking him violently.

The empty bottle fell to the floor with a muddled thump, rolling off to the edge of the room.

"Who the…? Where? What the hell's the matter with you Dimitrov?" the Sergeant yelled as he emerged from his alcohol-induced slumber, staring defiantly into the Corporal's eyes.

"I'm sorry Sergeant, I had no choice. We knocked, but you…" Dimitrov babbled.

"We were attacked!" yelled Taz from the doorway, trying to save the Corporal from the barrage of insults he was sure to endure if he didn't make his point quickly.

The Sergeant froze, looking first towards Taz and then shifting his gaze back to the Corporal.

"Attacked? Attacked by who? The locals?" Sergeant Lance asked, obviously confused.

"No, you sent us out to find the missing boy, remember?" Reid chimed in.

"Oh yeah, right. Did you find him?" Lance asked, rising up to sit on the foot of the bed as Dimitrov backed off, giving him room to breathe.

"No," replied the Corporal. "We found something else. Or rather, something else found us."

"I'm listening," the Sergeant replied, his eyes half opened and bleary.

"We found a rotting carcass, some dead animal, probably a camel," Dimitrov explained.

"So you were attacked by a dead camel? Give me a break Corporal, it's late, and I'm tired and I just want to get some sleep," the Sergeant interrupted.

"NO! You're not listening Sergeant," the Corporal yelled in frustration. "Becks is dead!"

"What?" the Sergeant bellowed with renewed interest.

"There were some creatures there, Sergeant, gorging on the carcass I'm guessing. When we approached they let off this god-awful deafening shriek. We were taken completely by surprise, disoriented, we couldn't hear a thing. Then they jumped us. One of them bit Becks right on the neck. He was dead before we could do anything to help him."

"What kind of creatures?" the Sergeant asked.

"I've never seen anything like them sir, none of us have. They had pale gray skin, about a meter tall, razor sharp teeth, and a nasty looking tail. They were obviously predatory, Sergeant. Albano got one, but there were at least six more circling us, and who knows how many more lurking in the darkness."

"So you ran?"

"Yes Sergeant. We didn't know what else to do. There could have been dozens more for all we knew," the Corporal confessed.

"You did the right thing. Informing me was your top priority. I think it's time we go wake up Rory, and send a message back to HQ. They need to know about these... shriekers," the Sergeant stated.

"But what about Becks' body?" blurted Marcus, who had remained quiet up to that point.

"Becks' body? Weren't you there, Grey?" the Sergeant barked. "There probably won't be anything left of Becks' body by the time you'd get back to it. Nothing recognizable, at least."

Marcus held his tongue, afraid that he wouldn't be able to contain his rage and would say something that would get him into trouble with the Sergeant.

* * * * *

Dawn was starting to creep over the horizon before they managed to wake Rory, who was even less cheerful than Lance about being so rudely awoken. It took all five of them to convince him to allow them to use the communications tower to contact the Alamo, and even then he wasn't all too happy about it.

ENCOUNTERED HOSTILE NON-INDIGINOUS ALIEN LIFEFORMS. ORIGINS: UNKOWN. NUMBERS: UNKOWN. PRIVATE BECKS, RICHARD KIA. PLEASE ADVISE.

The message was short and to the point. They would have to wait at least fourteen minutes for a reply.

"We have to do something," Taz bellowed. "We can't just sit around and wait for the Alamo to send backup. We're stuck here for another two weeks with those things out there."

"Pipe down Private. I'm thinking," Sergeant Lance ordered him.

"Judging by the number of missing cattle that have been reported, I think it's safe to assume that we're dealing with a lot more of them than those we saw, Sergeant," Dimitrov offered.

FORTIFY POSITION. NO CURRENT SHIPS AVAILABLE. BACKUP ETA: 4 WEEKS.

"Four weeks! We're going to need our weapons. I don't give a shit what the Sheikh says. He can kiss my ass," Lance exclaimed.

"What about the camp?" Dimitrov asked.

"We better move the camp into town. We'll set up inside the GeoDynamics compound," Lance ordered. "Get everyone in here."

"What about the locals?" Marcus inquired, concerned that their safety wouldn't be high on the Sergeant's list of priorities.

"The locals?" the Sergeant fumed. "Screw the locals. They have their Hajari, or whatever they're called."

Dimitrov exchanged a concerned look with Marcus before attempting to persuade the Sergeant. "Sir, HQ would certainly see the rescue of the locals as an act of extreme heroism on your part," he prompted.

The Sergeant raised his eyebrow. The Corporal had made a good point. Certainly if he were successful in rescuing the town, his superiors would be unable to overlook his courageous deeds. They would have to promote him.

"You're right Dimitrov," he finally decided, after weighing the potential implications for his career. "We'll set up guard posts at each of the town's three main access points and seal off any others. That should assure the safety of the locals. But if even one of those Hajari gives you any trouble, you shoot the bastard!"

* * * * *

The squad was deeply disturbed to receive the news of Becks' death. Jenna jumped straight into Jago's monstrous arms. Jago looked mortified, and peered over her head at the rest of his squadmates to see if anyone had noticed. Although it did little to reassure them, Beck's death had brought the squad back into the settlement and, more importantly, given them access to their weapons.

They'd set up their tents in the wide, walled-off area inside the GeoDynamics compound, within reach of the barracuda. Since all the reports of missing cattle had specified that the abductions had taken place during the night, Taylor had suggested that the creatures were undoubtedly nocturnal, reducing the need for daytime guard duties.

Sergeant Lance had ordered them to don their armor, and, despite the blazing heat of the sun, his orders weren't met with any objections. They slept during the hottest part of the day. The tents provided them with little comfort from the scorching sun, making falling asleep extremely difficult. That night, Lance stationed guards at each of the three main entrances to the walled-off settlement.

The Sergeant himself and his men occupied the northern gate, which was furthest away from the reported abductions, and thus the least likely entrance to see any action. It was also the closest to the GeoDynamics compound, providing Lance easy access to the barracuda. Spielman and his men were stationed at the southwestern gate, a small, rarely-used entrance situated in a courtyard in front of a tall residential building, with several smaller structures forming the walls of the courtyard. Corporal Dimitrov's team guarded the southeastern gate, the busiest of the three, located at the end of the settlement's largest street. The gates Dimitrov and Spielman's teams were guarding weren't far apart, but they were separated by a block of buildings, with no easy or quick route between them.

The night after Becks' death was eerily quiet. Tensions were high, among both the squad members and the villagers. Taz's exaggerated description of their assailants had done little to quiet anyone's nerves. The teams had built up barricades of sandbags at each guard station. They huddled behind them as the squad's snipers kept watch from nearby rooftops, from which they could see over the town's walls and survey the surrounding countryside. The night seemed almost eternal. The whole squad remained silent, waiting for the sweet release daybreak would bring. Shutters creaked in the wind that battered them mercilessly through the night, making the squad jump at the unexpected sounds. Somewhere in the distance a dog barked sporadically. The waiting was unbearable, Marcus thought. He almost wished that the creatures would come. At least now they were ready for them.

"Why did you want to go to Alpha Terra?" Corporal Dimitrov asked Marcus when Taz had wondered off to relieve himself, leaving the two alone behind their sandbags.

The question took Marcus by surprise. None of the others had ever asked him about his decision before.

"I don't really know," confided Marcus. "I guess I was afraid."

"Afraid of what?" the Corporal asked.

"The war… dying," Marcus confessed, trying to hide his shame.

"There's nothing wrong with being afraid of death, Marcus," Dimitrov confided, noting Marcus's reaction. "We're all afraid, even the Sergeant. Especially the Sergeant," the Corporal laughed softly. "Except he's more afraid of unimportant things, like missing out on a promotion, and that others might not think the best of him."

Marcus had never really thought about it that way before.

"Fear keeps you on your toes, keeps you alive. Just don't let yourself get too afraid, or eventually it'll consume you," the Corporal counseled.

Marcus thought long and hard about Dimitrov's serious words throughout the night. Fear had indeed been the deciding factor in most of his decisions. The only times he'd been truly pleased with himself was when he'd let go of his fears before acting. Perhaps the Corporal was right. He had been afraid of the war, just as Steven had. Was that the only reason why he'd wanted to leave the squad? Had he latched onto the first likeminded clone to find solace? As the first rays began making their way over the horizon, Marcus breathed a sigh of relief, pleased that the night had been uneventful, but continued to ponder Dimitrov's advice.

* * * * *

As the days went by, the reports of missing cattle turned into reports of missing children and farmers. All around the Last Oasis, it was clear that the creatures had been keeping busy. Corporal Dimitrov had tried to persuade Lance to send out a team to try bringing the local farmers into the main settlement for their own protection, but the Sergeant had refused him, shouting that he wouldn't risk any more of his men on a fool's errand.

When not actively on guard duty, Marcus spent most of his time catching up on his technical training. He read through countless manuals and educational material, learning the inns and outs of everything from computer security to technical engineering. He enjoyed taking his mind off the situation, and reading managed to keep him occupied.

By the fifth day, there was no need to send out men to warn the farmers. The news had spread far and wide, and the southern gates were filled by long lines of farmers and their families, all seeking shelter within the walls of the Last Oasis. The Sheikh sent his Hajari to speak with the Sergeant on several occasions, not to squabble over the squad's use of weaponry and technology, but to try to elicit aid for his people. The Sergeant had refused all requests and invitations to meet with the Sheikh.

The local townsfolk mostly stayed indoors during the day, making only short trips to their gardens to harvest food for their families, and to the local temple to pray for the safety of the settlement. Marcus felt the urge to join them in prayer. He hadn't thought much about a god, or any higher power, watching over him, but he wanted to believe. He wanted to know what it was like to have faith, to know that, no matter what happened, someone or something would keep them safe.

Chapter 27

The reports had been pouring in all day long. The outlying regions had been completely evacuated. Every single household in the Last Oasis now housed at least two or three families, and Sheikh Abdul's palace courtyard was overflowing with tents and refugees. The creatures' ravenous appetites had far exceeded everyone's expectations, indicating that their numbers had to be in the hundreds at least. Marcus knew that conflict was now inevitable, and in all likelihood, tonight would be the night that the creatures would work up the courage to attack the main settlement.

As the sun set, the squad was on high alert. The snipers scoped out the horizon for any signs of an incoming attack. Apart from mumbled prayers and the moaning of the bereaved, the Last Oasis could have been mistaken for a ghost town. Even Taz was silent.

Marcus looked at Corporal Dimitrov, who seemed calmer than most of the squad, as the two of them joined Taz in their sandbag-lined dugout. How was it that the Corporal was able to retain his composure when everyone else was so unnerved? Marcus had assured himself that this was not a fight that he wanted to miss. Not because he was looking forward to the confrontation, but because somebody needed to stand up for the Children of the Wastes. If it weren't for the squad, all that would stand between these peaceful people and a horde of hungry predators were a few select men with swords. No, this was indeed a noble cause, one that he wouldn't miss out on for anything.

So why couldn't he keep his hand steady? How was it that the Corporal was so calm and collected when Marcus was so tense?

As if Dimitrov had sensed Marcus's musings, the Corporal looked at him reassuringly, placing a hand on his shoulder as he'd done in the past.

"Don't worry Marcus. We may be outnumbered, but we have a good defensive position and we'll see them coming a mile away. All you have to do is point and shoot, and rely on the rest of us to do the same," Dimitrov reassured him.

"I know you're right. In my mind, I know you're right. My body's just a bit slow to accept it," Marcus grinned nervously, trying to steady his hand as he peered over the barricade to survey the deserted landscape. "Maybe they won't come tonight," he added as he sat back down, leaning up against the sand filled sacks that made up the barricade walls.

"Perhaps," replied the Corporal. "But I wouldn't bet on it."

"Corp," Reid came over the comms. "I've got movement on the horizon, eighteen degrees south-east."

Reid was positioned on top of the building next to the team's barricade, a three-storey house belonging to one of the local families. Marcus could see the outline of Reid's sniper rifle jutting from the edge of the rooftop.

"Numbers?" Dimitrov inquired.

"Unclear. They're at least three kilometers out. I can just make out the outlines with my scope, but they're all huddled together. Could be anywhere from ten to a hundred," Reid replied.

"Roger that. Let me know when they get closer," the Corporal ordered.

"Will do. They don't appear to be moving," added Reid.

Several minutes passed as they nervously awaited more information on the horde's movements.

"What's going on out there Albano?" Dimitrov asked , breaking the silence.

"Nothing yet Corp. It's as if they're waiting for something," Reid responded.

"Waiting for what?" Sergeant Lance chimed in on the comms.

"Your guess is as good as mine, Sergeant," Reid replied.

"Hughes, anything on your side?" the Sergeant anxiously inquired.

Hughes was a part of Corporal Spielman's team, positioned at the southwest gate.

"Nothing Sergeant. No movement at all."

"Sergeant," Reid broke in. "I have a group of three, maybe four, breaking away from the rest, approaching the southeast gate, fast!"

"Look alive, Dimitrov," Lance ordered. "Don't let them get past that barricade."

"Roger that," the Corporal replied.

Marcus leaned over the barricade, his SGC K-660 aimed out into the desert, the creatures still too far away for him to make out. Dimitrov and Taz leaned out over the barricade as well. The three of them took aim, ready to fire the second the creatures came into sight.

"Albano, hold your fire until they're within our range. We don't want to scare them off before we can take them all out at once," the Corporal ordered.

"Man those things can run!" Reid blurted. "I'd say fifty or sixty kilometers an hour judging by what I'm seeing. Four targets, should be coming into view any second now."

Marcus peered out into the darkness. His helmet's night-vision didn't have nearly as long a range as that built into Reid's scope, but he was sure it would still be more than enough for the range of his carbine.

Suddenly they came into view, four of the beasts, their powerful legs propelling them straight towards the barricade at a tremendous speed.

"Fire!" the Corporal bellowed.

Marcus's squeezed his carbine's trigger, letting off a full burst at the center of the group, hitting one of the creatures in its hind leg and another right in the center of its torso. Reid dropped the one on the left with a carefully aimed shot to the head, ripping it clean off the creature's narrow shoulders, as Taz and Dimitrov also let fly a hail of bullets. As the dust settled, all four of them lay still in the sand.

"Targets down," informed Reid.

"Whew. That wasn't so bad," Taz blurted.

"Maybe so," the Corporal replied. "Nonetheless, we should conserve ammunition. We used way too many rounds on just those four. Use three-round bursts from now on. That should…"

A series of short, successive high-pitched shrieks from one of the four downed creatures interrupted the Corporal. The piercing wail, although not as terrible as the boom of sonic energy they'd been hit with during their first encounter, was enough to awaken even the soundest sleeper in the Last Oasis. Reid cocked his rifle and quickly ended the creature's suffering with a well placed shot.

"What the hell was that?" Lance asked on the comms.

"One of them was still alive," Dimitrov informed him. "Reid, what's the status of the rest of the pack?"

Marcus saw Reid's rifle once again swing out over the dark horizon.

"They're gone!" Reid gasped, astonished.

"What do you mean gone?"

"They're gone Corp. Must have run off during the shooting," added Reid.

"It couldn't have been that easy," Dimitrov replied. "Hughes, anything on your side?"

"Still nothing," Hughes replied, perched on a rooftop only a few hundred meters from their position.

"What about you Sergeant, any movement by the north gate?"

"Quiet as the grave," Lance replied.

"I guess we must have scared them off," Taz chimed in.

"Jittery little buggers," Spielman mused.

"Well, let's not pack our bags just yet. They might be back," the Sergeant ordered.

Marcus sighed. He'd been hoping that their brief firefight had been enough to deter the shrieking beasts from another attempt on the settlement. Deep in his gut, however, he knew they'd try again.

"I've got movement, nine degrees south-west," Hughes called from his rooftop.

"How many?" Lance asked.

"Not sure. They're pretty far off. Maybe five," Hughes replied.

"Don't let them out of your sight Private," the Sergeant barked.

"No Sergeant."

A sudden outburst of screams, emanating from the western quarter of the settlement, cut through the silence. Somewhere inside the walls a woman screamed in terror, her cries joined shortly afterwards by the screams of children and men.

"What the hell's going on over there?" Lance bellowed.

A series of terrifying shrieks erupted from inside the settlement, a short distance from the south-western gate.

"They're inside the walls!" yelled Corporal Spielman.

"How the hell did they get past you?" Sergeant Lance almost screamed, demanding an answer.

A series of shots went off from a distant rooftop. From the muffled sound of the discharges, Marcus figured it had to be Hughes firing his sniper rifle.

"They're coming over the western wall!" Hughes barked over the comms, continuing to fire.

"Suarez, Orseau, Kitamura, move in, fast!" Spielman ordered.

Marcus and his team awaited orders. Marcus could see Reid was no longer focused on the horizon, but that the sniper was actively surveying the settlement's walls in every direction.

Marcus heard short bursts of fire off to the west, followed by more screams and cries for help.

"Corp, shouldn't we go help?" asked Marcus.

"No, we have to stay put. We can't run off and leave our position vulnerable," Dimitrov replied.

Reid's rifle went off, first once, then a second time. Marcus couldn't see which direction he was firing.

"What's going on up there Albano?" Dimitrov demanded.

"Two of them were trying to sneak over the east wall Corporal. They're down," Reid replied.

On the western side of the settlement, frequent bursts from carbines could be heard, followed by the boom of Hughes's powerful sniper rifle. Marcus tensed up. He felt as if the creatures were coming at them from all sides, circling them, just as they'd tried to when he and his team had investigated the carcass.

"We need backup!" Spielman demanded. "They're all over the place!"

"Stand your ground Corporal," Lance ordered him.

"Kitamura's down, we have to fall back!" Spielman bellowed.

"Negative Corporal, stand your ground!" commanded Sergeant Lance. "We can't afford to fall back. You must hold position!"

Reid's rifle fired again.

All of a sudden, Marcus saw several shapes creep over the wall between the southeast and north gates.

"Over there!" he shouted, pointing towards the wall. They were gone. "They were coming over the walls. I just saw them!" he assured his team.

"Sergeant, we're too spread out," Dimitrov said over the radio. "They're coming over the walls. Our defensive positions are meaningless. We need to fall back."

"We can't let those creatures run around inside the settlement Corporal. The locals are defenseless against them," Lance barked back.

Although Marcus was indeed worried about what might happen to the locals if the squad were to retreat, he could see that the situation was spiraling out of control. Dimitrov tapped Marcus and Taz on the shoulder to get their attention. He raised two fingers, looked each of them in the eye, then pointed towards the western part of the settlement, silently ordering them to go and reinforce Spielman's team. The two of them nodded in approval before heading off down the main street, searching for the nearest west-bound alley.

"Hughes, behind you!" they heard Reid shout.

Marcus looked up just in time to spot three of the creatures climbing up the back of the tall building where Hughes was positioned, no more than a hundred and fifty meters away. Hughes spun around just as Reid fired off a shot, hitting one of the creatures square in the chest. It hung limp, its sharp claws still embedded in the wall. The other two increased their pace, one of them grabbing the edge of the roof with both clawed forepaws before arching its neck backwards, its head peering over the edge just enough to let out a deafening shriek at the sniper. Hughes fell to his knees, clutching his ears in pain, as the third creature clambered onto the roof.

Reid fired another shot, barely missing the shrieker's head. The shot ricocheted off the building behind it just as the creature leapt onto the prostrated Hughes and began prying his helmet loose. Sprinting down the main street, Marcus spotted another pair of pale silhouettes starting to climb the walls to the roof when Reid let out a cry of his own.

Spinning around, Marcus saw that one of the shrieking creatures had managed to sneak up the side of Reid's building when the dark-skinned clone had been busy defending Hughes. It was now clutching his back, its powerful claws latched onto his shoulder.

Marcus shouldered his carbine, aiming towards the roof, unsure whether or not he should risk trying to shoot the damned thing off Reid's back. The sniper twisted and turned, trying to shake it off. The creature writhed, managing to wrap its tail around Reid's midsection. Marcus frantically tried to control his breathing, taking great care to aim as best he could. His hand shook. Not now, not now!

Suddenly Reid threw himself backwards, slamming his back down on the ground as hard as he could, dropping out of Marcus' line of sight, but stunning the creature just as it readied itself to shriek directly into his ear. Marcus could hear Reid fumbling around on the rooftop. He waited eagerly for him to pop back up, desperately hoping that his teammate would survive.

"Orseau's down, Orseau's down!" Spielman yelled on the comms.

Marcus looked left and right, first to Reid and then to Hughes, who was being savaged by four creatures, who had managed to pry off his helmet.

"Fuck," Lance moaned. "Ok ok, I'm sending backup. Simone, Clarke, go now!"

Suddenly Marcus heard the popping of Reid's sidearm going off, firing rapidly just as Marcus spotted another creature coming up the side wall. He raised his carbine and let loose a hail of bullets at the wall, drowning the creature in lead. It hung there limp for a few seconds before its claws came loose, then plummeting back to the ground.

Reid stuck his head up from the edge of the roof, kicking down the lifeless corpse of his assailant. He caught Marcus' eye, and the two exchanged nods as the sniper bent to pickup his rifle.

"Shit, Hughes is down," Reid cried. "I repeat; Hughes is down."

"Sergeant!" Dimitrov yelled. "We have to pull back. They're already inside the walls and coming at us from all directions."

"Don't you think I know that!" Lance roared, bursting with rage. "Fuck, fuck, ok ok. Strategic retreat, everyone. Fall back to the compound!"

Taz shook his head at Marcus, raising his hand, middle finger extended, in the direction of the north gate.

Marcus covered the main street as Corporal Dimitrov began falling back towards their position, keeping his carbine pointing at the side walls of the nearby buildings as Reid started to rappel down to the ground, his long rifle slung over a shoulder.

All over the settlement, screams of women and children could be heard as the shriekers forced their way through windows and un-barricaded doors while the local men tried to fend them off with shovels and pitchforks. Looking over his shoulder, Marcus saw two shadows, which his helmet identified as Simone and Clarke, run across the street, trying to get to Corporal Spielman and support his team's retreat.

Marcus and Taz waited for Dimitrov and Reid to catch up with them. "Should we still go over there and try and help them?" asked Marcus when the other two arrived, gesturing towards the western part of the settlement.

"No," Dimitrov decided. "The order's been given. We're to fall back to the compound. Simone and Clarke will cover them. Let's keep an eye on the main street as we go."

The four of them started making their way back along the widest street of the Last Oasis, each of them watching a different direction. Six more of the shriekers fell as they caught a hail of bullets from Taz and Dimitrov.

Finally Marcus spotted Spielman's small frame burst from an alley behind them, his carbine spewing a steady stream of lead as he let loose an inarticulate scream of rage, running backwards into the open.

"Sanjay!" yelled Marcus, suddenly realizing what he had seen in his dream on the veranda of the Black Lotus Inn.

"No, where are you…" Dimitrov bellowed. But he was too late. Marcus had already charged headfirst into a nearby alley.

As if reborn from the fire, Marcus's hands steadied and his fear dissipated. He ran like he'd never run before, ducking left and right around the narrow corners. Somewhere along the way a shrieker that tried to leap onto him from a low-hanging rooftop fell to the ground with three rounds in its chest. Faster, he thought. I have to go faster!

As he turned the last corner, he was greeted by the sight of several bodies lying on the ground in the open area in front of the Inn.

Marcus lowered his weapon, taking short, careful steps into the open. There he was. Little Sanjay lay at the base of the terrace, his leg bent back awkwardly, his neck smeared in blood.

Marcus staggered to the small shape, then slung his carbine and lifted the poor boy off the ground. He felt as if he couldn't breathe. Tears swelled up in his eyes as his knees began to buckle.

"He's dead! Can't you see that? They're all dead!" Dimitrov shouted as he came running up behind him.

The Corporal had followed him to the Black Lotus Inn, and was now busy emptying his clip into a group of three shriekers who'd taken up position in one of the alleyways next to the Inn. Marcus looked down at the wound on Sanjay's neck. Blood trickled from the open wound. Marcus felt dizzy. He'd seen this. This had happened before.

"Forget about him, we need to get back to the compound, stat!" Dimitrov shouted into his face as the Corporal grabbed Marcus by the shoulder, pulling him away from the Black Lotus, blood soaked bodies littering the terrace behind them.

"They're all dead Marcus. We have to go before..." Dimitrov was cut short as Marcus, still clutching little Sanjay with one arm, lifted his carbine over the Corporal's shoulder and, without looking, emptied his entire clip.

The shrieker that had been about to land on the Corporal's back fell to the ground, stone dead.

*   *   *   *   *

Marcus and the astonished Corporal had managed to make their way back to the entrance of the compound without saying a word, ducking through the gate to where the rest of the squad had been eagerly awaiting their arrival. Once the Sergeant had hurled a slew of insults at them for taking so long, Dimitrov and Marcus joined the squad's defensive position around the Compound's perimeter. Marcus could still hear the screams and whimpers in between the deafening shrieks from throughout the settlement.

"Can't we do something?" asked Marcus.

"Pipe down Grey," ordered the Sergeant.

"We can't just let all those people die trying to defend themselves," Marcus went on, hoping to persuade the Sergeant.

"We've lost four to those vile beasts already Private, how many more have to die before you finally accept the fact that this is a lost cause?" Lance roared.

Marcus was saddened by the loss of the men who'd given their lives in defense of the settlement, but even more so by the knowledge that many more like little Sanjay would follow.

"Clarke, I want you to get to high ground. We need someone surveying the area, making sure none of those creatures slip past our defenses. Pick one of those chemical tanks over there and take up position on top," Lance ordered. "Raven, Adler, Doc, fall back to the ship. We'll use that as our base of operations," he added. "Suarez, you're with Spielman and Raleigh. I want you guarding the main entrance. Dimitrov, you and your men stay in the back of the compound, watch the walls, and secure the bottleneck. Raynes, Simone and I will stay mobile and provide backup as needed."

"How's everyone on ammo?" Dimitrov inquired as the rest of the squad moved into position.

"One clip left for the carbine, and a full clip in my sidearm," Marcus replied.

"I've got two full clips for the carbine, and a full clip for the sidearm," Taz said, inspecting his weapon.

"I'm good," was all that Reid had to say.

"Alright. Reid, why don't you climb up on one of those tanks and see if you can help Clarke out," the Corporal suggested.

"I've got movement!" yelled Clarke from the center tank.

Marcus and his team ran towards the bottleneck formed where the tanks crowded up against the refinery complex, Marcus and Dimitrov taking up position on the left and Taz on the right. Almost immediately they began hearing shots fired from the compound's main entrance. Spielman and his men were laying down suppressive fire, trying to keep the creatures at bay.

"There's too many of them!" Spielman yelled. "Some are climbing over the walls."

"I've got them," Clarke called, taking aim with his carbine just as Reid came up the ladder behind him. Clarke fired off a few short bursts, taking down a few of the creatures that had managed to clamber up the compound's outer perimeter wall.

A deafening shriek erupted from somewhere close to the front gate. Someone screamed in terror. Marcus felt his heart racing, faster and faster, harder and harder. They were coming in. There would be no stopping them. There was no place left to run.

"Suarez is down!" Raleigh roared, emptying her clip into a nearby group of shriekers.

"Spielman, Raleigh, fall back!" Lance ordered.

"Albano, Clarke, you still have your grenades?" Dimitrov asked.

Reid fired off a couple of rounds at a pair of shriekers that had gotten over the walls and were getting ready to jump Spielman from behind.

221

"Yes Corp," Reid and Clarke confirmed.

"Good, we'll try and bait them into the bottleneck. You two use your grenades as soon as they're in position," Dimitrov ordered.

"Right," Reid acknowledged.

At the far end of the bottleneck, Corporal Spielman shoved Jenna away from the main gate, pushing her back as he covered her retreat. She turned and ran like hell down the bottleneck towards the ship. Reid and Clarke fired off a few rounds into the creatures thronging the gateway to try and distract them enough to allow Spielman to make a run for it. The beleaguered Corporal was backing slowly away from the main gate, firing as he went, but there were too many shriekers for him to turn and run. Finally they caught a break. There was a gap in the procession of shriekers piling in through the compound's entrance.

"Now Spielman, run!" Reid yelled.

Spielman, limping from a claw-wound to his calf, turned and sprinted as fast as he could. Dimitrov and Marcus covered him as he stumbled down the narrow corridor between the refinery and the silos, firing off every round in their clips as the throng of creatures behind him pushed forward, trying to seize Spielman as he ran on through the bottleneck. Taz kept his rounds in reserve, firing only when Dimitrov had to stop to swap clips.

"DO IT!" the Corporal roared.

Clarke held a bundle of four Nova Labs' frag grenades over the edge of the tank. He pulled the pins as Reid continued to fire off shots into the mass of shriekers, trying to herd them closer together.

"Look out!" yelled Marcus, as he spotted one of the shriekers pulling itself up the side of the tank, completely unnoticed. The creature arched its head just as Clarke turned, getting ready to throw the

222

grenades into the crowd below. The creature shrieked. Marcus could almost see the sonic blast as it hit Clarke head on, knocking him over the edge, into the waiting maws of the pack below.

"NOOOOO!" Marcus yelled in despair.

Reid looked to the side just as Clarke's bundle of grenades landed on the roof of the tank beside him. Marcus' heart skipped, sure that this would be the last he would ever see of Reid. Time seemed to stand still as he watched the sniper bend his knees in a futile attempt to jump for cover. He leapt into the air, away from the deadly stack of explosives, clear over the edge of the tank and straight towards the throng of ravenous shriekers beneath him as the grenades went off in a cacophony of explosions, tearing through the tank and throwing a magnificent fireball into the night sky.

Marcus cringed as he turned to cover his eyes from the blast. He lifted his head a few seconds later, confused as to why, once the initial boom of the grenades had sounded, the rumble of roaring thunder had continued. As he turned to see if he could spot the origins of the unexpected sound, he was greeted with the strangest of sights. The throng of shriekers was desperately trying to escape back down the narrow corridor as a massive wave of water crashed down from the torn tank and into the bottleneck. The creatures tore each other apart as they clambered over each other in an effort to escape.

Jago came running up from behind Marcus, lugging his weapon in both hands.

"Boss says to get to the ship!" the behemoth yelled as he opened fire into the chaotic blend of water and frantic shriekers.

"No wait!" yelled Marcus, shoving the muzzle of the machinegun down to the ground as he spotted Reid at the front of the wave, unconscious and being carried down the corridor in their direction. "Do you see him?" asked Marcus, pointing towards the sniper.

"Yes, I see," Jago rumbled.

"Don't hit him," Marcus instructed, releasing the muzzle of the KRS-56.

Jago nodded his approval before bringing the gun back to bear.

The wave of water began to disperse, leaving Reid stranded, lying face down in ankle-deep water close to their end of the bottleneck. Marcus ran in, doubled over as low as he could, Jago's weapon flaring behind him, surrounding him in a halo of bullets that cut through the confused shriekers as if they were made of butter. Marcus didn't even pause to think, he just grabbed Reid's arm and began pulling him back towards Jago as fast as he could.

"Die you bastards!" Jago roared as the stream of rounds spat from his massive weapon cut through the tumbling creatures like a saw. "Get to the ship!" he reiterated, waving Marcus off as he approached with the unconscious Reid.

"I'm trying!" Marcus shouted, Reid's weight slowing him down.

"Let me," Jago suggested, releasing the trigger and grabbing Reid with one arm, flinging him over his shoulder as if he were a ragdoll. Marcus hesitated for a split second, still amazed at the behemoth's monstrous strength, before springing away towards the downed barracuda. Dimitrov and Taz covered their retreat, following closely behind Marcus and Jago as they ran.

"Are you sure she'll fly?" Lance bellowed into his radio from the ship's open ramp.

"Fly yes, land no!" Raven yelled back.

As the Sergeant helped bring Reid aboard the barracuda, he glanced over the compound, making sure no one was being left behind. "The

224

probe!" he shouted, spotting the damaged warehouse in the corner of the compound.

"Screw the probe," Dimitrov barked. "We can come back for it later."

The Sergeant glared defiantly at his Corporal, then grimaced and looked away as he realized Dimitrov was right.

"Fine. Leave it for now, but make no mistake Corporal, we'll come back for it. This place isn't safe anymore."

The ship's engines came online with the familiar low, droning hum. Lance ran towards the back of the ship, and began to climb the rungs to the second deck. The barracuda slowly began to lift off the ground. The sound of something cracking underneath them was unmistakable as the landing gear was torn clean off.

Dimitrov pulled Marcus over to the left side door with him, sliding it open to give them a better view of the ground as the ship listed at an altitude of some twenty meters off the ground, turning west to fly over the settlement.

Chapter 28

Her limousine had just arrived on the rooftop landing. Takahashi always observed anxiously by the window when she arrived.

"I really abhor those infernal machines," he said when she came down the elevator. "I really wish you wouldn't use them."

"I'm fine, Father," she assured him. "Really, they're quite safe."

"I know. I'm just afraid that…" he stuttered, unable to finish the sentence.

"…that I'll end up like her?" she finished, snidely.

His lack of response did little to ease the tension between them.

"So, have you eaten?" he spoke, finally.

"No, and I don't have time. I'm sorry to have to rush you, but I have to give a speech at a trade convention at 4:30," Mariko responded.

"You have to eat. Dominic has prepared a late lunch for us," he gestured towards a lavish table in the solarium.

A wide slanting window, nearly three stories tall, allowed the sun to soak the room in its basking glow. A variety of trees and flowers in a myriad of colors adorned the perimeter of the stone-tiled floor, creating the illusion of an outdoor setting. It was the only room in the enormous penthouse suite Takahashi enjoyed.

"Alright Father, but I must be brief," she submitted, rifling through her briefcase as she strode ahead of him towards the solarium. "You look tired, Father. Have you been spending all your time on the net again?" she asked, without taking her eyes off her files.

Takahashi took a seat at the end of the table, facing the striking view through the window.

"I'm fine. I'm more worried about you," he assured her.

Mariko reached for a platter with an array of miniature slices of bread with decorative toppings. She removed a single slice by means of an ornamental silver spade, only to leave it untouched on a plate engraved with floral patterns while she sifted through a stack of documents, arranging them in order.

"You need to sign these before I leave," Mariko informed him.

"Did you have any trouble locating him?" Takahashi asked.

"Not much," she said as she subconsciously poked and prodded her lunch with a silver fork.

She brought out her datapad and began reading through her messages.

"And he's agreed to work with us?"

"He has. It didn't take much convincing," she replied, not lifting her eyes from the screen.

"So everything is in place?"

"All the wheels are in motion," she said, raising her eyebrows and tilting her head patronizingly.

"You know you don't have to work so hard all the time."

"I like to keep myself busy. It helps me keep my mind off things…" she said, trailing off when she realized she'd revealed too much.

"But you haven't forgotten. You haven't moved on. Drowning yourself in work may distance you from what happened, but it isn't healthy," he tried to convince her.

"You're one to talk, Father! You spend nearly every waking hour on the net. You haven't been home since God knows when, and now you're lecturing me on how to live my life?" she burst out.

"That's different Mariko. I'm an old man. I've lived my life. Yours is just beginning," he appealed to her.

"I am living my life. I'm trying to make a difference!" she barked.

"Not like this. You should find a nice man, settle down. Forget about the quarterly reports for once, and leave the business to the old men," he wheedled, instantly regretting his last words.

"Old men? I'm just as good at this as any of you are! And why would I want to drag a man into my sad little life? So he can end up just like Mom?" she snarled.

"Sweetie, that was an accident. You can't expect that to happen to you. Your mother loved you more than life itself. She would never have wanted you to become like me. You know that."

"We both know that it wasn't an accident. Your ambition is what killed her. Those long hours, all those deals you made over the years. You made her a target. Even if it was an accident, it would only have been a matter of time before someone…" she growled.

Deep down, he knew that she was right. His worst fears had been exceeded. He'd always thought that she had just distanced herself from him because he reminded her too much of her mother. He'd never imagined that she blamed him for her death. He felt his aging heart breaking. If only she knew. She wouldn't forgive him, but perhaps with time she would come to understand.

"Can you please sign these, I really have to run," she said, with a visible effort to control herself, pocketing her datapad and pushing her plate to the side, her food still untouched.

"Alright. Have it your way," he responded, hurriedly signing each document in turn before pushing them back to her.

He could barely stand to look at her, to see the blame in her eyes. But he was loath to have her leave.

"Will you be back tonight? Dominic is making your favorite. Baked ziti with lamb and garlic ragou," he urged, half-hoping to solicit a positive response.

"I can't. I have a dinner meeting with Senator Alstrom regarding the new defense contract. The Republic is trying to short change us on the new CTC models. The whole thing is a mess, and I really need to sort it out," she concluded, grabbing the files and stuffing them back in her briefcase.

"At least let me find you a proper driver," he pleaded. "This new guy of yours doesn't have the experience."

"He's fine, Father. He comes highly recommended. He used to work for Intelligence, Division 4, so he knows how to handle himself."

She strode towards the elevator without as much as a word of goodbye.

Takahashi paced slowly towards the window, waiting to observe her departure. It wasn't long before her sleek craft emerged into view, jetting towards the busy skyline. He stood poised by the window, gazing at the city in all its splendor.

He was almost finished. The point of no return was coming up soon, and he would have to decide on how to proceed. He'd trusted his mentor up until now. With billions of lives hanging in the balance, how could he not be at least a little apprehensive?

It was fated to happen. Who was he to argue with fate? His mentor had been right about everything so far. He'd sacrificed so much for his vision for a better future, for all of them. Yet there were still so many forces working against him, and things could still go horribly wrong.

"Have faith," his mentor had told him.

Everything was about to change. The entire structure of Terran society would be thrown into turmoil.

It wasn't his faith that was lacking. It was theirs.

Takahashi caught himself once more staring at his own reflection. So many years had gone by. He had dedicated his life to his mentor. Now was not the time to have doubts.

His mind was at war with itself. He knew it was the right thing to do, yet he feared the outcome.

"Suzie, could you come in here for a moment?" he called.

"Yes Taki?" his assistant replied as she emerged from the hallway.

She was always so cheerful around him. He couldn't believe how much she reminded him of his daughter, back when she was still young and carefree. Back when she still loved him.

"Would you like to join me for a late lunch?" he asked with a half-forced smile.

Chapter 29

Heavily damaged as it was, Raven had severe trouble maintaining the barracuda's altitude as it soared over the Last Oasis. Packs of shriekers roamed the streets below, gorging themselves on the dead bodies littering the ground.

Marcus was devastated as he surveyed the scene from his vantage point in the ship's port-side hatch. The screaming had mostly subsided, although Marcus wasn't sure he'd have been able to hear it over the barracuda's engines if it hadn't. Most of the shriekers had already found their source of food for the night, and the rest roamed the streets in search of an unclaimed corpse as the Children of the Wastes huddled together inside their homes, desperately hoping to avoid alerting the shriekers to their presence. There were so many of them, Marcus thought.

Suddenly the cannon slung beneath the hull fired a round. The recoil vibrated through the ship. The shell impacted on the ground below, incinerating a small group of shriekers that had been intently feeding off a pair of bodies, tearing a hole in a nearby wall as it did so. Marcus nearly lost his grip on the rappelling bar as the blast went off.

"Is she insane?" Dimitrov blurted.

"Raven, don't fire the cannon! The streets are way too narrow, you'll just make matters worse," the Corporal shouted over the comms.

"It's not me," Raven replied. "The Sergeant is the one doing the shooting."

"Sergeant!" the Corporal called, just as another shot went off.

The front side of the building opposite the Black Lotus Inn collapsed as the Sergeant's aim missed its mark. The three shriekers that had been feeding off the bodies lying on the terrace scattered off into a nearby alleyway.

"Sergeant, what are you doing? There are people in those houses!" Dimitrov yelled, desperately trying to stop the Sergeant making a fatal mistake.

On the deck, Reid had begun regaining consciousness, doubtless due to the tremors reverberating through the ship each time the cannon went off. Taylor was at his side, making sure he hadn't sustained any permanent injuries.

"You're a lucky man Albano. Most people would have broken both legs after a fall like that," the medic told him.

The cannon went off again, this time killing a pair of shriekers at the end of a narrow street. Luckily, the damage to the surrounding structures was minimal, but the sudden screams of children from the nearest building, loud enough to be heard over the barracuda's humming engines, was quick to draw a crowd of hungry shriekers.

"We've got to stop him," Dimitrov yelled. "Marcus, with me."

The two of them withdrew from the side opening, and scrambled up the rungs to the second deck. The ship shook as the cannon fired once more. They burst through the door to the cockpit to find Lance sitting in the copilot's chair, with Adler lying unconscious on the floor next to him and Raven furiously trying to prevent him from firing another round with one hand while still attempting to keep the ship steady with the other.

"Sergeant!" Dimitrov shouted. "Have you gone stark raving mad?"

The Sergeant spun around angrily in his seat, glaring at the frantic Corporal.

232

"Have you forgotten your place, Corporal?" Lance barked.

"No, but you're firing a cannon into a narrow street. Those houses are filled with refugees!"

"He wouldn't listen," complained Raven, both hands back on the controls, desperately trying to gain altitude. "He knocked Scott out."

"He refused to follow orders!" the Sergeant yelled.

Marcus could see the palace through the ship's front window. A few of the shriekers were trying to climb over its walls. Just as they would get about midway up, they would lose their grip and slide back down to the ground.

"There!" pointed Marcus. "We should be safe inside the palace."

"Well spotted Grey," replied Raven. "I'm taking us in."

The Sergeant got up from his seat, turning to face Corporal Dimitrov.

"There are always casualties in war, Corporal," the Sergeant proclaimed, putting his hand on the Corporal's shoulder in a pathetic attempt to appease him. "See if you can wake Adler up, would you?" he added before darting past them into the stasis chamber, on his way down to the lower deck.

"That man needs a good slap in the face," Raven confided as she swerved around one of the palace towers.

Marcus and the Corporal managed to get Adler into his chair and, after a few moments of shaking and slapping the poor copilot across the cheek, he began to regain consciousness.

"That's a lot of tents down there!" Raven proclaimed as the ship hovered over the palace courtyard.

Marcus could see them too. The entire courtyard was filled to the brim with a chaotic arrangement of tents and refugees, many of whom had come out to see the ship hovering overhead. Some stood staring upwards, while others banked smoldering fires in an effort to dispel the darkness.

"There's no room to land. Any ideas Corporal?" Raven pleaded.

"We could rappel down and try and clear some room for you to land," Dimitrov suggested.

"Good enough for me."

"Sergeant," Raven called over the comms. "You're going to have to have everyone rappel down to the courtyard and clear some room for the ship." She flicked a series of switches on the control panel in front of her, then looked over her should at Marcus and Dimitrov. "You two'd better hurry downstairs too," she added before turning back to concentrate on keeping the ship steady.

Marcus and Corporal Dimitrov ran through the stasis chamber and slid down the ladder to the lower deck just as the squad began preparing their rappelling harnesses.

"Shrieker!" shouted Taz from the open left side door.

In one fluid motion, Reid grabbed his sniper rifle and rolled over on the deck, coming to one knee, rifle raised at the ready. He fired. The shrieker that had managed to climb to the top of the palace wall disappeared from view as its body fell back outside the wall, its head a mist of fragmented bone, skin and blood.

"Reid, keep a lookout while the squad rappels down," Lance ordered. "The rest of you, as soon as you touch ground I want you all to start clearing space for the ship to land. I don't care how you do it, just get it done!"

"Yes Sergeant!" the squad responded in unison.

Spielman and Raleigh were the first to descend, followed closely by Jago and Taylor. The ship tilted slightly as the monstrous behemoth jumped out of the ship and began rappelling down the rope.

"Dimitrov, Sobieski, Grey, you're next," the Sergeant barked.

Marcus hit the ground a bit too hard, sending a pain shooting up through his ankles to his knees. He'd landed in a small passage between two rows of dust-colored tents. Dimitrov and Taz landed more gracefully, and immediately began helping the others to convince the still half-asleep refugees to move their tents to make room for the ship's landing.

Most were reluctant at first. Many of them were too busy staring up at the ship in silent awe. As the squad fought to explain what their pilot needed to do, the refugees gradually took to packing up the closest tents and moving their belongings to a more suitable location.

Marcus glanced up and saw that the Sergeant and PFC Simone, the cute auburn-haired girl with the freckles, were getting ready to rappel down. Reid, his identification icon floating above the door on the far side of the barracuda from Marcus, was clearly still scanning the walls for any signs of shriekers. Simone slid down first, sharing a rope with the Sergeant, who followed quickly after her.

Marcus saw as Reid suddenly turned his rifle, focusing intently on a point at the top of the far wall. A lone shrieker had managed to clamber up the walls and was rearing its head. As Marcus watched, it let out a deafening, high-pitched shriek, aimed directly at Lance, a split second before Reid blew it apart with his rifle. Even though the Sergeant was at least twenty meters away, the sudden shock made him lose his grip on his descender. Lance plummeted down, landing straight on top of the unsuspecting Tara Simone, who likewise relinquished her harness.

Marcus gasped as he watched helplessly while the pair came crashing down to the ground. The Sergeant landed right on his ass. Marcus could hear the resounding crack when his back snapped.

Simone wasn't so lucky. She had spun in the air from her sudden impact with the Sergeant, leaving her to plunge headfirst into the stone-tiled floor. Her neck snapped, killing her instantly.

"Medic!" Marcus yelled, rushing to their aid.

Taylor heard the call and was quick to respond. A quick finger on Simone's pulse confirmed Marcus's fears. There was nothing they could do. The Sergeant lay unconscious as Taylor grabbed a pair of tent poles he found lying in the remains of a half-moved tent and placed them on either side of Lance. He then threaded and fastened an array of straps underneath the Sergeant, having Marcus assist him so as to avoid further damaging the Sergeant's spine.

"We've got to move him. The ship's about to land," Taylor said, gesturing Marcus to grab the other end of their makeshift stretcher.

"Taz!" Marcus shouted. "Clear a tent for us."

Taz snapped into action and ran to a nearby tent, and began asking the refugees to let them use the tent for emergency medical treatment. Marcus helped Taylor carry the Sergeant into the tent as the last of the refugees ducked out, staring wide-eyed at the unconscious Lance. Once Marcus had set down his end of the stretcher Taylor promptly dismissed him, assuring him that he would be more useful outside, helping the others secure the perimeter.

As Marcus emerged from the tent, the barracuda was just touching down in the clearing the squad had managed to form in the center of the courtyard. Reid jumped from the ship and immediately ran towards the closest tower, searching for a good vantage point from which to use his rifle. Dimitrov was busy shouting orders to the squad, as well as trying to get the Sheikh's Hajari to secure the courtyard and organize the refugees. With Lance incapacitated, he had clearly taken charge of the situation.

With less than two hours to go until sunrise, the squad took to the walls. The shriekers had a more difficult time climbing the palace walls than with the common buildings of the settlement, making it much easier to maintain the perimeter. Pretty soon the creatures had learned to stay clear of the building, feasting instead on the bodies already lying in the streets.

Marcus couldn't bear to think of little Sanjay, still lying there in front of the Black Lotus Inn, being devoured by some hellish beast. He felt such anger, such unbearable hatred. He wanted to open the gates and kill every last one of the aliens. He stood there on the walls as dawn crept over the horizon, tears swelling in his eyes. They'd lost so much in a single night. Only eleven of the squad still survived, and although he didn't think too fondly of the Sergeant, Marcus caught himself worrying whether or not he would survive the night.

Chapter 30

Dawn brought with it a complicated mixture of hope and despair as the creatures vanished shortly before the sun appeared on the horizon. Refugees inside the palace walls found comfort in the presence of the troops they had shunned only days before. Outside the walls locals and refugees alike sobbed and mourned the loss of their loved ones. A long line of worshipers waited their turn in front of the local temple, spilling well into the nearby streets. The remains of those who had lost their lives during the night were being attended to by the Sheikh's servants, who wandered the streets with camel-drawn carts. Each cart was already stacked with bodies, covered with canvas to hide their hideous state.

Taylor had emerged from the tent to smoke a cigarette and inform the newly-gathered squad of the Sergeant's state. Although still alive, the Sergeant was paralyzed from the waist down. Taylor assured the squad that the damage could be repaired, given the proper facilities, but for now there was nothing that could be done, save pain relief.

Marcus was amongst the first ordered to get some rest. They were supposed to sleep in short shifts during the early hours of the day, but Marcus couldn't sleep. His mind was tormented with the loss of his squadmates. Although he'd not felt particularly close to many of them, they were still among the few people he'd known his entire life. Mostly though, he mourned the loss of little Sanjay. For someone so young to experience such a horrible fate was beyond Marcus' imagining. He could only hope that the young boy had not been made to suffer too long.

More than anything he wanted to head out and hunt down the rest of the shriekers. He estimated that they must have killed nearly sixty the previous night, probably close to a third of them, still leaving a sizeable force to be reckoned with.

The familiar face of Doc Taylor appeared underneath the flap of the tent Marcus had claimed when the refugees headed out into the settlement to help with the clean-up, his usual half-smoked cigarette jutting from his lips as he peered down at his datapad, not even glancing at Marcus.

"Need something to help you sleep, Grey?" he inquired.

"What do you mean?" replied Marcus.

"Some of the others are having trouble falling asleep. If you want I can give you something to knock you right out. You really ought to get some rest," Taylor explained.

"I guess," said Marcus, halfheartedly. He didn't really care if he slept or not. His heart burned with too much hate. Sleep was the furthest thing from his mind.

He almost didn't even notice as the medic produced a small air hypo and injected him in the neck before departing once more. Marcus's anger lingered even as sleep began to overcome him. Hopefully this new day would grant him a release for his anger, some means to repay the shriekers for all the hurt and pain they had caused on this remote moon on the outskirts of the Terran solar system.

*　*　*　*　*

"Wake up Marcus," Dimitrov whispered, nudging him repeatedly.

Marcus opened his eyes. The heat in his tent was unbearable. He had slept no more than four hours, which meant the sun was already high overhead.

"Is something wrong?" asked Marcus, sitting up to perch on the edge of his cot.

"The Sergeant is insisting on keeping command of the squad, despite his injuries," Dimitrov informed him. "I need you to come with me to the GeoDynamics compound. I'm going to attempt to contact Alamo Station, and inform them that Taylor and I are relieving him from duty on account of his injuries."

"You can do that?"

"According to military law, yes. Although, given the Sergeant's demeanor of late, I think it's safer to inform the Alamo before we do so. It also gives us the opportunity to let them know what's been going on here."

Lance's actions had been exceedingly reckless and poorly thought-out during last night's engagements. And his temperament had been becoming increasingly erratic. He might not go so quietly.

"I'll come with you," Marcus proclaimed.

* * * * *

Rory wasn't all too pleased to see them, what with all the damage caused to his refinery. The steel walls of the main refinery building had provided him and his workers with the perfect shelter from the shriekers, but the damage to the water storage silo was beyond repair, and it would be costly to replace.

Luckily, Dimitrov approached him with humility and understanding. After a series of apologies, Rory allowed them to use his communications tower.

SERGEANT DAVID LANCE WOUNDED IN BATTLE, DEEMED UNFIT FOR DUTY BY SENIOR MEDICAL OFFICER PRESENT. DOUBTS REGARDING THE SERGEANT'S MENTAL STATUS. UNDER ARTICLE 3-A, CORPORAL DIMITROV WILL ASSUME COMMAND OF THE SQUAD.

THE LAST OASIS UNDER HEAVY ATTACK BY HOSTILE ALIEN LIFEFORMS. NUMBERS IN THE HUNDREDS. CIVILIAN CASUALTIES: HEAVY. MILITARY CASUALTIES: 9. REMAINING MILITARY PERSONEL FIT FOR DUTY: 10.

Dimitrov waited nearly twenty minutes for a reply. Although the message was merely a formality, confirmation would strengthen the Corporal's resolve, not to mention his position when he confronted Lance.

HQ CONCURS WITH MEDICAL ASSESSMENT. CORPORAL DIMITROV TO ASSUME COMMAND. REINFORCEMENTS INBOUND, ETA: 19 DAYS.

"Do you think he'll give you any trouble?" Marcus inquired.

"The Sergeant? No, I don't think so," the Corporal replied. "Lance is a bootlicker born and bred. He won't defy military law, unless he wants his career to come to an abrupt end." Dimitrov chuckled at the thought. "Come on, let's get back and see how he's doing."

* * * * *

Upon their return, Marcus and Dimitrov were greeted by Taylor. He'd been waiting for them to return outside the palace gates. Marcus was relieved to get back to the palace. He had averted his eyes as they had made their way through the settlement, carefully avoiding walking past the Black Lotus Inn. The smell of blood baking in the sun hung heavily in the air.

"Corporal, there's been a development," the medic informed Dimitrov, seemingly unalarmed as he lit a new cigarette and dragged the pair of them off to a side alcove just inside the palace.

"What's the problem?" Dimitrov sighed.

"In addition to the Sergeant's paralysis, my scanners indicate he's suffering from radiation poisoning."

"What?" the Corporal blurted, shocked at the medic's discovery.

"That's not all. The strange part is that my scanners can't classify the type of radiation he's been subjected to."

"How high a dose has he received?"

"It appears to have been a concentrated dose. Strangely though, it doesn't seem to be having any harmful effects on his physiology."

"Could this be what's been causing his strange behavior?"

"It could," Taylor concurred. "However, after everyone settled in this morning and I'd seen to the Sergeant's needs, I began running tests on the others."

"And…?" Dimitrov prompted.

"They've all been exposed. Even me."

"Then why hasn't anyone else's behavior been affected?"

"It's possible that the Sergeant's model had a more adverse reaction to this particular type of radiation," the medic theorized. "But there's no way to make sure."

"Alright Doc. We have to relieve him of his command," Dimitrov said. "Furthermore, I want you to keep a keen eye on everyone's behavior. If anyone starts to act irrationally, or displays any symptoms that might indicate they've been... compromised, I want you to act accordingly."

"Agreed."

"Let's go see the Sergeant. This ought to be interesting," Dimitrov mused.

"What about me, Corporal?" prompted Marcus.

"You'd best go gather the others. I'll need to address them after I'm finished with the Sergeant."

Marcus recruited Reid to assist him with rounding up the rest of the squad. They all gathered outside Sergeant Lance's medical tent. The squad could easily hear the argument taking place inside.

"Under Article 3, Section A, any Officer or Enlisted Personnel unfit to perform his duties due to mental or physical ailments can be relieved from duty by the ranking medical officer present!" Dimitrov shouted.

"He's a fucking medic, not a doctor!" the Sergeant yelled in response. "You can't relieve me of my command. This is MY squad."

"Doctor or not, we've received confirmation of Taylor's assessment from HQ. You're to be relieved of your command until you're physically fit to resume your duties," the Corporal overrode Lance's protests.

The rest of the squad grinned to each other, pleased to finally be rid of the Sergeant's authority. Marcus couldn't wait for Corporal

Dimitrov to assume command. He had great faith in his leadership, and saw him not only as a role model but also as someone he could confide in.

There was a sudden crack as a sidearm went off, startling them all. A dark stain spread across the side of the tent, blood, fragments of skull and gray matter.

Marcus's heart skipped a beat. He refused to believe what he'd just seen. Surely the Sergeant couldn't have…?

The members of the squad turned to each other in astonishment, a stunned expression on everyone's face. Marcus's lips quivered as he tried to scream out loud, but found himself unable to utter a single sound. Not Dimitrov, he thought. Surely Lance couldn't have…

He staggered forward, his legs barely moving. Reid grabbed him, seeing that he might fall to his knees.

Seconds later, Taylor emerged from the tent. Marcus had never seen him so serious and full of regret.

"He… he just… shot him," Taylor stammered.

The muscles in Marcus's face spasmed as tears began to form at the corners of his eyes.

"I've sedated him and removed his weapon," the medic informed them somberly, gesturing to a sidearm shoved roughly through his belt. The look on his face was one of wracking shame, as if the blame were entirely his.

Marcus couldn't believe it, refused to believe it. Every time he got close to someone they were taken away from him. First Steven, then Eve, and now Corporal Dimitrov. He staggered to his feet, wanting nothing more than to rush into the tent and end Lance's miserable existence then and there, but somehow he knew that wasn't what Dimitrov would have wanted.

As the initial shock wore off, the squad turned to one another for some indication of how they were to proceed.

"What do we do now?" Taz blurted.

There was no immediate answer.

"Well, Spielman is Acting Sergeant for now," Taylor informed them. They all looked to the newly-promoted Sergeant Spielman, who didn't seem all too enthusiastic about his new role. "Grey, you're Acting Corporal," Taylor added, almost muttering under his breath.

Spielman stepped into the center of the group, looking around at his squadmates and taking a moment to ponder how best to proceed. "We've taken some heavy losses, there's no denying that," confessed the newly-appointed Sergeant. "But that doesn't mean we can't still function as a squad."

Marcus wasn't too pleased to be appointed Acting Corporal. He didn't feel worthy to replace Corporal Dimitrov. He just stared down at the ground in quiet resolution.

"Given that we only have nine men fit for duty, I think it best to split the squad into two teams, not three. Since the ship is out of order, we'll have to repurpose our pilots as well. We'll need every man and woman for the fight ahead. Those creatures will be back," Spielman said. "Corporal Grey, you'll lead Sobieski, Albano and Adler. Raynes, Raleigh, the Doc and Raven are with me." He looked around, taking the squad's silent nods for assent.

"Did you hear me Grey?"

Marcus hadn't been paying particular attention to his new Sergeant's speech. His mind was still overcome with sadness, a feeling he was becoming so accustomed to.

"Yes Sergeant," he replied, half-heartedly.

"Now, we know these beasts are nocturnal, right Doc?" Spielman asked.

"That's correct Sergeant."

"Good. Then I say we take the fight to them."

"But they outnumber us at least ten to one!" Taz blurted.

Spielman grinned, a sly smile crossing his lips. "True. But if we engage the enemy during daylight, we can catch them by surprise as they sleep."

The squad nodded in approval, looking to one another for assurance.

"I say we go and give those sons of bitches everything we've got. It's time for payback!" the Sergeant roared, to the sudden cheering of the crowd.

Marcus felt his blood burning with eager anticipation. Revenge, he thought. His grip tightened around the pistol-grip of his carbine, his teeth grinding at the thought of avenging the deaths of his squad mates, of little Sanjay, and all the others who had been lost to the shriekers.

* * * * *

The GeoDynamics communications tower was empty as a shadowy figure crept towards the control room. It kept to the shadows. Avoiding the few outdated security cameras proved all too easy. The figure produced a small device which it promptly attached to a port on the communication console.

A series of lights began to blink in rapid succession as the device decrypted the console's security cipher. The figure took a seat, just as the device blinked green.

ACCESS GRANTED.

STILL NO APPARENT SYMPTOMS. SUBJECTS IN IMMEDIATE DANGER.
REQUEST REINFORCEMENTS.

The response only took two minutes, suggesting that its source had to be much closer than the shadowy figure had anticipated.

REINFORCEMENTS ALREADY EN ROUTE. ETA: 28 HOURS. CONTINUE TO MONITOR SUBJECTS. SUBJECTS' SURVIVAL PARAMOUNT.

The figure pressed a button on the decoder, which promptly erased any trace of the communication, before stealthily exiting through the tower's back door and slipping silently away.

Chapter 31

They had to act quickly if they were to make use of the remaining daylight. Knowing full well that the settlement could not withstand another attack, the squad had marched into the GeoDynamics facility in order to commandeer one of Rory's mining trucks. It was already midday, and it would take them at least a couple of hours to drive to the crash site, where they hoped to find the shriekers.

The vehicle they chose resembled a tank more than a truck. Gray metal plating was riveted over its sturdy frame. A cockpit protruded from above the formidable drilling machinery it mounted behind the engine block. The cockpit's reinforced windows were framed in orange-painted steel, with ladders running to it from the thin platforms that ran the length of the vehicle above a row of four tires on each side. There was only room for one person in the cockpit, but the rest of the squad easily fit on top of the running boards.

"Ye can't take my driller!" Rory roared, his motorized cart kicking up clouds of dust as it whizzed back and forth around the compound, trying to prevent the squad from scavenging what they needed for their journey.

"We'll have it back to you in a few hours," Spielman tried to explain to him, if only the refinery manager would stay still long enough to hear him out.

Marcus was busy scrounging through a pile of canisters searching for something to fuel the massive vehicle.

"Grey, check the warehouse!" Spielman shouted, taking note of Marcus's plight.

The massive doors of the warehouse stood open. The motor that usually powered them had malfunctioned in the flooding caused by the rupture of the water silo. Marcus passed Jago, who was returning from the palace with cases of ammunition from the barracuda, before entering the massive structure. Inside, the ceiling was easily five times his height. Stacks of crates and barrels filled every corner of the warehouse, casting gloomy shadows over the narrow corridors between them.

Marcus made his way along the corridors, reminded suddenly of the training they'd been subjected to in the simulation room back on the Alamo. How much he missed those days! Back when he still had no idea what was ahead, before everything got so complicated. The path swerved back around towards the entrance. Marcus's gaze was suddenly drawn to an area off to the side of the door, where a stack had toppled over during the ruckus the night before. Half buried under a pile of crates and boxes, Marcus saw the probe the squad had returned upon their arrival on New Io.

It's good that Lance hadn't seen this, he thought, amusing himself with the notion.

Nonetheless, he approached the pile and began digging the probe out. Taber had died because of the damned thing. Marcus might as well make sure he hadn't died in vain. As the probe was slowly revealed, Marcus saw that it had indeed been damaged. Its front panel was heavily dented, and loose on all but one side. As he dragged the probe out of the pile, the loose panel came off entirely, clanging as it hit the floor.

Marcus bent down to pick it up. As he knelt to fix it back into position, he stopped. All his recent technical training came flooding to the front of his mind, manuals and guides, speed-read over the long days and nights on guard duty.

This was no probe.

He had limited training, and most of what he had learned he had crammed into his brain in such a short amount of time that he had very little familiarity with it, but his curiosity spurred him onward. He rushed to an old toolbox lying haphazardly on the floor next to an old engine that someone had clearly been trying to repair, grabbing a powered screwdriver and an old tech scanner before returning to the false probe.

He began removing the casing entirely, stripping the circuitry from its protective shell. As the plates came away, Marcus could see that the digital readout on the control panel wasn't even connected to the device in the probe's main body. Although the keypad initiated the actual device, the readout displayed pre-recorded data stored on a memory device embedded in the back of the readout.

Was it all a lie? Why would someone send them half way across the solar system to perform a fake reading on an abandoned ball of rock? Questions flooded his mind as he continued to study the peculiar-looking device. This is a field amplifier, he thought as he inspected one of the device's subcomponents. These coils would exponentially increase the buildup of power from the generator down there at the bottom, fueling some sort of reaction.

But what did it do?

"Grey!" came Spielman's voice from outside the warehouse. "Sobieski found some fuel in one of the smaller sheds. We have to move now if we want to have any chance of catching them before sunset," the Sergeant called.

Marcus paused briefly as he contemplated whether or not he should call Spielman over and show him his discovery. No, it would have to wait. As the Sergeant had said, they had no time. The safety of the settlement had to come first. He pocketed the tech scanner and the powered screwdriver, thinking they might come in use later.

"I'm coming," he shouted back as he began piling debris in front of the probe so no one would tamper with it in their absence.

* * * * *

As the mining vehicle's engines began to drone, the vehicle shook violently. Marcus and the others were perched on the running boards above the wheels, while Raven sat in the cockpit steering the massive truck. They had to go out through a massive gate in the outer wall of the GeoDynamics compound. Rory had ordered his workers to keep the gate closed, but when Spielman had threatened to have Raven drive right through it, the refinery manager had caved in. The immense steel door slid sideways into the wall, slowly allowing their passage out into the wasteland.

As the massive vehicle made its way around the settlement's walls, heading southeast in the direction of the crash site, Marcus turned to look back at the settlement. He couldn't help but wonder what would happen to the Children of the Wastes if they were to fail in their mission. Still, he was pleased that they were finally taking matters into their own hands. For the whole of his short existence he'd been told to do things, ordered to do things, or manipulated into doing things he didn't want to do. Worse yet, their first real mission had been a lie that had cost lives. That truly made his blood boil with anger.

Who knows what the device had been doing on Triton? Marcus mused. Perhaps it was the so-called 'probe' that had caused the radiation poisoning that had affected Sergeant Lance, resulting in the death of Corporal Dimitrov. His friend. Marcus was tired of being pushed around and not told what was going on. Now their mission was simple, and one of their own choosing.

Chapter 32

Marcus gazed intently at the horizon, where the Last Oasis was slowly disappearing from sight.

"He spoke very highly of you, you know," Reid confided, leaning in close to Marcus to be heard over the roar of the drilling rig, clearly not wanting to talk over their helmets' comms, through which the rest of the squad could overhear what they were saying.

Marcus knew that he was just trying to make him feel better, but the thought of Dimitrov having spoken of him to the others with such regard gave him some measure of assurance.

"He said you had great potential," Reid continued.

Marcus didn't reply. He merely smiled disingenuously at the sniper, hoping he would take the hint and let the matter drop. He didn't really feel like discussing anything to do with the recently-deceased Corporal.

"He's watching you, you know. Somewhere, out there," Reid went on.

Marcus furrowed his brow. The idea of an incorporeal Dimitrov somehow monitoring his every move, perhaps even judging him, didn't really appeal to him.

The mining truck diligently continued its long trek across the wasteland, headed towards the site of the crashed asteroid. The going was slower than they'd anticipated, and the sun was already closing in on the horizon. It would be dark in an hour or so. The worried expression on Sergeant Spielman's face said more about their dilemma than any words could.

"What do you want to do after your tour of duty?" Reid asked at a more normal volume as the truck dipped across the ridge of yet another sand dune.

"I… I haven't really given it much thought," Marcus confessed.

Reid followed Marcus's gaze to where the Last Oasis, now completely vanished from view, had been.

"I want to see the world, spread the word of God," Reid told him.

"A priest?" Taz chimed in from the back of the truck, having listened in on their conversation.

"Something wrong with that Taz?" Reid barked, grimacing.

"Not at all, I think its genius! It's probably a great way to meet girls. Think about it! Who are they gonna trust more than a priest? Tell their intimate secrets, all vulnerable and stuff," piped Taz.

"You're disgusting!" Reid bellowed.

"Well excuse me, Mr. High and Mighty."

"What about you Taz? What are you going to do when you're free?" Marcus broke in, hoping to avoid a full-scale argument.

"I'm gonna open up a bar or a nightclub. I want to be my own boss and have someplace where I'll be surrounded by enough booze and gorgeous girls to last me a lifetime."

"How are you going to afford that? You spend all your money on booze and girls as it is," Reid jeered.

"I'm gonna find me a nice rich girl," Taz professed, proudly.

Marcus and Reid burst out in laughter. Taz's antics never ceased to amaze them.

"What about you Ape?" probed Marcus, nudging the dozing giant.

"What?" Jago muttered, startled by their sudden interest in him.

"What do you want to do once all this is over? When you're finished with the military?"

"Hmm. I dunno. Maybe find a town like this. Someplace small, in the middle of nowhere. Where there's no Sergeants or guard duty, only simple people, farmers and such. In a place like that a big guy like me can be king. Everyone's afraid of big guys," Jago told them, his enthusiasm clearly genuine.

When the laughter had subsided, Marcus allowed his mind to wander. He'd dreamed of what it would be like to live out his life on Alpha Terra before making his choice, but since his betrayal he hadn't allowed himself to consider what his future might have in store for him. He'd seen what Beta Terra looked like on the viewscreen in Eve's quarters on the Alamo. While it had looked intriguing, he hadn't found all the chaos and clutter of Terran society all that appealing.

No, Marcus wanted something simpler. The life of the Children of the Wastes spoke to him. The truth and honesty of such a simple way of life felt much more alluring than what little he knew of life on Beta Terra. Perhaps he would live out his life here, among these people who had shunned the squad when they first arrived. Perhaps when he was free from the military, they would accept him with open arms.

"Sergeant," Raven prompted from the cockpit. "I've got an incoming transmission from Rory."

"Patch it through to my comms," Spielman ordered.

Marcus heard over the comms as the Sergeant stepped over the clones on the other running board to get to the back of the platform, where the noise from the massive vehicle's engine wasn't as loud. Marcus couldn't see him for the drilling equipment slung between the platforms, but a few moments later he addressed the squad on the comms, his tone troubled.

"Have any of you heard of a ship called the *TFS Genesis*?" he asked.

The squad looked inquisitively at one another.

"Isn't that Captain Intari's battleship?" Taz asked after a moment's pause.

"How do you know that?" Spielman asked.

"Well, I… it's just a rumor that I heard on the Alamo," Taz professed, sounding unsure of himself.

"What is?" the Sergeant pressed.

"Well, they say that Captain Intari is a high-ranking member of Division 6," Taz went on. "But there's no proof, of course. Hell, I'm not even sure that Division 6 is real."

"What's Division 6?" Marcus asked, his curiosity spurring him to join in the conversation.

"Well, officially, there are five divisions in the military intelligence hierarchy, right? But there are rumors that there's a sixth division too, and that it has jurisdiction over anything to do with psionic abilities."

"Psionics abilities? What are psionics abilities?" the Sergeant asked, clearly skeptical.

"Psionics is a term used for people with highly-developed mental abilities. Some of them are said to be able to read minds, others can see the future," Taz explained, thrilled that the others were finally taking an interest in his wild theories.

"That stuff really exists?" Reid asked.

"Oh yeah! There are some theories that people like that have existed throughout the ages. Division 6 is said to be working on breeding more powerful psionics through DNA manipulation and gruesome experiments."

"And this ship is one of theirs?" the Sergeant prompted.

"That's what the rumors say. Of course, none of this can be proven. But then, it wouldn't be a very good secret conspiracy if it could," Taz mused.

"Sergeant, why are you so interested in this?" Reid probed.

"Because it's headed our way," Spielman announced. "Rory told me that it's just appeared on his sensors. It'll be here in approximately twenty five hours."

"The *Genesis* is coming here?" blurted Taz, alarmed.

Marcus couldn't help but wonder how this tied in with his discovery of the probe. He suddenly felt an urge to confide in the others what he'd learned. They had as much right to know as he did. Even if there was nothing they could do about it at the moment.

"There's more," interjected Marcus.

The others stared at him intently.

"You knew about this?" Spielman asked.

"No. I had no idea. But there's something else that came to my attention just before we left the settlement. I had thought it'd be best to wait until we were back in the Last Oasis before I told you, but, given all this about Division 6, I think you should all know now."

"Well, what is it?" Taz whispered, his anxiety reaching new heights.

"The probe we brought with us to Triton and delivered to the GeoDynamics facility. I saw it in the warehouse when I was looking for fuel for the truck earlier. It was all dented and bent out of shape, and one of the panels had come loose." He paused, his mouth dry.

"…and?" the Sergeant prompted.

"I don't know what it was, but I know what it wasn't. That thing was no probe," Marcus revealed to the others' astonishment.

"How do you know that?" protested Taz.

"Because Lance asked me to fill in for Taber as the squad's technician a few days ago. Since then I've been reading a lot of material on engineering, technical manuals, electronics courses, things like that. Whatever that device was, it wasn't meant to take any readings whatsoever. The results were already present on a data-storage device embedded in the display screen."

"What the hell is going on?" Spielman pondered.

"Could this be what made Lance so sick?" Taz asked, excitedly starting to form his own theories.

"I don't know. There's no way to tell unless we strip that thing down and study it thoroughly," Marcus claimed.

"I knew it. I knew there was something wrong," Taz proclaimed hysterically. "Division 6 did this. They're experimenting with us like we're fucking lab rats. When the *Genesis* gets here, they're gonna do all kinds of horrible experiments on us then dissect us!"

"Calm down Sobieski," the Sergeant ordered.

"Taz might be right Sergeant. I've got an itch. Something doesn't feel right," Reid offered.

"Whether he's right or not, there's no use getting everyone riled up. We have to approach this with caution. We can't just assume the worst and act accordingly. Taz said it himself, Division 6 is just a rumor," the Sergeant replied. "Besides, we've got other, more pressing, things to worry about."

Deep down, Marcus suspected that Taz was right. What else could explain his dream? He'd foreseen the attack on the settlement. He'd seen little Sanjay dead on the ground outside the Black Lotus Inn before it had happened. His dream had even helped him save Dimitrov.

Nothing like that had ever happened to him before they'd taken the probe to Triton. Had it changed him somehow? Changed all of them? If only he'd acted on his dream sooner, then perhaps he could have prevented the whole thing from ever taking place – the attack, all those deaths.

The sun was beginning to set on the horizon. The shriekers would be awake soon, and they were still several miles from the crash site.

"Raven, we have to go faster," bellowed Sergeant Spielman.

"It won't go any faster than this Sergeant," she replied.

Gloom swept over the squad as they realized that they wouldn't make it in time to catch the creatures in their sleep. Silence overcame them as they each contemplated their predicament. The shriekers would be awake, and attack them in full force out in the open. If they survived the night, which didn't seem likely, the *TFS Genesis* would be arriving the very next evening, bringing salvation, and, quite possibly, a whole new range of problems.

Minutes dragged by like hours as Marcus began giving up hope.

"Sergeant, this thing's survey scanners are picking up something big," Raven called.

"Where?"

"Just over the next ridge. Whatever it is, it's massive, and almost pure metal."

"Helmets on people, and ready weapons," the Sergeant ordered.

As the mining vehicle made the steep climb over the last ridge, the squad huddled at the front of the platforms, ready to engage the horde of ferocious beasts they were expecting to fall upon them at any moment. The truck dipped slowly down at the crest of the ridge, its suspension giving way as the front end hit the ground. Before them, roughly half a kilometer away, lay the smoldering ruins, not of a meteorite or falling star, but of an awe–inspiringly massive starship. Its alien structure, easily over a kilometer long and more than a hundred meters wide, towered over the surrounding landscape. The dark-gray, organically-shaped hull was adorned with strange, glowing red runes. It had carved a long, deep trench into the ground as it had come hurtling down and collided with the surface of New Io. Smoldering rubble lay strewn about the surrounding valley.

None of them had even noticed that the truck had stopped. They stared in quiet wonder, their mouths agape, their eyes filled with amazement.

Chapter 33

The dark gray alloy of the ship's hull shimmered hues of magenta as the evening light refracted from it. The squad had approached from the left rear side of the ship, searching for any sign of an opening. The ship towered some forty meters above them. Judging by what they'd seen on their approach, it was dug in pretty deep, suggesting that at least some of the ship's many decks were below the surface.

"Over there!" Taz pointed.

It was a small alcove just above ground level that seemed to have once been covered by a two by three meter panel, which had doubtlessly been broken off in the crash. Spielman gestured for the squad to approach with caution. There had been no signs of the shriekers so far, which had them all nervous. Inside the alcove was an entryway, and alien symbols written in red were prominent both on one side of the door blocking their progress and on a small panel covered in buttons.

"Corporal Grey, see if you can get this door open," the Sergeant called.

Marcus took out the scanner he'd taken from the GeoDynamics warehouse, and tried to use it on the panel. The readings were inconclusive. The scanner couldn't even manage to register the type of energy the device was using. Marcus began pressing the buttons at random in the hope of exciting a reaction, praying the keypad wasn't password protected.

"Any time now Grey," Spielman muttered.

Marcus continued to press the rows of buttons randomly. Suddenly there was the hiss of air escaping and the door flew open. Startled, the men jumped back half a step.

Inside, a short corridor ran to a T-junction up ahead. Everything was bathed in a dim red light. Marcus looked to the Sergeant for orders.

"Sobieski, take the lead," the Sergeant called.

Taz hesitated momentarily before stalking into the corridor. As soon as he'd taken a couple of steps inside a heavy door at the end of the corridor slammed down, blocking further passage.

"Wahona hawilimi tsi kadu lidoya," a deep booming voice resounded through the corridor, repeating the phrase again before falling silent.

"Um, that doesn't sound so good," Taz muttered as he began backing up again. "I think I may have triggered something."

"Is there a panel? Some way of opening that door?" the Sergeant asked.

Marcus crept cautiously down the short corridor to get a better look, peering into every corner and shadowy indentation. "Nothing Sergeant. We must have triggered some sort of alarm," Marcus informed him.

"Can we cut through it?"

"I don't have the necessary tools. We could blast through, but that would ruin any chance of surprise we have left."

"In that case, we'll have to find another way in," Spielman decided. "Let's move to the other side of the ship. Perhaps we'll have better luck there."

The team quickly reorganized, and began making their way around the backside of the vessel. One of the massive thrusters had broken off, and lay embedded in the sand behind the ship. It was nearly five times as tall as a man, with wires and tubes sticking out from the shattered connection that had held it in place on the hull. Marcus had seen the massive ships of the Terran Forces, but they'd always been too far away for him to truly appreciate their size. This downed alien craft provided him with a new perspective.

The squad kept their weapons at the ready, as if they expected to run into a horde of angry shriekers at any moment. Most likely they had made their den in the wreckage of the ship, Marcus thought. He wondered who or what had been piloting the massive vessel. Surely the shriekers weren't the ones operating it. Such savage beasts wouldn't possess the intelligence needed for such a task. As they circumvented the rear section of the ship, the damage to the starboard side of the hull became apparent. The hull plating was all twisted and bent out of shape, with long tears running its length and three wide cracks gaping in the gray metal.

"Raleigh, I'm assigning you scout duty," Spielman proclaimed.

"What? Why me?" Jenna protested.

"Because our team needs a scout. I can't risk Raven or the Doc, and the Ape is just too damn big. You're it," the Sergeant ordered.

"Crap," Jenna blurted, realizing there was no way out of it.

Marcus couldn't help but be slightly amused. Jenna had always been able to get around having to pull her weight by using her feminine wiles, appealing to the macho instincts of some of the male clones. This was the first time Marcus had ever seen her having to take point instead of cowering behind Jago.

"We'll test our luck with the first opening. Jenna, you go ahead and see if it's clear," the Sergeant prompted.

Jenna dragged her feet as she approached the mound of sand and debris leading up to the tear in the ship's hull, as if prolonging the task would somehow get the Sergeant to change his mind. She cleared away some of the rubble blocking the gap, shouldering her carbine as she was forced to use both hands to steady herself as she waded through the debris. She finally reached the opening. It was a good meter and a half up from the ground, but large enough that even Jago could fit through it.

Not the most graceful person, Jenna threw her carbine through the opening before trying to climb up herself. Her armor weighed her down heavily as she clambered up, struggling to lift her leg high enough to get through. The squad amused themselves at her expense. Marcus felt slightly ashamed that he could so easily take pleasure in someone else's shortcomings. She paused just as she managed to get one leg up on the rim. Spielman shook his head in disbelief as she hung there, not moving.

"Any time now, Private Raleigh," prompted the Sergeant.

Jenna gave no response, still clinging to the ledge, her foot planted in the corner of the gaping wound to the ship's hull.

"Raleigh, get your ass moving!" Spielman barked, losing his patience.

Still, Jenna didn't respond.

Suddenly her other leg, dangling down the side of the hull, began to spasm, subtly at first, then kicking the side of the hull until she lost her grip on the ledge and plummeted down the mound of debris. She landed on her back and began rolling down the mound as the squad sprang forward to help her.

"Wait!" Reid shouted.

They stopped in their tracks, looking back at Reid for an explanation, as Jenna slid to a stop at the base of the mound of rubble.

"Radiation spike," Reid informed them, pointing to his helmet.

Marcus looked at all the little readouts on his heads-up display, and saw that Reid was right. The readout was displaying near dangerous levels of radiation. The squad took several steps back, all but Taylor, who cautiously approached Jenna. He knelt down, and began removing her helmet. As her face came into view, the medic cringed, turning his head away in disgust. Marcus leaned over to see, knowing even as he did that he shouldn't.

He saw it. Jenna's face was distorted, her skin half melted away, her nose drooping, exposing the cartilage underneath. He wanted to look away, but he couldn't. Her eyes were milky white, her pupils no longer visible.

"Can you fix her?" Jago asked, naively. Marcus couldn't help but hear the subtle hint of anguish in the huge man's voice.

"She's gone," the medic exclaimed. "There's nothing I can do."

Marcus was in shock. He was so ashamed that, mere moments earlier, he'd laughed to himself at what he'd mistakenly thought to be her clumsiness. Taylor stepped back, removing his helmet so that he could swallow a pair of anti-radiation pills from his medical kit.

"What do we do now?" inquired Taz.

There was a long pause before the Sergeant finally replied. "We continue. We can't afford to stop now. We've come all this way. If we leave now, she'll have died for nothing."

"What about the radiation?" asked Taz.

"We don't know how spread out it is. It might be localized to the rear section of the ship. Just keep watch on your readouts, and we should be ok," Reid interjected.

"Should we try the second tear?"

"No, it looks too high up. The third seems a better option. It's also further away from the radiation," the Sergeant said.

"What about Jenna?" asked Jago, the poor Ape's heart reaching breaking point. "We can't leave her here."

"We can't move her," explained Taylor. "Just carrying her back to the mining truck would…"

"I'll do it!" yelled the Ape, lunging forward to grab Jenna's body firmly and lifting it over his monstrous shoulders.

"No Jago!" Spielman shouted, but it was too late. The behemoth was already sprinting as fast as he could back to the truck, with Taylor fast on his heels.

The squad waited in silence for their return. Jago was popping anti-radiation pills as if they were candied treats, and even then he didn't look so good.

"He'll be fine," Taylor said. "The pills should do the trick in about an hour or two."

Jago was breathing heavily, sweat pouring down his brow, as he set his helmet back in place.

"You ok Jago?" the Sergeant inquired, placing his hand on the huge man's monstrous shoulder in reassurance.

"I'm ok boss," he replied wearily.

"Good. Then let's move. Taz, you take the lead."

"Lucky me," replied Taz sarcastically.

The squad moved forwards, past the center crack in the hull and onward to the third, all the while keeping their weapons at the ready, still expecting the shriekers to jump from even the smallest crevasse at any moment.

"Where the hell are they?" Spielman blurted after a few tense moments.

"Maybe they had their fill yesterday," Taz suggested.

"Maybe."

Nearing the last and largest tear in the hull, the Sergeant ordered Taz and Marcus to scout the interior, reminding them to keep an eye on their radiation meters. Taz went in first, taking small, calculated steps and diving immediately to the side once he was through the gap, keeping his back to the wall and looking every which way for the slightest sign of movement. Marcus moved in behind him, taking the other side of the opening. He started to scan the room for any signs of the shriekers, but was quickly overcome with the sight before him.

The compartment they were in was roughly as wide as the ship, and about thirty meters long. A pair of half-open heavy-set doors, nearly five meters high, led towards the rear of the ship. A smaller pair of doors in the center of the opposite wall, to Marcus' right, allowed access to the front section of the ship. A third set of doors, also leading forward, was off to the side, but higher than, the main doors, approachable via a series of metal steps and a catwalk. Wide cracks had formed in the center of the chamber floor, urging caution when Marcus stepped forward to examine the room more closely.

The dim blue light emanating from a series of computer consoles and panels filling most of the room served as the chamber's only light source. The sheer number of them gave Marcus the impression that, whatever this room was, it had to serve an important function, integral to the ship's operation. A low droning noise echoed throughout the chamber, originating from somewhere below him. There was no movement, but Marcus was filled with an imminent sense of foreboding as he mustered up the courage to wave the rest of the squad to enter. The others poured through the crack, one by one, each one pausing briefly to take in the scene before spreading out to cover the doors.

"Holi odaw nogadimi!" the same deep, booming voice from their first entrance resounded through the chamber, repeating the phrase again and again at short intervals.

"Visiting hours are over?" Taz jested, somewhat more comfortable now that the others were with them.

"Cut it out Sobieski," Spielman ordered. "Grey, see what you can find out from those controls."

Marcus moved over to the centermost console, taking great care not to step too close to any of the cracks in the deck. The symbols on the screen were completely alien to Marcus, and the arrangement was unlike anything he had ever seen. The display screen showed a series of boxes, each one with several rows of symbols and diagrams, of which Marcus could make neither heads nor tails. The tech scanner was of little help.

"Uh, Sergeant. I really have no idea what I'm dealing with here." Marcus admitted.

Spielman paused briefly, pondering how best to proceed. "Ok. We'll check the rear section first."

As the squad carefully made their way past the tall, heavy doors to the rear section of the ship, they all kept one keen eye on the radiation meter. Once through, they were greeted with the sight of a long hallway, lined with thick glass on either side. The space on each side of the hallway was segmented with thick metal walls to create dozens of compartments. Dim, shadowy figures loomed in the far corners of each cell as they made their way down the deck. The hallway itself was dimly lit via illuminated panels in the ceiling, bathing the otherwise dark cells in a faint glow.

"What are they?" the Sergeant whispered, taking slow steps from cell to cell as he peered inside, trying to catch a glimpse of their occupants.

Marcus went further into the hallway, spotting a larger cell further down the hallway, on the left side. There was something inside it, something big. As he approached the glass, the occupant began to take shape. A massive fractured skeleton, at least ten meters long, lay inside the cell. It was in such poor condition that Marcus wasn't able to even begin to imagine what it had looked like when it was alive, nor did he particularly want to. Light pierced through a large tear in the back wall, exposing the compartment to the desert.

"Eaten," blurted Marcus.

Taz leaned up against the glass of a nearby cell, trying to see what was inside. Without warning, a pair of slimy, grotesque creatures slammed into the window, splattering the glass with a layer of obscuring ooze and sending the poor scout flying back across the hallway, crying out in fear. A pair of circular maws with small, sharp teeth along their rims sucked fervently on the glass, as if oblivious to their owners' incarceration.

"What the hell is this place?" Taz blurted frantically.

"A freak show," the words escaped Marcus's lips without him even realizing it.

Chapter 34

"The shriekers must have come from this cage," Spielman said, looking down at another compartment open to the desert.

"They must have gotten out through the tear in the hull. But where's the crew?" Reid asked.

The creatures in the rest of the cells were keeping quiet, all but a pair of grotesque, winged specimens that looked like a cross between a giant bug and a lizard with a wide-rimmed sucker lined with teeth. They were all too fond of propping themselves up against the glass whenever anyone ventured too close, flaring their fangs in an aggressive territorial display.

"We should carry on. They have to be around here somewhere," the Sergeant said.

They returned once more to the first chamber, where Spielman decided to split the squad in two to cover more ground. He ordered Marcus to lead his team up the catwalk to the second door leading towards the front section of the ship, while he himself took the rest of the squad through the doorway below.

To their surprise, the doors flew open as soon as the clones approached. A strong smell of chlorine filled their noses as Marcus and his team entered a long, narrow corridor, filled waist-high with misty vapors that slowly began to disperse as they waded forward. As the smell of chlorine began to dissipate, an even fouler stench took its place. Everywhere the team looked, the surface of the corridor's walls and ceiling was stained with years, if not decades, of accumulated crud and grease. It was as if it had never been cleaned.

"They must not be partial to hygiene," Taz mused.

"Careful," urged Marcus, waving Taz forwards to take point.

"I really don't like the looks of this," the scout complained as he took the lead.

"We've got your back Taz," Reid assured him, slinging his rifle over his shoulder and drawing his sidearm.

"It's not my back I'm worried about," Taz sighed.

The sides of the hallway were lined with heavy support beams every three meters, slanted slightly inwards towards the center of the corridor. Between each of them was a metal door and access panel. The same alien runes they'd seen on the control panels below were engraved above each panel on a plaque of burnt-crimson stone. Each carried a different arrangement of symbols.

"What do you suppose these are?" Marcus asked, barely taking his eyes off the far end of the corridor, afraid that if he would look away even for a split second, a shrieker would emerge from the slowly-fading mist and devour him.

"Storage, cells, crew quarters, could be anything," Adler, the copilot, offered. He seemed remarkably unafraid, excited even.

"We should check one. Perhaps there are survivors," Reid suggested.

Marcus nodded his approval, and gestured towards the nearest door.

Taz and Reid backed up to nearby adjoining support beams, using them for cover as they scanned the two ends of corridor, while Marcus and Adler approached the door. The keypad had only two buttons, one blue and the other red, both of them emitting a soft glow.

Marcus looked to Adler, who simply shrugged his shoulders. Marcus pressed the blue button and quickly took a step back, raising his carbine in anticipation.

The door stood still.

Adler leaned forward and pressed the red button. The door promptly flew open, revealing a narrow compartment faintly illuminated with the same eerie red light as the first access point the team had tried. The chlorine vapors that had filled the corridor now seeped out from inside the room. Marcus held his weapon at the ready as he stepped lightly into the room.

The same stench and lack of visible hygiene soon became evident. It was compartmentalized into three distinct areas, one after the other, accessible via arched entryways in the center of the dividing walls. The first compartment held a small table and round stool with a peculiar device embedded firmly in the table's center. An orange holographic sphere, flickering constantly on and off, floated above the device. Marcus despaired of trying to understand the ship's technology on such short notice, and proceeded quickly into the next compartment.

On his left, a tube, roughly the size of a man, the bottom half made from shimmering, grease-stained metal, the upper half from a slightly milky glass, housed a bizarre looking suit of armor in a strangely-proportioned, humanoid form. Marcus stopped to stare at it. It seemed to be made out of faded red chitin, painted with white patterns and symbols. There was no visible means by which to open the tube, so Marcus quickly shifted his focus to the other side of the narrow room. A sand-colored oval basin, around three meters wide, lay up against the far wall, leaving only a narrow space for Marcus to edge down to the next chamber. Five intensely bright red lights arranged in a circle shone from the ceiling over the basin, and Marcus tilted his head as he wondered what sort of function the arrangement served.

The last partition housed a single wide, flat platform. A thin crimson sheet stretched tightly over what Marcus took to be a mattress, discolored and tainted by years of continuous use, suggested the arrangement was some sort of bed, although there were no pillows or covers. On the wall over the bed, an assortment of bizarre and monstrous instruments, all spikes and blades, were arranged as a display. Marcus could only assume they were some sort of close combat weaponry, although they looked nothing like anything he'd seen before, even back in the lectures on the Alamo. Each item was blackened and serrated, engraved with runes and ornate symbols. The craftsmanship was spectacular, far superior to anything he'd ever seen, yet Marcus was loath to attempt to claim one for himself. If its owner was still alive, Marcus could only imagine what it would do to someone carrying its own weapon.

Still, there was no sign of any owner, and apart from the weapons and armor, Marcus could find no sign of personal items inside the alien's quarters.

"There's no one here," Marcus shouted out to the others in the corridor.

"There has to be someone somewhere," Taz replied. "The ship couldn't have flown itself."

Adler eyed the odd suit of armor intently, studying it with something approaching reverence.

"Scott, we should keep moving," Marcus said as he passed him by.

Adler paused briefly in his study of the peculiar armor, before finally giving in and following Marcus back out into the corridor. The team huddled together as Marcus described what he'd found inside the room.

"We should go back and bring the others here," Taz suggested.

"No Taz," Marcus overrode him. "We have to continue. The crew has to be here somewhere."

They carried on down the hallway, ignoring the rest of the doors, until the corridor split before them. Marcus ordered Taz and Reid to take the left fork, keeping Adler with himself as backup. As the two of them ventured right, the path swerved, first left and then right, passing through several more open areas devoid of any sign of life but cluttered with debris from the crash. Suddenly the path stopped abruptly in front of a wide stairway, leading up towards another corridor that disappeared into the shadows.

The tread of each step glowed a deep red, the half-meter thick cloud of chlorine vapor at the bottom of the staircase glowing from the light beneath its surface, swirling as Marcus and Adler waded through, approaching the steps. Marcus ran his hands through the surface of the mist, fascinated how it seemed to settle back into place within seconds of being disturbed. He began the steep climb up the steps, Adler following closely behind him.

As they ascended the staircase, the hallway up ahead came further into view. A few meters from the head of the stairs, the walls of the corridor gave way to a semi-circular hall, the flat end of which was lined with wide windows facing the darkening desert. Many of the windows had cracked during the crash, allowing sand to pour in, accumulating in vast deposits against a line of still-glowing consoles beneath the windows. Dirt and grime stained every visible surface.

Several corpses lay strewn about the floor, on top of pools of dried blood. Their flesh had been stripped clean from their blackened bones.

Clearly the shriekers had feasted on the crew before venturing further afield in search of food. Marcus and Scott stopped to take in their surroundings, with first Marcus, then Adler removing his helmet to view the scene with his bare eyes.

Marcus knelt down by one of the bodies. Unlike the Terrans, the crew of the ship had hands with only four digits, longer than those of a human and ending in sharp claws. The skull too was vastly different to that of a Terran. A bony protrusion where a human's nose would be extended up over the head, widening as it arched over the back of the skull. Its ocular cavities were much higher than those of a Terran, and were set wider apart, almost on the sides of the skull. Overall though, the humanoid skeleton was roughly the same size as most Terrans, if not as large as Jago.

"Daoa naholi nogadimi," the now familiar alien voice echoed through the chamber.

It was then that Marcus spotted the raised central dais, upon which stood a pedestal supporting a circular console pulsing a faint blue glow periodically. Leaving Adler, who continued to examine the bodies, going through the heaps of torn dark colored clothing on the floor, Marcus stood up and approached the circular console. A shimmering blue crystal roughly the size of Marcus' fist was implanted in its center.

"Daoa naholi nogadimi," the voice repeated, echoing across the room.

Marcus removed his right gauntlet, and ran the tips of his fingers over the surface of the dazzling crystal. The light seemed to intensify with the pressure of his touch. Instinctively, he clutched the magnificent crystal and pulled. With a quick jerk, the crystal snapped loose from its socket.

"Gatsivi nitli owohalimi. Odena nadu," the voice droned, just as all the consoles began to power down.

"What did you do?" Scott demanded, rising quickly to see what had happened.

"I… I just," Marcus blurted, holding his hand out, displaying the crystal.

Adler stared at it intently. It had stopped glowing when it had been disconnected from the device, but it was no less spectacular to behold. Marcus still couldn't stop staring at it.

"It was just sitting there," he tried to explain, unable to tear his eyes away from the glittering object.

Marcus heard a click from a couple of meters in front of him. He looked up and saw Scott, aiming his sidearm directly at him. The copilot's youthful face was no longer a picture of naive innocence, but was now distorted in a menacing scowl, the likes of which Marcus had never seen before.

"Hand it over, slowly," Scott commanded, reaching out his left hand to take the crystal.

Chapter 35

The consoles had powered down. If not for the warm glow of Oberon looming outside the windows, the chamber would have been shrouded in total darkness. The right side of Scott's visage was painted in unearthly orange and purple hues, shadowing his grim expression. The pistol remained steady in his hand, pointed straight at Marcus's head.

"Why are you doing this?" Marcus begged. "We're brothers."

"I'm not your brother," Adler sneered. "In fact, I was hatched more than two years before the rest of you morons."

Confusion built up in Marcus. He'd heard that pilots and copilots were usually hatched earlier than the rest of the squad to allow time for the extensive training they had to undergo before being deemed fit for service, but… two years?

"Then is Raven…?"

"Bah," Scott sneered. "That bitch is as clueless as the rest of you."

"Then, why are you doing this?" Marcus reiterated.

"Have you any idea how much my superiors in Division 6 will appreciate something like this?"

"You're Division 6?" gasped Marcus, stunned at the young copilot's revelation. "It's real? Then why are you here? Was this all a plot to get to this?" Marcus blurted, staring at the blue crystal in his outstretched hand.

"No, you idiot. I'm here to monitor you. Nobody could have predicted that an alien ship would crash out here in the ass end of the system!" Scott retorted.

"Monitor us? The probe! You planted the probe!" Marcus gasped in sheer astonishment.

"No, actually, I didn't, and neither did Division 6. But we did discover that someone was paying a fortune for this little experiment, whatever it might be, and Division 6 wants to know why. Who would go through all this trouble, and what were they hoping to gain?" Scott explained, steadying his grip on the handgun.

"So… you're as clueless as we are?" Marcus said, trying to maintain some measure of confidence.

"Shut your fucking mouth. I know enough," Adler barked.

"So Division 6 had you infiltrate our squad in order to discover what was really going on? In that case, what happened to the real Scott Adler?" he asked.

"Well, there's really only room for one," Scott sneered. "Anyway, the experiment was hardly successful. From what we could tell, you were supposed to be altered, made… different somehow. But there's nothing special about you. There's nothing special about any of you! You can't even stand up to a bunch of mindless beasts. So I might as well take the crystal and have something to show for all my hard work."

"Did you call the *Genesis* here?"

"Of course. It's a magnificent ship. Too bad you won't be there to see it. This squad is dropping like flies, and I don't want to share the glory. Who's going to notice one more dead body?"

Marcus had never imagined that anyone could be so vile, so utterly devoid of human compassion. His anger flared. Not like this, he thought. Not at the hands of someone he'd considered a brother. He couldn't believe that they'd all been deceived so easily. He himself, his squadmates, his friends, all manipulated in some psychotic mind game orchestrated by someone he didn't even know, and for what? To be tossed aside like puppets when the experiment failed? For a moment, Marcus felt nothing. It was as if his heart had stopped beating and his mind had simply been turned off. Perhaps he really was no better than a puppet.

Suddenly he was overcome with pure hatred, rage swelling up inside him. He'd been angry before – at Lance, at the world – but nothing even remotely close to the magnitude of the fury he now felt for Adler, who was sneering as he raised his finger to the trigger of his sidearm.

Marcus' lips began to tremble, his nostrils flared, and his eyes started to twitch. His hands were clenched so firmly that he was sure that the crystal would shatter in his hands. He was so overcome with rage that he felt that if he couldn't contain it, it would lash out at his enemy and burn him alive where he stood. But Marcus didn't want to contain it. He'd had enough of cowering in fear, of giving in and bowing down. No more!

All of a sudden Scott dropped his weapon, clutching at his ears in a vain attempt to shield himself from the piercing pain. Marcus barely even noticed. He focused his rage, harnessing every last drop of willpower within his being to lash out at the cowering traitor before him.

Droplets of crimson blood began trickling down Scott's nose, his mouth wide open as he emptied his lungs, screaming in pain. Marcus, so wrapped up in his rage, wanted him dead so badly that he didn't realize what he was doing, let alone stop to wonder at how he was doing it. The blood was spewing forth from Scott's bloody nostrils and

279

pouring from his ears, covering his hands and fingers. Through his fury, Marcus even saw blood forming at the corners of his eyes. The traitor's legs buckled and he fell to his knees, steadying himself with one hand on the floor, desperately trying to keep the other one covering his ear.

"Stop it!" he screamed, pleading for his life.

But Marcus would not stop, unable to contain the volcanic fury erupting inside him.

"Please, no, God!" Adler gurgled, as blood began to run from his nose into his mouth.

Finally, Scott's limp body toppled over, quite dead. Marcus stared intently at the corpse. His anger began to fade as he breathed wearily in and out. He stood perfectly still. Trying to comprehend what had just transpired. With a shock, he realized that, for the first time in his life, Marcus had killed a man. He tried to justify it to himself as self defense, it didn't make the horrible knot of emotions in his chest any easier.

Scott had been wrong. Marcus had been altered. He couldn't understand how, or even why. At first, when he'd seen the attack on the settlement before it had even happened, he'd written it off as mere coincidence. But, given what he'd just done, there could be no denying it. He was no longer the same.

He suddenly remembered something Taz had said to the squad when they'd first discussed Division 6. He'd told them that some people had the ability to do strange things with the power of their minds. Psionics, he'd called them. That had to be it. Marcus had to be one of them.

Marcus looked once more at the crystal he was clutching in his hand. It was still intact. He placed it carefully in one of his belt pouches before quietly exiting the windowed chamber, heading back to join up with the others.

What would he tell them? How was he going to explain Adler's absence? Marcus didn't know how he could explain his actions, or even if the others would believe him.

*　*　*　*　*

Taz and Reid came veering round a corner when Marcus almost stumbled into them. Taz was so on edge that he nearly emptied a full clip into Marcus before he realized who it was.

"Wow, easy there," Reid cried, pushing Taz's gun barrel down so he wouldn't accidently kill someone.

"Shit. Sorry Marcus," Taz apologized. "I thought you were one of those shriekers."

"Did you find anything?" Reid asked.

"No, I…" Marcus started to reply.

"Where's Adler?" Reid interrupted him.

"He… uh… Scott's dead," Marcus confessed.

"Dead? Shit. Shriekers?" Taz yelped.

"No… it was me. I killed him," Marcus confided.

"You?" Reid blurted. "What do you mean, you?"

"He… uh … Scott wasn't who he said he was."

"What are you talking about?" Reid growled.

"He was a traitor. He was Division 6," Marcus tried to explain. "He pulled his pistol on me. He was going to shoot! I didn't know what else to do."

"That rat bastard," Taz bellowed. "I knew there was something off about him. See, I told you guys, Division 6 is real! You never listen to me!"

"Yeah yeah, pipe down," Reid barked. "Why did he try to kill you?"

"He wanted this," Marcus said, producing the shimmering blue crystal from his pouch.

"What the hell is it?" Taz blurted.

"I'm not sure. But I think it's sort of like the heart of the ship. It was embedded in a central console in a big room, the bridge I guess. As soon as I removed it, everything powered down. Whatever it is, it must be important."

"You must be one hell of a quick shot to get the drop on him if he'd got his sidearm trained on you," coaxed Reid.

"I… uh… yeah. I guess," Marcus stuttered, convinced that the truth would sound simply too absurd. "What about you guys, any signs of the shriekers?" he asked, desperately changing the subject.

"Nothing whatsoever. If they were here, they're long gone by now," Reid replied.

"Come on. We'd better go tell the others," Marcus ordered, before heading back down the long, winding corridor.

* * * * *

They appeared in the darkest hour of the night. With no one but the few remaining Hajari to oppose them, the shriekers had torn through the settlement like an enormous wave crashing onto a rocky shore. The number of casualties was enormous, rivaling that of the previous night, despite the diminished numbers of the Terrans.

As a horde of enraged shriekers managed to claw their way over the palace walls, Lance discovered his sidearm in a chest in the corner of his tent. He dragged himself up against the back of the tent. He wanted to go out and fight them, to show these monsters who they were dealing with, but his body refused to cooperate. His hand shook as he pointed the gun at the entrance of the tent, unable to do anything but wait.

The desperate cries of the women and children in the courtyard were deafening, tearing at his very soul.

Lance sobbed, shaking his head in disbelief. "This isn't happening. This can't be happening," he muttered to himself.

A shadow loomed at the edge of his tent, creeping ever closer. He squeezed the trigger, firing three shots right into the center of the shadowy figure.

Eight left, he thought as he looked at the small digital readout on the side of the pistol. "*08*" it flashed, showing the state of the magazine. The SGC N-11 medium handgun was a fine weapon, but he only had so many rounds. He had to use them sparingly.

The flap on the edge of the tent's entrance blew open, startling Lance, who blindly fired off another couple of rounds.

"Fuck, fuck, fuck, fuck," the crippled Sergeant blurted repeatedly as he desperately surveyed the contents of his tent, hoping he would spot another clip or ammo case. Nothing. He paused to regain his composure, breathing heavily in and out, his eyes closed, trying to distance his mind from his predicament.

Suddenly a three-pronged claw gripped the edge of the tent flap and slowly pulled it open, a shrieker peering its hideous head in towards Lance. He took aim, and, just as the creature bent its knees, readying its charge, fired.

The creature lunged. Although bleeding heavily, it latched its claws onto Lance's hip and thigh. He screamed in agony, lowering his weapon and firing off several more shots, straight down through the creature's skull. The shrieker's grip loosened, and it fell, limp, to the floor.

Lance clutched his hip, which was bleeding profusely. Luckily, the wound on his thigh didn't look as severe, and given his condition, he was numb from the waist down anyway.

"*01*", the readout on the gun flashed.

Lance bit his lower lip, ignoring the pain as he stared intently at the weapon he gripped so firmly in his hand. He shifted his focus to the dead shrieker on the floor, gazing at the rows of razor-sharp teeth protruding from its massive maw.

Lance raised the pistol as another pair of shriekers appeared in the opening. This time he pointed the weapon at his own head. He closed his eyes, his finger firmly on the trigger as his hand started to shake.

He pulled the trigger.

Lance opened his eyes in quiet disbelief, turning the weapon over to look at the readout.

"*Jammed.*"

Chapter 36

The squad had regrouped in the chamber where they'd entered the ship. Spielman and his team were already there when Marcus, Taz and Reid returned. Seeing the Sergeant run his eyes over Marcus' diminished team, Marcus knew he wouldn't be able to avoid admitting that Adler was dead, but he wasn't yet ready to trust the others with the full truth yet. What if one of them was also a mole?

"Alder's dead. We split up to cover more ground, and when he didn't make it back to the RV I went looking for him. He'd been in a control room of some sort, maybe the ship's bridge, but... well, I found the crews' bodies there too. The shriekers got them." Marcus lied.

"Damn." Spielman sighed. "Well, we didn't see a single sign of them. I guess there might not be many left here. I'm sure if there were enough of them to attack us they would have by now. Did you see any yourself?

"Well, I didn't see any, but I fear the worst. If they're still hungry after yesterday's slaughter, they're bound to be back. Without us, the settlement is defenseless," Marcus confessed.

"With Division 6 on the way and most of our squad dead, we're going to have a lot to answer for," Reid responded.

"Albano's right. However, if we were able to divert their curiosity with something more substantial, we might be able to keep control of the situation," the Sergeant suggested.

"How do you mean?" Marcus asked.

"All we found was smashed up cargo and empty rooms. Wasn't there anything that might be of value on the upper decks?"

Shooting Taz and Reid a look, praying they wouldn't mention the crystal, Marcus briefly outlined what he and Adler had found in the alien quarters. He knew that whatever Spielman hoped, Division 6 wouldn't be distracted by the ship. The probe, sending Adler to infiltrate the squad – they'd invested too much already.

Spielman listened with considerable interest, but quickly realized the trinkets Marcus' team had found wouldn't protect the squad. "Grey, is there anything you can do with those consoles?" he asked. "We need every bit of information we can get."

Marcus turned to the consoles, now powered down, no doubt due to his removal of the crystal.

"I… I can try," he responded.

"Do it," the Sergeant ordered.

Marcus crossed to the nearest rank of consoles, taking care to avoid the deep cracks in the chamber's floor. He could hear bits of rubble coming loose underneath him, cascading down to the floor of the level below. He gripped the edge of the console, trying to divine some manner of operating it. He began poking and prodding the array of buttons next to the screen, but the device gave no response.

"I think it's powered down Sergeant," Marcus called, turning to survey the rest of the chamber, trying to look as if he was hoping to find a solution.

All of a sudden, his foot slipped, knocking a larger piece of debris into one of the wider cracks. He caught himself on the edge of the gaping hole, his heart racing.

"Whew, that was close," he sighed.

A series of clicks and snaps suddenly sounded from below, followed by a deep hum that reverberated through the floor.

"Um, Sergeant. I've got an itch," Reid bellowed.

Marcus stood perfectly still, his hands outstretched, not wanting to move even a finger.

"What was that?" the Sergeant spat.

Suddenly something shot up through the crack by Marcus's foot, something powerful shaking and tearing at the deck. Startled, Marcus and the others jumped back immediately. With the rest of the squad close to the tear in the hull leading out to the desert, Marcus was left alone in the center of the room, gawking at the two-meter-long serrated pincer protruding through the floor. It was covered in a thick, milky-white substance that glistened as if it were semi-transparent.

Marcus was stunned, unsure whether he should shoulder his weapon or simply make a run for the rest of the squad as fast as he could. Suddenly the pincer withdrew, disappearing quickly back below the surface. There was a loaded pause, then Marcus turned to the others, starting to move towards them.

"What..." he got out, just as a large section of the floor collapsed from under him. He tumbled down into darkness.

He rolled down a slanting section of the floor, slamming to a stop on the deck of the level below. He had landed face down, and lay there, half-stunned. As the seconds passed, Marcus became aware that he wasn't alone. The same deep, humming sound he'd heard before, followed shortly afterwards by the clicking and clacking of bone hitting bone, were enough to send his mind reeling into deep dark places.

He tried to force himself to move, to get up, but his body refused to comply. Finally, he mustered enough self control to lift his head high enough to survey his surroundings. As his eyes shifted upwards, he saw it. The air was filled with dust from the collapse, just enough to render all but the creature's huge head invisible. It reared up over the cloud, its one red, glowing eye staring back at him, studying him. Hundreds of teeth lined its vertical maw, the long gash of a mouth disappearing down the front of its body into the clouds of dust, unlike anything Marcus would ever have envisioned in even his darkest nightmares. Its lips moved in and out, displaying waves of hungry teeth ready to dig into the monster's prey. The top portion of the creature's head was a deep red, almost black color, as if painted so as to provide a better contrast with its single glowing eye. A pair of multi-jointed, articulate limbs ending in serrated stubs, protruded from the base of its neckless head like mock arms.

"Marcus, run!" came the cry from above.

Marcus snapped his head around, seeing the squad staring down at him from the rim. He rolled, just as one of the creature's pincers came crashing down towards him, missing his stomach by a hair's breadth and smashing through the floor. He jumped to his feet, casting around for somewhere to run to. Spotting a crashed beam leading up to the upper level, he sprang for it.

The beast's droning hum rose in intensity as it screeched and clacked its teeth in excitement. Marcus sprinted up the beam as fast as he could. As he neared the top, the beast thrashed at it with its pincers, making the beam roll off to the right. Marcus dropped onto his stomach and clung to the metal in desperation as he was twirled around in the air before the beam came to a full stop, leaving Marcus lying half on, half off the girder.

"Marcus, grab my hand!" Reid shouted.

Marcus looked up. Reid was lying on the deck above, stretching down his arm, trying to reach Marcus. The beast roared beneath him. Marcus looked over his shoulder, and saw the wave of teeth clashing with increased momentum. He managed to get back on his feet, both hands still on the beam for support he started to climb, trying to get high enough to reach Reid's arm.

The beast sprang again, colliding with the beam, which jerked upwards. Marcus was knocked loose, his arms windmilling, only to have something fasten firmly around one wrist. He cried out, flailing his free arm against whatever was holding him, trying to get a clear look at it as he did so.

It was Reid's hand. He could barely believe his luck. Spielman helped Reid pull Marcus back up onto the upper level, where the squad was hurrying out into the desert through the opening in the hull.

"Grey, we've got to move!" the Sergeant shouted as they hurried him out into the gloomy, star-lit desert.

They ran as fast as they could along the length of the ship, back towards the mining truck. Raven was firing up the engines and turning on the truck's powerful floodlights as Marcus and the others began climbing the ladder up to the platforms over the wheels. They'd made it.

Without warning, a section of the alien ship's hull only two hundred meters away exploded in a cloud of dust and debris as the terrifying creature burst through in full force. Marcus could finally see the creature in all its glory, shining in the powerful lights of the mining rig. Its six fearsomely-muscular legs, each a towering three meters long with more joints than Marcus could count, scurried about its low-slung, lumpy body as the creature oriented itself to its surroundings. It reared back on its hindmost four legs, baring the vertical maw that ran from between its first pair of legs up the front of its torso to its squat, blocky head.

"DRIVE!" Taz screamed hysterically.

The horrifying beast spotted them as Raven hit the accelerator as hard as she could. The truck sped off in a storm of sand, the creature springing after them with a screech.

"Shoot the fucking thing!" the Sergeant bellowed, readying his weapon.

Marcus fumbled his carbine from where it was still slung over his back, but had trouble aiming straight as the truck bumped violently across the dunes. There were bullets flying from over the drilling rig as the squad emptied their clips at the terrifying monster that was fast closing the distance between them. As the reassuring storm of gunfire echoed in his ears, Marcus began to think that they'd pull through after all.

But, one by one, the weapons fell silent as the clips emptied. The beast hadn't even slowed down, and was now only two or three meters behind the speeding truck.

"It's not working!" Taz screamed, backing away from the back of the vehicle.

They were almost finished exchanging their magazines as a pincer came down hard, bursting through the end of platform where Spielman had just finished locking his clip into place. The Sergeant threw himself away, barely managing to cling to the railing to avoid tumbling off the truck. Reid reached out to help him back up as the rest of the squad provided cover, firing a hail of bullets at the monstrous beast at point-blank range. Even as he fired, Marcus noticed that the bullets barely even penetrated the monster's thick skin.

"Look out!" he shouted, as the creature brought its powerful pincers to bear once more.

Reid and Spielman looked up just as the pincer came down, fast as a lightning strike, piercing the Sergeant's thigh. He screamed in agony, the blunt claw embedded clean through his leg. Reid, throwing an arm around the Sergeant, tried to pull him back up the truck, but the creature resisted.

Spielman looked back at them, his face curiously calm. Knowing it was all over for him, he deliberately let go of the railing and clutched instead at a cluster of fragmentation grenades hanging from Reid's belt. Despite Reid's muscular frame, he was no match for the monstrous strength of the beast, and Spielman was torn from his grip, the grenades coming loose from the sniper's gear. The Sergeant flew off the truck, dangling on the creature's serrated pincer like a marionette. He grasped the pins on the four grenades, paused for a split second, and pulled.

The nightmarish beast threw him to the ground, thrusting its other pincer deep into his shoulder. Using its forelegs, it began to twist the Sergeant's body in ways that a human body was never meant to bend. Spielman was still twitching as the creature knelt down, parting its wave of teeth to envelop him entirely. To Marcus, its mouth resembled a giant zipper, closing leisurely around its prey.

Just as the last pair of clacking teeth snapped into place, the beast disappeared in an explosion of orange goo. Large fragments of bone and chunks of flesh flew all over as an orange rain drowned the sands in alien blood.

"Stop the truck!" Marcus bellowed.

The truck ground to a halt and Marcus peered through the dust to see if he could spot any remains of their Sergeant. There were none. Having been at the center of the explosion, Marcus knew he would have been lucky to even find pieces of the Sergeant's armor.

He knew that Spielman had given his life to save them. There was no other way. He'd given the ultimate sacrifice for his men. Even though his mind was racing to find fault in how things had played out, Marcus knew there had been no way they could have saved him.

"Drive," he sighed, knowing there was nothing more anyone could do.

The truck began moving once more, starting its long journey back to the Last Oasis.

Marcus sat in silence at the back of the platform, staring back at the gory scene as it fell out of the pool of light from the truck's lamps. He'd thought so much about bravery over the last few days, especially since his discussions with Corporal Dimitrov. Yet only now, after seeing it in person, watching someone willing to make the ultimate sacrifice for others, did he finally understand.

Marcus had always felt out of place. Although he'd talked frequently with some of the men in his squad, he had only really ever had two friends, first Steven and then Dimitrov. This was the first time that Marcus felt that he truly belonged with these men, who risked their lives together every day of their lives in the service of something greater than themselves. Despite all the sadness and anger he had experienced since making his choice to serve, for the first time in his life Marcus was truly happy that he had chosen to stay. He was proud to stand beside such great men, his family.

Chapter 37

The sun was easing into its steady climb over the horizon when the settlement came into view. Stark shadows tainted the landscape in the calm after the storm. There had been no sign of the shriekers during their long ride back to the Last Oasis, and Marcus's mind was frantic with worry. As the truck drew closer, the squad began to discover the consequences of their absence. The few souls that wandered aimlessly about the streets were quiet as the grave, like specters hovering over a field of a long lost battle.

What disturbed Marcus the most was the lack of sound. There were no cries, no sobbing mothers weeping for their children, or husbands cursing the death of their wives. The morning air was still. These people, who had remained so unshaken in their faith through so much, had finally abandoned all hope.

Marcus couldn't even begin to count the bodies.

It was their fault. They had left these poor, defenseless people completely alone in the night against an enemy they had no chance of defeating. The squad had taken a great risk in heading out into the desert to attack their assailants in what they'd hoped would be a more vulnerable position. It had cost them all dearly. The loss of Sergeant Spielman weighed heavily on the clones. Jago was perhaps the most distraught among them, for Jenna's death had affected him more than Marcus could ever have imagined.

"What now boss?" The Ape asked him, his watery eyes seeking guidance.

Marcus thought it odd to hear those words directed at himself. The chain of command dictated that he was the unit's new acting Sergeant. Considering how he and the Ape had gotten on in their earlier encounters, the irony of hearing the behemoth looking to him for leadership was not lost on Marcus.

"We do what we can to help," Marcus somberly ordered.

The truck came to a stop near the southeastern gate, where the remainder of the squad promptly descended from the platforms. There were only six of them left, and morale was at an all-time low. Taz seemed more stressed and on edge than ever, and Jago was starting to transition from deep sadness to pure anger. Even the usually stoic Reid hung his head low in mourning. Taylor appeared to be unmoved, but the number of cigarettes he had gotten through since their escape spoke otherwise. The only one of them who still kept her cool was Raven.

Marcus had assumed that her cocky demeanor was a front to hide some vulnerability, but he was beginning to suspect that he may have been wrong. She seemed completely unshaken as she waded through the gory streets alongside the rest of the squad, on their way to the palace. The stench of death and decay tainted the air as the temperature began to rise, a bane to even the most courageous of souls. Dozens of bodies were in the process of being stacked into piles outside the palace walls as the squad approached the open gate to the courtyard. Not a single Hajari guarded the entrance.

As they entered, Marcus ordered Taz and Reid to go and check on Lance. The aging Aman, the Sheikh's servant, stood inside the courtyard, a swarm of troubled refugees clamoring at him from every angle, begging for aid. Marcus and the others made their way through the crowd, trying to avoid the use of too much force.

"Aman, where are the Hajari?" Marcus shouted over the crowd.

The wrinkled old man waved the refugees aside as he peered through his spectacles at the squad's approach.

"Ah, Mr. Grey. I'm so glad you survived the night," he proclaimed, with a hint of sarcasm. "We were all so worried about you."

"I… I'm sorry we weren't here when they… when we were needed," Marcus confessed, genuinely humble. "We had hoped to stop this from happening."

"And what a marvelous plan that must have been," the servant spat.

Marcus couldn't bear to look him in the eye, his guilt for the role he and his squad had played in the town's demise simply too great.

"Where are the Hajari?" he reiterated.

"Dead! They're all dead. They gave their lives trying to defend the palace," the servant sneered.

"And the Sheikh?"

"His Holiness escaped the onslaught. He is secure in the lower levels of the palace."

"Why didn't the others join him?" Marcus asked, puzzled.

"We crammed in as many as we possibly could, but there wasn't enough room for all of them."

"Do you know how many were lost?" inquired Marcus.

"We don't have the final numbers, but I estimate at least seventy. Of course, with the refugees, our numbers are much higher now. There simply wasn't room for them all."

Just then, Reid and Taz returned from Sergeant Lance's tent. "Marcus," Taz called, shouting above the rustle. "We found him. Or what's left of him."

Marcus excused himself from Aman and went to speak with his squadmates in private.

"He's dead?" Marcus asked as they moved to one of the deserted corners of the courtyard.

"Afraid so, although it's impossible to say for sure," Taz snorted.

"What do you mean? Either he's dead or he's not," Marcus snapped.

"Well," Taz paused to exchange troubled looks with Reid. "We're not really sure if it's him or not. There isn't much left."

Marcus winced in disgust at the image.

"Then it's official. Only six of us left," Marcus pondered. "And the shriekers will be back as soon as the sun sets."

"There's also the *Genesis*," Taz interjected.

"Thank you, Taz," Marcus said.

"What do we do boss?" Jago rumbled.

Marcus couldn't decide how best to spend the daylight hours. If the creatures came before the *Genesis*, there would be nothing the squad could do to stop them, not with their numbers so diminished. If the *Genesis* were to arrive first, there was no telling what fate would await them. Whatever happened, there was no way they'd escape. They'd probably all be dead within the day.

"Do whatever you want," he finally replied, utterly defeated.

"What?" they blurted in unison, startled at Marcus's answer.

"This might be our very last day. I think it's only fair that you get to spend it however you want," he explained.

There was a pause as they each considered how they wanted to spend what could very well be their final hours.

"I'll go pray, and help the locals bury their loved ones," Reid decided, before promptly disappearing from the palace courtyard.

"I'll come with you," shouted Jago. "I'm gonna bury Jenna's body."

"I guess he'll need these," Taylor proclaimed, producing the bottle of anti-radiation pills before following the retreating behemoth.

"What about you Raven?" Taz asked, shooting her a sly look. "This could very well be our last day alive. You don't want to die a vir-"

"In your dreams," Raven laughed, throwing her middle finger into the air as she turned to walk away. "I'm going to go get some sleep."

"I guess I'll go for a walk," Taz sighed.

Marcus was left alone with his thoughts. There was really nothing he could think of that he wanted to do. He could go help the others, but there'd be still more bodies that would need burying tomorrow. He wasn't quite ready to give up hope, but he harbored no illusions about the gravity of their situation.

His mind wandered to the crystal he had pocketed earlier. As he withdrew it from his pouch and held it out in the sun, the light refracted off of it, creating a dazzling display of azure rays. It was obviously very important. Adler had said that it would be of great interest to Division 6. Perhaps he could use it as a bargaining chip. Weary from the night's adventures, Marcus headed deeper into the courtyard to find a tent and get some rest. But before doing so, he crept to a vacant corner of the palace and buried the crystal in the soil of one of the flowerpots.

* * * * *

The last few rays of daylight peered over the palace walls as Marcus emerged from his tent, rubbing sleep from the corners of his eyes. Taylor was sitting outside the tent, deep in conversation with one of the locals, who appeared to have accepted his presence despite their differences. Instead of his usual cigarette, the medic had a raggedy-looking rollup in his mouth, and his eyes appeared red and weary.

"Marcus," he grinned. "Come, join us."

As the bubbly-looking local spotted Marcus's approach, he quickly got to his feet and scurried off towards a crowd of refugees in the center of the courtyard.

"You should try this," Taylor said, handing Marcus the dubious-looking cigarette.

Marcus declined with a wave of his hand, but sat down beside him nonetheless.

"It really is quite fascinating. I got it from one of the locals," the medic went on, producing a small plastic bag half-filled with an olive-hued herb. "It really takes the edge off things."

Marcus just smiled, pleased that the Doc appeared to be enjoying himself. They'd seen so little joy in their short lives. If this was to be their last day, he'd rather they make the most of it. Taylor drew heavily on his joint. A thick billow of milky smoke clung to the air in front of him, slowly dispersing before being replaced by a new, thicker cloud.

"This is all we are, you know," the medic mused. "We're a puff of smoke, just waiting to be dispersed."

His epiphany was not without some level of truth. The extent of human frailty dawned on Marcus as he thought back over how easily their numbers had dwindled in the past few days. Wafts of smoke blowing in the wind indeed.

"They'll be coming soon," sighed Marcus.

"Who? The shriekers or Division 6?" Taylor asked.

"Does it matter?"

"I guess not," the medic replied after a short moment of contemplation.

A sudden piercing shriek at the edge of the settlement broke the silence. A startled crowd of restless refugees hurried towards the palace doors, hoping to find asylum.

"Come on. We should go get the others," Marcus said.

*   *   *   *   *

The squad huddled together on top of the palace walls, ready to strike as soon as the shriekers appeared on the streets below. With little more than a magazine each, they were running dangerously low on ammunition. A cry for help at the outskirts of the town disturbed Marcus greatly, but he knew there was nothing they could do for those still outside the palace walls. If they were to venture out on the streets they would be vulnerable, and the shriekers would easily pick them off one by one.

They stood quietly, each second more unbearable than the next, waiting for death.

Suddenly the thunderous roar of four barracuda dropships racing across the sky above the palace split the sky. The resulting cheers from the crowd of terrified refugees in the courtyard brought new hope as the squad turned to one another, as if reassuring themselves that what they saw was indeed real.

Marcus leaned his back on the battlements for support as he slid down them to sit on the stone floor. A sigh of relief escaped his lips as a barrage of cannon fire erupted on the outskirts of the town, followed shortly by a hail of gunfire as troops began rappelling down to the ground below.

Chapter 38

The four barracuda dropships lined up just outside the Last Oasis' southeast gate were an impressive sight, made all the more so by the blazing spotlights mounted on each ship, illuminating the scene and driving the darkness back into the desert. A full complement of eighteen soldiers stood at attention in front of each ship, an inspiring, if intimidating, sight for the squad of six who now faced them.

Marcus could see the *Genesis* soaring overhead, silhouetted against the towering orb of Oberon. Even at this great distance, it was truly formidable to behold.

The clanking of boots hitting the open ramp of one of the barracudas signaled the approach of a pair of men in mid-conversation. Judging by his insignia, Marcus quickly determined one to be the dreaded Captain Intari. He wore an officer's dress uniform, dark gray pants and jacket, with a short, unbroken collar fastened together with seven square clasps of polished silver. A row of multicolored ribbon bars adorned the left side of his chest, signifying his achievements within the Terran Forces.

As Marcus had expected, the Captain had a grim visage. A square jaw, formidable cheekbones and a slightly hooked nose made him seem every bit as fearsome as his reputation suggested. A heavy brow and sunken eyes spoke of his unforgiving nature and strong convictions, although there was a certain degree of nobility in his carriage and sleek dark hair, graying at the temples.

Marcus was shocked when he finally focused his attention on the man the Captain was engaged in conversation with, an older version of the now-deceased Sergeant Lance. The resemblance was striking. Apart from graying hair and a fading scar clear across his cheek and eyebrow, the new arrival looked identical to Marcus' former Sergeant. Two days' stubble grew on his cheeks and chin, a marked divergence from Lance's clean shave. As he spoke, in a raspy voice that hinted at a life of experience, his stern gaze inspected the scene, his impassive face clearly hiding a calculating mind. Despite his great resemblance to Sergeant Lance, he wore the insignia of Lieutenant on his collar, and limped down the ramp with the aid of a motorized brace encircling his left knee.

Marcus didn't know quite how to react as the two men approached. After a series of awkward stances, he finally settled on a salute, his squad quickly coming to attention behind him. The officers halted in front of the squad, suspiciously eyeing each of them in turn.

"I am Captain Virge Intari, and this is Lieutenant Mitchell. Where's the rest of your squad?" Intari barked.

"KIA sir," Marcus replied, taken aback.

"All of them?" Lieutenant Mitchell inquired, raising an eyebrow.

"Yes sir. So are many of the civilians."

"These… civilians are none of our concern" the Captain interjected. "As they themselves have made so abundantly clear, they aren't a part of the Terran Republic, they are therefore entitled to neither our protection nor our sympathy," he sneered.

"Yes sir," Marcus replied, unnerved by the Captain's lack of compassion.

"Sergeant, you and your squad will stay put, while Lieutenant Mitchell and I appropriate a suitable location for a debriefing," the

Captain ordered. "Sergeant Haines, follow me," he barked as he and the Lieutenant marched away through the southeastern gate into town, one of the four squads following close on their heels.

Lieutenant Mitchell had surprised Marcus. He'd taken Lance as typical of his model and had been expecting a sniveling weasel, lapping up the Captain's attention and milking him for praise, but this older clone had seemed uninterested in, or unimpressed by, the company he kept.

As soon as the officers were out of earshot, the three remaining squads eased up, chatting amongst themselves, some lighting cigarettes.

"The new boss is a bit of a jerk," Jago muttered, much to the amusement of the others.

Some of the clones from one of the three squads approached them defiantly, one of them swaggering to a stop mere inches in front of Marcus.

"So, you're the one in charge of this sorry excuse for a squad?" a familiar voice asked.

"Eve?" Marcus gasped, his heart skipping a beat.

As she pulled her helmet off, Marcus was dazzled at the sight of her hypnotic brown eyes flaked with gold, her smooth brown hair dancing in the wind.

She jumped straight into his arms, kissing him deeply.

"Do I get one too?" Taz called.

Marcus shot him a mocking scowl.

"Surprised to see me?" she chuckled.

"I... I... I can't believe it!" Marcus confessed. "How did you...?"

"I guess you're not the only one who wasn't destined for Nyramar," she proclaimed, grinning from ear to ear.

Marcus grabbed her quickly by the waist, pulling her close enough to steal another kiss. Her lips were every bit as soft as he had remembered. In that moment, all his worries evaporated. No matter what fate awaited him at the hands of the infamous Captain Intari, this moment belonged to him.

* * * * *

Intari had commandeered one of the structures on the main street. It was a two-storey structure of sun-washed mud bricks stacked around wooden beams. The squad had been separated, each member locked in a separate room awaiting interrogation.

"Let me out you fuckers!" Jago shouted as he banged repeatedly on the door of his room.

Marcus wondered how long the door would hold up against the Ape's massive fists.

The Captain had informed them that he wished to debrief them each in turn. Until then, they were to remain in lockdown. Despite their predicament, Marcus couldn't help but smile as he sat on the floor with his back against the wall, thinking about Eve. This changed everything. She was here, not light years away fighting a war where she had no chance of survival. She was here!

Of course, as far as he knew he might never see her again, but the thought that she was out there, maybe even just outside his room, comforted him greatly. Who knew, when this was all over, maybe they could build a life together.

As the hours passed, Marcus entertained the notion of life outside the military with Eve at his side. He was no longer afraid. He was proud to serve in the Terran forces, just as she was. He hadn't even had time to tell her that, but with luck he would still get the chance.

Eventually, dawn broke, and a blank-faced clone entered Marcus' cell bearing a ration-pack and a bucket for him to relieve himself. After eating, Marcus, exhausted by the stress of the mission, dozed in a fitful sleep that was interrupted around noon when he heard the door of one his squadmates' cells open, than slam shut as they were led in front of Captain Intari. The voices he heard were muffled and drowned out, making it impossible for him to understand what they were saying, but tempers were definitely flaring. Too worried to sleep again, Marcus stayed awake, fretting, through the long afternoon, listening to doors opening and closing as the rest of his squad was taken away for interrogation. Every interview seemed to culminate in a heated argument, and at one point Marcus was sure he had heard the Captain threatening to have Jago shot if he didn't calm down. Thankfully, no shots were fired. Not long afterwards, the same blank-faced clone that had brought him breakfast returned with another ration pack, which Marcus was too nervous to do more than pick at.

As the last few gossamer strands of daylight faded away from the miniature window in Marcus's room, he got up on his toes and peered out into the streets. The familiar sound of a barracuda firing up its engines could be heard in the distance, and then another quickly followed after. Two of the four dropships parked outside the settlement began to rise up from behind the settlement walls. The ships banked sharply, still hovering in place, before their pilots engaged the thrusters, sending the ships racing off into the distance, en route to the wreckage of the alien ship.

"Shit," Marcus muttered to himself. "They're going to find Adler."

He needed an explanation. Surely they would see that the traitor's death wasn't the result of a pack of shriekers. If only he'd thought of it earlier! Perhaps he should have hidden the body, or at least made it look like an accident. The state he'd left Adler in left too many questions to answer.

It was several hours later, almost the middle of the night, before he heard the approaching footsteps. The interval was slightly off, leading Marcus to draw the conclusion that it was Lieutenant Mitchell who was limping towards his door. It was too late. He had no excuse. He would have to try his luck to talk his way out of it.

The chair that had been propped up against the handle on the outside was removed and pushed to one side. The door flew open. Mitchell stared at him from the doorway.

"You're next," he gestured emotionlessly, waving Marcus up from his seat on the floor.

Chapter 39

"Have a seat Sergeant," Captain Intari ordered, peering at his datapad, which bathed him an almost ghostly aura of pale blue light.

A disk-shaped drone with a camera lens hovered off to one side, a series of three red lights blinking periodically on the edge of its thin metal frame. Marcus took a seat on the opposite end of a desk that had been moved to the center of what seemed to have been the living room of the house Intari had commandeered. Lieutenant Mitchell had taken up position behind Marcus. Although he couldn't see him, Marcus thought he could feel the Lieutenant's breath on his neck. The Captain poked and prodded the screen on his handheld device, rubbing the stubble on his chin.

"Private Eric Taber," the Captain spat. "He was your first casualty?"

Marcus's mind raced back to their first mission on the moon Triton, where the squad's technician had lost his life in a raging meteor storm.

"Yes sir," he replied. "He was struck by a meteor."

"That's quite a coincidence Sergeant," the Captain responded.

"Uh… excuse me?" Marcus stuttered, unsure what the Captain meant.

"And your mission. Successful was it?" Intari probed.

"Uh… yes sir. Successful," Marcus confirmed.

"Excellent. It says here you took a GeoDynamics survey probe to collect some readings. Where exactly is the probe now?" The Captain finally raised his gaze from his device, staring intently at Marcus.

Marcus couldn't help but wonder why the Captain was so interested in their first mission, and not what had happened afterwards. Knowing full well that the probe was buried beneath a pile of rubble inside the GeoDynamics warehouse, Marcus decided to proceed with caution.

"I believe it was destroyed sir," he stated. "During the first shrieker attack. There was a lot of damage to the GeoDynamics compound."

As he spoke, Marcus felt a subtle pain begin to form at the base of his skull.

The Captain averted his gaze and peered briefly over Marcus's shoulder before continuing. "I see," he said. "Have you experienced anything out of the ordinary since leaving Triton?"

"What do you mean sir?"

The Captain eyed him suspiciously again, studying every minute reaction.

"Any dizziness, strange… thoughts… or dreams?" he probed.

"No sir. Nothing like that," Marcus lied, thinking it best to keep his experiences to himself.

The Captain glanced over Marcus' shoulder once again, and the throbbing of Marcus's headache continued to increase.

"Any physical abnormalities?"

"Physical… no sir," Marcus stated.

"So nothing unusual at all?"

"Well, other than Sergeant Lance losing his mind and a horde of alien monsters trying to kill us… no sir."

"Don't get funny with me Sergeant," the Captain scowled, furrowing his brow and revealing several lines of wrinkles on his forehead. "Now, it says here that what appeared to be a shooting star hit the ground due southeast of here. Is that correct?"

"Yes Captain," Marcus confirmed.

"And the attacks on the settlement began shortly after?"

"Well, at first the shriek… creatures… attacked farm animals on the outlying farms. Then a local boy went missing. Things escalated after that."

"I see," the Captain said, his voice devoid of any apparent emotion. "And the attack on the settlement. I require a detailed description of the events as you remember them."

Marcus recanted the long night of the attack in as much detail as he could, leaving nothing out but his recollection of the dream he'd experienced foretelling the horrendous events of that night. Intari listened intently, glancing over Marcus' shoulder at Mitchell every now and then. Marcus's headache continued to rise, to the point where his whole head was throbbing in sync with his heartbeat.

"And this Sergeant Lance, can you confirm that after a series of questionable incidents, he discharged his weapon on a…" the Captain paused to consult his records, "Corporal Dimitrov?"

Marcus couldn't help but relive that terrible moment. The pain he'd felt when he'd heard the gunshot and had realized what had happened. Weirdly, his headache began to subside almost as soon as he relived that moment. It was as if his sorrow had somehow overcome it.

"Well?" the Captain urged him.

"Yes sir," Marcus finally replied. "I can confirm that."

"What of the others? Were any of them acting strangely or performing in any way out of the ordinary?"

Marcus shook his head in silent response.

"Now, this alien vessel you discovered. According to these statements, you were alone with Private Scott Adler when he died. Is that correct?"

"No sir. I mean, yes sir. But Adler and I had split up to scout different directions from a T-junction. When he didn't return, I went looking for him. I found him lying on the floor," Marcus explained, trying as best he could to sound genuine.

The sharp pain inside Marcus's skull suddenly spiked. He resisted the urge to clutch the side of his head in an attempt to relieve the pain.

"How convenient," the Captain replied, eyeing Lieutenant Mitchell behind Marcus. "You expect me to believe that while you were wondering off on your own, inside what you took to be a hostile alien ship, Private Adler simply keeled over and died, without any obvious cause?" the Captain snarled.

"Yes sir. We were short handed. In retrospect, it might not have been the best decision to allow Private Adler to operate alone."

"No, I suppose it wasn't," the Captain sneered.

"Lieutenant Mitchell will escort you back to your room. My physician, Dr. Drechsler, will be running a series of tests on you and what's left of your squad. I have a suspicion that his examinations will yield some interesting results. Pending his findings, you are to remain under lockdown."

"But sir, there's nothing wrong with me," Marcus objected, just as a tall, scrawny-looking man in uniform came bursting through the door.

"Captain Intari, there's a communiqué for you. It's urgent," the messenger informed him.

"Mitchell, take him back to his cell," the Captain ordered before storming out of the room.

Marcus had waited in his room for the better part of the night, unable to sleep for anxiety over what Captain Intari's physician would discover during his examination. Could his experiments reveal that Marcus had indeed been altered in some way? And what of the others? Was he the only one? There were so many questions racing through his head, and the few answers he had filled his heart with dread for what was to come.

As he heard the chair that had been propped up against the other side of his door begin to move, Marcus felt his heart skip a beat. If this Dr. Drechsler could expose what had been done to him, Marcus could well end up being strapped to an operating table, being dissected and studied whether he consented or not. Or perhaps he had just been listening too much to Taz's conspiracy theories.

"Seems you've got friends in high places," came the voice of Lieutenant Mitchell as the door swung open.

"What?" Marcus blurted, rising from the floor.

"You're free to go," the Lieutenant explained.

"How? I mean… so there won't be any physical examination?" Marcus asked, astonished.

"Not unless you're in the mood to cough while a grown man fondles your privates," the Lieutenant responded, his piercing blue eyes boring into Marcus.

"Uh… what?"

"Get out of here. You and your men are free to go. We've set up camp just outside the palace gates. There's a tent there reserved for your squad until we can figure out what to do with you."

"Yes sir!" Marcus cheerfully complied, anxious to join his squadmates.

*　*　*　*　*

After being cooped up in his tiny room for the better part of two days, Marcus's squadmates were a welcome sight, but his relief at seeing them didn't even come close to the euphoric feeling that overcame him when he saw Eve again. The two of them had to wait the whole scorching day to get any time alone, finally sneaking out of the camp late in the evening, when, save for a pair of guards keeping watch, most of the other clones were fast asleep.

Somewhere in the distance, the muffled sounds of the ongoing battle with the shriekers raged on. They'd wandered through the settlement towards the calm oasis, where they came upon a small wooden bench by its banks.

Neither of them spoke much, preferring instead the silent company and the warm reassurance of each other's presence. They held hands as they sat there, quietly gazing up at the stars and the magnificent Oberon, whose majestic rings radiated in a spectacular display of cosmic beauty. When they parted ways in the dawn's early light, they vowed that they would never allow anything to keep them apart for long.

Before returning to the camp, Marcus snuck back into the palace courtyard to retrieve the crystal, his only bargaining chip if things took a turn for the worse.

*　*　*　*　*

"A new ship? What about the old one?" Raven objected.

"It's pretty fried, not worth trying to repair. We've been ordered to hand over one of ours so you can get your squad back to Alamo Station," replied Sergeant Grant, who was in charge of one of the four squads currently residing in the camp.

"What about your squad? Won't they need a ship?" Marcus asked.

"There are six more aboard the *Genesis*. We'll requisition a new one the next time we're in port. For our purposes here we've more than we need. This one's all yours," the Sergeant explained.

"You might want to have your pilot take some lessons though," chimed Sergeant Grant's pilot, a cocky blond man with a narrow chin.

"What did you say?" barked Raven, bristling in a clear display of aggression.

"Calm down Raven," Marcus urged her.

"You'd better watch your mouth. I can fly circles around your incompetent ass any day of the week!" she yelled as Reid and Taz tried to restrain her from beating the blond pilot into a bloody pulp.

"Oh. There's just one more thing," Sergeant Grant added, drawing Marcus aside. "Given your lack of experience in a leadership role, your squad has been assigned a new officer. Sorry, but you're no longer Acting Sergeant."

Secretly relieved, Marcus didn't respond immediately. When Grant continued to stare at him, clearly expecting some reaction, Marcus finally asked "So who's our new Sergeant then?"

"That's him right there," said Sergeant Grant, gesturing towards a figure approaching from the gate, too far for them to make out.

Although he couldn't see his face, Marcus could easily make out the slight limp as Lieutenant Robert Mitchell inched his way towards his new squad.

312

Chapter 40

Having Lieutenant Mitchell as their new squad-leader was daunting. His resemblance to Sergeant Lance made them all wary of his leadership capabilities, and they all knew that the only reason he'd been assigned to their squad was so he could keep an eye on them and report back to Captain Intari the second anything seemed out of place. Jago kept giving the new Lieutenant the evil eye, his interrogation still weighing heavily on his mind. Mitchell remained quiet for the most part, except when he was barking out the orders that soon had the squad aboard their new barracuda.

As their ship climbed towards the stars above New Io, the squad was more than happy to finally see the moon in their wake. Marcus was the only one who felt anything was amiss. Yet again he'd been forced to leave Eve behind, not knowing when they'd see each other again. This time though, his feelings of loss were mixed with the promise of future meetings. He warmed at the thought of how her lower lip enveloped its other half when she pretended to frown.

As the blissful calmness of empty space overcame the ship, the new Lieutenant ordered everyone put to stasis for the long ride home to the Alamo. Marcus was slightly hesitant to go to sleep, not knowing whether he would dream of Eve, or all the horrible things he'd encountered on their voyage. Either way, they would be home soon.

It was odd how the Alamo suddenly felt like home. Before this voyage, Marcus had dreamt of leaving, of finding his own path in the world. Now he was proud to serve, and looking forward to returning to the base with what was left of his squad.

Taylor engaged the stasis cycle for the rest of the squad's pods, and, one by one, they drifted off to sleep. As the last man awake, the medic reveled in the stillness that had fallen over the ship. With all but the bare necessities powered down, he withdrew the small pouch from his pocket, and spread a pinch of the green herbs it contained across a thin sheet of paper, which he subsequently rolled with his nimble fingers.

He stood by the small window at the rear of the ship, gazing out at the stars as the soothing herbs began to relax his mind.

*   *   *   *   *

Marcus found himself standing at the base of a giant old tree, its branches gnarled and blackened, devoid of leaves. The roots protruded from the ground in several places, so thick that he knew he wouldn't be able to wrap his arms around even one of them.

The ground was laid with sleek tiles of dark-gray natural stone, with veins of white adorning their surface.

The sky overhead was dark and cast with heavy clouds. Delicate white flakes drifted slowly from the air. There must have been millions of them, millions upon millions. Even though he'd never seen such a sight before, the word "snow" popped into Marcus' mind.

He held out his hand, allowing the gentle flakes to accumulate on his open palm. They weren't cold, he thought. Snow should be cold. Were his resonant memories failing him? Perhaps due to an error in their programming?

There was no sound. He couldn't even hear the breeze that gently caressed his cheeks.

He was surprised to suddenly see the people around him, running every which way in panic. He reached down to hold the folds of his white robe in his hands, rubbing the fabric with his fingers. He had never seen anything like it before. It glistened in the moonlight that illuminated the scene. Suddenly there was a thick cloud of smoke off to his side, flowing across the smooth surface of the stone like water.

The ground cracked beneath him.

Without warning, beams of light tore through the darkened clouds, touching the ground in the distance.

Marcus gazed in amazement as the people around him became even more frantic. Spheres of light appeared in each of the places where the beams had hit the ground, so bright that Marcus had to shield his eyes with his forearm.

As the spheres grew at an alarming rate, so did the panic of the people around him. Many dropped to their knees, keeling over and weeping in surrender. The ground around the spheres evaporated, rising up along the edge of light like plumes of smoke, merging with them, fueling their growth.

There was no escape.

*   *   *   *   *

Marcus awoke, covered in sweat and panting heavily. Taylor stood in front of him, forcing his eyelids open, and peering into his pupils with a small flashlight.

"Get that away from me," Marcus snapped.

"Sorry Grey, just checking to see if you're ok."

"I'm fine. Just didn't sleep too well," Marcus lied.

"Alright, suit yourself."

The squad's new Lieutenant stood in the open pod across from Marcus, pouring the contents of a bottle of pills into his mouth, chewing through nearly a half a dozen of them, all the while rubbing his left knee. While the rest of the squad was cheerful, grateful to emerge from stasis despite the nausea and dizziness that followed, the Lieutenant was as surly as could be.

"What is that god-awful smell?" he demanded after swallowing his pills.

"Probably just a malfunction in the air filtration system," the medic was quick to reply. "What are those pills, Lieutenant?"

"It's for the pain," the officer sullenly retorted.

"Might I ask what happened to your knee?" Taylor asked, eager to take the Lieutenant's mind off the smell, which, much to the medic's surprise, had managed to linger in the air for the duration of their long journey.

"Nyari seeker drone," Mitchell replied, stretching his leg and continuing to rub his aching knee. "Damn, I hate those things. The damn thing got me just as I was returning back to base with a wounded man on my shoulder. I never even saw it coming."

"You were in the war?" Taz blurted.

The Lieutenant shot him a threatening glance.

"Of course I was in the war. Where do you think I got this?" the Lieutenant scolded, pointing to the scar which cut clear across his cheek and his eyebrow. "I was damned lucky to keep the eye."

"What was it like boss?" Jago rumbled, momentarily forgetting about his issues with their new leader.

"You don't want to know, son. A lot of good men have died on Nyramar," he sighed, looking sincerely regretful. "A lot of good men."

It was then that Marcus saw how different Mitchell was to Sergeant Lance. Despite their physical resemblance, the two were almost nothing alike. Perhaps the Lieutenant's experiences during the war had made him into a different man altogether.

"Are we winning the war?" Taz asked, genuinely intrigued.

"This war can't be won, by either side. We're both just too damned stubborn to admit it," the Lieutenant snorted.

"We're approaching Alamo Station. Four minutes people," Raven's voice echoed on the comms from the cockpit.

"Well, we best get ready," Mitchell ordered.

It had been six weeks since they'd left New Io and, despite their diminished numbers and new leadership, the squad's morale was running high.

"Man, I can't wait to get back to the Zonaka, throw back some cold ones, chat up a couple of hotties. Last time I was there, I met this gorgeous blonde. She was all over me, like... eggs... on... cheese. Just goes to show, no girl can resist my charms," Taz boasted.

"I didn't know they kept coma victims in the Zonaka," Reid quipped, much to everyone's amusement.

The Lieutenant swallowed a couple more pills before heading off to the cockpit.

"Hey Marcus, what do you think of the Lieutenant?" Taz asked.

Marcus stared at the door leading to the cockpit, making sure it had closed properly behind Mitchell.

"I don't trust him. He's Division 6," Marcus whispered.

"He told you?"

"No, but he's one of Intari's men," Marcus explained.

"Then what's he doing here?" Taz asked.

"I'm not sure. Nothing good," Marcus replied, looking back towards the door.

Raven had received docking clearance, and the new barracuda approached the array of hangar bays on the far side of the Alamo complex. Given Callisto's relatively thin atmosphere, the ride was a lot less bumpy than they'd gotten used to.

The doors to hangar bay 3-14 slid open and Raven eased the ship into position.

"It's about time we got a proper landing," Taz sniggered. "I was starting to think they'd forgotten to program her resonant memories."

The squad chuckled, all but Jago, who was still trying to understand the joke.

"Last one to the Zonaka buys the beer!" Taz bellowed as he ran for the hatch to the lower deck.

It was good to be home.

Chapter 41

Takahashi's limousine skimmed past a long line of hovercraft making slow progress in the busy afternoon traffic, the executive lane allowing swift travel between the city's more lavish sectors. Rain poured constantly from dark, billowing clouds that loomed eerily overhead. Most of the inhabitants of Sol, the capital of Beta Terra, cursed the relentless downpour, but Takahashi found it soothing, almost therapeutic.

A small screen embedded in his armrest displayed news of the latest scandal to hit the Tomiko family. Takahashi sneered in disgust. The corruption associated with the Tomiko clan was legendary in Terran society, and Takahashi had long ago decided that they were merely a symptom of the decay of Terran society.

"Do you ever think about where we're heading, Leonard?" Takahashi asked, half-heartedly.

"To the C-CORE headquarters," replied his driver, furrowing his brow in bewilderment.

"I mean as a people, Leonard," Takahashi corrected him.

The driver paused briefly, searching for an answer which wouldn't display his ignorance. Finally he decided against entering into a philosophical discussion with the eccentric old man, and simply remained quiet.

An icon on Takahashi's screen flashed green.

The old man fidgeted with the touch-sensitive surface of the screen, raising the divider between himself and the driver before accepting the incoming call. The silhouette of a man on the streets below flickered into view, accompanied by the noise of the busy ground-traffic mixed with the sounds of the heavy downpour.

"Mr. Muromoto," the shadowy figure greeted him. "I have what you requested. I had to go through a lot of back channels to get this information. If anyone finds out…"

"I think you'll find that the amount I'm adding to your fee will more than make up for the risk," Takahashi interrupted him.

The shadowy figure withdrew a datapad from inside his wet coat and proceeded to check his credit statement. The astonishment in his eyes was exactly what Takahashi had expected.

"You can transfer the information over this link," Takahashi instructed. "I have secured the connection between my account and yours. I assure you, it's quite safe."

The man on the screen looked apprehensively into the camera for a moment before transmitting the data.

"I trust that fulfills my mission?" he inquired, half expecting the old man to add further stipulations to the contract, especially given the exorbitant fee he'd just received.

Takahashi pressed a series of icons on the screen to call up the newly-received data. A devious smile slowly crept its way across his lips, lips which slowly began to quiver as the smile transformed into a vengeful scowl.

"It does indeed," Takahashi answered. "Thank you for your service."

The screen went momentarily blank before flickering back to the news report. Takahashi leaned back in his seat, arching his head to gaze up at the weeping sky as the limousine neared the administrative plaza.

Ahrend Benz, the head of C-CORE, was not a man particularly known for his patience. He had an odd look about him, the kind which, to the unobservant, might have seemed trustworthy, even saintly. He often feigned ignorance in the face of adversity, preying on those who would show sympathy. Yet, when the tables were turned, his demeanor quickly turned malicious. Takahashi knew that a man who knew nothing about compassion lay behind his deep-set eyes and crooked nose.

Benz was well known for his ravenous appetite for fine cuisine, something his bulging neckline did little to hide. However, his appetites also extended to sordid affairs with underage boys, a fact that he'd managed to keep hidden his entire career.

"We were friends once, you and I," Benz pleaded, feigning innocence. "Why are you doing this to me?"

Takahashi stood poised in front of a marvelously-crafted bloodwood desk. Benz's office reeked of opulence. The same exotic wood that made up the colossal desk lined the curving walls, intermingled with viewscreens that ranged from floor to ceiling. Paintings by the most famous Terran artists hung on the walls, works by Krause, Jiliad, Asuka, any one of which could have financed a mission to the deepest sectors of uncharted space.

The closest viewscreen depicted a muted news report citing allegations of child abuse by Benz.

"Friends?" Takahashi could barely contain his hatred. His clenched fists trembled, his nostrils flared with loathing. "How dare you utter that word in my presence?"

Benz slouched over the lavish desk, pressing his weight onto it with heavy hands, the glass countertop quickly fogging up around his pudgy fingers. His feigned innocence evaporated, leaving only disappointment and surrender.

"I… I couldn't help myself," he tried to explain. "I tried so many times to stop, but something inside me, something dark, kept creeping back up, wanting more."

Benz had begun sobbing hysterically, fumbling to wipe away the tears with the sleeve of his suit jacket, the cost of which could have fed a family of four for several months.

"You have to help me. We were friends once, you and I. Please, I beg you…" Mr. Benz pleaded as they began to hear sirens in the distance.

Takahashi's fists slowly began to unclench, his nostrils stopped flaring, and his pinched brow eased.

"What you did to those children is monstrous, but to call yourself my friend after what you did to my Lilly…" he whispered, drawing a wide-eyed look of astonishment from the weeping man.

"What…?" Benz started to ask.

"You covered your tracks quite well, old friend," Takahashi snarled sarcastically, "but not well enough."

He produced a small device from his jacket pocket and pointed it towards the viewscreen, calling up the documents he had received just prior to his meeting with Benz.

The display showed a trace of payments, through various shell corporations, to Takahashi's former driver, who'd also perished in the accident that had killed his wife, a man who Takahashi had had the utmost trust for. The documents also dictated payments to a terrorist organization in Coraya 4, an organization known for its inventive use of explosive devices.

"I never meant to hurt her," Benz sobbed. "The device was meant for you!"

"I know," Takahashi replied. "You wanted power even more than you wanted those boys."

"You'd just been named head of C-CORE," Mr. Benz laughed through his tears, turning to see the procession of law enforcement vehicles approaching, lights flashing. "They promoted you ahead of me. I knew that I'd be stuck in my old job. I panicked. It wasn't personal."

"Neither is this," Takahashi exclaimed, turning his back on the whimpering man. "It's just a means to an end."

Chapter 42

As one of the more popular hangouts on the promenade, the Zonaka was usually filled to capacity well into the early hours of the morning. The squad was seated on the bar's lower tier, up against a spacious, slanting windowpane which provided them with a view of Alpha Terra. A crowd of fresh clones erupted into cheers on the second tier above them as the Wako flared, hurling yet another batch of clueless clones off to the war.

The turquoise-tinted neon lights and the heavy mist of smoke formed an atmosphere of anonymity and intrigue, a welcome escape from the featureless halls of Alamo Station. Rows of glass shelves, stocked to the brim with an assortment of bottles, lined the wall behind the bar just below the second tier balcony.

"Let me see it again Corp!" Taz jostled.

Marcus, whose new rank had just been confirmed by the military hierarchy, produced the medal to the team once more, dumping it on the table with obvious disdain like a trinket he couldn't care less about.

It was the Iron Service Cross, awarded for acts of extraordinary heroism.

After their debriefing, their new Lieutenant had put Marcus forward for the medal for his brave actions that had saved the lives of the entire squad when their ship had crash-landed on New Io.

"That's some medal," Raven praised him, throwing back a shot. "You're damn lucky to be alive after that one Marcus."

"We all are," Marcus sighed.

"Do you remember how Suarez used to get drunk off his ass and start shouting shit at the officers? How that ass didn't wind up in the brig I'll never know," Taz joked. "I never did like him. It's weird, but… I'm gonna miss that asshole."

There was no reply. They all stared quietly at the bottom of their glasses.

"To Suarez," slurred Reid, having had more than his fair share to drink.

"To Suarez," confirmed the rest of the squad, raising their glasses in his memory.

"May they rest in peace, with God's blessing," Reid added.

"God? Listen to the reverend here. Why do you always have to go on about God?" Taz blurted.

"Reverend. I like that," chimed Raven, slapping Reid so hard on the shoulder that he spilled his drink down his shirt. "Yeah Rev, what's with this whole obsession about God?"

Reid was so drunk that he didn't even bother trying to drying himself off.

"Why not? What's wrong with the idea of someone watching over us? God keeps us safe," he mumbled, having trouble even sitting up straight.

"What do you guys think of the name 'Striker'?" Taz asked.

"For what? You knock up some poor girl?" Raven quipped.

"No, for me! I need a cool nickname," Taz explained.

"Yeah right! In your dreams, Romeo," Raven scoffed. "Actually… that's not bad!"

"You like it?" Taz asked, raising his eyebrows in surprised optimism.

"Not 'Striker' you moron! I meant Romeo," Raven protested.

"Romeo? What does it mean?" Taz queried, unfamiliar with the name and not recognizing Raven's attempt at sarcasm.

"Don't worry about it. Trust me, you're a total Romeo," she insisted.

"Hmpf… Romeo. It has a ring to it," Taz conceded.

"Where's the Lieutenant?" Taylor asked.

"Too good to drink with the rest of us grunts, I guess," Raven responded, throwing back yet another shot.

"I'm glad he's not here," Marcus confided. "I don't trust him any further than I can throw him."

"Neither do I," Raven admitted. "But there's nothing we can do about it now. He's here to stay. The best we can do is keep an eye on him, and hope for the best."

"Hey Ape, It's your turn," Taz beckoned, gesturing to the phalanx of empty glasses on the table.

Jago stood up and wobbled his way over to the bar, bumping into a jittery Taz lookalike, sending him crashing into the squad's table.

"Watch it freak!" Taz yelled, jumping to his feet to shove his twin away.

"What's your problem?" the other 6-28 yelled, backing off.

"You are!" Taz snarled.

"Wow, calm down boys!" Raven pleaded, grabbing Taz with one arm and pushing his lookalike away with the other.

The two scouts stared intently at one another, nostrils flaring, eyes locked, before quietly backing off.

"Why do you always get so worked up around your own model?" Raven sighed. "It's not like you're the same person. You just look alike!"

"Yeah, yeah, yeah. I've had it with the whole 'we're all special little snowflakes' crap," Taz snapped.

"Will you calm down! It's not like it's his fault," Raven responded, driving him back to his seat.

Taz sat tensely, clutching the edge of the table. Marcus could see that he was just waiting for an excuse or an opportunity to act up again. "Maybe you should have one of the Doc's special cigarettes," he suggested.

"Can't. It's not exactly... sanctioned in military regs," Taylor confided.

Taz finally eased up when he spotted Jago getting into a confrontation with one of the newbies at the bar.

"Did you know they can barely read?" Taylor blurted.

"Who?" Marcus asked.

"The Apes. The 6-17s. Well, some of them can. But I hear it's a big problem. They just keep breeding them for their overwhelming combat capabilities. The W.R.D. has been trying to make them more intelligent for years."

"Are you serious?" roared Taz, nearly bursting out into laughter.

"Yes, I'm serious. But I wouldn't joke about it if I were you. They can get a bit... defensive," the medic warned him, fighting not to laugh himself.

Just then, Jago returned to the table with his monstrous hands clutching six large glasses of beer, carefully trying not to spill anything.

"Thanks Ape," Taz sniggered, desperately trying not to laugh.

Marcus was quick to interject, drawing attention away from the sniggering duo. "To fallen friends," he said, raising his glass for a toast.

"To Jenna," Jago added, taking a huge gulp of his beer.

Marcus began to zone out. He was just beginning to see how unique they all were. He'd wondered so many times before whether or not they were just the same as all the other clones. Now he finally understood that, despite their appearances, it was their experiences that made them unique.

"Do you think they're watching us?" blurted Reid, practically unconscious, face-down on the table in a pool of spilt beer.

"Do we think who's watching us?" Raven asked.

"You know… Tony, Lance, all of them…"

"Easy there Rev. I think it's time you got back to the clubhouse," Taylor laughed. "I'm gonna go make sure he gets back safely and then find someplace where I can light one of these," he added, patting the pocket where he kept his herbal remedies.

The medic grabbed Reid by the shoulders, steadying him as he got up from his seat.

"You take him straight to bed Doc, no hanky-panky," Raven grinned, earning her an angry glare from Taylor.

"I can help Doc," Jago said, rising up to grab Reid from the other side.

The two helped carry him out of the Zonaka, past the countless clones drinking away their fear of the war they were destined for.

"So Raven, you want to go and…" Taz started to say.

"No!" bellowed Raven, interrupting him mid-sentence.

"But you don't even know what I was gonna say!" Taz protested.

"Forget it Romeo. It's never going to happen," she declared, rising to leave.

"Oh come on! You don't know what you're missing," Taz clamored as he tried to go after her.

"You're a walking hard-on and waste of a breeding tube Romeo! Leave me the fuck alone," Raven roared, storming out of the club.

Taz stood stock still, his hands at his sides in quiet surrender.

"Ouch," Marcus said after a short, awkward pause. "That was harsh."

Taz snapped, slamming his clenched fist into the table. Much to their surprise, the table snapped in half, spilling drinks and throwing empty glasses all over the place. Marcus knew that Taz was strong, but not that strong.

"Whoa there, Romeo. Calm down," Marcus consoled him. "How the hell did you do that?"

Taz didn't answer. He was staring at the giant viewscreen above the bar.

"Hey Marcus. Isn't that your old friend up there?" Taz said, gesturing towards the screen.

Marcus turned around sharply in his seat, the shattered table forgotten. Nothing could have prepared him for the image above the bar. There he was, the man he had abandoned, betrayed, on Alpha Terra. His old friend Steven Meer.

Once the initial shock wore off, Marcus raced to the bar, shouting for the bartender to turn up the volume.

"...will not waver, until Alpha Terrans have a representative on the Council. Unless our demands are met, we will begin to execute the hostages. We have taken this action only as a last resort. The people of Alpha Terra are crying out for help! We have been ignored for too long! No longer will we be a dumping ground for the Republic's problems. We will no longer be ignored," Steven was proclaiming.

Shortly after Steven's speech, the announcer came on. She was a blonde, fair-skinned woman with slanted eyes and a petite nose.

"This striking footage was sent to the network just moments ago from the Strom sensor outpost on the edge of the Terran solar system. Given recent developments in the war on Nyramar, the facility has been operating with a minimal staff. Nevertheless, military intelligence claims that as many as a hundred Beta Terrans were present when the terrorists stormed the outpost."

Terrorist? Steven, a terrorist? That couldn't be right. Marcus couldn't believe what he was hearing.

"Most of the staff consists of scientists and custodians, left over to maintain minimal functionality and to conduct research vital to the war efforts," the announcer continued. "Our sources say that the terrorists gained entry to the base by means of a stolen supply frigate, scheduled to bring provisions to the outpost. We'll bring you more information as the story develops."

Almost as soon as the announcer had fallen silent, Marcus's wrist comm began to sound. He hit the button to answer the call.

"Corporal Grey," came the voice of Lieutenant Mitchell. "We have an urgent mission. Report to the hangar bay immediately."

Chapter 43

The squad had assembled and geared up in a hurry. Lieutenant Mitchell was shouting orders at the top of his lungs, urging the squad to move like there was no tomorrow. They'd all been issued with new armor, the same make and model as their old suits, but painted an off-white mottled with streaks of gray and black, and Marcus also received a technician's toolkit. Taylor had had to give them all anti-intoxicants to relieve their inebriation, but they were still forced to dress and carry Reid to the ship, as the pills required at least a half an hour to take effect. As soon as the last of them had made it to the lower deck, the barracuda blasted off into space, engines flaring, en route to the Wako station.

"You mean we're finally gonna get to use that thing?" Taz asked, excited as could be.

"Pipe down Sobieski," the Lieutenant ordered, going through the mission parameters on his datapad. An optical lens at its base projected a holographic map of the Strom sensor outpost, zooming in and out, panning across various sections as the Lieutenant went through the diagram.

"Alright, you overgrown jizz bags, listen up. We've got at least eight hostiles holding a little over a hundred hostages. The reason we were chosen for this mission is that one of the hostage takers, Steven Meer, used to belong to this squad. The higher ups are hoping that it will provide us with the edge we need to resolve this matter as quickly as possible, with a minimal number of casualties," Mitchell briefed them.

"Conditions will be rough. Strom is a ball of ice with sub-zero atmospheric conditions, so we'll have to limit our exposure. Our suits can only withstand so much. Now, being a sensor outpost, we're going to have to come in from the other side of the planet and make our way along the ground. Raven's going to have to pull of some fancy maneuvers to keep us as low as possible if we are to stay below their sensor range," the Lieutenant continued.

"Time for another crash landing!" Taz joked.

"Shut it, Sobieski!" Mitchell flared.

"What about defenses?" Marcus asked.

"The base is fitted with a pair of high-powered siege cannons. Their tracking speed is no match for a dropship, but we can't afford to be spotted. That eliminates the use of the station's docking bay. Raven will have to drop us off as close as she can, and we'll proceed on foot," Mitchell responded. "The hostages are most likely being held inside the main tower, so we'll gain entry through the old control tower on the opposite side of the base, and make our way from there. Understood?"

"Yes sir," the squad responded in unison, all but Reid, who lay strapped into his stasis pod, slowly starting to recuperate.

"I don't want you to take any chances. If anything moves, shoot it!" Mitchell instructed.

The implications of what they were about to do left Marcus wondering if there was any way to end this peacefully. The thought of having to pull a gun on his old friend was unimaginable. Maybe that was what the Lieutenant had meant. Perhaps they were hoping that Steven would feel the same way, and, when it came down to it, he would surrender without a fight. No, that wouldn't happen. Marcus knew that Steven was a man of great conviction, a man who felt betrayed by someone he'd thought was his best friend. No, if there was a peaceful resolution, it wouldn't be that easy.

There were also other things to consider. In the light of his realization that it was the clones' experiences that made them unique, not their genetic code or their programming, Marcus pondered what could have happened to Steven on Alpha Terra to make him want to harm innocent civilians. Steven had always felt out of place on the Alamo. Perhaps it was just Marcus's betrayal that pushed him over the edge. For all he knew, this could all be his fault.

"Coming up on Wako station Lieutenant," Raven called on the comms. "I need your authorization code."

"I'd hold on to something if I were you. We're in for quite a ride," the Lieutenant advised the squad as he made his way to the cockpit.

"Won't we get squashed like bugs pulling that many Gs?" Taz mumbled, leaning towards Reid so the others wouldn't hear.

"Don't worry. The inertial dampeners counteract the effects. Well, most of them," Reid responded, clutching his head in an attempt to stave off the massive headache that was slowly making its way to the back of his neck.

"Most of them?" Taz squeaked.

"There have been some accidents in the past. But it's rare."

"What kind of accidents?"

"Well, syncing up the increase in the dampeners to the thrust of the mass accelerator is a tricky thing. I heard some stories about ships arriving at Nyramar that were filled with Terran goo. The troops just… liquefied under the immense pressure," Reid explained, grinning at Taz's reaction.

"Fuck me! Are you for real?" Taz blurted.

333

"It's even more dangerous with such a short distance. If they calculate the trajectory wrong, or if we don't manage to slow down in time, we'll end up in the ass end of space, or splattered across the planet's surface," Reid went on, adding to Taz's worry. "Like the Lieutenant said, I'd hold on to something," he concluded.

Taz whimpered, digging his nails so deep into the rim of his pod Marcus was sure they'd need a welding torch to pry him loose.

"Entering the chute," Raven called. "Get ready."

The barracuda was dwarfed by the massive barrel of the Wako, capable of firing entire battleships.

"Counting down, 10… 9… 8…" she yelled.

"I don't wanna do this," Taz bellowed. "There has to be another way."

"5… 4…."

The buildup of energy surrounding the ship crackled up against the hull.

"3… 2… 1… engage!"

The ship's inertial dampeners were just a split second out of sync with the tremendous force of the mass accelerator. Marcus and the other struggled as they were pressed forcefully against the sides of their pods. If it weren't for the heightened tension of the situation, they would have looked ridiculous as their lips and cheeks warbled, warped away from their skulls by the unseen force of their acceleration. Even if they'd wanted to scream, they were unable to, their lungs compressed by the high g forces they were undergoing.

Luckily, it only lasted about half a minute. As the barracuda reached its optimal velocity and immediately began its lengthy deceleration procedure, the air came back into their lungs and they were able to relax and breathe normally. Reid threw up almost immediately, and the others were severely disoriented.

The Lieutenant came wobbling back from the cockpit just a few moments later, still slightly dizzy.

"We've got a couple of hours to kill before we reach Strom. I suggest we all get some sleep. I want everyone at their best for the mission," he suggested.

Remarkable, thought Marcus. Only two hours. It would have taken nine weeks with the barracuda's own thrusters. It made him truly appreciate the distance to Nyramar, given that it was a six month journey with the mass accelerator. It would take hundreds of years without it.

"Something to help you sleep there Corporal?" Taylor offered, holding up an air hypo.

The others were already drifting off to sleep, having received their dose. With his mind wandering all over the place, Marcus was too anxious to fall asleep on his own, so he nodded at the offer of an injection. The medic pressed the pen-shaped device up against his neck and pressed the trigger. Marcus felt a diffused pressure as the serum was thrust into his bloodstream.

His vision blurred sharply and, within seconds, Marcus was fast asleep.

* * * * *

A stark contrast to New Io, Strom was a frozen and barren world, incapable of sustaining life. So far out in the solar system, very little light or warmth made its way to the tiny, insignificant planet.

"Is everyone ready?" asked Raven, rhetorically.

Reid made an odd gesture, touching his forehead, his stomach and the left and right sides of his chest in sequence, all the while muttering to himself under his breath.

"Nervous Albano?" the Lieutenant asked, shooting the sniper a weird look.

"We don't have the best luck when it comes to landing, sir," Reid explained.

Jago and Taylor chuckled in response.

The usual vibrations began making their way through the ship's hull as it entered Strom's atmosphere.

"Here we go again," Raven bellowed over the ship's comms.

Whether due to the cold weather, or perhaps the atmosphere being thinner than they were used to, the turbulence was less severe than the squad had expected. As the shaking failed to escalate to the levels they'd known before, they half expected that something had gone wrong and they'd been forced to back out, but after a few minutes of smooth sailing tensions began to ease.

"Approaching the Sah'jyra trench," Raven informed them. "Twenty eight minutes to the DZ."

The ship dived left and right, enormous cliffs of rock and ice shooting past the windows at the back of the deck. Raven had the arduous task of trying to prevent the bulky ship from slamming head on into a cliff face. Small rocks and sheets of snow crumbled down into the chasm behind them as the roaring engines blasted them loose. The squad, strapped into their pods, gritted their teeth and bore the flight in silence.

"Two minutes," Raven's voice came again. "Get everyone down below and ready to deploy."

"You heard the lady," Mitchell yelled. "Get your sorry asses down below."

"Pfff, she's no lady," Taz sighed, too quietly for the Lieutenant to hear.

The squad made their way to the lower deck, steadying themselves against the bulkheads as best they could as the ship still thundered along an icy chasm, swerving periodically to avoid a collision. Although Jago's oversized stasis pod was at the rear of the ship, next to the ladder leading below, it took him so long to unfold himself from the cramped confines of the equipment that he let the others descend first. The towering giant held his helmet in one hand and steadied himself with the other, waiting for Reid, the last person before him, to slide down the rungs.

Suddenly the ship veered sharply, sending Jago crashing into the rim of the small window beside the hatch, slamming his face against the hard metal. Shaking his head to ease the shock, the huge man stared at his reflection in the window, inspecting the cut lip and grazes he'd received, only to see the edges of the wounds slowly pulling together, healing completely, leaving not even the smallest mark behind. Not knowing any better, he simply shrugged his shoulders, and began climbing down the rungs to the lower deck.

"I think I can get close to a ledge up ahead. It's the only place I can drop you anywhere near the outpost. You might be better off using the forward ramp," Raven called.

"Does everyone have the proper atmos canister installed?" Mitchell asked, tilting back the squad's helmets in turn to make sure everything was in order.

"Ready when you are Raven," the Lieutenant confirmed.

The pilot engaged the ship's deceleration thrusters and the ship came to an abrupt stop, swerving a full ninety degrees and tilting violently, the squad nearly crashing into the left bulkhead.

"Depressurizing," Raven warned them as she activated the pumps.

The squad held their breath in anticipation, waiting for her to lower the ramp.

"Deck's clear. Opening the hatch," Raven called, as the forward ramp began to descend.

Unlike Lance, who'd always hung back, Lieutenant Mitchell was the first to exit, followed quickly by Jago and Reid. As Marcus emerged onto the ramp, he was buffeted by the sharp icy winds of Strom. Stumbling down the ramp to the narrow ledge of solid ice, the breathtaking scenery unfolded before him stole his attention.

"Keep it moving people," Mitchell urged them. "The outpost is almost three hundred meters from here, and we've got some climbing to do. Excellent flying there Raven. You're good to go," the Lieutenant added when Taz and Taylor had joined them on the ledge.

They could see Raven through the windshield just above them, nodding her approval as the ship spun about, dipping down into the chasm as it began gaining momentum, before disappearing behind a column of frozen rock.

Chapter 44

Getting to the outpost wasn't as simple as the squad had hoped. The ledge didn't run directly towards the outpost, some hundred meters above them and three times that distant, and the wall of the cliff rising above them was too steep to scale where the barracuda had dropped them off. Making their way along the narrow ledge also proved more treacherous than they'd anticipated. More often than not, their footing gave way at the slightest pressure, making them constantly have to probe and double check before moving on. It was closing in on an hour and a half when the squad finally found a position secure enough to climb.

"This is insane," blurted Taz, for the fifth time.

Lieutenant Mitchell had given up trying to silence him.

Their latest staging point was a tapered crevasse in a formation of rock and ice that trailed almost forty meters up, slanting somewhat to the left as it did so.

"Sobieski, you're up," the Lieutenant ordered.

Taz prepared the climbing gear, specifically designed for ice climbing, that had come with the squad's winter-pattern armor. It included a pair of spiked soles that he clasped onto the bottom of his boots, and a specialized pistol that fired spring-loaded cams attached to a length of rope. Taz secured the rope to his rappelling harness and fired off one of the cams. It pierced through the ice above them, digging in so deep that all they could see was the black slender rope trailing out of the hole. The scout slung his carbine over his shoulder and started climbing, with the others waiting patiently below.

"Ape, you're last. I can't risk those cams coming loose on account of your weight," Mitchell ordered.

"Yes boss," acknowledged Jago, somewhat disappointed.

"What if he falls?" Marcus asked pointedly, thinking it unfair to discriminate against Jago on account of his size and weight.

"He won't," the Lieutenant snapped. "That's why we're going first. So that if anything happens there will be more of us up there to pull him up."

Jago nodded, somewhat reassured by the Lieutenant's reasoning.

In the meantime, Taz had reached the first cam. He leaned back, away from the wall he'd climbed, bracing himself against the other side of the crevasse, and fired off another cam.

"Keep it steady Sobieski," Lieutenant Mitchell ordered.

They had already been out in the cold for way too long, and the wind had picked up its pace, promising to turn into a raging storm. Despite the insulation of his armor, Marcus could barely feel his fingers, and was beginning to worry about having to climb such a steep incline.

"In position," Taz proclaimed as he flung his leg over a ledge high above. "Just give me a minute to fire off a few more of these just in case."

"You're up Albano," the Lieutenant urged, handing Reid the dangling piece of rope.

Reid grabbed it and deftly began a steady climb up the wall of ice. Marcus was impressed at how easy he made it seem.

"Careful Reid, that part's slippery as hell," Taz informed him, watching Reid approach a hazardous spot.

Reid pushed himself away from the ice with his feet, shimmying himself off to the side to avoid the slippery area. In only a couple of minutes, Reid had reached the top and the Lieutenant was already gesturing for Taylor to proceed.

Marcus watched nervously as the medic made his way up. He wasn't as physically fit as the rest of the squad, and Marcus was loath to imagine what would happen if he were to lose his grip on the slender rope. Of course, the belay device on his harness would stop him from plummeting to his death at the bottom of the chasm, but things could always go wrong.

Fortunately the Doc had studied Reid's ascent with great care, and followed his footings precisely.

"You're up Grey," Mitchell prompted.

Marcus grabbed the rope and attached his belay device, a clasp meant to generate enough friction to prevent a climber from falling if he were to lose his footing. A pair of ascenders followed suit, metallic clamps with handles and triggers that locked onto the rope when pressed, allowing the climber to move more quickly without having to rely on his own hands.

Marcus pressed the trigger on the ascender in his left hand, locking the rope in place. He moved his right ascender further up the rope, bracing himself against the wall with his legs as he stretched up. The right ascender locked into place and Marcus released the left one, pulling himself up before reattaching it and sliding the right ascender up once more. It was hard work, especially given the weight of his armor, but he quickly began to pick up pace as his blood started to flow, warming his achingly cold fingers and toes.

After clearing the initial streak of ice, the rest of the first half of the climb was relatively easy. Marcus kept finding clear footing on the barren rock as he continued pushing one ascender above the other, slowly pulling himself up twenty centimeters at a time.

"You're coming up on the rough spot there Grey," Taz called as Marcus approached what appeared to be a solid block of ice, covering the upper middle part of the crevasse. Following Reid's moves, Marcus prepared to spring from the wall, propelling himself to the side where he could shimmy up around the edge of the ice. As he leaned into the wall, bracing himself for the push, his foot slipped out from under him as he kicked.

Marcus was sent spinning into thin air, the wall of the crevasse shooting by him. In shock, he lost his grip on his ascenders, but it took a moment for him to understand that he really had fallen. When the realization hit him, his eyes popped wide open and he gasped, his stomach feeling like it had jumped up into his chest. He frantically flailed his arms in the air, desperately trying to grab the slender rope. All of a sudden, Marcus felt his stomach come crashing back down as the belay device caught on, stopping his fall dead in its tracks with a jolt, leaving him dangling on the rope like a fly caught in a spider's web.

"Shit! You ok Marcus?" yelled Taz, leaning over the ledge to monitor the situation.

Marcus took a second to regain his senses. He had fallen only a few meters, but he was still spinning and panting heavily. He reached over to where one of the cams protruded from a rocky outcropping and pulled himself towards the wall, steadying himself. Luckily, the ascenders had trailed down the rope after him and now clung to the belay device secured to his belt. Marcus grabbed the ascenders and, slowly but surely, began climbing back up.

He reached the hazardous sheet of ice again, and took more care to secure his footing this time. As he sprung from the wall, sailing through the air, he reached out, ready to grab the lip of the crevasse.

"Nicely done," Reid congratulated him as Marcus caught a grip on one of the large rocks protruding from the ice.

It was easy climbing from there, and the others were ready and waiting to help pull him up. To their surprise, the Lieutenant made even Reid seem like an amateur. Securing the rope between his crossed legs and foregoing footing altogether, Mitchell swarmed directly up the rope, a method that allowed him an even greater degree of control over his climb.

"Not a bad trick for an old dog," Reid mused as Mitchell made it to the top more than a minute faster than he had.

"Can we hurry this up? I really need to smoke," Taylor snapped.

"You really need to lay off those," Reid yelled back.

"Hey, smoking is a dying art my friend. I'm just trying to keep it alive," the medic retorted.

"Alright Ape, we're ready for you," the Lieutenant called down. "Just take it nice and slow."

The cams trembled under the behemoth's tremendous weight as he started to make his way up the rope. The squad grabbed the rope, each latching on with their ascenders to support Jago, making sure he wouldn't tear the cams right out of the wall. Despite his weight, Marcus was impressed by Jago's monstrous strength as he confidently hauled himself almost half a meter up with every movement.

When it came to the slippery part of the slope, Jago decided against swinging to the side to find a better spot, but simply kept on going, his legs frantically running and kicking in place on the frictionless ice as if he were suffering a seizure. Although it slowed him down some, his tactic worked and he was quickly almost at the top.

Suddenly one of the cams burst out of the side of the wall, crashing down and almost hitting Jago right in the face.

"Grab him!" shouted the Lieutenant.

The squad dropped the rope and knelt at the lip of the ledge, reaching down, ready to pull their huge squadmate up to safety. Without warning, a cam in the wall behind them shot loose, and the rest creaked, seemingly ready to break free at any moment.

"Give us your hand!" Reid yelled.

Jago lunged up, stretching his arm as far as he could. Reid had the longest arms, and was just able to hook his fingers onto Jago's stubby hand. The huge man kicked away from the wall, jumping a few centimeters up into the air before coming crashing back down again. Luckily, that was enough of an edge for Reid to get a firm grip.

It took all of their combined strength to drag Jago up over the edge, and even then he almost took half of the squad down with him to an untimely death.

"Let's hope we don't have to go back the same way," Taz panted as the squad finally surveyed their surroundings.

They were stood on an icy shelf roughly eight meters wide, more than enough to allow for an easy passage. They started off westwards in the direction of their objective, the path before them turning a sharp corner to reveal the Strom sensor outpost.

The base consisted of several structures scattered over both walls of a huge gorge in the mountainside, linked via tunnels and chambers that had been carved into the rock. The nearest structure was a small tower looming almost directly overhead, perched atop a low-hanging cliff, a pair of massive dual-barrel siege cannons resting firmly beside it, each one easily the size of a small frigate. Further away to the west two circular towers, merged together along their long axes to form a single spire, jutted from the opposite side of the gorge which sheltered the outpost from the planet's harsh elements. A forty-meter wide sensor dish was erected on the ice shelf lying on the floor of the gorge below them. The docking bay, a massive airlock embedded into the side of the mountain at the far end of the gorge, served as the outpost's only means of ingress.

"Most of the structures are inside the mountain. It's a lot bigger than it looks," Mitchell informed the squad. "We'll get in through the control tower above us. There's an access panel we can cut through."

A short hike up the side of the mountain lead the squad to the base of the small control tower, whose purpose it was to monitor traffic around Strom. Over the years, as budget cuts led to fewer workers, its functions had been gradually rerouted to one of the main towers on the other side of the gorge.

"Given the terrorists' numbers, the control tower should be empty. It wouldn't make sense for them to spread out and stretch themselves so thin. Still, keep an eye out," Mitchell ordered.

Marcus knelt by the access panel, pulling a miniature cutting torch from the toolkit he'd been issued with back on the Alamo. The flame intensified as he adjusted the nozzle, focusing it to a narrow point. It took a few minutes to heat the metal properly, but as soon as he had made a hole in the metal sheet, cutting the rest was easy work. The panel soon came loose, falling to the frozen ground and sliding down the side of the mountain. Steam poured out of the opening as the warm air flowed out through the gaping hole.

"Let's hustle," Mitchell ordered. "We've got to get past the control tower's airlock and close it before the internal sensors pick up the leak and alert the targets to our presence."

The squad rushed through the opening, past a semi-circular bank of computer consoles and chairs below a steam-covered window.

"Move, move, move!" the Lieutenant urged as they dived through the door on the opposite side of the tower, sealing it shut behind them. They were in.

Chapter 45

"This whole eastern section is the military part of the base. It hasn't seen much use since we took the fight to Nyramar," Lieutenant Mitchell told the squad as they made their way along a corridor.

The squad had deftly threaded their way through a virtual labyrinth of passages. Had the Lieutenant not possessed the schematics for the installation, they would surely have gotten lost. Great care was taken in clearing each chamber, making sure that none of the terrorists would be able to sneak up behind them from an unchecked room.

"How much further?" Taz asked as he and Reid caught up with the others after clearing the administrative section.

"Another eighty meters before we reach the security check point," the Lieutenant answered, consulting the schematics on his datapad as they moved. "From there we should be able to access the hangar bay, and get into the main tower."

The hallway curved gently ahead and behind them, rows of doors on the west leading to the now-disused barracks, the occasional larger entryway on the east to larger areas such as the mess hall and admin section.

"Grey, you and the Ape go seal off quarters E-1 through E-12. Albano and Sobieski, you two seal off D-1 through D-12. Me and the Doc will take care of F block. We'll rendezvous at the armory up ahead in five," Mitchell ordered.

As the squad's technician, Marcus produced several lengths of thick metallic tape from his pouch and handed out one each to the

Lieutenant and Taz, keeping one handy for himself and placing the rest back in his pouch.

"Place it over the door and the frame and just pull on the little tab there," Marcus instructed them.

The living quarters were underground towers, made up of twelve floors of ten rooms stacked on top of one another and accessible from the common hallway via a series of elevators. By sealing off each entry to the hallway, the squad was able to save valuable time by not having to search hundreds of small rooms.

Jago kept a look out as Marcus knelt in front of the door, attaching the thick piece of tape vertically where the door met the doorframe.

"What's that boss?" Jago boomed, peering over Marcus's shoulder.

"Shush, not so loud," Marcus scolded. "Watch and learn."

Marcus took off his gloves to allow for a finer degree of manipulation before grabbing the protruding tab of the thin piece of plastic film covering its surface, tearing it off abruptly.

"Get back," Marcus ordered as the metallic tape suddenly ignited, burning intensely.

The pair of them jumped back to the opposite side of the corridor, shielding their eyes from the white-hot flames. In just a few seconds the fire had died out, leaving the door welded to the frame.

"That's pretty hot boss," Jago grinned.

"Come on, we'd better get to the armory," said Marcus, slapping Jago encouragingly on the shoulder.

Taz and Reid were just finishing up the job when Marcus and Jago came strutting down the corridor.

"Everything ok?" asked Marcus.

"We're all set. Let's go scope out the armory. Who knows, maybe we can find something useful," Taz answered.

The armory was just twenty meters ahead. Taz and Reid went in first to gauge if it was safe, Marcus and Jago following quickly behind them. It was an L-shaped chamber, with racks of dust-covered rifles and carbines lining the far wall. Crates of ammo were stacked on the floor in the far corner. A door on the far left side led to a firing range that seemed not to have seen any use since the dawn of the war.

"This shit's ancient," Taz moaned, rifling through the weapon racks.

"You won't find much of use there," the Lieutenant declared, storming through the door.

Behind him, Taylor was grinning from ear to ear with his helmet under one arm and a half finished cigarette between his lips. Reid just shook his head, smiling in disbelief.

"Let's move. The security check point is just up ahead," Mitchell ordered, snatching Taylor's cigarette from his mouth and tossing it on the ground.

The medic hurriedly put his helmet back on as the squad stormed back out into the corridor.

They quickly cleared the corner leading to the security room, a dimly-lit square chamber with three security consoles forming a horseshoe in its center, two of which were sprayed with still-wet blood. A series of gray metal cabinets lined the walls. Another hallway to the left led, via a large airlock, to the docking bay. To their right there were two sets of doors, one small and unremarkable, the other a huge, circular portal that wouldn't have looked out of place on a starship. A series of lights on the farthest console flashed red at short intervals, indicating that something was amiss. A pair of security guards lay face-down on the floor between the consoles, each shot twice through the torso and once through the head.

"I guess they were lying about there being no casualties," Taz snarled.

"Grey, go check that console. Albano and Sobieski, you two clear the detention area. The terrorists may have used the cells to secure hostages," the Lieutenant barked, pointing to the smaller doorway in the right-hand wall.

Taz and Reid went for the door, kicking it open into a narrow corridor while Marcus inspected the flashing console.

--- IMMINENT REACTOR OVERLOAD --
-- MALFUNCTION IN RELEASE VALVE(S): 1, 2, 3 --

"Lieutenant, we've got sabotage. The reactor's been compromised," warned Marcus.

"Can you bypass it?" Mitchell asked.

"I'm trying," Marcus responded, attempting a series of commands, all of which came up empty. "It's not responding to any of my commands. We'll have to do it manually."

"Will that be an issue?" asked the Lieutenant.

"No problem sir. It's just a matter of turning the handles in there," he answered, nodding to the thickly-shielded circular door to the left of the detention area. "The sabotage means the levels of radiation in the core are dangerous, but the shutdown itself is easy. Even a trained ape could do it," Marcus told him. "Sorry Jago."

"What?" Jago rumbled.

"Then get it done," Mitchell ordered him.

Marcus nodded in approval and started searching through the cabinets lining the rooms for a radiation suit.

"Sir, the detention area is clear," Reid called as he and Taz came bursting back through the door they'd disappeared through a moment before.

"But we may have a problem," Taz added.

"My lucky day," Mitchell sighed. "What is it now?"

"Not sure sir. All the cells are open," Taz explained.

"So?"

"I've got an itch sir," Reid interjected. "I just want to check the logs to confirm it."

Lieutenant Mitchell shook his head wearily before gesturing for them to proceed. Reid went straight for the closest console, calling up the daily logs.

Marcus finally found the right cabinet, but to his distress he found that both the primary and backup radiation suits had been slashed to pieces.

He held them up for the Lieutenant to see.

"Fan-fucking-tastic. How long 'til it blows?" the Lieutenant barked.

"Less than half an hour," Marcus confessed.

"Until what blows?" Taz almost shrieked, his anxiety obvious.

"The reactor… it's going critical," Marcus told him.

"What? We should get out of here!" Taz yelled.

"There's no time. If that thing blows it'll cause a thermonuclear explosion that would take out the entire base and everything else within several kilometers," Mitchell barked.

"Well that's just fucking great," Taz roared.

"It gets better," Reid added. "I found our missing detainee."

"Let's hear it," sighed Lieutenant Mitchell.

"A logistics frigate called the *TLS Caecius* arrived four days ago with three Nyari prisoners for study. According to the logs, two of the three have been removed from the cell block for tests."

"What happened to the third?" asked Taz, shouldering his carbine and peering into every corner of the room, clearly expecting a crazed Nyari assassin to jump on him from the shadows.

"I guess whoever it was that messed with the reactor must have accidentally released the locks on the detention cells," Reid proposed.

"We're so screwed!"

"Forget the Nyari. The fact that the terrorists messed with the reactor tells us something," presented Lieutenant Mitchell.

"What?" Taylor replied.

"They know there's no way in hell that the Republic will cut them a deal. They're here to martyr themselves."

"What's a martyr?" Jago rumbled.

"They're here to die, stupid!" Taz stormed, losing his patience.

Taylor threw his helmet to the floor and pulled out one of the chairs from beneath the computer console, dropping into it with a groan.

"What the hell do you think you're doing?" Mitchell roared.

"If we're all going die, we might as well enjoy the time we've got left," Taylor explained, lighting the end of one of his cigarettes. "At least until we come up with a plan."

The Lieutenant snarled, but didn't order Taylor back to his feet.

"Can I have one too?" Jago asked.

Chapter 46

Marcus's thoughts were wracked with turmoil as he tried to imagine what could lead Steven to not only attack innocent civilians and hold them hostage, but to be willing to kill himself in the process, all to prove some kind of point to the Republic.

No, that wasn't the Steven he knew. The Steven he had known would have done anything to survive, to be free.

"Someone's got to go in there," Taz declared.

Morale was low, and tempers were flaring as the squad weighed their options in the security room. Jago and Taylor had already finished smoking, much to Mitchell's displeasure.

"I agree. We have to do something, and we have to do it fast," the Lieutenant conceded.

"Whoever's going in there isn't coming back out," Taylor warned them, looking askance at the heavy door leading to the reactor. "We've got no protective suit, and, judging by the readout, the levels of radiation in there are lethal, even with only a short exposure."

"Doc, how are we on anti-rads?" Mitchell asked, hoping for a solution.

"We're low. Those pills are incredibly expensive and the military only hands out so many," Taylor confided.

"I'm not going in there," Taz barked defiantly. "There's no fucking way I'm gonna end up like Jenna."

"Fuck you!" roared Jago, lunging forward ready to break Taz's jaw.

"I'm sorry Ape, but if you wanna test your luck in there, go right ahead!" Taz shouted at the huge man.

"I'll do it," snapped Marcus, silencing both of them before things got out of hand. "I'm the most logical choice anyway, being the squad's technician and all."

"I thought you said even a trained monkey could do it," Mitchell eyed him seriously.

"Well, yes, but who knows what else could go wrong? It's better if someone who's trained…" Marcus began before Reid interrupted him.

"No Marcus. I'll do it. You've already played the hero card. It's time for someone else to step up," Reid said quietly. "And besides, I'm not afraid of dying."

The Lieutenant put a hand on the sniper's shoulder, gripping him firmly. Marcus wasn't sure, but he thought he sensed a measure of pride in the officer's eyes, which struck him as odd, since he was certain that the only reason Mitchell had been assigned as their leader was to monitor them and report back to Division 6.

"Won't his armor protect him?" Taz blurted in concern.

"I'm afraid not. Not against radiation. It's made from a light-weight polymer with some special padding. If anything, it'd just slow him down," Mitchell predicted.

"So what do I do?" Reid finally asked after a moment of silent contemplation.

Taz's eyes were swelling up with tears at the thought of losing yet another member of the team. Despite their usual quipping and ribbing, Marcus had suspected that the two of them had developed a strong bond. A bond that would soon be broken.

"It's simple," Marcus began to explain. "There are three manual release valves. Each one should have a pressure gauge. Just turn each of them clockwise until you see the pressure begin to decrease."

"I'll stay with him," Taz declared. "In case one of the terrorists doubles back and tries to stop him fixing it."

Mitchell nodded his approval. "I'd better notify Raven," the Lieutenant said, configuring his comms.

"Raven, do you read me?"

"Loud and clear sir. What's your status?"

"Where are you parked?" the Lieutenant asked.

"I'm just over two clicks south of the outpost," she replied.

"I need you to take the ship out further, six kilometers minimum. We've got a potentially disastrous situation here."

"Aye aye sir. Relocating now," Raven acknowledged.

"We should go. Those terrorists won't kill themselves," Mitchell went on, looking at the rest of the squad.

"Actually...," Taz started to interject.

"Oh, right. Very funny Sobieski," the Lieutenant groaned.

The squad chuckled, the atmosphere lightening as they gathered their gear and prepared to leave Taz and Reid behind.

Marcus looked towards Reid for one last time. Reid stared confidently back at him, as if trying to reassure him that this was really what he wanted.

"Go," Reid finally urged them.

*   *   *   *   *

Lieutenant Mitchell led from the front with Marcus, Jago and Taylor trailing behind him through the docking bay. The hijacked supply frigate stood docked in one corner, opposite a row of four massive fuel tanks, a wide segmented hose connecting the ship to the reservoirs, as if it had been abandoned during refueling. The space closest to the wall was divided into different sections, most of which seemed to facilitate visiting ships. Three rusted and worn interceptors jutted from rapid deployment harnesses in the far wall, long past their prime. A pair of small enclosed atmospheric shuttle craft rested in the opposite corner, no doubt used for scouting Strom's inhospitable terrain.

They ran across the massive floor, Mitchell limping the whole way, between the main airlock and the hallway to warehouse storage, heading straight for the door that separated the research facility from the rest of the base.

"They've got to be in the main tower. We've got no time to lose," the Lieutenant shouted, spurring them onwards.

The automatic door didn't open as they approached, so Marcus ran straight for the door controls. The screen indicated that the door had been locked from the other side, and that an eight digit access code was required to open it.

"Can you get it done?" the Lieutenant asked, panting heavily.

"I think so. Give me a minute," Marcus replied, pulling out his toolkit.

He unscrewed the panel, removing the plastic cover to get to the wiring. Sifting through the wires, he spotted a yellow wire with a black stripe and secured it between his fingers before grabbing his wire clippers. After cutting the first wire, he did the same with a pair of red and blue wires and removed the plastic sheath from their tips, twisting the copper threads together to form a feedback loop.

"Why would they lock the door?" Taylor asked.

"There could be a Nyari on the loose. They probably locked themselves in for safety," Marcus muttered as he worked.

"Any minute now?" Mitchell prompted.

"Almost there," Marcus assured him, grabbing a small electronic device and hooking it up to the yellow wire with the black stripe.

At the push of a button the device began deciphering the access code, one digit at a time. Lieutenant Mitchell consulted his datapad while they waited.

"Ok, up ahead we've got small secondary armory on the left, then past that there's the mess hall and kitchen, followed by living quarters B-1 through B-7. Off to the left we've got what appears to be a bar and a complex which includes living quarters A-1 through A-10, C-1 through C-8, as well as a gym and the rec-room. There're too many ways in and out for us to seal off, so hopefully my hunch is right and all the targets will have converged with the hostages in the main tower. We just don't have time to check the rest," explained the Lieutenant, stowing his datapad. Marcus's device finished deciphering the last digit and the locking mechanism on the door gave way.

"The main tower is at the very end of this corridor. We'll rush through it hot and heavy. Understood?"

"Yes boss," Jago confirmed, and the others nodded their approval.

The four of them charged in head on, ignoring the few doors they passed by. Even if Reid managed to prevent the reactor from going critical, the terrorists would realize that they weren't alone. They had to get to the hostages before that happened, and there simply wasn't time to scout the living quarters of several hundred personnel. They had to take a chance.

* * * * *

"Wait, don't go just yet," Taz begged. "There's still plenty of time."

Reid forced a smile, taking a seat next to him. He'd already divested himself of his armor. It would just weigh him down anyway. The two of them sat there quietly, not sure what to say. The silence grew, overshadowing them until they couldn't bear it any longer.

"Where's a cold beer when you need one?" Reid mused, finally disrupting the painful silence.

Taz almost had to force a laugh.

"I can't believe you're really going," he admitted.

"Don't worry Taz. This isn't the end. It's only the beginning," Reid confided. "We'll see each other again. You've got all of eternity to get on my nerves."

Taz chuckled half-heartedly, unable to look Reid in the eye. "Why do you believe in God?" he asked, trying to understand how Reid could be so calm given the circumstances.

"How can you not?" Reid coaxed. "With all this chaos, I find it impossible not to impose some sort of meaning to it."

"I never really thought about it," Taz confessed.

Reid pinched his shirt over his chest and pulled it out, sticking his other hand down the neckline to produce a gilded cross dangling from an intricate but frail-looking necklace. He stared at it in silent wonder as it spun about slowly in front of his eyes.

"Take it," he gestured, pulling it over his head and handing it over to Taz. "For luck. Who knows, maybe when I'm gone, you'll find God yourself."

Taz reached over hesitantly and caught the shimmering necklace in his grasp.

"Or maybe he'll find you," Reid concluded.

Taz smiled faintly, sensing that they were nearing the end of their conversation. The last conversation they would ever have.

"Twelve minutes left. I'd better get going," Reid decided. "Will you pray for me when I'm gone?"

"I promise," Taz whispered.

Reid opened the seal on the circular airlock leading to the reactor's antechamber. It was a tube-shaped, sterile white room lit by fluorescent lights. Nozzles in the ceiling would spray the occupant with a special absorbent chemical to wash away contaminants and cool their radiation suit.

Reid slowly pushed the door back behind him, locking it in place. Taz stared at him through the small square-shaped window in the center of the door. It felt so out of place seeing him inside the sterile chamber in his black t-shirt and pants while Taz looked in from outside, still wearing his armor.

Reid placed his hand on the glass, a thin line of fog tracing the outline of his fingers and palm. Taz raised his hand and placed it on the glass on top of Reid's.

"Goodbye, dear friend," Taz muttered under his breath as Reid let go of the glass.

Chapter 47

"Why are they locking themselves in from the escaped Nyari if they were just going to blow everything up anyway?" Marcus asked as he started rewiring the door's controls.

Their charge down the corridor had met no resistance, and the four of them were now stood in front of the door separating them from the main tower. Things were much better maintained here, and it was clear they were back in the inhabited section of the outpost. The Lieutenant pondered the implications of Marcus' revelation and what it might say about the mindset of the men they were about to engage.

"You're right. This whole thing doesn't make much sense. And how did they get to the frigate anyway? Alpha Terrans don't have access to anything even remotely spaceworthy," Mitchell wondered. "We don't have time to find out right now. We have to move."

Marcus knew he was right. There was no time now to ascertain the motives or the reasoning behind what was going on. It would have to wait.

"Ape here is too big for a stealth approach, and his S-56 isn't suited for breach tactics, so I think it's best if Grey, Doc and I burst through the door first and then Ape provides covering fire. We hit them fast and hard," Mitchell instructed them. "This is the only entrance to the tower, and we only have a few minutes before the terrorists find out that there isn't going to be an explosion. As soon as that happens they'll know they're not alone. We can't take the risk that they won't start shooting hostages once they find out."

Jago looked hesitant, but still acknowledged the order.

"You'll be fine Ape. Just move fast and try and find some cover. You're a pretty big target. Hopefully the terrorists will panic when they see us come rushing in, then me and Grey can take them out one by one."

"Yes boss," Jago confirmed, somewhat reassured.

Mitchell crouched by the right side of the door, with Marcus and Taylor on the left side, all of them ready to pounce as soon as the door sprung open. Marcus had finished rewiring the door controls and all that was left was to press the button to open the massive door.

"Ready?" Mitchell asked, raising his hand to initiate the countdown.

They nodded, taking deep breaths in preparation. Five, four, three, two, one, and the Lieutenant gave the signal.

Marcus pressed the button and the door instantly flew open. Forgoing all logic, Jago charged through the open doorway, his weapon raised and ready, bellowing out a fierce battle cry.

Mitchell and Marcus were dumbfounded that the behemoth had completely disregarded the plan, but soon gathered their senses, clearing the door as quickly as they could, checking every possible corner.

They emerged a quarter of the way up the taller of the main spire's two circular structures. A shaft ran the entire height of the larger tower, creating levels of balconies from which one could see clear to the top and bottom, with offices and compartments lining the outer walls. Common areas were located in the central space where the two cylinders met, through which a visitor had to go to reach the most important areas, housed in the smaller tower. Although mostly dug into the base of the mountainside, the tips of both cylinders rose above the rock and ice, windows letting in what little light managed to

361

make its way this far out into the solar system. Embedded in the roof over the central shaft, a circle of glowing light bathed the main tower in a seemingly natural glow.

The clones were immediately greeted by a pair of guards in simple black clothing, who'd taken up position on the same level on the other side of the shaft. Jago ran as fast as he could, circumventing the gaping hole in the center of the larger tower structure, while the terrorists crouched behind the glass balustrade for cover, firing a few random shots with automatic weapons.

They were almost thirty meters away, not an optimal distance for Marcus and Mitchell to fire their carbines on the run. Marcus dived into cover behind the glass, raising his carbine to fire a few bursts in the closest terrorist's direction, buying Jago more time to reach them. As soon as the gunfire started, screams erupted from the floor above in the smaller tower.

"That's the hostages. They're in the infirmary," shouted Lieutenant Mitchell. "Grey, you stay here, keep Jago covered. Taylor, you're with me."

They ran off towards a flight of stairs a few meters from the doorway they'd entered through, the Lieutenant limping profusely.

A hail of bullets trailed past Jago as one of the terrorists jumped out of cover, emptying his clip from the hip. Marcus grabbed the opportunity and squeezed his trigger, yanking his carbine across from his first target toward the firing terrorist. With no time to aim, most of Marcus's bullets impacted on the glass balustrade and metal railing, ricocheting off into the distance. Luckily, a few of the shots hit the target square in the chest, sending him straight to the floor.

Marcus hoped sincerely that Steven wasn't in the infirmary. He wanted to confront him himself. Having him shot by a Division 6 mole wasn't the fate Marcus had imagined for his old friend. He had to give him the chance he deserved, an opportunity to explain his actions.

Jago was almost on the terrorists. The second guard was getting anxious, keeping his head down to avoid Marcus's aim. Suddenly Marcus saw him fire, a barrage of rounds hitting home all across Jago's upper torso. The massive behemoth didn't so much as slow down. If anything, he picked up his pace, slamming into his assailant so hard that the man was flung into the air, coming crashing down a good four meters from his original position.

Marcus couldn't help but admire Jago's incredible brutish strength, but Jago didn't stop there. Stomping to a halt, he aimed his huge weapon down at his assailant, lying spread-eagled on the floor, and fired a hail of rounds, decimating the prone and helpless target.

"If you come in, we'll kill them all!" came the faint cry of one of the terrorists in the infirmary.

Marcus ran for it. With the two guards down, his job here was done. Lieutenant Mitchell would need all the help he could get. The stairs rose up around a squared-off U-turn, with the same tapered metal railings as the balconies. Marcus ran straight up, glancing over his shoulder to make sure that Jago was still ok. He could see the giant's massive chest rising and falling rapidly with his labored breathing as the behemoth stood over the remains of the terrorists.

"Are you ok Ape?" he asked on the comms.

"I'm fine boss," Jago informed him.

The terrorists had set up a camera on a tripod on the balcony right outside the infirmary, and had been using it to send feeds to the news networks. Mitchell was propped up against a pillar in front of the entrance to the infirmary proper, and Taylor was crouched behind a metal cabinet. As Marcus approached, they waved him into position behind an overturned desk. The infirmary faced the light well of the central shaft, but the glass walls that faced outward were made of one-way glass, meaning the terrorists inside could see Marcus, Mitchell and Taylor, but the clones couldn't see them.

"Switch to thermo" the Lieutenant whispered over the comms.

Marcus turned on his helmet's built-in thermographic vision and, within seconds, the darkened glass walls of the infirmary dissipated, revealing the heat signatures of the people inside.

A large crowd of figures was cowering on the floor up against the near wall, with three men standing behind them, weapons aimed at the ready.

"Stay back and no one will get hurt," one of the standing figures called.

He's not in there, Marcus thought, surveying the targets. It was difficult to make out, but judging from their height and build, none of the terrorists inside the infirmary was Steven. Where the hell could he be? Marcus went back over the layout of the base in his mind, tracing their steps. Could he have been in the part of the complex they hadn't checked? Or somewhere above them in the tower? Marcus knew better than to underestimate Steven's intelligence. How could he have been so stupid as to get himself trapped here? Marcus had started to believe that Steven had come here in order to martyr himself, but if there was one quality that Steven possessed, it was his will to survive. He wasn't a mindless drone, willing to sacrifice himself for some cause. He'd have a plan to escape.

It was like a light bulb going off inside Marcus's head. The ship! The supply frigate in the docking bay had been connected to the refueling tanks. Steven was going to get away in the ship while the squad was distracted by the hostages.

"You with me, Grey?" Mitchell asked, interrupting Marcus' train of thought.

"I'm with you," Marcus confirmed.

"I'll take the one on the right and you take the one on the left. Taylor, you take the center," the Lieutenant ordered. "Aim high."

He gave the signal, and the three of them burst out of cover, guns blazing. The sheets of glass separating them from the terrorists shattered as a barrage of rounds raged through. The hostages screamed in terror as the upper half of Marcus's target disappeared in a mist of blood and fragments of bone before falling limply to the floor.

The Lieutenant's target received the same fate. Unfortunately, Taylor's aim was off, and before he managed to take his target down, the man got off a round that shot straight into the head of the hostage he'd been aiming at.

"Clear," Mitchell confirmed.

Marcus took a moment to breathe and compose himself, switching out his clip as he did so. "We good?" he finally asked.

Lieutenant Mitchell strode forward, knocking open the door to the infirmary.

"We're good. One casualty," the Lieutenant informed him.

"I have to check on something. Can you handle them on your own?" Marcus asked, not wanting to reveal his intention to go after Steven by himself to the rest of the squad.

Mitchell looked at him for a suspiciously long time before replying.

"Go ahead. The Doc and I will mop this up."

Marcus nodded and ran off, heading back for the corridor which led to the hangar bay.

* * * * *

Steven had been hiding in the warehouse, waiting for the right time to claim the frigate for himself. He knew the Republic would send a squad to deal with the threat, and he had to make everything look just right.

He'd just returned from the hangar control room, where he'd transferred controls of the hangar doors to the ship. He strode confidently to the fuel hose, and knelt down by the ship's hull to disengage it. Everything was in place. It was time for him to make his grand escape. He didn't have that long to get to the minimum safe distance, but a few minutes would be more than enough time.

"Steven!" Marcus shouted, rushing through the door behind him.

Steven froze, recognizing the voice. He knew the Republic would send someone, but never in his wildest dreams had he thought they might send *him*. It was a most fortunate coincidence.

"Steven, you have to stop!" Marcus yelled, slowing his pace and slinging his carbine over his shoulder to free his hands so he could pull his helmet off.

Steven rose slowly, turning to face him.

"Hello old friend," he said with a sly smile, lowering his hands to rest at his sides, a short distance from the pistol that hung from his belt.

"So you're a terrorist now?" Marcus remarked, stopping in front of him.

"You're one to talk. If you had any idea of the insurmountable amount of terror inflicted on Alpha Terra by the Republic, you wouldn't be calling me that," Steven claimed.

"I know you've never come to terms with the way things are, but this is lunacy. You think you and your new friends coming here and blowing up a Republic outpost, killing over a hundred innocent civilians, is going to change things?" Marcus blurted, throwing his helmet to the floor and pointing an accusing finger at Steven.

"There's no such thing as an innocent Beta Terran. Their apathy and negligence is the very reason why the Republic has been able to go unchecked for so long. Someone has to stop them," Steven grimaced.

Marcus couldn't believe it. In just a few short months his friend had transformed from the innocent philosopher he once knew into an atrocious monster.

"These people you're with, they're using you Steven! They've turned you into something you're not," Marcus pleaded.

"Those fools? This was my idea," Steven bridled. "They don't even know that I've rigged the reactor to blow. They'll die like martyrs. I, on the other hand, have bigger plans."

"I don't believe you. The Steven I knew could never have done such monstrous things. Someone has to be pulling your strings. How else could you have gotten off of Alpha Terra?" Marcus argued.

"I have powerful benefactors, people who believe in a free Alpha Terra," Steven declared, his pride shining through. "You once believed that every man had the right to be free. What happened to you?"

"I was afraid," Marcus conceded. "Afraid of dying for a cause I didn't believe in. I'm not afraid anymore."

"Then you're a fool!"

"And do you really believe that these benefactors will stand by you when things go wrong? You're being used and you can't even see it! Whoever they are, they'll toss you to the wolves at the first opportunity," Marcus sneered.

"No, they would never betray me. The only one who'd betray me... is you!" Steven roared.

In the blink of an eye, Steven's hand flashed, gripping the weapon at his side. Before Marcus could react, he was staring down the barrel aimed straight at his head. They stood there, silently staring at each other. A silent storm raged behind Steven's eyes.

"You told me once that you could never shoot me," Marcus reminded him.

Steven's nostrils flared in outrage, his mouth contorted.

"I guess I was wrong," Steven sneered, pulling the trigger.

* * * * *

Taz sat by the console, monitoring the feed from the security cameras inside the reactor chamber. Reid had already finished turning the first valve, and was making his way towards the second. It was slow going. Rotating the manual release valves had turned out to be a lot more straining than they'd anticipated. Reid was already showing signs of radiation sickness. Taz worriedly cheered him on, gripping the edge of the console for support.

He didn't even notice when the lid on the air vent behind him swung down, hanging loose from the ceiling. Shrouded in shadows, the escaped Nyari soldier lowered itself down from the vent. It slowly crept its way up behind Taz, raising its razor sharp claws, ready to carve into his flesh.

Chapter 48

His strength was slowly escaping him. Reid knew he didn't have much time left. The reactor was still approaching critical, even though he'd managed to slow its progression somewhat by opening the first valve. With his diminishing strength, he was beginning to worry that he wouldn't be able to release them all in time. The chamber was half-filled with scorching steam, tainted by radiation.

He gripped the second valve tightly and began exerting his strength upon it. It turned slowly.

Reid could feel his skin starting to burn.

"You fucking pussy, you can do this!" he roared, trying to drive himself on.

He took a deep breath, only to inhale the toxic fumes and immediately start coughing uncontrollably, nearly collapsing on the floor. Once he'd finally stopped coughing, he mustered enough strength to turn the wheel. It moved slowly, but steadily. When he saw the pressure gauge begin to move at last, he began to ease up on the wheel.

"One more," he sighed.

*   *   *   *   *

Taz instinctively threw himself to one side when he saw movement reflected on the console's viewscreen, narrowly escaping the Nyari's razor-sharp claws as it charged, throwing itself an impossibly long distance across the room and crashing into the console, breaking it in half.

"Shit, shit, shit!" was all he could shout as he sprung away, searching the room for his weapon.

He'd laid it out on the console when he began monitoring Reid's progress, but when the creature had come crashing into the unit, the carbine had scattered somewhere out of view.

"Jaher hooman, ya stir na'ang ti nald!" roared the grotesque alien, its mandibles writhing to form the sounds of its incomprehensible language.

He was face to face with death incarnate, and Taz knew his demise was approaching fast. The Nyari was circling him now, studying his every move.

Taz pulled his knife, slowly. He knew that there was no chance he could beat it in hand to hand combat. Even with the knife, his chances were slim to none. Nyari were stronger and faster than any human, and their claws were more than a match for his puny Terran blade.

The creature lunged once more, raking its claws against his side and tearing a great gash in his armor as he narrowly escaped the brunt of the impact. Its beady little eyes stared at him, unflinching and filled with hatred.

It had blocked the passage to the research section of the base, making it impossible for him to run towards the rest of the squad. He was cornered. There was nothing left to do.

Taz mustered all the courage he had and hurled the knife straight towards the Nyari's chitinous torso. He didn't even wait to see if his throw had connected or not, he simply turned towards the hallway leading back towards the control tower and ran as fast as he could.

370

* * * * *

Marcus slowly opened his eyes. Had Steven missed? He couldn't believe that he could miss. With less than five meters between them, Steven's pistol was aimed straight at his head.

Steven looked at the gun in his hand in disbelief and then quickly turned it back on Marcus, firing again, rapidly emptying the entire clip. To their mutual astonishment, as the bullets closed in on their target they swerved away to the side, as if they were being pulled away by an unseen hand, slamming them into the wall behind Marcus.

"No," Steven roared. "That's impossible!"

Marcus couldn't believe it either. It defied reason that a hail of bullets would simply veer away from him. Not about to question his newfound luck, Marcus hurriedly grabbed the carbine slung over his shoulder and aimed it, sling dangling loose, at Steven.

"Alright, I give up!" Steven persuaded, dropping the pistol and raising his hands in surrender. "You win."

"I know I betrayed you Steven. I can't even begin to explain how terrible it felt. The guilt was unbearable. But you know what? I finally realized that I made the right choice. Even if it's not what I wanted to do with my life at first, I'm doing something good and noble," Marcus declared, taking a step forward.

"Being bred for war is noble? The Beta Terrans don't give a shit about you, they just made you so they didn't have to fight their own battles!" Steven sneered.

"I've seen the faces of the innocent. Who'll defend them if not us?" Marcus countered.

"They can defend themselves!" Steven roared in outrage.

"They have too much to lose! They have wives, children and other responsibilities. We have none of those things. We were born with a clean slate. I'd rather die protecting them than to see one more innocent child fall into the hands of the enemy, or see a wife struggle to feed her starving children because her husband was taken away from them. I may not have realized it until recently Steven, but I am where I want to be. Now turn around and place your hands behind your back."

Steven scowled, and quietly complied with Marcus's orders.

Marcus stepped forward, preparing to bind Steven's wrists. As he lowered his weapon, Steven suddenly snapped his head backwards, hitting Marcus square in the jaw. Stunned by the blow, Marcus dropped his carbine.

Steven kicked the weapon, sending it sliding far out of reach before spinning and charging Marcus head on, slamming into his chest and roaring like a rabid beast.

* * * * *

Reid screamed in agony. He had prayed to God for strength. The third valve was proving to be exceptionally tough to open. Either that, or he was simply growing weaker. His skin was so scorching hot that some spots were starting to turn black.

The reactor itself was vibrating. The metal frame was starting to come loose, with waves of radiation creating visual distortions across the chamber. The wheel was so burning hot that Reid felt the skin on his fingertips starting to sear, and then melt, as he gripped it with all his strength. He felt the heat piercing through his flesh, singeing his bones.

Rearing back in agony, Reid released the wheel, arched his back and screamed with rage. "I will not fail," he roared, grabbing the wheel once more.

It felt cool to the touch.

Reid assumed that the nerve endings in his fingers were dying. He couldn't feel the heat on his face either. Or anywhere else for that matter. As he looked down at his skin in despair, he noticed that an aura of azure light was emanating from his skin.

It was everywhere, a shimmering halo insulating him from the deadly radiation. He stared down at his blackened fingers, shrouded in waves of dancing light. He raised his head and gave praise to the Almighty, and, his hope renewed, he clutched the wheel and turned.

* * * * *

The Nyari moved like nothing Taz had ever seen before. With its four powerful arms, it was able to use the walls and even the ceiling to propel itself forward, leaping incredible distances in a single bound. Taz sprinted past the mess hall with the ferocious alien hot on his tail and rapidly gaining on him. He knew that it would be futile to run much longer. He had to try to double back and reach the others.

With all the doors on the right, to the living quarters, welded shut, his only option was the admin section. There were two ways in, one to the office complex and a separate entrance to an auditorium along a secondary corridor. If he could lure the creature in there after him, he might stand a chance of reaching the others.

Taz burst through the door of the office complex and dived for the entrance to the auditorium corridor, throwing a trash can by the wall back to try and slow his pursuer. It didn't work, the Nyari simply ramming straight through it as if it wasn't even there. Taz turned right, clearing the corner to the auditorium. His heart was beating so fast he thought it would burst at any moment.

The auditorium fell away in front of him, towards a stage at the far end, with rows of seats lining both sides of the aisle he was running down. Without thinking, Taz grabbed one of his grenades, removed the pin and dropped it to the floor as he ran down the ramp between the seats, heading for the exit on the right. He dared not even look to see if it had worked, so, as the blast came, sending shrapnel and debris flying through the hall, he just kept running.

His assailant squealed, an inhumanly high sound.

"Steek naldakur!" the Nyari roared as it leapt through the cloud of dust and debris.

Ducking through the exit, Taz was back in the main corridor, heading back to the security room. He threw off his gloves and even unstrapped his chestplate as he ran, trying to lessen the weight he was carrying so that he could run faster.

Suddenly the Nyari jumped, slamming right into his back. Taz tumbled onto the floor, landing face down. His back ached like never before, his flesh torn from where the beast's claws had raked clear across his shoulder blades. The clacking sound of the Nyari's claws tapping the floor in front of him nearly stopped his heart from beating as he attempted to muster enough courage to stand back up.

He'd barely gotten to his knees when a sharp punch to the chest sent him crashing back, knocking the air from his lungs. The creature flung its weight on him before he even landed, two of its arms gripping his shoulders, its claws digging into his flesh as its knee slammed him to the ground, pinning him there.

The Nyari puffed out its chest, its free arms arching back, its gruesome claws ready to rend Taz into oblivion.

His adrenalin spiked to new heights as he tried to fight back, snarling and frothing at the mouth. His blood rushed to his muscles, the veins in his hands popping out, thicker and more prominent than he'd ever seen them before. There was a distinct pinging sound as the clasps on Taz's bracers shot through the air and hit the wall. Though his genetic template and training had made him strong, the power he now felt coursing through his veins was unlike anything he had ever experienced. It was as if his muscles were made out of carbon fiber interlaced with cables of steel wire. He could feel the dual plates that made up his bracers bending and twisting out of shape.

* * * * *

Marcus tried to reach for his knife. Steven had him face down with one hand pinned behind his back.

"Fucking die!" Steven raged as he tried to slam Marcus's head into the floor.

Marcus struggled to keep his head up. His fingers were almost on the knife's handle. Suddenly Marcus rolled, slamming Steven's left side into the ground. His grip came loose, allowing Marcus to roll away to freedom.

Marcus rose to his feet, unsheathing his knife and turning to face Steven. The two stared intently at one another, sizing each other up as they paced defiantly, circling one another, looking for an opening.

Marcus lunged straight for Steven's stomach, the sharp serrated blade missing by a hair's breadth as the blond man jumped back.

Steven countered by sending his elbow square into Marcus's jaw. Marcus quickly staggered back, brushing the blood from his lip.

Steven took up the familiar stance of the Terran rapid assault martial arts they had been trained in on the Alamo, his hands raised and ready, his feet planted firmly on the ground, keeping his center of gravity low.

Marcus lunged again, this time thrusting the tip of the blade straight towards Steven's neck. Steven raised his arms to block just in the nick of time. The blade cut clean through the skin on his upper arm, a stream of blood trickling down his side.

"Give up Steven. It doesn't have to end like this," Marcus pleaded.

"Fuck you, you traitor," Steven roared, charging forward to send his palm crashing into Marcus's larynx.

Marcus turned to counter, raising his right hand, which held the knife, to block the attack. But Steven had feinted, pulling his blow at the last minute and grabbing hold of Marcus's arm and pulling it hard, twisting his wrist. Marcus realized it was a bluff a moment too late, and the knife was hurled to the ground, Steven following with a quick sweep under Marcus's legs, sending him crashing to the floor.

Steven threw himself on top of Marcus, his knee on his thigh and one hand firmly on his neck, the other fumbling to reach for Marcus's knife. Blood was flowing down Steven's arm, smearing Marcus's chestplate as he tried to shake loose. Steven finally caught hold of the knife and turned it straight towards Marcus's face. Marcus grabbed both of Steven's arms, trying to prevent him from forcing the blade down upon him with one hand, the other desperately trying to pry loose Steven's chocking grip.

As he gasped for air, Marcus began to lose hope. The knife came closer with every passing second, almost scraping the skin below his left eye. It was almost over.

* * * * *

With the third valve opened, Reid dragged his feet along the floor, desperate to reach the sealed door to the antechamber. The glowing aura protected him from the lethal radiation, but the damage was already done. Still, something inside him drove him forward, urging him not to give up just yet.

Steaming vapors rose from his skin as he forced himself to drag his feet forward, inching on a few centimeters at a time, his dangling arms held awkwardly away from his body like a reanimated corpse. As he reached the sealed door, Reid grabbed a hold of the lever, using the full weight of his body to push it down. He slumped to the floor just as the door creaked open.

Clutching the metal grating on the floor, Reid pulled himself into the antechamber on all fours, slowly but steadily, the skin on his legs and hands sloughing off as it scraped against the floor. As soon as he'd managed to drag himself completely into the antechamber, Reid kicked the door shut behind and collapsed, his vision blurred and the halo of light surrounding him evaporating. Then everything finally went black.

* * * * *

Taz threw the Nyari off as if it weighed no more than a child, a feat of enormous strength that rivaled even the monstrous Jago's might.

Unable to control his adrenalin-fuelled rage, Taz could do nothing but charge the alien head on.

Seizing the Nyari's throat, Taz lifted it right off the ground with one hand and slammed it back into the floor with all his might, cracking its chitinous shell. The creature shrilled in pain. Taz arched his back, his fists clenched, as he roared like a savage beast.

With the tables suddenly turned, the Nyari turned in terror and fled down the corridor. Spurred by his rage, Taz wasn't about to let it get away, so he raced on after it, screaming in frustration. Unfortunately, despite Taz's newfound strength, the Nyari was quickly able to increase the distance between them.

Instinctively, Taz reached out and grabbed the door to the mess hall as he passed it, tearing it right off its hinges with a minimum of effort and flinging it in the Nyari's direction. The door soared through the air, slamming right into the back of the Nyari's head, sending it crashing to the floor. Taz was on it in seconds, planting his booted feet firmly on top of the Nyari's scrabbling upper arms. He knelt, fastening his grip on its chitinous skull, and, with a heave, tore the alien's head clean off of its shoulders.

* * * * *

Steven put his weight on the knife, forcing it down. The blade slowly began to sink into Marcus's cheek. Marcus struggled as much as he possibly could to try and pry Steven's grip on the weapon loose, but it only increased his pain as the knife tore up the wound. He had to think fast. Time was running out.

Marcus tried to kick Steven in the groin, but the snarling clone was too quick to adapt his position, anticipating the move. He tried rolling to the side so that Steven would be tossed off of him, but he was pinned down too hard. With Steven's hand firmly on Marcus's larynx, his mind was slowly going dull from lack of oxygen.

"Die, you traitorous piece of shit!" Steven spat in his face.

Suddenly Marcus released his grip of the arm pressing down on his neck, instead fumbling through his pouches for anything of use. Steven used the opportunity, pressing down harder with both hands. The knife began sinking in, grating against the bone in Marcus's cheek, sliding up in the direction of his ocular cavity. Marcus screamed, grabbing the first thing he could from his pouch.

He slammed the strip of metallic tape against Steven's neck, its adhesive coating attaching itself to his skin. Steven was startled, not knowing what it was that Marcus was attempting to wrap around his neck. He relinquished his hold on Marcus's throat, instead pressing down on the blade with both hands, trying to force an end to the confrontation.

Marcus ran his fingers along the length of the tape, desperately trying to keep the knife at bay with his one free arm. There it was. Marcus grabbed the small protruding tab of plastic and ripped with all his strength, clenching his eyes shut in anticipation. Steven suddenly let loose a scream as horrendous as Marcus could ever have imagined. Marcus could feel the release as Steven let go of the knife, clawing at the glowing hot tape as it burned through the skin on his neck, crying out in unimaginable agony.

Marcus threw him to the side and rolled away, shielding his eyes from the flames. He thought Steven's hellish screams would never die out. Eventually, Steven's horrendous shrieks were replaced with an inhuman gurgling sound. Marcus was loath to look, but his curiosity finally got the better of him.

He raised his head and peered through the smoke. He was nearly overcome by the smell of burnt flesh. Steven's smoldering neck was virtually non-existent. He knelt down to reclaim his knife and stopped to stare silently at the corpse of Steven, his once and former friend.

Chapter 49

The office chair creaked under Jago's tremendous weight. He had taken the seat to let the Doc have a look at his wounds. Although his condition didn't appear critical, some of the bullets had managed to pierce his chestplate.

"Let's get this armor off of you so I can have a look," Taylor said, releasing the clasps on the shoulders and hips, lighting a cigarette as he did so.

Lieutenant Mitchell came up behind him to monitor the proceedings, having already released the hostages. Most of them were consoling one another, although a few outraged individuals were kicking and cursing the bodies of their former captors.

As Jago's blood-smeared chest came into view, three rounds fell to the floor, soaked in blood.

"Well, that's unusual," muttered the medic, unconsciously blowing smoke in Jago's face.

"Is it serious?" Jago gasped, half expecting the Doc to tell him he wasn't long for this life.

Taylor didn't answer. Instead he reached for a piece of gauze and used it to wipe the blood from Jago's heaving chest.

"Where did the blood come from?" Mitchell asked, peering over the medic's shoulder.

"There are no wounds," Taylor proclaimed with some astonishment.

"What, they didn't hit me?" Jago blurted in confusion.

"No, they definitely hit you. These bullets pierced your armor and…" the Doc stopped, moving closer to examine Jago's skin more closely. "As far as I can tell, they went through your armor and just stopped, which is impossible. Or…"

"Or what, Doc?" the Lieutenant prompted.

"Or his body simply ejected the bullets from the wounds and healed itself, which is simply ridiculous," Taylor muttered.

They didn't have time to discuss the matter further, their comms interrupting them without warning.

"Doc, we need you A.S.A.P.!" Taz yelled.

"What's wrong? I'm in the middle of…" Taylor tried to interject.

"Reid's alive!" Taz shouted. "We need you right away. Can you get to the security station?"

"I'm on my way," the medic replied, grabbing his gear and running for the corridor.

* * * * *

Marcus had heard the call too, and came running through the door from the docking bay. Taz had opened the door to the antechamber and was kneeling by Reid's severely burnt body, urging him to stay alive.

"He's not dead?" Marcus asked incredulously, coming to Taz's aid.

"He's dropping in and out of consciousness. Do you have any anti-rads?" Taz pleaded, eying the huge tear down Marcus' cheek, but too fixated on Reid to comment on it.

"No, only Doc has them," Marcus replied. "How is he still alive?"

"I don't know. But if the Doc doesn't get his ass here soon, he won't be for much longer."

382

As if on cue, they heard rapid footsteps approaching.

"In here!" Taz shouted.

Taylor burst through the door, dropping his medical kit beside Reid's smoldering body.

"Step aside," the medic ordered. "I need room to work."

Rifling through his medical kit, he produced a syringe and a small vial of anesthetics. He hurriedly filled the syringe and grabbed Reid's arm to prepare for injection. The skin peeled off like burnt paper.

"Reid, can you hear me?" the medic shouted as he depressed the plunger on the syringe. "This will help with the pain."

"Grey, get Raven on the comms. I'm going to need that ship in the hangar bay as soon as possible. Maybe if I can get him into cryo, he might survive the ride home and he can get proper treatment."

"You got it," Marcus acknowledged, switching his comms to the ship's frequency.

"Raven, do you read me?"

"I read you Grey. What's your status?" prompted Raven.

"The mission is complete, hostages secure and targets down. We need the ship, now!" Marcus yelled.

"On my way. I need those hangar doors open if I'm gonna join the party," Raven responded, forbearing from asking more questions.

Marcus could hear the engines coming online in the background.

"I'll take care of it," Marcus promised.

"Doc, pump him full of whatever anti-rads we've got. The rest of us will just have to do without," Marcus ordered.

"Already done. Just get that ship in here," the medic replied.

*   *   *   *   *

On his way to the hangar bay control room, Marcus met Jago and Mitchell coming to check on Reid's status.

"What the hell's going on?" the Lieutenant demanded.

"Reid's alive. Raven's bringing the ship in. The Doc's gonna put him in cryo. I have to get the doors open," Marcus blurted, pausing just long enough to get the message across. "They probably need help carrying him to the ship."

"Alright. Ape, let's go give them a hand," Lieutenant Mitchell confirmed. "Oh, and Grey," he went on, looking at the gaping wound across Marcus' face, "get the Doc to patch you up once he's got Reid in stasis. I take it whatever caused that's been taken care of?"

Marcus nodded, then turned and ran for the control room. It was a small, narrow room with a wide window, overlooking an airlock large enough to accommodate a medium-sized frigate. Marcus took a seat at the console, bringing up the display for the airlock controls. The password prompt came into view. He reached for his decryption device and hooked it up to the data port.

"I'm almost there," came Raven's voice on the comms. "You'd better get that door open."

"Almost there," Marcus agreed, just as the device gave him the correct password to access the controls.

He engaged the airlock's outer hatch, and watched through the window as the massive door began to move. When the door was halfway open, the barracuda came soaring through the gap. Marcus overrode the door, ordering it to close again and switching the outer hatch to sealed mode. As soon as he could, he engaged the inner hatch with a throw of a switch.

"The ship's in the hangar," Marcus informed the rest of the squad.

"We'll be right there," Taylor responded.

384

Marcus unhooked his decryption device from the data port and was preparing to leave the control room when a small icon at the bottom-right corner of one of the viewscreens caught his eye. It was an indicator for an outgoing data stream. On a hunch, he clicked on the symbol, bringing up the bandwidth of all outgoing transmissions.

"That can't be right," he muttered to himself.

The stream was much higher than anything he could have justified, given the lack of current operations at the outpost. Sensing that something was amiss, he began sifting through the records, trying to locate the outgoing data packets. A series of requests later, he found what he was looking for.

Someone had hacked into the security feed for all the cameras in the outpost and was piggybacking off the outpost's signal. But where was it coming from? Judging by the strength of the signal, it had to be somewhere awfully close. But where?

Marcus brought up the logs for the communications array, checking the destination for all outgoing transmissions. Most of the items he discovered were routine automated tasks, sensor logs for deep space radar being sent back to Beta Terra, but one of the streams caught his attention.

It was an encoded narrow-beam transmission being sent directly into space, its destination less than a few hours journey by ship. Marcus quickly brought up the commands for the sensor array and input the coordinates for the data stream's destination, then engaged the scanners.

"That's not possible," he blurted as the image of the *TFS Genesis* came into view, on course for Strom.

"Fuck…" Marcus sighed in defeat tinged with anger. "They know everything!"

Through the open inner airlock, he could see the others carrying the unconscious Reid's burnt body up the forward ramp of the barracuda. Lieutenant Mitchell was waving him to join them. Marcus glared back at him, feeling rage swelling up inside him. Mitchell had betrayed them all. Marcus quickly rerouted the hangar bay controls to their ship's onboard computer and notified Raven that the doors were under her command. He grabbed his carbine from the chair next to him and stalked through the door, ready to confront Mitchell at the first opportunity.

Marcus stormed across the bay and up the barracuda's forward ramp to the empty lower deck and, without so much as pausing, went straight for the ladder. As he emerged from the hatch, Taylor and Taz were strapping Reid into his stasis pod. Marcus hesitated, not wanting to confront the Lieutenant before Reid was in stasis. Every second could mean the difference between life and death.

As soon as the medic had closed the lid on Reid's pod and engaged the stasis cycle, Marcus sprang into action, bringing his carbine to bear right into the Lieutenant's face with a snarl. Mitchell cautiously raised his hands, taking a step back.

"What the hell do you think you're doing Grey?" he asked nervously, the others backing away as well.

"What I should have done from the start, you piece of shit!" Marcus flared. "You sold us out to Division 6!"

"What are you talking about?" Taylor asked.

"This whole thing, this whole mission was a setup right from the start!" Marcus told them, much to their astonishment.

"How do you know?" asked Taz.

"The security feeds for the entire base are being beamed to the *Genesis* as we speak. They've seen... what I can do," Marcus explained.

"What you can... you too?" Taz gasped.

"Me too? What do you mean?" asked Marcus, confused.

"That escaped Nyari found me and tried to make me his lunch," Taz explained. "Just when I thought it was all over, I suddenly... got strong. I mean freakishly strong. I could have taken on the Ape. Did it happen to you too?"

"No... mine was different," Marcus confessed. "I, uh, stopped bullets."

"Stopped bullets?"

"And this Division 6 piece of shit right here is gonna have us all carved up to find out what makes us tick!" Marcus scowled, snapping his attention back to Mitchell and pushing the barrel of his carbine up against the Lieutenant's cheek.

"That would explain how the Ape survived those bullet wounds," Taylor chimed in.

"We've got to get out of here, now!" roared Taz, hysterically.

"The *Genesis* is only a few hours away. We'll need to move fast," Marcus snarled.

"Grey, I understand that you're upset," Mitchell tried to explain.

"Upset! That's a fucking understatement," Marcus spat.

"But I'm not who you think I am," the Lieutenant confessed. "I'm an agent working deep undercover within Division 6."

"What? You really think we're going to believe you now, after all this?" Marcus persisted.

"I'm telling you the truth. I work for an organization called C-CORE," Mitchell declared.

"Bullshit!" Marcus shouted, dropping his carbine and grabbing the Lieutenant by the throat, slamming him back against a bulkhead.

"I've heard about them," Taz started. "They're the ones who do all that deep space recon."

"Among other things," Lieutenant Mitchell added, his face starting to flush from Marcus's grip on his neck. "If anyone can keep you safe, it's C-CORE."

"You were probing my mind during the interrogation on New Io, weren't you?" Marcus protested. "If you're not Division 6, then why were you trying to help them bring us in?"

"Yes, I was probing your mind. You have to understand, every member of Division 6 is a telepath. That's why I was chosen to infiltrate their ranks. There are very few people outside of the Division with the ability. They're extremely efficient in their recruitment. When your mind began reliving the moment of Corporal Dimitrov's death, I felt your pain, and couldn't go through with it any longer," the Lieutenant explained, trying to convince them that he wasn't the monster they'd taken him for.

Marcus lessened his grip, suddenly unsure.

"I don't know Marcus. I say we shoot the bastard," Taz snarled from the corner.

"And then what?" Mitchell asked. "Are you going to run and hide? There's nowhere you can go where they won't find you. You need my help. It's the only way you'll stay alive."

Despite his rage, Marcus was somehow sure that the Lieutenant was indeed sincere. Besides, there was nowhere they could run too.

Marcus sighed, releasing Mitchell. "This doesn't mean that I trust you. What do you propose?" he asked, feeling that the squad was out of options.

"We run," Mitchell answered simply.

"What about the hostages?" Taylor broke in.

"The *Genesis* will be here soon enough, and they have everything they need to survive long enough without our help. We have to move, and we have to move now," the officer urged.

"But where? You just said that there's no place we can go," Marcus refuted.

The Lieutenant turned on his wrist comm and patched through to the cockpit. "Raven, fire up the engines, fast as you can. As soon as we break orbit I want you to set course for Beta Terra."

Chapter 50

They'd set the stasis cycle of their twelve-week journey to end a few hours before they would reach their destination, giving them time to prepare for the worst. Although the squad had narrowly managed to outrun the *TFS Genesis*, as soon as their barracuda approached the space lanes around Beta Terra's massive orbital station they were flagged and hailed by customs officials.

"Don't answer," Mitchell ordered from the copilot's seat.

"I have to," replied Raven nervously. "Regulations state that any ship that doesn't abide by Republic customs laws will be disabled and boarded."

"TFS-407-818 Barracuda, your ship has been flagged for inspection. You will be escorted to Unity Station by customs officials where you will be detained for questioning. Acknowledge," came the incoming transmission from a pair of Terran fighters on an intercept course.

"We have to lose them," Mitchell urged Raven.

"Are you insane? There's no way in hell I can outmaneuver those fighters in this bucket of bolts." she countered. "We're flying a fucking metal crate with an engine."

"Division 6 has managed to infiltrate every civilian and government agency we know of. If they capture us, we're all dead. They'll shoot me in the head for betraying them, and that's a damn sight better than what they've got in store for you. I can promise you that."

"I thought you were the best," Marcus prompted Raven from his position standing behind the pilots' seats, knowing it would only push her to prove herself.

Raven's dead-eye stare was enough to force them to step back to the rear of the cockpit. She turned sharply in her seat and pushed the throttle to maximum, angling the ship for a head on collision with the incoming fighters.

"What are you doing?" Marcus snapped.

The engines whined so loud he could barely hear the sound of his own voice.

"TFS-407-818 Barracuda, stand down!" ordered one of the fighter pilots.

The fighters were coming in awfully fast, and neither party appeared to have any intention of breaking off.

"818 Barracuda, stand down. I order you!" the pilot yelled once more on the comms.

What had been a small speck on the horizon just seconds earlier was now an intimidating bird of prey about to collide head on with their ship. Marcus grabbed the back of Raven's seat with all his strength, afraid what would happen if he let go.

"Pull up, pull up!" the Lieutenant roared from behind them.

Raven didn't even flinch, maintaining her course and coaxing every last bit of thrust from the engines. At the last possible second, the fighters broke away, nearly giving Marcus and the Lieutenant heart attacks.

"You are one crazy piece of work," Mitchell commended the pilot. "How did you know they'd break off?"

"They want us alive don't they?" Raven reasoned. "They'll come around and target the engines. We're not out of the woods yet."

"Set course for 16.28 degrees north and 47.51 degrees west planetside. That's our rendezvous point just outside Sol. You think you can shake them off our tail?" Mitchell asked, claiming the copilot's chair for himself.

"You're pushing it. Those fighters can kick some serious ass," Raven told him.

"Then I better get us some help," suggested Lieutenant Mitchell, producing his datapad.

He interfaced with the ship's onboard computer, and accessed the Terran Information Network to relay a message.

"We're being targeted," Raven gasped at a shrill beeping from her instruments, frantically trying to maneuver the ship out of harm's way.

"Can you get us closer to that super-freighter?" Mitchell gestured towards a massive container ship bearing the logo of Uruhara Industrial Complex.

"I see it!" confirmed Raven, sending the ship spinning sharply to the right, narrowly escaping a hail of high-velocity rounds aimed for the barracuda's engines.

The freighter drew closer as Raven threw the ship back and forth, the massive segmented hull they were diving for able to provide them with the shelter they needed.

"They won't risk hitting the freighter," Mitchell ventured.

The sensors indicated that one of the fighters was breaking formation, probing for a better vantage point as the other continued the chase. Raven tugged at the controls, pulling the ship up moments before it slammed into the freighter's hull.

"Look at the size of that thing," Marcus gasped as they skimmed across its surface, rows of panels and bulkheads racing past the cockpit's window like a landscape.

"Where's the other one?" Raven asked, barely able to take her eyes off the artificial terrain in front of her, as one of the blips disappeared off the sensor screen.

Marcus and the Lieutenant jumped to the side windows, trying to catch a glimpse of the missing fighter.

"I don't see it," Marcus called, peering through the glass.

They were nearing the bow of the massive freighter when they heard the distinct thud of bullets ripping through the hull below them.

"Where's that coming from?" roared Raven hysterically, pressing the buttons to seal off the lower deck, now venting oxygen.

The blip suddenly reappeared on the sensor screen, right on top of them.

"Where the hell is he?" Raven screamed, leaning forward and arching her neck to peer up through the window. "Hang on," she yelled, before executing a barrel roll.

The growing view of Beta Terra's magnificent landscape above them spun sharply, a full two and a half circles as the ship rotated, dipping below a steady stream of projectiles.

"I see him," Raven shouted, spotting the fighter, which had been hiding directly below them, now a short distance off their starboard flank.

Suddenly another pair of blips on the sensor screen caught their attention, climbing fast from the planet.

"We're fucked!" Raven cried, no longer knowing which way to turn.

A series of missiles shot from the oncoming fighters, in the face of which Raven just shook her head, gasping in surrender.

"I can't do this," she whispered.

The two blips behind them suddenly changed course, splitting up and increasing their speed rapidly. As the missiles blew past the cockpit window, Raven gasped.

The ship shook momentarily as a sudden burst of light engulfed one of the fighters behind them, the flames quickly extinguished by the surrounding vacuum of space.

"TFS-407-818 Barracuda, We've been assigned to escort you to your rendezvous point," came the voice of one of the pilots from up ahead as the other chased off the remaining fighter.

*　*　*　*　*

Their LZ was a parking lot outside an abandoned warehouse district a few kilometers outside the capital. With the sun already set, the surrounding landscape looked bleak and unwelcoming. The streetlights had been blackened in anticipation of their arrival, and an armed escort of two dozen armed men stood guard by a pair of unmarked hover trucks. As the squad made their way down the forward ramp, a team of technicians emerged from one of the trucks and greeted Lieutenant Mitchell.

"He's still in the pod. Can you remove it without waking him?" the Lieutenant asked without further explanation.

"Yes Captain. We'll have to dismantle parts of the ship to get the pod out, but as soon as we're done we'll secure the pod for transport. The surgeons are already in place and awaiting his arrival," the head technician replied.

"Excellent. I'll proceed with the others," Mitchell informed him.

The technicians continued up the ramp, carrying a portable power generator and an assortment of tools and scanners.

"Captain?" Raven eyed Mitchell suspiciously, her chest still heaving from the adrenalin rush of dodging the fighters.

"My true rank," he explained. "Come on, we'd better get going. I've arranged a place for us to lay low."

The team was hustled into one of the two hover trucks, a simple vehicle consisting of a cockpit and a wide platform, on top of which rested a large gray container. Although the interior of the cargo container wasn't as uncomfortable as he'd expected, Marcus couldn't relax. He had no idea where Mitchell was taking them, or if the pretend Lieutenant was telling them the truth about who he worked for. Marcus sat on the cold metal floor with his back to the wall, unable to see the magnificent cityscape of Sol as the truck raced through the low-hanging clouds, picking at the bandage Taylor had wrapped around his face, thinking hard.

Whatever was going on, Mitchell had gotten them away from the *Genesis*. If he was Division 6 after all, why would he have gone to so much trouble? Maybe he'd misjudged Captain Mitchell, or whoever the man really was. Marcus suddenly felt the need to apologize to the man who'd now saved them from what was certain to have been a terrible demise.

"Mitchell," he beckoned.

"Yes Marcus?" Mitchell answered, swaying over against the movement of the truck to sit by his side.

"I just wanted to say that I'm sorry for having accused you of all those things I said before. I don't know what's going to happen to us now, but I'm grateful you got us away from Intari."

"It's quite alright. Under the same circumstances I don't think I would have reacted any differently myself," Mitchell smiled. "You know, you really should hand that crystal over to me for safekeeping."

"How did you know?" Marcus asked, astonished at the depth of the Captain's knowledge.

"From the interrogation on New Io. Just because I didn't say anything to Intari doesn't mean I didn't see it in your mind," he smiled.

Marcus reached into his pouch. He'd managed to keep the crystal from the crashed alien ship for so long, he'd almost forgotten about it, and Mitchell's keeping his knowledge of it from Intari was yet more evidence that he didn't mean the squad any harm. Anyway, it wasn't as if they had any choice but to trust Mitchell and his C-CORE bosses.

"Don't worry Marcus. I'll keep it safe," Mitchell assured him as he placed the crystal in one the pouches of his own armor.

"Put that out," moaned Raven as Taylor lit a cigarette across from her.

"Give me a break. This is the first time I've been able to relax since I was fucking born!" the medic bickered, Raven shaking her head in disgust.

Starting to feel that maybe, just maybe, they might finally be safe, Marcus closed his eyes and began to zone out, allowing the soothing vibrations of the truck to rock him to sleep.

* * * * *

"Grey, get your ass out here! There's someone I want you to meet," Mitchell called, nudging Marcus out of his slumber.

Marcus wiped the drool from his chin with the back of his hand, peering out of the cargo container and through the darkness to the cloud-cast skies over Sol.

The squad emerged from the vehicle on a landing platform on top of one of the taller towers of Sol's corporate plaza, its floodlights also extinguished. The guards, who'd apparently travelled in the second truck, had got out ahead of them and formed a line from the rear of the truck to the entrance of a small structure on top of the platform.

An elderly man dressed in a flawless gray suit approached them from an entrance in the small building, a female assistant shadowing his every move.

"I'm glad you could make it Captain," he smiled gently, shaking Mitchell's hand in the dim light.

The rest of the team paused awkwardly as the old man finished his greeting. He turned his attention to them, eyeing them each rapidly in turn.

"I am Takahashi Muromoto. I am honored to welcome you to my home."

Chapter 51

After almost two weeks of being cooped up in the lavish penthouse suite of the Muromoto Tower, the squad was starting to feel restless. Taylor spent most of his time lounging on the elegant loveseat by one of the suite's many windows, chain-smoking cigarettes and sipping expensive whiskey chilled with ice, immersing himself in the comings and goings of Terran city life. Taz had discovered Takahashi's personal supercomputer and, with his permission, had spent every waking hour jacked into the Terran Information Network. The kitchen proved to be Jago's favorite room in the enormous suite, where he spent most of his time hassling Dominic, Takahashi's live-in chef. Not as content as the rest of them to lie around in luxurious comfort, Raven spent a good part of each day pacing back and forth or trying to start arguments, most of which revolved around the lack of information regarding Reid's condition.

Marcus spent most of his days in quiet reverie in front of a viewscreen, mesmerized by every aspect of Terran society displayed on the news. He didn't much want to dwell on past events. Unlike the rapidly-healing wound on his face, his memories were still too painful, even though he whole-heartedly believed that he'd had no choice in the way things had turned out. At least his doubts about Mitchell had proved unfounded. The squad had been exceptionally well treated since their arrival on Beta Terra, even if Takahashi and Mitchell had been somewhat tight-lipped about their plans for the squad's future.

On the viewscreen, the news anchor had just begun an update on the situation on New Io. "After over four months, New Io is still under quarantine after an outbreak of the deadly Tokiwa virus. Officials from the Terran Health Initiative, in cooperation with military officials, are struggling to keep the situation contained. The death toll is said to be nearing two hundred, with no end in sight to the epidemic."

"Can you believe this shit?" Raven bellowed, pacing back and forth behind Marcus's couch. "You know, Taz is right. I'm really starting to buy into his whole conspiracy bullshit."

Raven's anger was suddenly interrupted by the now-familiar sound that preceded the arrival of the elevator, which opened up directly into the living room. Having anticipated another errand boy from the Muromoto Group, the group was ecstatic when Reid, supported by Captain Mitchell, stepped out of the elevator.

"Look who I found wandering around out in the street," the Captain grinned.

"Rev!" Taz rejoiced, having just unjacked from the system after a lengthy stint.

"I can't believe you made it!" Marcus laughed. "You're one tough ass bastard."

"What happened to your arms and legs?" inquired Raven, lacking any inkling of discretion.

Marcus suddenly noticed that the skin on Reid's arms and legs was slightly discolored.

"Good to see you too Raven," said Reid in jest.

"The doctors had to amputate all of his limbs to increase the effectiveness of the anti-radiation therapy," Mitchell explained. "Even then, they were afraid that the saturation levels required for his bloodstream to repair the radiation damage would kill him. But once he began showing signs of improvement they were able to graft on cloned tissue to replace what was lost."

"Just as well," Taylor chimed in from the rear of the crowd. "His right hand was all used up anyway. It was bound to need replacing."

The squad's cheering turned to laughter as their missing teammate came back into the fold.

"I believe this is yours," Taz stated, producing Reid's necklace with the golden cross. "I can't tell you how happy I am to be giving this back to you."

Reid smiled as he accepted the return of his most prized possession. "I hope it's had a positive influence on you, at least a little… although knowing you I'm not so sure," Reid jested.

A few minutes later Takahashi Muromoto returned to the suite after a busy day of making arrangements. He cleared his voice and gathered them all to hear what he had to say.

"I do believe that Captain Mitchell has already informed you that Division 6 has agents throughout the entire Terran solar system. There is nowhere you can run, and no place you can hide for long. I have therefore used my influence within C-CORE to arrange the only viable option left. I've arranged for you all do depart on the deep space exploration cruiser *Tengri*, departing two days from now, should you wish to," Takahashi told them.

"Aren't those one way trips?" Taz asked, skeptically.

"They are, which is why I urge you all to consider this opportunity with the utmost care," Takahashi replied.

"What about new identities, cosmetic surgery… that kind of thing?" Taylor suggested.

"It's certainly possible, but you'd be on the run for the rest of your lives, always looking over your shoulders. Given the sophisticated nature of the Division's intelligence and resources, I'm sorry to say that it would only be a matter of time before they found you," the old man explained.

"I don't know," sighed Taz. "This sounds awfully risky."

"Before you consider the matter, there is one more piece of information that you need to be aware of. This will show you the lengths Division 6 is willing to go to achieve its goals," Takahashi told them, walking over to his console and pressing a series of buttons. "This is a recording I made while you were en route from Strom."

A piece of news footage began to play on the main viewscreen, an attractive female reporter addressing the camera.

"This is Carol Agnessi with Lumacorp News, bringing you the latest update on the hostage situation on Strom. The Republic battleship *TFS Genesis* entered orbit less than two hours ago in response to a terrorist threat, only to discover that the terrorists had already taken the lives of all 104 civilians and 8 military personnel stationed at the Strom sensor outpost. Sources say that the terrorists then proceeded to take their own lives. More updates at 11:30."

The screen went blank.

It took several seconds for them to come to terms with the reality of the situation.

"But, all those people?" blurted Taz. "All of them dead?"

"I think you're starting to see the gravity of your situation," Takahashi nodded.

"But we saved them! Why would they have them all killed?" Marcus argued, aghast.

"They're witnesses. As far as Division 6 is concerned, they have proof of what you can do," Takahashi replied. "The only way you'll ever be safe is if we get you as far away from here as possible."

"But these exploration voyages... there's no guarantee that the crews have ever been able to establish a basis for sustaining life at the other end, is there?" Taylor asked.

"Actually..." Takahashi started, reaching into his jacket pocket and producing the shimmering crystal that Marcus had handed over to Mitchell. "This little gem should prove quite valuable in that regard."

"What is it?" Taz asked, sneaking closer to steal a better look at the sparkling crystal.

"I... I found it in the alien ship on New Io," Marcus stuttered, unsure of how the others would take to his lack of disclosure. "With a Division 6 ship on approach, and, having just dealt with one traitor, I wasn't sure whom I could trust."

Having accepted Marcus' actions when he'd told them about his confrontation with Adler, the squad seemed to accept his reasoning.

"So, what is it exactly?" Reid asked, fascinated with Marcus's souvenir.

"As far as my scientists have been able to make out, it's a navigational crystal," Takahashi explained. "With it, we were able to discover several of the coordinates your alien vessel visited prior to its unfortunate crash on New Io."

"So?" Taz asked, impatiently.

"So... these are genuine coordinates for worlds visited by an advanced alien race. The implications are unfathomable," Takahashi proclaimed with great enthusiasm. "Think about it. We can send the *Tengri* to one of those coordinates. You might become the first of our race to make peaceful contact with an alien race. Just imagine the untold opportunities that await you at the other end of your journey."

Marcus warmed to the thought. Not having to worry about looking over his shoulder for the rest of his life was definitely appealing, and this would give his life the purpose he so desired. He could still serve humanity by venturing into the unknown. As he looked at the others, he saw the same look on all their faces, one of approval mixed with a hint of excitement.

"I think they're all on board Mr. Muromoto," Mitchell ventured.

"And you, Captain?" Takahashi probed. "I've convinced C-CORE to hold off on appointing the Tengri's commander. Will you take the appointment? Go with them, look after them?"

Mitchell grunted, and nodded his agreement.

* * * * *

The limousine crept along the busy traffic lanes, on its way to an undisclosed hangar bay belonging to C-CORE. In his hasty acceptance of Takahashi's proposal, Marcus had neglected to take one very important thing into account. He would never see Eve again. He'd seriously considered changing his mind, but the more he contemplated what that would entail, the more he was sure he was doing the right thing, for both of them. If he were to stay, not only would he be hounded by Division 6 for the rest of his life, but so too would anyone he was close too. Eve too would have to live on the run, constantly hiding, in fear of what would happen if ever they were to let their guard down for even a second.

If he truly loved her, he would have to let her go. Given time, she would forget all about him, and hopefully find someone who would treat her as well as she deserved, someone better than him. No, this was the right thing to do, especially for her.

The limousine began its slow descent towards a series of massive hangar structures in a northwestern industrial district on the outskirts of Sol. The doors of one hangar stood open, a series of container trucks and tankers parked haphazardly outside, a slew of workers unloading provisions onto a wide conveyer belt leading up to the ship that lay inside. The few rays of sun capable of piercing through the thick veil of clouds sparkled off the ship's bow, which protruded from the hangar's doors.

"I'm sorry there isn't much time to enjoy the sights. We waited until the last possible moment to bring you out here. We didn't want to risk you being seen," Takahashi explained inside the limousine. "The loaders are just about finished working, and the ship is scheduled to depart within the hour."

The driver brought the vehicle to a stop inside the hangar, right next to an open lift. As the team gathered for the ride up to the main airlock, Marcus felt a knot forming in his stomach as his nerves started to get the best of him.

Takahashi rode with them all the way to the top, wishing them good luck on their journey. Without much time to get to know the rest of the crew, they agreed it would be best for them to stow their belongings in their quarters and meet on the bridge, ready to say farewell to the world they had all hoped to one day call their home.

Marcus had had another vision in his dreams the previous night, a dream he was excited to share with the others when the time was right. He had dreamt of a magnificent city among the stars, surrounded by hundreds, if not thousands, of ships, all so incredibly alien in design that he could barely contemplate them, all different, all coming and going. It was a vision of hope, holding the promise of untold opportunity and adventure.

As the *Tengri* slowly made its way out of the hangar and began its steady climb into space, the squad stood in silence, gazing out into space. Even though they were setting sail into the abyss, Marcus was unafraid. He had the promise of new friends ahead of him, but, more importantly, he had his old friends at his side. His very own family.

Chapter 52

Takahashi stood at the window, nursing his drink. He enjoyed the sound the ice cubes made as he swirled the glass in the palm of his hand. The sun had just set behind the tapered headquarters of DynaCorre Industries, one of Takahashi's chief rivals in the corporate world.

This was his favorite part of the day, when the sun had just set and the stars were beginning to make their appearance in the early evening sky. He glanced at the timepiece on his left wrist, an action he'd repeated several times in the last few minutes. It was a plain watch of stainless steel. His daughter had often berated him for not wearing something more fashionable, more fitting for a man of his stature.

Yet despite all his wealth, he'd always been more interested in function than appearance. He carried no special sentiment for the unremarkable device, except that it had been with him through most of his life's journey, and it kept perfect time. He'd occasionally had to replace some of its components, and he'd often amused himself at the thought that he could have built at least two or three whole watches from the parts it had absorbed over the years.

The launch was only a few seconds away. Even though he couldn't see the Wako flaring from such a distance, Takahashi stood by the window and gazed at the stars, imagining himself going with them. His watch emitted a series of three faint beeps. Takahashi sighed, lowering his head in resignation.

"Goodbye, old friend," he murmured to himself, staring sightlessly into his glass until the last of the ice had all but melted away.

"Father," Mariko prompted, arriving unexpectedly, interrupting his thoughts. "Are you alright?" she asked, trying not to sound disingenuous.

Takahashi sighed once more, turning to look his daughter in the eye.

"I'll be fine dear," he declared, taking a sip from the glass.

"I was just contacted by Ms. Torres at GeoDynamics. She asked that I give you a message," Mariko told him. "The retrieval of the field emitter went without a hitch. She had some trouble getting clearance for her agents to land on New Io, but once there, they were able to locate the device in the GeoDynamics warehouse. She expressed her certainty that it had remained undiscovered."

"That's good news," he said, forcing a smile. She stared into his eyes, trying to find even a hint of what the old man had been up to all this time.

"So you're not going to tell me what this was all about?" she asked.

Takahashi remained silent, taking another sip from his glass.

"I don't understand why you would go through all this trouble only to let them get away now?" Mariko moaned.

"Everything is as it should be," Takahashi proclaimed, swirling his glass. "After all…" he began, pausing briefly to swallow the remainder of his drink. "This is only the beginning."